BY JENNIFER RYAN

*The Underground Library*

*The Wedding Dress Sewing Circle*

*The Kitchen Front*

*The Spies of Shilling Lane*

*The Chilbury Ladies' Choir*

THE
UNDERGROUND
LIBRARY

*The*

# UNDERGROUND
# LIBRARY · *A Novel*

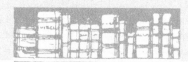

## JENNIFER RYAN

 BALLANTINE BOOKS · NEW YORK

Published in the United States by Ballantine Books, an imprint of Random House, a division of Penguin Random House LLC, New York.

BALLANTINE is a registered trademark and the colophon is a trademark of Penguin Random House LLC.

LIBRARY OF CONGRESS CATALOGING-IN-PUBLICATION DATA
NAMES: Ryan, Jennifer (Jennifer L.), author.
TITLE: The underground library: a novel / Jennifer Ryan.
DESCRIPTION: First edition. | New York: Ballantine Books, [2024]
IDENTIFIERS: LCCN 2023013953 (print) | LCCN 2023013954 (ebook) | ISBN 9780593500385 (Hardback) | ISBN 9780593500392 (Ebook)
SUBJECTS: LCGFT: Novels.
CLASSIFICATION: LCC PR6118.Y3546 U54 2024 (print) | LCC PR6118.Y3546 (ebook) | DDC 823/.92—dc23/eng/20230327
LC record available at https://lccn.loc.gov/2023013953
LC ebook record available at https://lccn.loc.gov/2023013954

Printed in the United States of America on acid-free paper
randomhousebooks.com

9 8 7 6 5 4 3 2 1

FIRST EDITION

*Title-page image from Adobe Stock*
*Book design by Barbara M. Bachman*

With love and thanks to
my grandmother,
Mrs. Irene Mussett

"To thine own self be true."

—*Hamlet,* Act I, Scene III

THE
UNDERGROUND
LIBRARY

# SOFIE BAUMANN

## THE BAUMANN RESIDENCE, BERLIN

*May 1939*

"HURRY, SOFIE!" HER SISTER'S VOICE FLOATED THROUGH THE open door, echoing past the bookcases lining the walls.

It reached her as Sofie sat in a world of her own, lounging in the window seat in her father's library, her favorite spot in the house. A book lay open in her hands, but her eyes were gazing out to the pale pink softness of the cherry blossom petals fluttering down from the tree on the street below.

"There you are!" Rachel hurried into the library, and Sofie could hear the tenderness in her elder sister's voice as she crossed the room. "I knew I'd find you in here." She smiled gently and rested a hand on Sofie's arm, and Sofie tried to imprint it into her memory, the essence of their nineteen years together—her entire childhood, and the only place she had ever known.

"I've decided not to go." Sofie trained her eyes on the page, trying to blot out reality. "You can tell Papa."

But Rachel's hand remained on her arm, her voice calm. "You know you have to go, Sofie. Think of Papa. He worries about you, and we'll follow you there very soon." She fixed Sofie with her firm smile, as if it were all agreed and there was nothing more to say. "We'll be together again before you know it."

Three years older, Rachel had always been the leader, serious and strong. Sofie, ever the youngest, had been the dreamy one with her head in a book. "Why can't you go in my place? You're far better suited for this than I am."

"I'm sorry, Sofie." She sat down beside her. "This job, the visa, they're in your name. I can't take your place, and even if I could, I wouldn't. I want you to be safe, and right now, Britain is one of the safest places in Europe." Rachel put an arm around her, and Sofie slumped into her with resignation, knowing that she was right, as usual. Ever since their mother's death ten years ago, Rachel had taken on much of the responsibility of their family. Sofie had been partially raised by her, not that she would admit it. As a result, Rachel was the person she always turned to when she didn't know what to do.

Pulling away, Sofie crushed her fists into her eyes with frustration. "But if they hadn't canceled your job, we'd have been leaving for London together. At least we would have each other."

"I know that it's daunting to go alone, Sofie, but a job will come up for me soon. I've been going to the British Embassy every day to check the advertisements and apply for posts. Yesterday there were two, one for a housekeeper and another for a cook—although I would have to learn some of that bland British cooking for the job." Rachel laughed, trying to make light of it, but they both knew how dire things were. Britain was the only place in Europe still offering visas to Jews; every other country was too scared of having a deluge of refugees, too scared of what that could mean in the coming war.

But the British visa came with a catch: you could only apply for one if you had already secured a job contract for domestic work. There was a shortage of servants in Britain, so the British humanitarian groups pressing to help Jews had finally struck a deal with the government: They would let Jews into the country if they were to fill a vacant servant's position.

"But it's not so easy anymore," Sofie said in despair. "Scores of people are swarming to the British Embassy every day to apply for only one or two new positions. Everyone I know is trying to get a visa. What will we do if you're not picked?"

"I will find a way to join you, visa or no visa. Frederick says that if things get any harder for us over here, we can cross the border into France."

"How much harder can it get?" Sofie countered. "We can't get jobs. We can't go to school or to college. They've forced us to sew these stars onto our clothes, and we're banned from shops and restaurants. Ever since Kristallnacht, we're being attacked on the streets and no one blinks an eye at it. Threats are painted on our doors and our property is vandalized for no reason. And what about those of us who simply vanish? No one's heard a word from Professor Reinhardt since he was called into the police station for questioning, and it's been more than a month now!"

"Don't work yourself up, Sofie. Things are never as bad as they seem. Both Frederick and I have exit visas, and we can go to Belgium or France. We're trying to get one for Papa to come with us, even though he's insisting on staying here, close to Mama's grave." She made a long sigh, then leaving the thought unsaid, she continued. "But we're still going to try to get the British visa, since it would also mean that we would have an income and a place to live when we arrive." She pulled away from Sofie, looking imploringly at her, eyes wide and insistent.

"But Frederick will never be able to get a work visa," Sofie said. Although their neighbor Frederick was like a cousin to them, Sofie couldn't see how a bookish medical student would be useful in helping them escape from Nazi Germany. "There are hardly any advertisements for male servants, only the occasional gardener or footman. The vacancies are always for women, maids and housekeepers. If you wait for him to get one, you'll never leave."

There was a moment of silence before Rachel said, "You're right, he might not. But if we have to travel through Germany to get to the border, he can help us. He looks more Aryan, and if I dye my hair blond, we can pretend to be regular Germans. I've heard people talk about it, how they just cut the stars off their coats and walk down the street with their heads held high, as if they have nothing to be scared about. We can do that if we need to, Frederick and me, and Papa, too.

We can hide in plain sight and escape." Rachel glanced out of the window at the cherry tree petals cascading down, then she got up and walked to the piano in the corner—arguably her favorite spot in the house.

Frustratedly, Sofie followed her. "Then why can't I wait here with you?"

"Because it isn't safe, Sofie, and the more of us that travel together, the greater the risk we'll be caught. You have to take this visa, for all of our sakes." Rachel let her fingers fall thoughtlessly onto the piano keys, playing the first few triplets of her usual piece, Beethoven's "Moonlight Sonata." Rachel was the musical one, the pianist, the notes an omnipresent echo through their home.

As she listened, Sofie tried to memorize it for the future—where would she ever hear piano music again? And where was she going to find a library like Papa's? What was she going to do without her books to escape to in these terrible times? A fear came over her for all that she was losing, and she clutched the slim volume of poetry in her hand, determined to slip it into her suitcase.

In the middle of the slower section, Rachel's fingers slowed and stopped, the last notes lingering like unfinished thoughts. "Sofie, you know that Papa will not let you stay, not when it means putting you in danger. If anything were to happen to you he wouldn't be able to bear it, not if you'd had the chance to leave. And our lives have already become so small here." Slowly, she got up and pulled Sofie toward the door, her voice a little more firm. "Now come on, it's time to go."

Sofie clenched her fists in frustration, but she knew she was no match for her older sister. No matter how much she argued, Rachel would put her onto the train regardless.

Reluctantly, she allowed herself to be led through the hallway to where her father waited, her small suitcase beside him. Quickly, she bent down and opened it, sliding in her volume of poems. Its company on this long, daunting trip would be both comforting and protective.

Her father came forward to hug her. "You know, Sofie, you have always been my special starry-eyed girl. Promise me to keep that light inside you alive. It's a pity we don't have any friends or connections in

Britain, but I'm sure the Wainwright family will treat you well. Work hard, keep your faith alive, and think of us, how we will be together again soon."

Tears came to her eyes as Rachel gently guided her out of the front door. "We have to leave if you're going to make the train."

But as she went out onto the front steps, Sofie turned back to the old house, her home for all her life, her eyes glancing one last time at the window in the library.

"I will come back," she murmured. "As soon as I can, I will come home."

And as she stood, the pink petals from the cherry tree blew from the tree in front of the house, some resting on her shoulders, and she suddenly felt the shiver of how transitory life was, how nothing ever stayed the same, every life fluttering in the wind.

It was a mile's walk to Friedrichstrasse Station. No one mentioned the future, no one mentioned the war, and no one mentioned how treacherous the journey across Europe could be, especially at the German border crossing. Despite the fact that she had both her British work visa and her German exit visa, the authorities were increasingly unpredictable where Jewish people were concerned. Safe passage was not guaranteed. One never knew if they might refuse you, confiscate your papers, or take you for questioning.

That's how people disappeared.

When the station came into view, Sofie's pace slowed, but Rachel laced an arm through hers to hurry her along. "We don't want you to miss the train."

The forecourt was loud and chaotic. Crowds pushed and shoved, so many trying to escape the country they no longer recognized. There was a sense of confusion, of urgency, while the threat of violence hung in the air like a sour stench. Children were crying, packages were being thrust into carriages, and all around them, people were holding each other, knowing they might be parting forever.

Sofie allowed herself to be pulled through the crowds like a shred of seaweed in high tide. The train was already at the platform, filled with women like her, heading for new lives in London. A well-groomed brunette in a fur coat sobbed as she clung to a man. An older woman holding a child scuttled into a carriage, the child's mother in hysterics on the platform.

"I know this is difficult, but at least you'll be safe until we get there." Rachel's voice was serious, instructive. "Work hard for the Wainwrights, make sure they don't have any reason to cancel your visa."

"But what if I can't?" Sofie couldn't help saying. "How can I be a good housemaid when the only knowledge I have comes from watching Mrs. Grun and Hilde at home? And what happens if there's a war? If the Nazis take Britain, what will happen then? How will I ever find you and Papa again?"

Her father folded her hand inside his. "This is the best chance for you. You have to be brave, Sofie."

Suddenly, she realized how difficult this was for him, the shadows beneath his eyes, the clenched jaw. He, too, did not want her to go, but this was the best of their few, dismal options.

The train whistle was blowing, the crowds shouting and the sound of carriage doors slamming around them.

Sofie's head dropped into her hands, heavy sobs coming out of her, and her father and Rachel put their arms around her. She tried to drink in their touch, wondering when she would feel it again.

It was Rachel who pulled away first, hastily wiping her tears as she softly drew her father back. His eyes were wet and red, and he was unable to speak, overcome with emotion.

"You have to go now, Sofie." Rachel's voice was hoarse with tears, and she turned Sofie toward the carriage door, handing her the small suitcase as she stepped on board.

Sofie could barely hear her through the cacophony of people and the whistle of the train, the buildup of steam as the engines prepared to leave.

Inside the carriage, Sofie pulled down the window to take their hands for one last time.

"Always know that we love you, Sofie," Rachel cried. "Every time you put your hand on your heart, you will feel us there."

Her dear sister and father swam in front of Sofie as her eyes welled up with tears.

Another whistle blew, and the train slowly began to shunt forward.

Their fingers were pulled apart, the white smoke of the train billowing between them, the noise as the train began to move deafening. Inside the carriage, everyone was pushing against the windows, shouting above the engines, waving arms and handkerchiefs.

For a moment, the smoke cleared, and Sofie's eyes met Rachel's one last time. Her guard had come down, and all that Sofie saw was her sister's raw, inconsolable grief tangled with a dense, unraveling fear.

And then Rachel was gone, the platform a sea of strangers, now disappearing into a blur.

Falling back into her seat, Sofie sank her face into her hands and cried as the thrum of the wheels carried her farther and farther away from everything she'd ever known. Minutes turned to hours, the time meaningless and misshapen. She had never felt so completely alone.

From now onward, she would have to make all decisions herself. Not Rachel, not Papa. Only her.

She watched through the window as the crush of city buildings slowly gave way to fields, and she silently waved goodbye to Berlin. Her sister and father would be home by now. They might have stopped for coffee, perhaps, although most of the coffeehouses had put up signs, JUDEN NICHT WILLKOMMEN. There weren't many places for them to go these days.

Her worries about Rachel and Papa seemed to increase the closer she got to safety. Germany was dangerous for Jews. People went missing, vanishing without a trace. No one knew for certain where they went, but the rumors of work camps had become more frequent and detailed. Papa's health wasn't good. He would never survive if he was sent to one.

Opposite Sofie sat a smartly dressed, middle-aged woman who eyed her, taking in the yellow star sewn onto her sleeve. Sofie quickly took off her coat, folding it to hide the star, placing it onto the luggage rack above her. Watching, the woman pursed her lips, then took out some knitting and focused on her stitches, the clickety-click of her needles keeping time with the wheels of the train.

Not knowing what to do with herself, Sofie took her suitcase out from behind her legs and pulled it onto her lap. Easing it open, she tried to stop herself from weeping into her last possessions, fingering her mother's heavy gold bracelet that she'd sewn into the hem of a skirt for safekeeping. She touched Rachel's mauve shawl, pulling it to her face. It still smelled of her, of their house. Carefully, she put it around her shoulders, its weight and warmth reminding her of the home and family she'd left behind.

There was a photograph of them, taken at Hanukkah in front of the menorah and the ladened dining table. Rachel was at the back, her arms over everyone's shoulders, with her dark hair curled elegantly. Beside her, Papa had a haunted look, his life reeling out of control. His business had been forced to close by the Nazis last year, and he'd had to sell his collection of first editions to afford the housekeeper. But then she'd left anyway, apologetic and weepy, but what could anyone say or do? People were vilifying her for working for a Jew. Papa's stature had shrunk first with his wife's death and now with the long, slow squeeze of the Nazis' relentless fist.

To Rachel's left, Sofie looked as if she were about to take off out of the picture, race to the library to read or work on her poetry. It was a good photograph of her. Her long wavy hair was a fraction darker than Rachel's and her wide smile full of life, so different from how she felt now, so many changes in just a few short months.

Her mind went back to the book she had found late one night, hidden in her father's library. It was titled *The Brown Book of Hitler's Terror*, written by those worried about the Nazis' tyranny. As she read page after page, the full realization of what could happen to her family descended on her.

"But how can they get away with this?" she'd demanded of her father, running into his study, pushing the book across his desk.

His eyes were steady as he said, "It will surprise you what people can do, especially if we go to war. Everyone will be looking the other way. No one will see what is happening under their very noses because they will not want to."

The train slowed as it entered the station of a large town. A number of people got off, and a group of nuns squashed into Sofie's carriage, an old one smiling kindly before sitting beside her. As the train began to move forward again, a younger nun led a prayer, the sound of the indecipherable Latin words mingled with the turn of the wheels and the clickety-click of the knitting needles. Sofie closed her eyes, and as she often did when she needed comfort, she let a book play inside her head. Looking ahead to her new home, she'd read *A Room with a View*—would the Wainwright's house be adorned with wisteria and croquet lawns? She tried to remember every description from the novel, letting the heartwarming tale comfort her, removing her from the strange, prickling fear that gripped her inside.

Suddenly, she was brought back with a jolt.

The train had stopped at a small station, seemingly in the middle of nowhere.

The nun's chanting had petered out, and some of the younger ones looked out of the window to see what had caused the stoppage.

"The Nazis are always disrupting the trains," the old nun beside her whispered to the others. "You never know why."

But the reason soon became apparent.

The speaker system crackled into life, and then came a sharp voice, either the police or the Gestapo. "All Jews must identify themselves."

With a sharp intake of breath, Sofie felt her heart pound.

Were they going to stop her from reaching the border? It couldn't be far away now. This couldn't be where her journey ended. She swallowed hard. In a flash, she remembered her sister's terrified face on the platform as the train pulled away, and she suddenly understood how dangerous this trip could be—and just how crucial it was for her to flee the country.

Sofie looked through the window down the platform. Noises and shouts indicated that a group of policemen were boarding the train.

She knew they would be checking people's papers, which were

clearly marked to show whether you were a Jew. You had to have identification papers in order to travel, so she couldn't pretend she'd forgotten them. And then there was the star on her coat, too. Her heart began racing, her face coloring. She couldn't help glancing around the carriage frantically, looking for a way out, but on one side the corridor was filled with police, and on the other the platform was guarded.

There was no escape.

Shouted commands came from other carriages farther up the corridor, policemen ordering people out onto the platform. Through the window, she watched as a trail of quietly resigned passengers were led away.

The woman opposite snapped down her knitting and pulled out her identity papers ready for the police. Evidently she had nothing to hide, and she quickly resumed her knitting. The stop was simply an inconvenience to her day, whereas for Sofie it could be the end of everything.

Fear clenched her heart. The shouted orders of the policemen were coming closer. They would be in her carriage within minutes, if not sooner.

Her papers were in her coat pocket, up on the luggage rack, and with her heart pounding, she realized she had no choice. As she stood, she pulled Rachel's shawl around her before reaching her hand up to feel inside the folds of fabric for the papers.

But then she felt a hand on her shoulder, and quietly, the old nun drew her back down into her seat, adjusting her mauve shawl to cover her head, tucking a bible into her hands. "You are with us, child."

Unsure, Sofie bent her head forward, petrified. This could be a very dangerous decision; if she was caught trying to lie, she had no doubt that whatever the police were going to do with the other Jewish passengers, they'd plan something much worse for her.

But before she could think it through, a large policeman was already at the door, demanding, "I need to see everyone's papers."

Sofie closed her eyes, barely breathing. She heard the young nun speak, the rustle of the papers being passed over. It was interminable.

From the corridor, orders were shouted through, urging the police to hurry.

Brusquely, the policeman flicked through the stack, barely pausing to check to which of the nuns each document belonged. "What about that one? Why does she have a shawl and not a habit?"

He was talking about Sofie. Fear gripped her like a vice. But then she felt a warm hand reaching over to pat hers. "She is a novice," the old nun said simply.

Silence hung in the air, only the clickity-click of the knitting needles slowing, the ball of wool dropping to the floor.

That's when Sofie remembered.

The woman with the knitting had seen Sofie's coat, the star sewn onto it. Would she tell the policeman that Sofie was deceiving him?

The needles stopped, and Sofie peered from under the shawl to see the woman handing over her own papers. As the policeman looked at them, the woman's eyes shifted to Sofie's, her gaze narrowing.

Sofie had seen that look before. Nazi propaganda had convinced the nation that Jews were the root of evil and hardship, that they were animals that had to be controlled. Did this woman believe it?

But then the old nun beside her reached down and picked up the woman's ball of wool. As she handed it to her, she murmured, "We all need help sometimes."

The woman inhaled sharply, an eyebrow raised to an indignant point, and as the policeman handed back her papers, the woman opened her mouth to speak. "I wanted to say——"

Sofie felt her throat tighten.

But then the old nun began to chant, her soft Latin words infusing the carriage with a calm serenity that clashed violently with the potentially horrific outcome.

"Yes?" the policeman grunted at the woman.

And as Sofie's heart stood still, the woman glanced from her to the nun and said, "How long is it to the border?"

"I am not a stationmaster," the policeman barked. "You will arrive when you arrive." He strode out, and soon his footsteps and shouts were heard in the next carriage.

Petrified for what might have happened, Sofie slowly let out a breath.

Within minutes, the doors were slammed shut and the train pulled away, the Gestapo's work done.

As the carriage passed the end of the platform, Sofie saw thirty people or more huddled together. Most were young women like Sofie, trying to escape Germany, now being organized into a marching line. The young brunette she'd seen at the station was there, her fur coat hideously juxtaposed to her new reality. Through the moving carriage window, Sofie caught her eye and saw only one thing: terror.

As the train rumbled out of the village, the old nun gently squeezed her hand, and Sofie shakily smiled at her with gratitude. A trail of tears oozed from her eyes, of fear and utter relief at what might have been the end of her voyage.

"Thank you," she croaked to the woman opposite, but the woman had gone back to her knitting, ignoring her with a small, cold sniff.

Sofie turned to the old nun beside her. "You saved my life."

But the old woman only smiled, patting her hand, just another small act of kindness in this horrific new world.

# JULIET LANSDOWN

## BETHNAL GREEN, LONDON

*August 1940*

IN THE LATE SUMMER HEAT, THE BUSY LONDON STREETS WERE A throng of activity, and as Juliet Lansdown stepped up from Bethnal Green Underground Station, she was almost bowled over by the bustle of pedestrians. People darted everywhere, the crowds dotted with uniforms as well as young women like her patriotically coming to the city to cover the jobs left by men going to the front.

Her suitcase in one hand and her gas mask box hanging from her shoulder, Juliet felt her pulse pounding. Finally, she was here. A wave of exhilaration washed through her, quickly followed by trepidation.

*I can't let this go wrong.*

The street was busy for the midafternoon, packed with buses, trams, and cars, the din of engines mingling with bicycle bells as a newspaper seller shouted the headline "Nazis Bomb South London Air Base."

She gazed up at the tall, terraced buildings, so far away from her little village. This was her chance. She had to make it count. It would prove what she could do, show the difference she could make. All the things she'd been through could be tucked away into the past once and for all: her oppressive parents, the disappearance of her fiancé on the front, and the secret that clenched her heart like a tight fist.

With determination, she straightened her pillbox hat and set off across the road.

Much thought had gone into choosing her prim navy blue skirt suit. Uniform-like clothes were all the rage, showing how women were doing their bit for the war. She'd curled her dark blond hair into a smart victory roll, and she wore patriotic red lipstick, making her look efficient, cheerful, and plucky.

At twenty-six, unmarried, and smart as a whip, she needed this new challenge. And challenge it most certainly was—it wasn't every day that a woman was offered a job as a deputy librarian, and in one of the grandest libraries in east London, too.

Her heart beat fast as she made her way across the street, dodging a double-decker bus and an old horse and cart piled high with salvaged metal railings, ready to be made into war planes.

She could hardly wait to see Bethnal Green Library itself.

And as she turned off the main road and into the park, it came into sight: the grand Victorian edifice presiding over the greenery. A hundred feet wide, the magnificent hall had sixteen tall windows and grand double doors in the center. A second story contained another row of windows, the roof divided by a great glassed dome.

Taking a deep breath, she headed inside.

The entrance led into a tall, marble vestibule, the walls covered with grand portraits of the solemn, side-whiskered industrialists who'd financed the library, bringing education to London's poor.

But it wasn't until she'd stepped into the main atrium that she halted in awe.

A shaft of afternoon sunshine threw a golden light through the glass dome, coating the dark wooden rows of books with a sense of antiquity. Tall shelves lined every wall, narrow spiral staircases taking you from one tier to the next as the books above became smaller and smaller. The smell of musty encyclopedias and floor wax permeated the still, silent air as a few readers shifted slowly through the aisles.

And all this was to be her domain.

To Juliet, a library was more than just a repository for books. It was a spiritual and intellectual adventure, a place to delve into the rich treasure trove of life. When she had first stepped into her village library in Upper Beeding as an intrepid six-year-old, she was struck by the sheer quantity of books—the endless escapes into different places, different families, different lives. The library made her small village feel expansive, her imagination unrestrained.

Once she was old enough, she volunteered there, staying away from the suffocating atmosphere at home. Being in the library reminded her of life's potential, of who she wanted to be, instead of what her strict parents had in store for her.

And now this big London library offered her even more than that: It gave her a sanctuary, a haven. For years, her parents had resolutely insisted that she live at home until she married, but with the war posters encouraging women to fill the London vacancies left by the men, even her mother couldn't object to her leaving, nettled as she was.

A retired country accountant and his humorless wife, her parents had been unconcerned with producing offspring until Juliet had surprised them late in life. Although she was their only child, she had been brought up by a dull nanny, barely knowing her parents, who seemed to belong to a different, stauncher era—one in which children were useful only in upholding the family's reputation. After he retired, her father had become increasingly reclusive, while her mother had bad-temperedly put herself to the task of finding Juliet a suitable husband, disdainfully instructing her to hide her shortcomings: bookishness, stubbornness, and a vulgar tendency to have ideas.

They lived in a solitary mansion on the edge of Upper Beeding, a house where visitors were discouraged. With no companions to keep her company, Juliet had found solace in books. Her friends had been Anne of Green Gables and Alice in Wonderland, her adventures in Narnia and the Secret Garden. When Juliet showed a flair for English at school, she had begged her parents to let her go to university, only to be told it would be the ruin of her.

"Too much education isn't good for girls," her mother decreed from the end of the dining table. "It puts ideas into their heads, and before you know it, a good marriage isn't enough. You're already a disaster as it is, surrounded by all your books. What about the suitable beaus I've paraded in front of you? The Hapfields' sons are perfect, and what about Sebastian Falconbury? I know you think him a mindless rake, but his father's the doctor, very well regarded. Really, Juliet, you need to stop this nonsense before those books turn you into a blue-stocking."

Little did her mother know it was already too late.

The pages had been read, the knowledge absorbed, the ideas around her already challenged. She didn't want to end up living her mother's life, shut up at home ministering to a high-classed husband who hardly acknowledged her. Privately, she became determined to remain single rather than risk being trapped in loveless duty like her mother.

But that was before Victor Manning had walked into her life.

He was different from anyone she had ever known. A political writer with published essays, he had come to her little library to speak. She remembered admiring him, reveling in his intellect, his charisma, the ability he had to capture a mood, a belief. He read aloud an excerpt from *Heart of Darkness,* delving into the heady symbolism and meta-phor before presenting his own prose, his ideals and meanings echoing Conrad's inner, complex reality.

How thoughtful, principled, and moral his writing had been; the opposite of his disappearance from the front line in Dunkirk three months ago.

Juliet's parents had not approved of Victor, and they'd watched coldly as his disappearance unraveled her. Of course, they didn't know the painful truth of how and why Victor vanished. No one did—and hopefully no one ever would.

At least the big, anonymous city would give her a chance to start afresh, make herself so busy that the terrible reality would be trampled under her rushing feet or crushed between the pages of books, unable to find air.

As she stood beneath the great, silent dome surrounded by book-shelf upon bookshelf, a peace washed over her, as it always did in li-braries. But the place had a different ambience to her little library at home. Instead of the bustle of people popping in, the quiet chatter, the children playing, Bethnal Green Library was hushed, the air still and stale with old volumes. The ornate balconies were empty, and a beautiful glass-paned reading room sat unused at the far side. Only a handful of people hovered in the nearest aisles, and just two elderly women perched at a table like a pair of silver-headed birds, spectacles on as they read the newspapers.

Opposite the double doors, the mahogany main desk was polished a deep brown, meticulously tidy with a single large register. Alongside it stretched a card-catalog cabinet, painstakingly labeled. Then there was a board for notices, which was meant for local events and library updates, but it contained only two government posters, neatly pinned: CARELESS TALK COSTS LIVES and CHILDREN ARE SAFER IN THE COUNTRYSIDE. It was quite the opposite of the noticeboard in Upper Beeding Library, which was full to bursting with community notices, events, and meetings, especially with all the wartime fundraising and volunteer groups.

"I'm here to see Mr. Pruitt," she said to the pretty auburn-haired girl behind the desk. In a summer dress, she looked young enough to still be at school, and there was a freshness to her bright eyes, a pencil stuck into her bun, forgotten.

She leaned forward with a smile. "Are you the new deputy? I'm one of the assistants, Katie." She gestured to the office door behind her. "Mr. Pruitt's in there, as usual."

Relieved to see a friendly face, Juliet introduced herself, adding, "I hope he's keen to try some of my new ideas."

Katie leaned forward to whisper, "I have to warn you, Mr. Pruitt isn't too keen on new things."

Trying not to let this unsettle her, Juliet fixed a smile on her face and knocked on the door.

A thin, nasal voice said, "Come," and Juliet stepped inside.

At around sixty, Mr. Pruitt was slim, unsmiling, and gray, from his three-piece suit to his receding hairline and small, penetrating eyes. Even his silver-rimmed spectacles failed to add any color to the man.

"Do take a seat." There was a dismal orderliness about him and the small office. She'd met librarians like him before. Every book in its place, every catalog card completed in the same black ink, every day the same strict routine. They knew the Dewey Decimal System by heart, enjoying the precision of it. To Juliet, organizing a library was a creative experience, not a rule-based system to be upheld before all else.

She stepped forward. "I'm Juliet Lansdown, the new deputy librarian." She put her hand forward to shake his, and he took the tips of her fingers, clearly uncertain whether women should be shaking hands at all.

"Pleased to meet you," he said, although the sentiment didn't seem to reach his eyes or mouth, which remained in an even grimace.

Looking her over critically, he took out a sheet of paper, which she recognized as her letter of application. "I hope you understand what a great responsibility it is, to be the deputy here?"

"Of course, and you'll find that I'm well qualified for the position." In her agitation, the words tumbled out of her chaotically. "I've been working in the library in Upper Beeding for several years. The head librarian there was a lovely fellow, and he let me take on a lot of extra duties, some of which I'd like to share with the library here—"

Mr. Pruitt put up a hand to stop her.

"Let it be known, Miss Lansdown, that you have been employed here not because of your experience, but rather in spite of it. Our former deputy insisted on rejoining his old regiment," he said with bitterness, "and had there been a man available to take the position, the job would have been his. But in the absence of one, I was instructed to find a suitable woman." He pursed his lips in displeasure. "We wish you to fill his shoes as best you can until his return."

Unsure, she murmured, "I plan to do so, and more, too. I formed a reading group in Upper Beeding, and it was incredibly popular, and I had an idea about a special section for children, too, that might do well here. . . ."

He placed his fingertips together in front of him, like a headmaster apprehending an errant pupil. "Miss Lansdown, may I remind you that this is one of the oldest libraries in London? We do things properly here, providing education and culture for the poor of the area. That is what our worthy patrons wished."

"But the poor are educated in schools these days." She knew her runaway tongue was getting the better of her, but she seemed unable to stop it. "And a much wider array of people use the library nowadays, and from all kinds of backgrounds, too, people who like to meet and talk about books they've enjoyed reading." Her voice trailed off. "That's why a reading group might be nice."

He stopped her, his voice more severe. "You will find, Miss Lansdown, that we do not hold with any of these new experiments in Bethnal Green." He sniffed dismissively. "I should also inform you that the council is considering scaling back or even closing the Bethnal Green branch. Everyone is too busy with the war, long work hours, and so forth, and they might need to put resources to better use."

Juliet's heart plunged. "The library might close?" Had she arrived just in time for it to be shut down? Was she to be sent back, her mission failed? Her mother would tell her how ridiculous she'd been to think that she could have independence and a career of her own. Then her mother would find the right kind of husband to keep Juliet in her place, just as her husband had done with her.

Mr. Pruitt nodded. "It might be better for us all if the library closes. We can move away from the dangers of the city with the evacuated. I'm considering an opening in Suffolk myself."

Her mind whirred. "But we have a duty to do all we can to keep the library open. You can't just give up, let the place close, not when it can be a source of comfort in times such as these."

Impatiently, he glowered at her. "You see, this is the problem with employing women. You get too emotional and simply don't understand how these things work."

"Perhaps with some of my new ideas, we'll have more people coming in. We can persuade the council—"

"May I remind you that this is a library, not a social club." He scowled, as if she were simply being awkward. "If you would prefer to work in a different sort of place, Miss Lansdown, I suggest you apply elsewhere."

Juliet reeled back. The threat was there. If she didn't like the way the library was run, he would have no trouble getting rid of her.

"I understand, Mr. Pruitt," she muttered contritely.

"Your duties will be to manage the day-to-day running of the place, ensuring the books are reshelved and that the registers are kept up-to-date. That will be all for now."

"Yes, Mr. Pruitt." She stood up to leave, but then turned back to him to ask something at the back of her mind. "Do you have any plans in case of invasion? France was taken in June, and they say the Nazis have their sights on Britain next, soldiers landing on the beaches, air raids over London. What are we going to do if the library is bombed?"

A snort of annoyance came from him. "The Nazis wouldn't dare," he said pompously. "We British aren't like the French, surrendering at the first turn. No, the Nazis know what they're up against with us."

Tentatively, she said, "But they're already bombing our factories and airfields. The city might be next."

He paused, his eyes glancing momentarily over a newspaper on his desk, the headlines reading "South London Aerodrome Bombed." But then he dismissed her with a sweeping motion of his hand. "I'm sure there will be further government instruction as to how to deal with any bombings." He secured his glasses on his nose and looked back at her, tired of their conversation. "You may go to your lodging now, Miss Lansdown, and I will expect you here and ready for work tomorrow morning at eight o'clock prompt."

Outside, she gave the auburn-haired girl a weak smile, and the girl's eyes flickered to Mr. Pruitt's door with a slight grimace, a sense of complicity between them giving Juliet a flicker of warmth in the otherwise chilly atmosphere.

Disheartened, she walked back out to the street. She'd hoped that in London people might have been more progressive, that the war might have changed things as women stepped up to replace the men lost to the front line. But in spite of this, men like Mr. Pruitt were still holding on to the past, protecting men's rights to lofty positions because women were supposedly too flighty to be of any practical use. Clinging onto this belief was in men's interest, after all; they got to keep their power, regardless whether they deserved it.

Beside the library, the pretty Bethnal Green Park lay before her, a lawn with a few trees and benches. One side had been given over to growing vegetables to help with food rationing, as had many of the city's parklands, and a few older men dug into the soil, their chatter carrying over the lawns.

As Juliet walked through the park, she looked for her new billet among the large Edwardian villas on the far side. Their front gardens gated and groomed, they were among the more prestigious houses in the area. Juliet had found the room by way of an advert pinned to the wall in the Upper Beeding doctor's office. His sister-in-law, a Mrs. Ottley, had a comfortable room to let.

As she approached number 41, Juliet noticed that the house wasn't quite as tidy as the others on Bethnal Green Park. The front garden was a little overgrown, and the paintwork on the windows needed attention. According to the doctor's wife, Mrs. Ottley had been instructed to take in lodgers by the local billeting officer; her evacuated children's bedrooms were needed for war workers.

*Mrs. Ottley might not want a lodger at all,* Juliet thought with a sigh. It was often the case these days, workers foisted onto anyone with a spare bed.

Taking a deep breath, Juliet reaffixed her pillbox hat and strode up the path to the door, giving it a cheery knock.

As she waited, she peered into the front window to see a cluttered living room, a piano with scores scattered over the top, a few battered orange-and-white Penguin paperbacks left on the table.

But other than that, there was no sign of life at all.

She went back to the front door, bent down, and opened the letter box, calling in her most friendly voice, "Mrs. Ottley! Are you there?"

"Yes, dear?" The voice came from behind her, and she turned to see a short, plump woman coming up the path carrying two string shopping bags filled with groceries. Around forty with short brown hair, she was dressed in a green Women's Voluntary Service skirt suit and a pair of low court shoes tight on her feet.

"Oh, let me help you." Juliet hurried forward to take a bag.

"Would you, dear?" She piled both onto her. "Now, let me find my key."

It was only once Juliet had followed her through the hallway to the kitchen, putting the bags down as directed, that Mrs. Ottley looked at her.

"Thank you, er . . . ?" She emitted a small groan as she eased herself into a chair at the kitchen table.

"I'm Juliet Lansdown. I wrote to you from Upper Beeding, about the room?"

"Oh, of course! Silly me! I forgot you were coming today. Let me put the kettle on."

As she laboriously prepared to get up from the chair, Juliet sprang to the stove. "I can do it."

"Thank you, dear." Only too happy to have someone to help, Mrs. Ottley settled herself back down. "There's milk in the parlor beside the back door, and you can find some cups in the sideboard. You look very handy around the kitchen. That'll be useful." She shuffled herself comfortably into the chair. "Now, dear, why don't you tell me a little about yourself? What brings you to London?"

"Well, I'm the new deputy librarian at Bethnal Green. Do you like reading?"

"Oh, I love a good murder mystery. Takes my mind off my children. They've been evacuated with the school to Wiltshire." She said *Wiltshire* with repulsion, as if the county itself were to blame. "They left at the beginning of the war, nearly a year ago now."

"You must miss them terribly, but Wiltshire's a lovely county. Are they with a nice family?"

She shrugged. "It's difficult to say. They're on a small farm, and they tell me about the animals in their letters. It breaks my heart to think of them growing up there, forgetting all about me. When I see some of the women around here bringing back their little ones, I wonder if I should fetch my Jake and little Ivy, too. We haven't had any bombs here, and it seems cruel to leave them away from their home for so long."

"But they're safe where they are, all the government posters say so." Juliet leaned closer to try to comfort her. "What you need is something to take your mind off it. Once I start work tomorrow, I'll be able to get some good books for you. Are you a member of the library?"

"I haven't the time, dear." She laughed at the mere thought. "But the two Miss Ridleys always pass books on to me—they're the old sisters who live next door. Although they don't seem to like mysteries as much as I do."

"Well, why don't you pop in and I can help you register? Then you can take out the books you want."

"I'm too busy now they've put me in charge of a canteen truck with the Women's Voluntary Service. All the women around here volunteer for the WVS if we can. It's good to be involved, but it doesn't give me much spare time." She glanced at the dishes in the sink with dismay. "And renting out rooms takes more effort than you'd think, too."

Juliet's hand stopped as she spooned tea leaves into the pot. "Rooms? Do you have other lodgers here?"

"Yes, there's a large annex in the attic, and my nephew's been renting it. He's not around a great deal, has some kind of job that takes him away a lot. He's a lovely chap, from Upper Beeding, too. Perhaps you know him? His name is Sebastian Falconbury."

Juliet's face fell. "Sebastian?" That was all she needed.

Seeing her expression, Mrs. Ottley said, "Oh, I hoped you'd be friends, since you come from the same place."

Trying to stay pleasant, Juliet said, "Well, we've crossed paths a few times."

"I'm sure you'll adore him once you get to know him better. Very popular with the young ladies he is! And clever, too." With great pride, Mrs. Ottley added, "Just before the war, he passed his law exams. He was at Oxford, you know?"

She did know. He was part of the set who idled away their time at university with picnics beside the river, drinking and debauching. Juliet's mind slid back to the various village events where Sebastian would turn on the charm to all the local girls, sweeping them off their feet only to end things a short while later.

But Juliet was far too clever to become one of his victims.

Deciding not to share this with his doting aunt, she made light of it. "Sebastian was one of the eligible young men my mother was always pressing me to meet, and as such he never stood a chance."

Mrs. Ottley gave her a wink, "All the more reason to like him, wouldn't you say?"

With a sigh, Juliet found herself replying, "Well, actually I was engaged to be married to someone else, so I wouldn't have been interested anyway."

With a glance at her ringless hands, Mrs. Ottley exclaimed, "Oh goodness, my dear! What happened?"

How Juliet wished that she hadn't brought it up! Slowly, she said, "Victor, my fiancé, went missing at the front in Dunkirk." It was the same story she always told, hoping that no one would ask for details, praying they'd drop the subject quickly. She didn't like to think about Victor, let alone talk about him. That was why she'd taken off her engagement ring—to put it all behind her.

"Oh, you poor dear!" Mrs. Ottley looked at her, aghast. "Were you engaged for long?"

"Quite a while," she said vaguely. "He was saving up so that we could live in a proper house. He was a writer, you see, expecting his next book to be his magnum opus, the one to put his name on the map." She didn't mention that the engagement had gone on for over three years. She could never press Victor about it as he would get moody, thinking that she was questioning the value of his work. That was the problem with being a genius; he could be emotional and temperamental. She often thought he was like Mr. Rochester, dark and tempestuous, capable of deep passion, and yet intelligent with a razor-sharp focus.

Mrs. Ottley reached an arm around her shoulders, and Juliet was pulled into a firm embrace. "That must be awful, my dear, but I'm sure another young man will come along and steal your heart. A good-looking young lady like you should have no trouble finding someone new."

Juliet gently pulled away. "It's all right, Mrs. Ottley. I'm better off on my own. In any case, I'm a little too old now—on the shelf almost."

She made a little laugh. "No, I focus on my work and my books, and Bethnal Green Library is my new challenge."

Mrs. Ottley patted a plump hand on hers. "You'll change your mind sooner or later, love. There's nothing quite like having a family of your own, little ones running around the place." Mrs. Ottley rummaged inside a capacious handbag and pulled out a large handkerchief. "Do you have a big family at home?"

"No, it's only me. My parents are older and, well, a little fusty. It's nice to move somewhere new. I always felt out of place there, like I was getting in the way with all my books and new ideas."

"Well, we're a warm happy family here, and you're welcome to be part of it."

Cautiously, Juliet asked, "And what about Mr. Ottley?" One never knew with the war.

But Mrs. Ottley flailed a hand out toward the window. "He's off with the navy, somewhere in the Atlantic, I think. His letters are so blacked out from the censors, it's hard to tell. Sometimes the only part I can read is, "Dearest Winnie, With love from your Gilbert.""

They both laughed, and as Juliet poured out the tea, she couldn't help feeling herself relax. There was a lazy lightheartedness to the place, distinctly different from her own home.

Mrs. Ottley drained her tea and got to her feet. "I'd better show you your room before I get dinner started. You'll have to give me your ration book if you want to eat here, though I'm not much of a cook, I'm afraid." She eyed Juliet hopefully as they went up the stairs. "I don't suppose you're any good?"

The last door on the landing opened into a large, light bedroom with floral wallpaper. On one side, a single bed with a dark pink counterpane looked soft and inviting, and on the opposite wall, there was a small wardrobe flanked by a chest of drawers, a dressing table, and a sink.

"It's my daughter's room." The woman smoothed the bedcover, leaving her hand to rest in the middle, and Juliet could sense the woman's quiet grief at missing little Ivy.

"Well, I'm very grateful to her for letting me stay here. The next

time you write to Ivy, tell her I promise to treat it as well as I can."
Juliet looked out of the window at the park in the front of the house. A
magnolia tree still bore the last of its white-pink petals, a breeze scattering them through the air, like soft snow slowly falling away.

"I'll leave you to unpack," Mrs. Ottley said. "Dinner will be ready
at seven o'clock or so. We're never very punctual, but you'll get used
to us."

After Mrs. Ottley left, Juliet went to the window, budging it open to
take a deep breath of the new London air, and instead of unpacking, she
found herself tempted into the low, cushioned chair beside the window,
a cozy nook for reading.

This is how a home should be, she thought as she settled into the
chair. She couldn't imagine her mother being so hospitable or welcoming to anyone—certainly not a stranger. As she looked around the
room, the hand-drawn pictures on the wall, the books and teddies on
the shelf, she saw the love that Mrs. Ottley had for her daughter. She'd
often assumed that most people existed in starchy families like hers, but
here, this was a different way of living, a warmer, more accepting place.

As predicted, dinner was late. Juliet was starving by the time she
came to find Mrs. Ottley in the kitchen, surrounded by probably every
bowl and pan she owned. Juliet quickly commandeered cooking the
vegetables, but it wasn't until they finally sat down at the dining table
that they heard keys in the front door.

"We're in here!" Mrs. Ottley called in a singsong voice. "You're
just in time for dinner!"

The door opened, and there was Sebastian Falconbury. He looked
much the same, his sandy-colored hair a little tidier, his good-looking
face more mature, his blue-green eyes sharp and amused. Dressed in-
formally in a beige blazer and brown twill trousers, the man looked like
he was strolling in from a weekend in the country, not a work trip. He
pulled out the chair to sit down as he appraised the situation, a half
smile creeping onto his lips as he saw Juliet.

Mrs. Ottley was fussing around him, heaping large spoonfuls of pie
onto his plate. "I think you know Juliet, don't you?"

"Juliet Lansdown, how lovely to see you." Sebastian gave her a charming smile. "Now, what brings you to this part of the world?"

"I'm the new deputy at the library," she said with spirit. She eyed him curiously. "What about you? I would have thought you'd have joined up, with all your athletic triumphs and so forth," adding in an aside to Mrs. Ottley, "Sebastian was the champion batsman of the village cricket team."

"Actually, I was in France," he said lightly. "But after a few bad knocks, they sent me home." It was said with ease, as if it had been a bit of a lark when it was probably rather grim. "Now they have me doing war work in one of the ministries."

She knew that this was a modest way of saying he was doing something important. A lot of jobs in London were high priority, filled by university men brought back from the front to work on coordination and planning, and it didn't surprise her that Sebastian Falconbury was one of them. It was the kind of thing that would happen to him, she thought with annoyance, to be entrusted with the fate of the nation.

"It's been quite a while since we met, hasn't it?" His eyes seemed to scrutinize hers. "Wasn't it at that garden party in Upper Beeding, about three years ago?"

"I think it must have been," she said, eager to move on.

She remembered it well. A garden party had been set up by both sets of parents as a last-ditch attempt to bring them together. Sebastian's father, she gathered, was keen to rein in his profligate son, and her own mother was eager to see off Victor. The event was uncomfortable for both of them, with Juliet lauding her intellectual fiancé over Sebastian, while he replied that Victor's writing was "plagiarized versions of the greats." Loyally, she snapped back at Sebastian that his Oxford set were "degenerate rakes who weren't worthy of the Bodleian Library."

Truth be told, both of them had been a bit rude.

Ever since, she'd been mulling over Sebastian's little put-down of Victor's writing, although sometimes she found herself re-reading it herself, half wondering if there was any truth in it.

Just as she was thinking this, Sebastian turned to her. "And what about you, Juliet? I imagine you've been through a lot since the last time we met." His eyes flickered to her hand. "I heard about Victor. I'm sorry. That must have been difficult for you." There was a quiet earnestness to his voice, disconcerting beside his usual ironic banter.

Flustered, she let her knife slip from her hand, and it clattered onto the plate. How much did he know about Victor's disappearance? They tended to put the men from Upper Beeding into the same platoon in the Royal Sussex Regiment. Had Sebastian been in Dunkirk when Victor vanished?

If he knew the truth about Victor, what would he think of her?

With anguish, she remembered the telephone calls from Victor's mother about the telegrams: The first notified them that he was absent without leave; the second that he was being treated as a deserter. When or if he was found, he would be subject to criminal charges.

She'd balked: There had to be a mistake.

Victor had always talked about loyalty and selflessness as if they were cornerstones of himself, of their relationship. It couldn't possibly be true.

After that awful telephone call, she'd taken off his ring, putting it into the very bottom of her jewelry case. She was determined to block it out of her mind, burying herself in work. If she ignored it long enough, hopefully it would all turn out to be a hideous mistake.

Avoiding Sebastian's gaze, she quickly changed the subject, turning her attention to their landlady. "Mrs. Ottley was telling me how she helps with a WVS mobile canteen. Such terrific work," Juliet said with spirit.

"I'm not the only one." Mrs. Ottley grinned. "Sebastian is in the Air Raid Precautions. The ARP are going to help with the bombing raids, if they ever happen."

"They'll come, all right," Sebastian said. "Nazi planes have been bombing closer to London every week. I wouldn't be surprised if they launch a massive aerial campaign, just as they did in Rotterdam before they invaded the Netherlands." For a moment, he looked concerned. "I only hope we're ready."

Mrs. Ottley looked proudly on. "Sebastian does the ARP three nights a week, *and* he has a full-time job, too."

He shrugged. "It's mostly blackout checks, walking the streets making sure people aren't showing any lights for the German planes to see."

"You'll be very busy if the planes start coming over." Mrs. Ottley grimaced. "We did a first-aid class last week, and they said it'll be all hands on deck if London's bombed. Everyone will have to volunteer." She glanced at Juliet expectantly.

"Well, absolutely," she said, unsure.

"If you can drive, there's a great need for more ambulance drivers." Sebastian raised an eyebrow. "Unless your library position keeps you too busy, of course."

"Well, perhaps I'll look into it once I've settled in," Juliet muttered, unsure how well suited she'd be. Like most well-to-do girls, she'd learned to drive on one of the cars at home. But what about the danger, the lack of sleep, the grisliness of it? She'd always been squeamish, unable to deal with blood and gore. She was a librarian, not a medic.

But Mrs. Ottley was beaming. "Oh, that's a wonderful idea, dear. The ambulances are attached to the ARP, so who knows, perhaps you'll run into each other."

Sebastian and Juliet's eyes met across the table as they acknowledged Mrs. Ottley's very obvious attempt at matchmaking. Then he asked, "How is your job going? I haven't had time to get over to the library recently."

"Well, I officially start tomorrow, but if today is any indication, it's a little bit too quiet."

"We're all too busy with this war." Mrs. Ottley helped herself to more cabbage. "Working where we're told, making sandwiches out of nothing, sending our children to stay with people we don't know."

To Juliet's surprise, instead of dismissing Mrs. Ottley, Sebastian reached over and patted her arm. "I know it's hard, but you're right not to bring them home. Have you heard from them?"

"No letters this week," she said dolefully. "But at least I have you here to keep me company, and Juliet now, too." She looked over at

Juliet. "Sebastian's marvelous with my little ones, giving piggybacks and playing trains."

"And they are both firm favorites of mine." He grinned. "In any case, I had to pass on my expertise in model trains to someone, didn't I?"

Juliet mused. "I didn't see you as the type of man who likes model trains, or spending time with children, for that matter."

"He's wonderful with them," Mrs. Ottley answered for him. "All his father's care mixed with his mother's sense of fun."

"I like to think so." He straightened his jacket with mock pride.

But Mrs. Ottley's mind had gone back to her children. "I do wish they were here."

"They're safer out there," Sebastian reassured her. "If London's bombed, life will become difficult and dangerous. At least they're out of harm's way, and it gives you the chance to do your WVS work. The mobile canteens you help run are invaluable. I know it's a sacrifice to let your children go, but you're helping to keep this country together."

Precisely what it was about this speech that baffled her, Juliet couldn't be sure. But she felt back-footed, as if she'd had Sebastian all wrong.

Hastily, she began eating again, famished as usual. The food rations always seemed to leave her feeling hungry, but tonight's pie had real meat, thank heavens. "This is absolutely delicious, Mrs. Ottley. Where did you manage to get steak? It's quite the best I've had for months."

The woman chuckled. "I got it from the fishmongers, of all places. They had it on sale. Big whopping steaks they were, lovely. I have no idea what the fishmonger was doing with meat. He must have run out of fish." She carried on eating, failing to notice that her two companions had put their cutlery down.

First Juliet and then Sebastian began to laugh.

"I never know what you young folk find funny these days," she said, picking up the serving spoon. "Anyone else for seconds?"

And then Juliet barely contained herself long enough to say, "It's whale, Mrs. Ottley. You bought a piece of whale meat," before laughing once again.

"Are you sure, dear? It looks just like steak."

"Some frozen whale steaks have been coming in, and they're being sold in the fishmongers," Sebastian explained. "Even though whales aren't fish at all, they're mammals, which is why it looks and tastes a little like beef."

"Well, I never!" Mrs. Ottley said, taking a piece on her fork and sniffing it. "I thought it had an odd smell."

Then she began to laugh, too, and somehow, somewhere along the way, the friction between the two lodgers broke, the conversation turning to the new clothes rations, a barrage balloon sailing loose over Hampstead, and a singing contest in the local church hall.

# KATIE UPWOOD

## BETHNAL GREEN LIBRARY

*August 1940*

To KATIE UPWOOD, BOOKS WERE EVERYTHING. FROM HER PRE-cious history tomes to the stretch of encyclopedias, she reveled in having the knowledge of the world at her fingertips. It might be just for the summer, between leaving school and starting university, but her library job was a joy and a privilege, offering plenty of quiet moments to creep into the history aisle.

This particular afternoon she stood among the shelves replacing the returns. The scent of almanacs mingled with the occasional waft of the rose perfume worn by the old Ridley sisters at the newspaper table, the sound of muted voices blending with the rustle of turning pages.

Although she was relishing her summer job, she couldn't wait to start university. She'd always been top of her class, and when the men went to war and more college places were offered to girls, her name had been put forward. Although she felt a little guilty, taking a spot from those on the front, she couldn't believe the opportunity she'd been given. The first girl in her school to go to university, she was the pride of her teachers and her adoring mother, too.

After a quick check that Mr. Pruitt was safely inside his office, she drew out a folded page from her pocket. Only that morning, she'd had a letter from Christopher, who was fighting on the front. She'd read it a few times already, smelling the page for any scent of him as she carefully opened it.

Like her, he was eighteen, and like her, he was one of the bookish ones at school. She'd been so proud of him when he signed up, the day after his eighteenth birthday in the spring, but how naïve it seemed now that the war was so real! Christopher wasn't built for fighting. What if something happened to him? She let out a soft moan: Why had she encouraged—yes, encouraged!—him to go?

*My dearest Katie,*

*Finally I have time to write, but you have to know that even though my letters are sparse, I think about you all the time. We are always so very active, going from one camp or battle to another. Luckily, I have managed to escape injury, but there have been a number of men down, and a whole platoon was taken POW yesterday, others MIA.*

*The men in my platoon are good fun. They call me "Old Boy" as I'm the youngest. I wish I'd brought along some books. Believe me, war can be as dull as it can be frightening.*

*They say we'll have leave at Christmas, and I can't wait to see you. I think of you in your job in the library—all those books, you must be in Heaven! Do you remember the day we hid behind the shelves in the biography section? I don't think I'll ever think of Darwin or Dickens in quite the same light!*

*Take care of yourself, my angel. I can't tell you how much I miss you. Enjoy university once it starts and write and tell me all that you learn.*

*Yours forever,*
*Christopher*

He would have been going to university as well if he hadn't joined up, she thought to herself as she quietly pocketed the letter.

It was three years ago that they'd first become friends. He was the tall, gangly boy in the history class, and she was the keen girl sitting at the front. He'd slipped her a book, *The Edwardians,* and she'd read it that night, barely able to wait until the next day to discuss it. Then they moved on to the Italian Renaissance, medieval fiefdoms, Greek trage- dies.

After a few months, they began to walk home together through the park, sitting on the bench under the magnolia tree, the long branches of pink-white blooms dappling the sunshine. That's where their hands accidentally touched, his fingers covering hers as she passed him a bat- tered copy of *The Rise of the Educated Classes.* It had felt electrical, as if her energy were suddenly fierce, alive, grounded.

If it hadn't been for the books, Katie would have felt self-conscious, unsure, shy. No one had ever shown interest in her before; why would they? Shorter than average and with a tendency to blush a lot, she seemed to blend into the background at school.

But with Christopher it was different. He wasn't handsome until you got to know him, with his pasty complexion and mid-brown hair. But to her, he was beautiful.

Tentatively, they'd begun to hold hands, and then one day, as they walked home, he asked if he could kiss her.

"All right," she'd replied, and there and then, on the corner beside the entrance to the underground station, he leaned his head down and pressed his lips onto hers.

Gradually, their meetings increased in intensity, but it wasn't until Christopher began to sneak Katie up to his bedroom that they began to explore each other more. Both of them naïve in the ways of the world, they let instinct drive them. The more they entwined, the more she felt of them as one: two separate halves that together made a whole.

As she gazed into the middle distance between the bookcases, she was shaken from her reverie by the two old ladies. They had risen from the newspaper table, stopping for a quiet word, as they often did.

"What do you think about the new deputy? She's bringing a bit of energy to the place, don't you think?" The elder Miss Ridley, Irene, had a no-nonsense approach to life. The local headmistress for many years, she only ever read the classics, with a special place in her heart for Shakespeare.

The younger sister, Dorothy, looked on eagerly. A former nurse, she was more whimsical than her sister, a lover of romance and drama.

Katie had got to know the Miss Ridleys well over the summer. They came to the library every day to read the newspapers and peruse the bookshelves, their silver heads bent to the side to read the titles on the book spines.

"Juliet certainly has plenty of spark," Katie agreed.

The new deputy was beautiful, cheerful, and exceedingly well-read. Beside her, Katie felt young and a bit scruffy, her ginger hair mismatching her dress, slightly tight now due to all the potatoes. The food rations meant lots of starch and vegetables, not ideal for the waistline.

"Mr. Pruitt isn't so keen, but Juliet has some wonderful new ideas," Katie went on. "She wants to start a reading group, meeting every week to talk about books."

"Golly, that sounds fun!" Dorothy rubbed her hands.

Irene had that determined glint in her pale blue eyes. "Well, Katie, you're the one who knows how to get around Mr. Pruitt. Why don't you give Juliet some tips?"

"Well, I'm not sure—"

"There's no harm in trying," Dorothy urged.

Virtually pushed by the old ladies, Katie was propelled back to the main desk, taking Juliet to one side. "Some of the regulars think your idea for a new reading group is wonderful, only—" She paused, unsure how to go on. "I've worked here for a while now, and Mr. Pruitt won't budge on something if you keep trying to press him into it." She leaned closer. "You have to be a bit more crafty."

"What do you mean?"

"You have to give him what he wants, and then you simply do what you want behind the scenes."

Juliet grinned. "Crafty indeed, Katie! The only trouble is, I can't make head or tail of him at all. What on earth could I do to keep him happy?"

Katie glanced over her shoulder to make sure he wasn't around. "He wants an easy life, sitting in his office, writing letters, and reading the newspaper." Katie laughed. "He used to leave the day-to-day running to the old deputy, so why don't you let him think he can do the same with you? Don't mention anything about the reading group. He takes every Saturday off work, so why don't we set up the first meeting for a Saturday morning?"

Baffled, Juliet said, "But how can we tell everyone about the meeting if we can't let Mr. Pruitt know?"

"The Miss Ridleys will spread the word, and maybe we could make a leaflet of sorts, quietly hand it around to people who might be interested instead of putting anything up on the noticeboard."

Juliet's eyes flitted to the old ladies, now back at the newspaper table. "Those two are quite the mischief makers, aren't they? Do they ever go anywhere without each other?"

"Not that I've ever known, even though they never seemed to agree with each other on anything. They already said they'd ask Marigold Saxby to come to the meeting, too."

"Is Marigold another regular?"

Katie nodded. "She's quite a character, used to be a singer, then she married Jason Saxby—a local gangster, or so they say. You can't miss her; she's about forty, very blond, and dresses like she's about to go on stage any minute." Katie made a little laugh. "But she's lovely and helps the Miss Ridleys a lot. She's completely addicted to romances."

"A gangster husband, you say?"

"Apparently he's making a fortune with forged ration books and identity papers. The war has caused all sorts of underground networks to pop up. I think Marigold's involved with some dodgy dealings, too. Word is, she's the one you need to see if you want a private detective or something on the black market . . . at least, that's what the Miss Ridleys say—they like to gossip more than they'd care to admit." As she laughed, she felt the thrill of excitement about the new reading group. "Do say you'll set it up, Juliet! I'm sure it'll be a great success."

"Well, why not? We'll call it the Library Book Club," Juliet declared, then added in a whisper, "Provided you don't think we'll get into trouble if Mr. Pruitt finds out."

"Take it from me, even if he does hear anything, he knows it'll be easier for him to pretend he didn't."

After work, Katie walked home through the park, her gas mask box banging against her side. She hadn't realized just how excited she'd be about a book club. It was something positive to lift their spirits amid all the talk of a Nazi invasion or mass bombing raids.

Katie's family lived in one of the larger houses on the park, the property bought by her father in the hopes of impressing his clients. A keen insurance businessman, he recognized how important it was to personify wealth and respectability. His customers knew the family personally; they were members of the church, parents at the school, friends from the neighborhood. Presenting the right impression was crucial to his success.

The entire family had been drawn into this, too. Katie's university place was peddled as a "means of meeting the right kind of husband." Her younger brother Rupert's ineptitude was brushed off with a jolly laugh: "Boys will be boys." And Mrs. Upwood's lower-class background was carefully covered up by elocution lessons and tips she'd read in society magazines.

But the more successful her father became, the more he seemed to loathe his family's deficiencies, especially Katie's mother's. He continually picked at her over small slips, angrily leaving the house to spend evenings with clients and his new set of friends instead of with his family.

Katie let herself in the front door. "Hello-o," she called. Taking off her coat, she peered into the front room. As usual, it was spotless, her father insisting on an exemplary interior just in case a client popped around unannounced. Expensive artworks and ornaments adorned the room, along with lush rugs and luxurious gold-tasseled drapes.

Her mother was usually at home, except when she had her women's groups, so Katie walked quickly through to the dining room to find her. But it, too, was empty.

*Where is everyone?*

Picking up speed, she strode down toward the kitchen. "Mum?"

And there she was. But instead of her usual upright form, dressed up for the WVS, she was sitting at the kitchen table, her hands winding through each other as a small fly buzzed at the window, its body tapping sporadically on the glass as it tried to get through.

"Mum?" Katie hurried over and pulled up a chair beside her. "Are you all right?"

But when her mother turned, there was a pallor to her face. "Katie? You're home early, I wasn't . . ." She paused, not knowing how to go on.

"I'm not early, Mum. Shall I make you some tea?" Katie felt her forehead, but it was cool, slightly damp.

"I'm fine," she said quietly. "It's you, my dear. You're the one who needs tea." Slowly, she pulled out a small official-looking envelope, the kind that contains a telegram. Placing it on the table, she pushed it over toward Katie.

"But it's not addressed to me," Katie said before registering the recipient. "Christopher's father," she murmured as she read the name.

There could only be one reason why this envelope was here.

A lightheadedness came over her as she pulled out the single, typed sheet.

MR. E. F. DONALDSON
46 HATCH ROAD BETHNAL GREEN

DEEPLY REGRET TO INFORM YOU THAT YOUR SON 46986 PVT CHRISTOPHER JOHN DONALDSON HAS BEEN REPORTED MISSING IN ACTION, PRESUMED DEAD. LETTER TO FOLLOW.

OC RICHARDS

Katie's world spun, the table swooping over and around, the kitchen taking on a gray blurriness.

"Christopher?" she whispered.

Her mother took her into her arms. "I'm so sorry. He was such a lovely boy, a fine young man. What a terrible thing to happen."

Katie felt her breathing stop, anything to make this news go away.

"I know. It seems too much to take in," her mother said, looking at the telegram in front of her. "His father could hardly speak when he came in, the poor man."

Katie's face paled with incomprehension. "But I had a letter from him this morning." She pulled it out of her bag, opening it as if it were proof. "He's alive, you see. He's fine."

Her mother put a hand on her arm, her eyes beseeching her. "But this telegram, it can't be a mistake, it came today. That's his father's name on it, their address. And your letter would have been written weeks ago."

Katie shook her head briskly. "It just doesn't feel like he's gone."

Her mother heaved a sigh, pulling her chair over. "I know it's not easy to take in."

Katie paused, something inside her crumbling. "But he can't be dead. He simply can't!"

Unable to find words, her mother put her arms around Katie, holding her as close as she could—always the solid, reliable person in her life.

Convulsing with hysterics, Katie buried her face in her mother's shoulder, but as her stomach heaved, she pulled away, barely making it to the bathroom before the entire contents of her stomach were ejected, as if her body simply couldn't bear to hear any more.

And she budged the window open, looking out into the sky.

"Where are you, Christopher?" she cried into the air. "Where are you?"

# SOFIE

## 36 BETHNAL GREEN PARK

*August 1940*

ARGUABLY THE BEST HOUSE ON BETHNAL GREEN PARK BELONGED to Mr. Wainwright, and he did everything he could to make sure everyone knew it. The rooms were splendid, albeit old-fashioned. The luxurious blue drapes and sofa fabrics were perfectly cleaned and ironed. The shelves and mantels ladened with statuettes were dusted daily. Before she had died a few years ago, his wife had been the self-appointed doyen of style in the locality, and now after her loss, her widowed husband was determined to maintain his wife's reputation in both upkeep and cleanliness.

Or rather, he was determined the housemaid would.

His voice bellowed from the living room. "Baumann!"

"Coming, Mr. Wainwright." Sofie left the half-finished washing up and hurried to see what he wanted. More than a year had passed since her arrival, and she still struggled to cope with the long hours, confusing work, and the sheer cold seclusion of the place—not to mention her unpleasant, abrasive employer.

Never had she felt so alone.

She awoke at five, alone in her gray little room in the cellar, dressing quickly in her gray maid's uniform. Then, also alone, she caught up with the laundry before making breakfast and waiting table for the most fussy, bad-tempered man who ever lived, making her wish that she was once again alone.

Inside her head, she replayed novels and poems as she polished and ironed, shopped and cooked, always alone. Her memories were her only company aside from the now-tattered copy of poetry beside her thin, gray cot.

At night she would collapse into it, exhausted, and read a poem or two, feel the words sink into her, become her, before falling asleep, the book clutched to her chest. Those poems were her friends, her family, and her sanity.

She hurried into the living room, where Mr. Wainwright had settled down to listen to the radio. A grim-faced, dogged man of over sixty, he didn't work, as far as Sofie could make out, and filled his days reading the papers, harrumphing at the radio, and making demands.

"You need to go to the library today, get a book with a map of Europe. I need to see the location of these places they're talking about on the news. The library's on the main road, beside the park. Mind you get a good map, none of that foreign rubbish."

"The library?"

She knew where it was, of course. Most days she made a detour to walk beside the beautiful building as she went to the grocer's, but never had she dared to go inside. If she did anything outside of Mr. Wainwright's instructions, he'd threaten to tell the authorities, have her visa canceled.

But now he was asking her to go.

Her mind soared. How she'd longed to go inside, feel that sensation of being surrounded by books again. And what about the people there? Would they be kinder than this odious man?

"Baumann?" Mr. Wainwright's voice roared through her thoughts. "I thought I told you to plant those winter vegetables." He jabbed a finger at his newspaper. "It says it's our patriotic duty to use every part of land we have to produce food. I know you're not British—and you should be grateful I don't hold that against you—but it must be done immediately."

"I'm sorry, sir, but I had to clear away the bushes, and some of them were difficult to get out." Pulling up the hydrangea and the hefty laburnum had wrecked her hands. The sores were still painful. "And I can't do the gardening in the evenings because we aren't allowed to have lights outside due to the blackout."

He grunted. "I know I can't expect you to think for yourself, but surely you should move the housework to the evening and use the daytime for the vegetable plot?"

She clenched her jaw shut to stop herself from barking back at him that she wasn't stupid, and he was the one that demanded she did the housework during the day so he could relax in the evenings without her "bustling about." She'd never done a job like this—never even cleaned or cooked before—but she knew his treatment of her wasn't right. She came from a good family, one where people were polite to their servants.

Calming herself, she spoke carefully. "I use the evenings to do the mending you wanted. Would you rather I set that aside in exchange for the housework?"

He flicked the newspaper down to look at her, a growl on his flabby mouth as he snarled, "You'll have to work faster then. Don't you understand you are a housemaid, you stupid girl? This is your job!"

Trembling, she made a small bob and muttered, "Yes, sir." It didn't pay to challenge Mr. Wainwright. The yellow-purple marks on her arm bore witness to his hot temper and spiteful dissatisfaction with life.

At the beginning of the war, the other maid and then the cook had quickly grabbed jobs in the new munitions factories, well away from Mr. Wainwright.

But Sofie couldn't leave.

Her visa was tied to the job. If she left or was fired, she would be forced onto the first boat back to the Nazis.

And it was a fact Mr. Wainwright never ceased to exploit.

As she sat on her bed, she pulled out her family photograph. How she wished Rachel and Papa were there, but there had been no domestic visas for either of them. Now she was stuck in London on her own.

She was barely holding herself together. How easy her old life had been, full of books, and music, and laughter. Now all those things were gone. She had no family, no friends, nothing except fear.

One of the calluses on her hands opened, blood oozing, and as she reached for a bandage to stop a drop of blood sliding down her wrist, she barely noticed the distant noise from outside growing louder.

It was the air-raid siren.

"Not again!" She let out a long, low groan, before getting up and plodding upstairs, the wail growing louder with every step.

The siren came every few weeks for no reason at all. At first, fear had gripped Sofie whenever she heard it, freezing her to the spot, unable to move. Had she come all this way, left dear Papa and Rachel, worked herself to the bone, only to be mowed down by a Nazi bomber?

Gradually, it became clear that the sirens were either false alarms or only small parties of planes bombing an aerodrome or factory. Other than overhearing Mr. Wainwright's radio, the only access to news she had was on the newspaper headlines in the shops or the snippets of gossip she heard while lining up at the butcher every morning. Despite her best efforts, she barely knew what was happening with the war.

At the top of the servants' stairs, she stopped, creeping up to the living room door. Mr. Wainwright never allowed her to listen to the news with him in the living room, but if she kept quiet, she could stand in the corridor and catch a few things.

"An air raid is in operation," the announcer said. "So we will be off air until the all clear sounds."

Sofie frowned. The BBC usually carried on broadcasting through false alarms.

"Baumann! Baumann!" Mr. Wainwright's voice thundered through the house.

"Yes, sir." She went in to see him on his feet, barging past furniture to the window.

A muscle pulsated in his cheek, forcing his eyelid to flicker uncontrollably. "Go outside." He flicked a fat finger toward the park. "See what's happening."

Grabbing the basket so that she could continue on to the shops if it was another false alarm, she hurried out into the sunshine. It had been a glorious late-summer day, and even now, at a quarter to four, the sun beamed warmth onto her exhausted face.

From the park, she could see across the rooftops and spires of the city, the sky speckled with silver-gray barrage balloons. Their cables forced Nazi planes to fly higher, which stopped the dive bombers that had crushed other cities. One of the balloons was positioned right above the park itself, the massive behemoth a bullet-shaped blob above her. Sofie gazed at their soft forms, wondering whether they were better at keeping the Nazis out or showing them where it would hurt the most.

On the green, other residents had gathered to gaze up at the horizon. Mostly neighborhood women, they smiled and greeted one another, wondering what to do.

A few planes could be seen in the distance, but that was all, and in a few minutes the all clear was sounding—the same air-raid wail, but played only once. Everyone began to return inside, and with a glance back to the house, Sofie hurried down to the main road.

Bethnal Green Library stood like a beacon, a reminder of her home, of the girl she had once been. It seemed a distant dream, a world of culture and words, of higher pursuits than planting vegetables and scrubbing the latrine.

As she walked inside, a stillness came over her, and then slowly, she breathed them in, the books. Even if she couldn't spend long there, something about the place made her feel normal, creative, full of stories, full of promises, and she felt a sudden longing to curl up among them, right there, and sleep for a thousand years.

The main atrium was breathtaking, and she stood in the center marveling at the expanse, the rows upon rows of books, their familiar scent infusing the air like magical revelations ready to change lives, to alter possibilities.

"Do you have a map book?" she asked a woman reshelving stock in the nearest aisle.

"We have some just down here," she said brightly, showing her the way. "I'm Juliet, the deputy here. Are you new to the area?"

She shook her head. "I'm just a housemaid."

Juliet eyed her curiously. "You live beside the park, don't you? I do, too. I think I've seen you coming and going." She glanced at the empty bag. "Would you like a library card?"

Usually, Sofie wasn't allowed to converse with strangers, but something in the way the woman smiled at her made her yearn for some kind of connection in her too-small world. "I would, very much." She felt a catch in her throat as she followed Juliet to the main desk, where the deputy opened a box of library cards and filled one in.

"Now, what's your full name?"

"Sofie Baumann."

"You must be from central Europe," Juliet said cheerily as she wrote.

Lowering her voice, Sofie murmured, "This is not very popular"— she glanced at the floor—"but I am from Germany." She waited for the woman to wince or pull away, but Juliet merely looked up from her writing.

"Well, if you're German," she said with a decisive smile, "there must be a very good reason why you're here."

"I'm Jewish," Sofie said simply. "I needed to escape, with the way things were going, and the only way to get a visa to live in Britain was to take a job as a servant."

Juliet nodded, looking her over: her stance, the look on her face. "But you weren't a servant back in Germany, were you?"

Slowly, Sofie shook her head, standing a little taller. "I lived with my family, and we had servants to clean for us." She let out a sad laugh at the irony. "It was our maid Hilde who taught me how to clean and cook before I came. But I am lucky just to be out of Germany. Grateful, too, only . . ."

"I can't imagine it's been easy." Juliet encouraged her on.

Sofie's eyes glanced uncomfortably at the kind woman. "I have no idea where my sister and father are. I haven't heard from them in nearly a year, and I worry all the time."

"Are they still in Germany?"

She shrugged. "In the last letter I received, my sister said she was leaving overland through France with a neighbor, but my father refused to go, certain that he would slow them down." She curled her fist with frustration at his stubbornness. "She said that our house had been taken by the government, and my father was forced to go to live with friends." Sofie wasn't sure why she was opening up to this woman, but the words came tumbling out, unstoppable. "I'm worried about him—about my sister, too. Now that France has been taken by the Nazis, it must be very dangerous. I want to help her, but I don't know how. I don't even know where she is. I feel like I'm letting her down—letting both of them down." Emotion welled up inside her.

"Do you know the route your sister was going to take through France?"

"She was going to try to get to the north coast and take a boat to Britain, that's what she said before I left." She glared into Juliet's eyes. "She is traveling with our neighbor Frederick. He has blond hair and can get away with being Aryan."

Juliet's face creased. "Is that so very necessary?"

"To get across the border, it is essential. But it is risky though. You could be spotted by someone who knows you, or your papers might be searched."

"How terrible, to have to hide yourself in your own country!"

"We became prisoners there. It was so gradual, first one law to close our shops, then another to stop us living in a certain area. Now the Nazis have so much control, I'm scared of what they will do with it."

"That must be agonizing, not to know where your family are, how they are."

"And all I can do is keep on working, keep on staying alive, praying that one day we will emerge from this nightmare, unscathed, and go back to where we were before."

"I'm so sorry." She paused, looking at Sofie's eyes and hands. "And is your work all right? Your employer seems a bit of a character."

Sofie frowned. "He knows how to keep me busy."

"What do you mean?" Juliet asked under her breath. "I hope he doesn't treat you badly."

Sofie instinctively put her hand on her arm to cover the marks where he'd grabbed her. "I need the job to keep my visa, and he knows that. Maybe that's why he hired a Jewish refugee. I don't know how he'd get anyone else to work for him."

"Some people are despicable," Juliet said with feeling. "Perhaps you could try to get another job. Your English is very good. Were you studying it before you came over?"

"Yes, I went to a Jewish school, and when the Nazis came to power, people began to think about joining relatives in America or here in Britain and they began teaching us English."

"What a horrific time you've had! You must come back to the library any time you can. Do you like to read?"

"I do, very much." Sofie heard a tremor in her voice, so incredible was it for someone to be so kind. "My father's library was my favorite place in our house." She gazed across to the spiral stairs running up the high shelves around the walls. "It feels so good to be here, like I can breathe again."

Juliet smiled. "That's how it is for me, too, the familiarity of bookshelves no matter where you are. All those stories to delve into, to lose yourself inside." There was something wistful in Juliet's gaze for a moment, and then she asked, "What books do you like?"

"I like short stories, but I think poetry is my favorite."

Juliet leaned forward. "We're holding a book club here on Saturday morning if you'd like to come? You could meet other people, feel a little less alone."

Sofie smiled, but then the fear came back, the utter dread that she might be caught. "I'll try to find an excuse to come for a while."

"It'll be a varied crowd, but I predict a spirited conversation and plenty of laughs." Juliet pondered for a moment. "And there might be someone who can help you find your family."

Sofie doubted it, but she appreciated the effort Juliet was making. "I will try to come."

Conscious of the time, Juliet helped her find a map book for Mr. Wainwright and then planted a second book in her hands. "This is for you. Something to keep you going, whether you've read it or not."

Sofie turned it over. "Short stories by Anton Chekov, how wonderful!"

"My favorite is the one called 'The Lady with the Dog,'" Juliet said.

Something inside Sofie seemed to both open and crush, and she longed for her father's old library—would she ever be there again? With a lump in her throat, she pinned the book to her chest. "It is perfect," she said, sliding it into her bag with the map book before glancing worriedly at the door. "Thank you, Juliet, for listening to me. I can't remember the last time anyone did." Before the tears that were building behind her eyes could escape, she darted out into the street.

And there she was again, back by the shops where she trudged every morning, back into the misery of her new life.

Only this time, as she dashed through the park, a new spring lifted her step. There was a book meeting to attend, and come hell or high water, she was going to get there.

But more than this, inside her bag, like a golden beam of light, was a new book, a vision of thought and hope and desire all engulfed in those slim, crowded pages.

# JULIET

---

## THE BETHNAL GREEN LIBRARY NEWSLETTER

---

### AUGUST 1940

*Welcome to our new monthly newsletter!*
*Keeping everyone up-to-date with what's*
*happening in the library.*

#### BETHNAL GREEN LIBRARY BOOK CLUB

*Every Saturday 10 a.m.*

*All are welcome!*

#### NEW MEMBERS

*The Bethnal Green Library needs*
*new members!*

*Please ask your family, friends,*
*and neighbors to join.*

JULIET HURRIED THROUGH THE OLD, VAULTED LIBRARY, WARMED BY the sunlight streaming through the dome. She'd handwritten a monthly newsletter—even though it was already halfway through August—passing it around to the regulars to keep it away from Mr. Pruitt's beady eyes.

After Katie's advice about keeping Mr. Pruitt away from her plans, she was getting into her stride. People were responding to her new ideas, and a number of newcomers had registered for library cards. Hopefully, word would spread, bringing more people to the library and stopping the council from closing it down.

Today she was bristling with nervous excitement. The first book club meeting was to be held in the reading room, and a great deal was riding on it. Mr. Pruitt was bound to hear about it sooner or later, and if it was a success, he could hardly put an end to it.

A flutter of light chatter came from the double doors as the Miss Ridleys arrived. Always neatly turned out, they were hotly debating something between them. Although at first they seemed indistinguishable, with their soft white hair pinned up behind their heads, Juliet had noticed that the older one, Irene, was daintier, even though she was clearly the one in charge. The younger one, Dorothy, was taller and more disorderly. She was always ready to disagree with her sister, a tang of rebellion in the jut of her chin.

As Juliet joined them heading into the leaded glass reading room, she saw that someone was already inside it.

"And you must be Mrs. Saxby."

The woman beamed up at her. "Call me Marigold," she said in a dramatic voice. A handsome woman, Marigold Saxby certainly made the most of what she had been given. Her heavy mascara and dyed blond curls made her look as if she were heading for a night spot rather than to a library. Draped languidly on a chair, she wore a knee-length blue silk dress with matching high-heeled shoes—so fancy, Juliet thought, that they must have been bought before the war. A mink coat was propped casually over her shoulders.

"Darlings!" she cried as the Miss Ridleys came in behind Juliet. "How wonderful of you to tell me about this!"

"We knew it would be more fun with you, Marigold," Dorothy said.

Quietly, Katie slipped in, taking a seat beside Dorothy.

"How are you, my dear?" Irene asked.

But the girl only murmured politely, "I'm fine, thank you," when she obviously wasn't. The news about her young man had put her into a tailspin.

"A nice chat will do you good," Dorothy said.

A voice from the door called, "Am I late?" and there was Mrs. Ottley with a grocery bag.

"Lovely to see you!" Juliet offered her a seat. "Shall we start?" And with aplomb, she moved to the front—as she'd done so many times in Upper Beeding.

"Welcome to the first meeting of the Library Book Club. First of all, I'd like to say a word about why we are here: Books." A few chuckles went around the small room before Juliet went on. "To me, books are like old friends, telling us great truths, holding our hands through the difficulties, showing us light and joy at the end of every tunnel." She gazed around at the faces. "Sometimes all I need is to see my battered copy of *Pride and Prejudice* to know that the characters are there inside me, warming my spirit, telling me to live life on my own terms, comforting me that everything will be all right in the end."

A hearty agreement went around the room.

"We all have our favorites," Juliet continued. "So I'd like to go around the group, introducing ourselves and saying what kinds of books we enjoy."

The Miss Ridleys went first, describing themselves as "literary doyens." Irene said she liked Virginia Woolf and Edith Wharton, and although Dorothy professed to liking Dickens, Irene stated, "But she has a proclivity for dramas, invariably those featuring a tragic love story, an inheritance battle, and someone dying under suspicious circumstances."

Marigold said that she only read romances—"especially those Regency ones, swashbuckling heroes and gutsy damsels."

Katie said that she liked history books. "Oh yes, and encyclopedias, too."

"And I like murder mysteries," Mrs. Ottley said, adding with relish: "A good Agatha Christie makes for a perfect evening."

"Oh, I agree heartily! There's nothing quite like a murder to perk up the spirits," Dorothy said, making everyone laugh.

Juliet grinned, delighted with how it was going. "Today I want to discuss what makes a favorite book so magical that you come back to it time and time again."

"We were just talking about that, weren't we, Irene?" Dorothy looked at her sister. "Shall we find out what the others think?"

"They'll agree with me, of course," Irene said, as if it were a foregone conclusion. "We were discussing which of the Brontë novels is the best, and there really is no contest. *Jane Eyre* is by far the superior one."

Secretly, Juliet smiled to herself. Of course the no-nonsense former headmistress liked the strong-willed heroine who spoke out and won respect.

Nonetheless, Dorothy was adamant. "But *Wuthering Heights* has Heathcliff! He absolutely trumps Mr. Rochester every time."

"Not that barbarian again! Jane is such a forthright woman, ahead of her time."

Marigold batted her mascaraed eyelids. "Well, I've always been a Heathcliff woman, plain and simple. Don't you want to rip his clothes off?" She let out a burst of raucous laughter, and Dorothy, part shocked, part delighted, joined in.

The battle ensued until a voice came from the door. "Has the meeting already started?" It was the young refugee. Thin and pale, she had haunted dark eyes in a heart-shaped face, her dark hair coming loose from beneath a beige cloche hat.

"Sofie, come and join us!" Juliet got up and pulled a chair over beside hers, turning to the others. "Sofie is a Jewish refugee. She's working as Mr. Wainwright's housemaid."

Before she could finish, Irene Ridley was already tutting loudly. "I hope that man is being agreeable. He's a bit of a swine is Ernest Wainwright."

"Well, he works me very hard." Sofie looked at her hands, and Juliet saw the scabs.

"Perhaps we could have a word with him." Dorothy's eyes followed Juliet's to the girl's wounds. "And maybe you could let me have a look at those sores, too. I have some antiseptic ointments at home."

Sofie looked at her uncertainly. "Th-thank you."

And that's when Juliet decided to broach the subject of helping Sofie find her family. It wasn't quite as she'd anticipated—in her mind Juliet would quietly introduce the topic—but needs must. She couldn't let the opportunity slip away.

"I asked Sofie to come today because I thought someone here might be able to help her," Juliet said, her eyes flickering uncontrollably to Marigold. "Sofie is trying to find her sister and their neighbor. They are traveling through France, trying to escape the Nazis."

The girl's eyes began to gleam with tears. "I want to help them, but I don't know how I can when I have no idea where they are—or if they're even alive."

There was silence for a moment, Dorothy putting a hand on Sofie's arm.

But then a voice came from the other side of the room. "I might be able to help." It was Marigold, pulling her fur closer around her neck. "I know a few people who earn a bob or two doing a spot of investigating. I'm sure someone might give you a few tips, for a small fee." She gave the girl a wink.

With apprehension, Sofie said, "Thank you, that is very kind. Will it be much?"

"A few pounds should do the trick. Why don't you write down the name of your sister, anything you can remember about their planned journey, and I'll pass it along. Put down your own address, too, and if they hear anything, you'll get a note through the door."

Carefully, Juliet tore a page from her notebook and passed it to Sofie with a pen.

Sofie began to write. "I'm very worried for them. Even before the war, my journey here was incredibly dangerous, and now with France occupied, anything could have happened."

"You poor thing." Marigold took the paper and tucked it into her handbag. "Leave it to me, love. I'll see what I can do."

Juliet was looking at a small pile of books on the table. "What you

ın the meantime is a good discussion to take your mind off every-
˛g."

"I do love to read," Sofie said. "Books are the only thing that keep
me going, a kind of home inside my heart." Her eyes went to the neat
pile on the table, and she pulled out a copy of *Ulysses*. "I haven't seen
this in years. James Joyce was one of the writers banned in Germany."

"Were a lot of books banned?" Irene asked.

Sofie's face clouded. "I remember the night of book burning in
Berlin, just after Hitler came into power in 1933. Papa took us with
him, even though I was still only thirteen. The whole of Opera Square
was a colossal fire, larger than any I'd ever seen. Young men were
shouting and chanting, throwing books into the flames. It was terrifying, monstrous, these people thinking they could obliterate history and
culture and reinvent it the way it suited them. My father wanted us to
see it so that we could understand what was coming."

"Books give people ideas, and they want only their Nazi ideas to
prosper," Irene said, her eyes meeting Sofie's.

"That's right," Sofie nodded. "The Nazis have this organization
called the Chamber of Culture, who are there to make sure everything published and broadcast backs Hitler and his ideologies. A list
of 'acceptable authors' came out, and we had to go through our own
bookshelves and bring the banned books to a collection point for the
burnings. They took place all over the country."

"Did you take your books down, too?" Dorothy asked.

"We had to. If you kept your books, they would burn down your
whole house. The warning was clear: Do what we say or we will burn
you."

"And was it the same for bookshops?" Irene asked.

Sofie nodded. "Most were burned, but libraries were kept open as
cultural centers. They were quickly filled with Hitler's books and new
authors pedaling Nazi propaganda. The banned authors fled the country. Papa told me that Brecht left immediately, saying, 'Where you
burn books, you ultimately burn people.'"

They sat in solemn silence until Dorothy asked, "Which authors
were banned?"

"Most of the good German authors and everyone Jewish, of
A lot of European authors were banned, too. I watched them strip li-
braries of Tolstoy, Huxley, and Dostoevsky, and American authors like
Hemingway and Scott Fitzgerald.

"Then we began to hear whispers about underground libraries.
People hid their favorites, shared them with others. It was risky, but it
was the small rebellions that made you feel alive, like you had power
over something in your life."

"Well, we'd better find some books for you to read," Dorothy said,
passing her a battered paperback. "Have you ever read *Wuthering
Heights*? If nothing else cheers you up, Heathcliff most certainly will.
It's like you're running through the Yorkshire Dales, feeling the fresh
air on your face, desperate for Heathcliff's body next to yours."

"Don't be vulgar, Dorothy," Irene snapped. But then she added, "It
is a classic though, Sofie dear. Although perhaps you would like to read
*Jane Eyre* afterward? You'll be saving the best for last."

As the discussion dissolved once more into the merits of each, Juliet
found herself sitting back, thinking about what was happening in Germany. How lucky their little group was to live in a country where libraries were still free to house the world's wealth of history and culture.

"What about you, Juliet, you're not a silly romantic, are you?"
Irene was looking for support. "What do you think about love?"

Juliet coughed, thinking of Victor and avoiding their gaze. "Well, it
isn't for everyone, is it?"

"Come on, love!" Marigold goaded her with a nudge. "There must
be a young man you have your eye on, isn't there?"

Shaking her head, Juliet declared, "Who needs a man when I have
this glorious library to manage, filled with fellow readers and books!
But to answer your original question, I'm not a romantic at all." And
she added with a grin, "I'm a librarian, a realist, and a thoroughly no-
nonsense person."

And as the laughter echoed through the windowed room, Juliet
couldn't help feeling her heart warming to this new place, this new
challenge, and these new, unlikely friends.

# KATIE

IMMERSED IN GRIEF OVER CHRISTOPHER'S DEATH, IT WASN'T UNTIL the following Tuesday that something bothering Katie began to take hold. She was in the library, the rain pattering on the dome, the place suddenly cool and dim as she went in search of the medical section.

The idea had been pressing her, at first a shadow wavering in the back of her brain, then a possibility, and now a potential reality. She'd moved the button on her skirts twice before discarding them for looser dresses, and why was she so exhausted all the time? She'd blamed it on the war, the rations, and then Christopher's death. But now, the inkling of another possibility nudged at her, unwilling to be set aside by excuses any longer.

She pulled out the great medical encyclopedia and heaved it to the newspaper table, empty now that the Miss Ridleys had left for the day. Hastily, she turned the pages to the right section.

And the moment she read it, Katie knew.

> If the patient is experiencing nausea, fatigue, weight gain, and her menstrual cycle has stopped, there is a chance she is pregnant.

Her breath caught in her throat.

The tightening of her clothes wasn't due to bloating or food rations, and nor were the disturbances inside due to indigestion.

The truth of it made her head spin. There was a baby growing inside her.

How could this have happened?

Frantically, she looked back to the book for more information. But it was a traditional Victorian tome, human reproduction being too immoral to describe in detail.

Her mother had been equally vague when she explained her monthlies to Katie a few years ago. The short discussion was conveyed hurriedly while she handed Katie the rags, briskly showing her how to loop the ends onto the belt to hold them in place. Her mother had simply said that pregnancy was something that happened to married couples who wanted a child.

But Katie wasn't married, and she didn't want a child.

Desperately, she went back to the bookcase, sliding out a guide to veterinarian practices, flicking through until she stopped abruptly at reproduction.

And even before she read, she knew. It all fit together; how natural it had seemed, how obvious, how instinctive. A seamless progression from a simple kiss to the creation of another human being. How clever nature was. How sly.

Panic shot through her.

*What am I going to do?*

It had been over four months since Christopher had left for war, but the pregnancy could have begun before then. Automatically, her hands went to her stomach, which bulged beneath her dress; she couldn't believe she'd been so naïve that she hadn't noticed how swollen it was.

Her mind spun as she felt the stirrings of a new life growing inside her. Although she always assumed she'd get married and have children at some point, it seemed years away, after college, when she was a proper married adult.

And suddenly, like an ice-cold wind, her new reality became crystal clear.

Without Christopher, without a ring on her finger, this baby—their baby—would be illegitimate. Both she and the child would be outcast from society.

About that, she wasn't naïve.

She'd witnessed a girl at the church fall into the same situation. Shunned by the community, she'd been sent to an unmarried mother's home, where they'd given her baby to "proper parents" for adoption. When she returned, she'd been a shell of herself, vilified by the locals, shunned by other men, left to do the best she could with her life while nursing her broken heart for the baby she'd had to give away.

A shudder went through Katie as she remembered her own mother joining the vitriol with the shrew-like Mrs. Baxter, the grande dame of Bethnal Green. "What else can she expect?" she'd muttered. "It's no wonder her mother is throwing her out."

Katie winced. Was she, too, to be thrown out? Would her own mother—the person who was so very dear to her—spurn her, too?

And what about her father? Surely this would cement his loathing for her once and for all; he would probably throw her out of the house for good. Where would she go if he did?

The more she thought about it, the more she realized what she would lose. Her precious university course would be gone, her plans for the future dissipating one by one: her studies, her career, her family.

If only Christopher were here. She knew that he would marry her in a heartbeat and her problems would be solved.

"Why did you have to get yourself killed, Christopher?" she murmured.

With a shudder she realized that this baby growing inside of her was the last small part of him living—that an element of him was still alive.

The wonder of it awed her: this child that was both hers and Christopher's. Not only was the baby the last remaining part of him, but it was also a mixture of them both—a product of their true love.

A sob caught in her throat.

"Why did you leave me?" she whimpered into the still air.

But there was no reply.

In the dregs of her despair, only one thing became clear: She couldn't let anyone know until she'd worked out what to do.

And that meant keeping it secret from her mother.

# SOFIE

HE LINE AT THE BUTCHER HAD SLOWED TO A CRAWL, AND AS Sofie stood waiting, she tried to ignore the smell of raw offal and the fat drops of rain that threatened a downpour. Time ticking by, her chance to get to the library was being curtailed with every extra minute she spent waiting. She'd taken to popping in whenever she could; Juliet and the Miss Ridleys had quickly become central to her day. The day before, Marigold had told her she'd asked a contact if he could find the whereabouts of her sister, and Sofie couldn't wait to hear if there was any news.

Worrying that the line was too long, she asked the woman ahead of her, "Do they have beef today?"

But to her horror, the woman spun around angrily as soon as she heard Sofie's accent. "Are you German? Come to take all our meat, after you've taken all our men?" She pulled up a fist, waving it in front of Sofie's face. "Well, you can tell them about my sister's lad, in the hospital with a broken pelvis. Your German friends would like that, wouldn't they?"

"Is she a Nazi?" another joined in, and soon Sofie was surrounded, a group of women raging at her.

"I'm not a Nazi, I'm Jewish," Sofie cried, begging them to listen, to understand. "I'm a refugee here, a housemaid. I hate the Nazis just as much as you—more even, much more. They're driving us out of our country. They're imprisoning us, sending us to work camps. . . ."

"How do we know you're not one of those Nazis in disguise?"

"I'm Jewish, really I am!" she pleaded.

But no one was listening. Either too eager to find someone to blame or unaware of what the Jews were going through, they carried on until she fled, tears in her eyes, back through Bethnal Green Park.

Only as she slowed did she think about her basket, still empty. Mr. Wainwright would be furious if she didn't have a good dinner on the table.

But she couldn't bear to go back to the butcher again.

And right there on the pavement, she bent her face into her hands and began to sob.

"Are you all right, dear?" A voice came from behind her, and she turned to see the Miss Ridleys, probably on their way back from the library. "Why don't you come home with us? A cup of tea will put you to rights in no time."

"We have fresh scones, too." Dorothy patted her shopping bag with a small grin.

Hastily, Sofie shook her head. "Thank you, but I have to get back. I didn't get any meat for dinner, and I don't know what I'm going to do."

Holding back tears, she told them what had happened, and they insisted on pulling her back to their house. "You can tell Ernest Wainwright that the lines were longer than usual," Irene said.

The Ridleys' house was large and dusty, the faint smell of mothballs freshened up by the scent of foliage randomly draping from a few vases and an umbrella stand in the hallway.

"Apologies for the state of the place," Dorothy explained. "Our maid went before the war, and that was it for us. But we muddle through, don't we?"

Looking less than happy about it, Irene pulled her into the warm kitchen. "Now sit down and tell us all about it."

Sofie soon had a cup of tea in her hands and a scone in front of her, butter melting on each half. A lump formed in her throat so hard that she struggled to speak, let alone eat anything.

"We have a little bacon if you'd like to take it for dinner?" Dorothy called from the pantry. "Not that Ernest Wainwright deserves it, but it'll keep you out of trouble. And we have some cheese, too. Perhaps you could make some kind of flan?"

"It's very kind, but I couldn't take your rations," she mumbled. The scone melted in her mouth, the butter creamy and comforting. Thinking of the time, she ate it fast, taking large, quick bites, barely chewing.

"But you must." Irene Ridley pressed the paper-wrapped package into her basket. "It's the least we can do. We can't have you thinking that all British people are as vile as he is—or like the people at the shops."

Sofie couldn't help but smile. "I couldn't possibly think that of you two. You've been so kind to me." She gulped back the tea, getting to her feet. "But now I really have to go. Thank you for everything."

"Wait a minute," Dorothy said, vanishing from the room; and as Irene and Sofie reached the front door, Dorothy returned with a book in her hands. "We have a few German language books in our collection, and I wondered if you'd like to read one?"

A strange sense of the two worlds colliding was quickly replaced by a desperation for something in her own tongue—something to make her feel less foreign, less alone.

"*Death in Venice*, by Thomas Mann," she murmured. "I remember reading this a few years ago. How miraculous it seems to see it here—it was banned, you see. How can I thank you?"

But the old ladies waved her away. "It's the least we can do."

Evening in the Wainwright house was as starchy as ever, but at least dinner went down without comment. Afterward, Mr. Wainwright retired upstairs, instructing Sofie to dust his precious ornaments. There were a dozen of them, his wife's pride and joy, priceless works of art according to Mr. Wainwright.

As she began to carefully pick up each one, Sofie wondered if Marigold's contact had found her family. She would have to pawn her mother's gold bracelet in order to pay for the information. It was still hidden in the hem of her blue skirt, the only thing she owned of her mother's. Funny how your priorities change, how your world can be broken down to the bare bones of necessity when you are pushed far enough.

She would take it to the pawnbroker she'd seen beside the grocer's shop on the main road. It would be worth at least ten pounds, if not more.

More than enough to buy her the information she needed.

As she dusted, the slow build of the sirens began. They came every few days now, usually only because of a few lone enemy planes, but the eerie wail was unsettling and she found herself hurrying through her dusting, eager to have it finished so she could return to her room in the cellar.

The sound of a plane droned in and out over the park, and the porcelain ornaments began to rattle on their shelves. She prayed nothing would break. Mr. Wainwright would murder her if something happened to one of his figurines, even if it wasn't her fault.

Her fingers worked fast over each statuette: one was a harlequin with a mandolin, another a woman with a torch held high in her hand like a monument of truth.

Suddenly, a low roar of aircraft rattled the panes in the windows, setting her heart pounding in her chest, and to her horror, the harlequin trembled in her hands. And then, as if in slow motion, she watched as it slipped through her fingers while she grappled to catch it, fumbling against its smooth surface.

But it was too late.

The great, precious ornament smashed onto the floor, shards cascading up and around her, the mandolin broken cleanly in two.

Panic swept over her as heavy footsteps came from the stairs.

"What was that noise?" Mr. Wainwright appeared at the door in his dressing gown, groggy and bad-tempered, glaring at the pieces of mandolin among the other fragments. "Do you have any idea how much that harlequin was worth?" he shouted, stepping toward her menacingly. "You'll have to pay for it."

"B-but I don't have any money." She staggered back, trying to get away.

"I'll bet you have some hidden somewhere."

"No, nothing at all! You have to believe me!" Sofie begged.

"We'll see about that." With a snarl, he strode off to the servants' stairs, storming down through the cellars to her room.

"I don't have anything," she called as she raced behind him.

By the time she reached her door, he was already inside, her suitcase upended, her clothes and belongings strewn everywhere.

On the bed, at the edge of the squall of clothes, lay her blue skirt, the gold bracelet safely hidden inside. Time slowed as she watched his hands pulling every garment, shaking and searching.

Would he reach for the skirt?

But he pulled away, panting from the exertion, his hands on his hips in annoyance. "You must have something."

"There's nothing. I promise." There was a pleading quake to her voice that she couldn't stop.

He took a deep breath, grunted at the clothes on the bed and turned toward the door.

Relief swept through her.

Then, in a final act of anger, he kicked the bed, and as the clothes shifted on top of the counterpane, the blue skirt slid off the bed, a small clunk as it hit the floorboards.

His eyes were on it.

Slowly, he bent down, lifting the skirt between forefinger and thumb, giving it two little shakes before wrenching open the stitches in the seam.

There, onto the bed, spilled the thick length of gold.

"You've got nothing, eh? I see you're a liar as well as an idiot." In one swift move, his hand scooped it up and put it into his pocket, then he shoved her angrily out of the way before plodding back upstairs.

It was over, and in more ways than one.

She first sat and then lay down on her small, hard bed. Then she turned toward the wall, and she cried.

He had taken her freedom, worked her to the bone, and now he had stolen her one means of getting the information about her family. She had nothing else to sell, no other way to get the few pounds she needed so desperately.

And that's when she realized the only other option she had: Since her employer had stolen the bracelet and her wages, she'd have to pawn something of his.

While cleaning his wardrobe, she had come across two false-bottomed drawers filled with jewelry boxes. From pearl necklaces to silver tiaras, the late Mrs. Wainwright's collection showed that she had been a woman with broad and expensive tastes.

He wouldn't notice if something small went missing, she reasoned, a ring or a brooch that should fetch a few pounds. In any case, she'd find the money to buy it back before he noticed.

It would be only temporary.

Her thoughts went to Rachel, and she whispered softly, "She'll help me buy it back once she gets here, if it takes that long."

The mere thought of her sister spurred her onward, as if this one small, desperate act could somehow bring her family back to her.

And as the idea cemented itself in her mind, she fixed a determined grimace on her face and strode upstairs to sweep up the fragments of the harlequin.

# JULIET

TRUE TO HIS WORD, SEBASTIAN WAS AWAY FROM HOME MOST OF the time, either due to work trips away or long hours in Westminster. Occasionally, Juliet saw him in his dark blue ARP uniform or a tailored suit, but more often she only heard him, creeping up the stairs in the early hours and collapsing into bed only to be gone again by the morning. Sometimes they'd meet in passing, in the corridor or on the front path, a quick "good morning" before going their separate ways.

And so it wasn't until she'd been there a few weeks that she arrived home from work to find him in the kitchen, the sound of sizzling accompanied by the mouthwatering smell of cooking meat. Looking rather comical with Mrs. Ottley's floral apron over his suit, Sebastian kneaded pastry in a basin, a half-hearted version of "Tea for Two" issuing from his mouth.

Faltering, she decided to creep away discreetly; but before she could turn, he'd spotted her, and she put on a smile, determined to be pleasant.

"Ah, 'tis the fair Juliet," he said, then continuing in mock Shakespearian, he added, "I do but dinner maketh, if thee careth for rabbit and vegetable pie?"

She eyed him, laughing. "Shakespearian now?" She glanced at the orderliness of the kitchen. "And what have you done with Mrs. Ottley?"

He resorted to his usual voice. "She complained of a sore throat, so I sent her to bed and took over the cooking."

As usual, Juliet was famished, and taking in the heavenly scent of rabbit gently browning in a pan, she looked at Sebastian. "I didn't know you could cook."

With that half smile of his, he replied, "I've learned to do many things since the war began. I hope it'll be to your satisfaction, although I'm a little pressed for time." He raised an eyebrow as he glanced from her to some vegetables expectantly.

Taking the hint, Juliet took off her coat. "All right, what do you want me to do?"

"Chop them, please." He pointed to a leek, some carrots, and a pile of stems freshly picked from the garden: parsley, sage, and thyme.

"You're far more domesticated than I imagined," she said as she began on the leek. "I always pictured you in your Oxford rooms mixing cocktails with glamorous women, or swanning around garden parties, full of flattery and charm."

"Oh, those were the days. It was a different world, wasn't it? But sadly, my wild era is no more." He sighed dramatically. "Is that why you were always so petulant around me, Juliet? Was I too debauched for you?"

"Not in the least," she said, focusing on her chopping. "But everything was so easy for you, wasn't it? A good family, Oxford, a choice of sports, entertainments, no end of pleasure."

He nodded, then after a pause, added more gently, "Yes, I was lucky. My mother always said that your parents were a bit strict."

Deftly, she scooped the chopped leeks into a pile. "Well, they put paid to any ideas I had about university long ago. 'Education isn't acceptable for women,' they told me. 'Too many books will make you into a bluestocking.' I had to focus my efforts on marrying some kind of privileged idiot who would expect me to serve him, just like my mother has done for my father all these years."

"A privileged idiot like me?" He grinned at her, as if he'd caught her out rather than been offended.

She shook her head, laughing. "I didn't mean it like that. If you must know, I loathed all the eligibles passed in front of me on principle:

If my mother liked them, they were bound to be odious." She eyed him. "I imagine you felt the same."

Liberally flouring the table, he set about rolling the pastry. "My parents thought a good marriage with a well-bred local girl would calm me down, and I confess I didn't mind them trying if it meant that I got to meet the occasional pretty girl, even if she were a bit abrupt with me." He shot her a sideways glance, and she knew he meant her, but then he carried on. "I think all parents find something wrong with their offspring. Mine thought I should be more studious when I was always running off to play cricket or tinker around in the stream in Beeding Glen. I found a badger's sett, and there were cubs every spring." He grinned. "I used to sneak out and feed them Dad's favorite smoked trout."

She laughed. "Did he ever find out?"

"I don't think so. I have been blessed with absent-minded parents. My father is always busy with his patients and Mum, well, Mum's just immersed in village life, helping out the neighbors and being the quartermaster of local gossip."

"They're certainly a lot more jovial than mine." She chopped the thyme, the parsley. "That's why I've come to London, to gain some independence. I've always wanted to be a librarian, and now I'm overseeing one of the grandest libraries in London." Outside, the sun went behind a cloud, casting a shade across the room, and she frowned in spite of herself. "All I need is to be surrounded by the books that I love: They are my friends, my adventures, my happy endings. Why would I need anything else?"

Although he still smiled, Sebastian had stopped rolling the flour and was looking over at her, a handprint of flour on his shirt sleeve. "But you can't live your whole life through books. It's *your* life, Juliet. You should be making it into a book in its own right, a novel packed with passions and excitement and escapades. You can't hide yourself away. You of all people."

"Why me of all people?"

He let out a laugh, as if it were obvious. "Because you're beautiful and clever. If only you could give yourself a chance to stop being so buttoned up, relax a little."

"Well, *I* choose to relax by reading," she said with a smile. "What is better than having an array of stories and characters at your fingertips, to pick what you like rather than plundering through life on your own?"

"But life isn't always about choosing the plot. It's about plunging in or plugging on, becoming submerged in your own story, having the courage to dip your head beneath the surface."

That was precisely what she had done with Victor, and look at what had happened. The whole mess could have been avoided if she'd stayed where she was comfortable, with her nose in a book. Living other people's lives protected her from her own.

Sebastian had gone back to rolling the pastry. "I'm sure you'd rather read about an evening of dancing than actually do it, wouldn't you?"

"Of course not," she snapped back. "I love to dance." But it came out hotly, as if it weren't something fun at all.

"All right, then," he laughed, "when was the last time you went to one?"

Try as she might, she couldn't remember. "There haven't been many dances since the war began," she said hurriedly, grabbing a carrot to peel.

"I think you'll find there are more dances than ever, Cinderella. One of these days I'll show you, and then you'll see." He chuckled. "Except you're too busy with your novels to pay attention."

"You shouldn't disparage my favorite habit just because you haven't tried it." She arched an eyebrow. "I can't imagine you read at all."

"I adore books, as it happens."

"What kind?" she said, challenging him.

He smiled. "Actually, I enjoy poetry."

"Poetry?" The word came out as almost accusatory. Was this the same man she'd met at that garden party only three years ago? But then she laughed at herself. Had she leaped to conclusions without giving him a chance?

He continued more pensively, "A friend introduced me to some of the poets from the last war, and I found that they spoke to me, especially after I came back. A line can stay with you for the rest of the day. Today I was reading T. S. Eliot writing about being stuck on the front in the last war: 'For us, there is only the trying. The rest is not our business.'"

The words lingered in the air, both of them stopping what they were doing, only sporadic birdsong spilling in from the garden.

Quietly, she said, "Is that how it feels when you're on the ground, that all you can do is follow orders?"

He nodded, his eyes going to the table. "But let's not talk about that. I feel rather guilty for not being still there, fighting with the others."

"But you're doing war work in the ministry. Surely that's something? What is it that you do there?"

"I'm in the legal department of the War Office. I'm part of a team making sure we're sticking to the Geneva Convention. We're trying to catch out the Nazis, too, as it's not always easy to prove after the event. It's good to stand up for what's right, expose the culprits not playing by the rules."

*Culprits like Victor,* she thought with a grimace.

But she put a smile on her face. "It sounds very important."

"I'm actually quite junior." He grinned bashfully. "When the war started, I'd only just qualified, but it's interesting work. I'm attached to the navy, which is why I spend so much time away in Portsmouth."

She watched him boning the rabbit meat, returning the bones into the pan to make a gravy. Gently, he began to hum again, "Tea for Two," swaying to the rhythm, and the sight of him in Mrs. Ottley's apron with a spring in his step made her laugh and join in. And before she knew it, he took her hand and made a few dance moves before twirling her by the hand, and suddenly she found herself doing a perfect spin. The two of them laughed as she went back to her chopping, a new flour handprint on her own sleeve.

And as she brought the chopping board to him to add the vegetables to the pan, they stood side by side, the closeness and aroma of him suddenly intimate and heady, and a quick image of them flashed into her mind, making dinner, talking, laughing. Something about his face, good-looking in a dapper, athletic sort of way, looked so focused and calm as he cooked, and she mused that it wasn't surprising so many women found him attractive. And as his arm brushed against hers, she wondered how it might feel to let it linger there, warming her through her sleeve.

Quickly she banished the thought.

What was she thinking?

She stepped away, clearing the other pans, taking them to the sink, filling the pastry bowl with water.

"I'm glad you've come here, Juliet," he said out of the blue, and she felt herself blush before he added, "It's good for Mrs. Ottley to have someone else to fuss over, a fuller house to make Jake and Ivy's absence a little less obvious."

"I'm glad I've found such a lovely landlady. She's already more like a friend."

"It's become quite jovial, with you around." He turned to her, their eyes meeting. "You've brought a new energy to the place."

She blushed. "And helped with the organization, too." She laughed, gesturing at the tidiness of the room. "But it's nice for her that you're here, too, Sebastian, helping with dinner and keeping her company."

And with a shrug, he said, "It's the least I can do." And then he smiled, not his half smile nor his polite one, but a genuine, gentle smile that somehow showed a trace of humility, a hint that he, too, might need a little kindness.

# KATIE

---

## THE BETHNAL GREEN LIBRARY
## NEWSLETTER

---

### SEPTEMBER 1940

#### THE NEW CHILDREN'S SECTION

---

*We now welcome little ones to come and read together.*
*Located at the far end of the fiction aisle.*

#### STORY TIME

---

*Every Saturday afternoon at 4 p.m.*

*Please bring a rug or cushion.*

NOW THAT SHE HAD A SECRET TO GUARD, THE LIBRARY HAD become the one place of normality in Katie's life. She hadn't told a soul about the pregnancy, least of all her mother, who'd only shown horrified disgust when Katie had tentatively brought up the subject of the "poor Knox girl at the church who'd got herself in trouble."

As she walked around the warm, musty bookshelves, there was that sense that all things endure, that life marches on regardless of her own world slowly collapsing. At the library, birth was merely part of the biology section, a rational process of reproduction. Katie's own reality was nothing but a background noise.

She'd had plenty of sleepless nights to think over her options. Although her urge was to keep hers and Christopher's beloved child, she knew she couldn't survive without her family, her home—and most of all, her mother.

And it was with this in mind that she approached Marigold Saxby in the romance section.

"Marigold," she whispered, trying to keep her voice relaxed and calm. "I wanted a quiet word with you, concerning a friend in a bit of trouble."

Ever buoyant, Marigold looked up from her copy of *Gone with the Wind* and smiled. "What kind of trouble?"

"The kind of trouble that might happen to an unmarried girl." Katie kept her voice soft, sympathetic for her poor imaginary friend. "She read in the newspapers that there are people who can, well, help to sort out the situation." Not wanting to meet Marigold's eyes, Katie glanced at the book cover, Rhett Butler swooping Scarlett O'Hara into an embrace. "I wondered if you might know someone."

"I do know someone, but I don't think I'd recommend it," Marigold said with a sigh. "Backstreet abortions are incredibly dangerous, you know. Are you sure your friend knows what she's doing, that this is really what she wants?"

Katie swallowed. "She's desperate, you see. Could you tell me what you know, and I can pass on the information to her?"

Unaware of Katie's awkwardness, Marigold crumpled her brow in thought. "The only one I know is Mrs. Dempsey. She's in Coalman Street, behind the old workhouse, number 6. She's been going for years." Marigold paused, leveling her eyes with Katie's. "But that doesn't mean she's safe. It's a risky business for everyone involved. I recommend that your friend finds another way to deal with her situation"—she raised an eyebrow—"or she might end up losing more than the baby."

Trying to keep her voice even, Katie said, "I don't know what other options she has."

"Well, there's always the unwed mothers' homes where they take the babies for adoption. It's not ideal, but unless you can find a relative to take the child, it's usually the best way."

A movement at the end of the aisle made Katie leap away from Marigold, and Katie quickly calmed herself as Sofie came down toward them with the Miss Ridleys.

"We're stocking a mini-library in our Anderson shelter," Dorothy was saying. "You should keep some books in yours, Sofie, just in case."

"Mr. Wainwright doesn't believe in shelters," Sofie replied with a heavy sigh. "He says that he'll stay at home if there's an air raid, and I have to remain at the house, too, in case he needs me."

"Well, if the bombers come, you're welcome to sneak over to our Anderson," Dorothy said. "It's a little tight, but at least you'll be safe."

"As safe as a small tin hut buried in a garden can be," Irene added with a twist of a smile.

"There's a spare bunk if you'd like to join us, too, Katie? After all, you're just a few doors down," Dorothy said, her warm eyes resting on Katie's as if she instinctively knew that something wasn't quite right.

"Thank you," Katie said quickly. "But my parents said we'll find a proper public shelter in town if it comes to that."

"Well, keep it in mind, dear," Irene said. "There aren't many public shelters, and the government is very strict that no one's to use the underground stations. They're to be reserved for transportation only."

"I can't think why," Marigold said. "There's an underground station on almost every corner of the city. It seems obvious to use them as shelters."

As the group discussed the various shelters, Katie's mind drifted. Now that she had the name and address of a woman who could end her problems once and for all, she felt herself relax a little, pushing aside Marigold's warnings.

After work, she shopped for dinner before trudging up from the main street, the slow build of the air-raid siren hurrying her along as she crossed the road to the house. A bag filled with vegetables weighed one arm lower than the other, making her hobble clumsily with every step.

The sunshine was still bright, even though it was late afternoon. If only the interminable siren would stop, she could have a moment to herself. She could barely hear herself think.

In fact, it was so loud that at first she didn't hear the sound of the planes.

It was the sight of the Miss Ridleys, ahead of her up the path, stopping to look up at the sky, that made her wonder what they'd seen.

Other neighbors were coming out to see before dashing frantically back into their houses. Katie began to hurry, dropping her bag in her haste, potatoes and onions spilling onto the pavement.

As she frantically gathered them up, she glanced over the rooftops, stopping in her tracks.

Above the horizon, a series of black shapes moved across the sky. There was something about the precision of their formation, the speed at which they came, that panicked Katie, fear coursing through her as she struggled on all fours, throwing the vegetables haphazardly back into her bag, leaving the ones that had rolled too far away.

The planes roared closer, and she ran into the house. "What are we going to do?"

"Get your things." Her father was storming around the hallway, her brother Rupert skulking in the background. "We need to find a shelter."

Trying not to panic, she dashed up the stairs.

"I'm in here, Katie!" Her mother called from her bedroom. "Help me take these bags down."

Inside, her mother was flustered, throwing blankets and clothes into a suitcase. "Oh, thank goodness you're here, love. Could you close this case and take it downstairs?"

Swallowing down her fear, Katie budged the case closed. "Are you all right, Mum?"

"I don't know—I just don't know!" Her mother panted as she ran behind Katie down to the front door. "We're just so exposed, bombs falling from the sky on our house—on us!"

"Where's the nearest shelter then, Helen?" her father barked at her mother.

For someone usually so composed and in control, her mother looked lost, frantic. As her husband shouted, she stood fixed, her mouth silently opening and closing.

"I-I don't know. I thought you'd found somewhere."

"You were supposed to check, you stupid woman!" he snarled, disgusted with her. "As usual, I have to do everything myself around here."

"I think there's a public shelter under the church on the corner," Katie said nervously.

With a scowl, her father set off, his balding head glinting in the sun. Katie hurried after him as best she could, hampered by the bags. It was unnerving to see her parents like that, fretting and unprepared, especially when it really mattered.

Even before they reached the main road, they could see the crowds being turned away at the church.

"It's full," a man's voice bellowed over the mayhem.

The sound of aircraft had intensified into a menacing drone, piercing and thunderous.

People turned, swarming around them.

"The railway arches," someone shouted, and the crowd changed direction like a shoal of fish, hurrying down the backstreet to where the overground railway line was supported by redbrick arches. Katie could feel her heart pounding as she tried to catch up with her family. She just needed cover. She needed to survive.

But the planes were getting closer.

As they ran, they watched as one by one the heads in front of them turned to the sky. First one, then three, then nine aircraft, and soon a whole deadly formation of planes became visible low over the houses.

The Nazis were finally descending on London.

Thuds came from the near distance, and it took a moment for Katie to register that they were bombs. With the startling booms, the crowd began to surge forward, bags being discarded on the side of the street, people screaming as they hunched their shoulders and ran. Some people put on their gas masks as smoke and the burnt stench of explosives seeped through the air. Others simply picked up their children and sprinted for their lives.

The arches were a series of caverns around twenty feet wide, each of them filling rapidly. People pushed inside until they were so full you could barely move.

Her nerves rattling, Katie pressed herself into an arch, gasping with gratefulness that they were at least under some kind of cover. Her mother stood beside her, and Katie reached for her hand, the sensation of her skin comforting in this stark new danger. Deep inside, Katie could only wonder if her mother would be so kind if she knew the whole truth. Would her mother's unwavering love suddenly be withdrawn?

The crowd hushed in fear as the bombers thundered overhead, explosions rumbling closer and closer. A child's scream was quelled, panic stamped out like forest fires.

"This is just the beginning." Beside her, a middle-aged woman in a headscarf murmured, "They'd better let us use the underground stations next time. They can't have half of London crowded beneath a railway arch. I'm not even sure it'll be of much use if a bomb comes down on us."

The truth of this statement bore down on Katie. A direct hit would kill them all.

Never had the city's population been in so much danger.

After a long, fraught hour, the sound of the planes receded, the danger dissipating, and the air-raid siren sounded once, marking the all clear.

Slowly, the shelterers began to trickle out onto the street, breathing in the acrid fumes, listening to the strange silence punctured by the occasional explosion from a mile or two away as fires raging through buildings found something volatile.

On the eastern horizon, an orange-red hue coated the sky. The great London docks were ablaze, incongruously mirroring the amber sunset in the west.

Out on the street, the crowds broke apart, everyone trying to find one another, people hurrying home, frightened and desperate for normality.

Katie searched for her father and found him standing in a side alley, lighting a cigarette for a pretty brunette in a red coat and then one for himself.

When he saw Katie coming, he pulled away, leading her hastily back onto the main street. "Thank goodness that's over." He grimaced as he looked Katie and her mother up and down, as if the pair of them were an embarrassment. "Come on. Let's go home."

They walked back in silence, exhausted and scared, unsure of what they might find. Would their road have been bombed? Their house?

Things would feel different from now on, Katie knew. With the occurrence of one raid—and a massive one by the looks of the intense glow of fire in the distance—there would, she had no doubt, be more.

The Nazis had set their sights on Britain.

As they walked up through the park, her father and Rupert slightly ahead, a familiar figure came into view. Prim in her tweed suit with matching hat, Mrs. Baxter bustled toward her house on the opposite green. A lean woman with a determined chin, she set her thin lips in a disgusted frown as her dark eyes darted over Katie and her mother, as if searching them for flaws or misdemeanors.

"That's all we need," Katie said under her breath.

But her mother, ever vigilant about her reputation, quickly stepped forward. "Mrs. Baxter, how are you?" The obsequiousness in her tone made Katie flinch.

"As well as can be expected," the woman replied tartly. "I was invited to join our neighbors in their cellar, and I have to say that it was far from ideal." She took in Katie's mother's slightly bedraggled appearance. "I hope you're ready for our WVS fundraising drive next week? We're counting on our more highly regarded members to bring in good money."

Katie heard her father's voice as he strode back toward them. "You can count on her full participation." He smiled unctuously at Mrs. Baxter, all politeness and good humor for one of his more lucrative clients—as were most of the more well-to-do families in the area. "Obviously, with our family standing and the business doing as well as it is, she'll be happy to put her all into fundraising."

For a moment, the woman seemed satisfied, but then she turned her attentions onto Katie. "And are you starting university soon?"

"I am," she said, giving a small bob. Mrs. Baxter was akin to royalty in Bethnal Green—especially where her family was concerned.

"Only a few weeks to go." Her mother put on her upper-class voice. "It's such an opportunity."

The woman's eyes roved over Katie's loose dress disparagingly. "I can see how it can be an option for certain young women."

Her meaning was plain: that Katie didn't have the elegance or looks to catch a good husband, and as Katie blushed heavily, her mother only nodded, giving Mrs. Baxter a polite smile. "We all do the best we can, don't we?"

After a disapproving look, Mrs. Baxter went on. "Well, at least it's better than the Knox girl." She leaned closer to whisper, "It was a sailor's, apparently. He had his way and wants nothing more to do with her."

Katie swallowed hard, but nothing could have prepared her for what the woman would say next.

"We had to let Mrs. Knox go, of course. It's a pity as she was a keen volunteer. Naturally, the church wants nothing to do with them, as well as a lot of other local groups, and Mr. Knox's employers, too. Such a shame, and just when the family was doing so well." Her eyes crinkled—was she enjoying the Knox's downfall?

It became imperative that Katie didn't meet the woman's eyes, and she began fussing with her dress, rearranging the gathering again and again. She couldn't give herself away.

Fortunately, Mrs. Baxter spotted some other neighbors to harass, and she took her leave and hurried on through the park, allowing the Upwood family to trudge on to their house, her father speeding ahead once more.

At her side, her mother began talking about Katie's university place. "I know some people don't think much of it, but it'll be good for you to have more education than I did. You can get on in the world," she said, adding with a whisper, "have more time to find a good husband."

It was the kind of thing her mother sometimes said, but only now did Katie realize that perhaps her mother might have wanted a better choice for herself. How angry her father had been when she didn't know where there was a shelter. How much he'd shouted at her when it was both of their faults.

The memory of their disorganized panic came back to Katie: When the bombers were zooming overhead, her parents hadn't had any plans at all.

It was her, Katie, who had led them to the public shelter and then to the railway arch, simply following a crowd who didn't understand arch mechanics.

What had she been thinking?

And she made a vow. Next time, she would be more prepared, find the best shelters. Next time, she would stop depending on her parents to know what was best.

Next time, she would trust herself.

# SOFIE

$\mathcal{S}$OFIE CLATTERED THE BREAKFAST PANS INTO THE SINK, FUMING as she hastily scrubbed. With the air raids going on and off through-out the night and Mr. Wainwright's resistance to finding shelter, her hatred of him had multiplied exponentially. After lying in bed quak-ing all night amid the sound of bombs and shouts, dogs barking, and wardens' whistles, a determination to get her own back on him took hold.

The news on the radio that morning had been grim. The late after-noon raid had simply been to pick out the targets—the East London dockyards—starting fires as markers for the bombers coming after dark to pummel the area with high explosives. The fires had burned until dawn. Hundreds of people had been made homeless, and just as many were injured. No one said how many were killed.

The last words from the radio broadcast held a portentous warning: "This could be the beginning of many more nights of bombing. The capital must prepare itself for the worst."

The words echoed through Sofie's head as fear transformed into loathing. How dare Mr. Wainwright keep her indoors during the raids? How dare he take her bracelet when she needed it so desperately? He'd left her no alternative: She had to steal back what was rightfully hers. Marigold had told her she'd found a contact, and Sofie would need money to pay him. Finding her sister was the most crucial thing in Sofie's heart.

She hurried through her chores with mounting resolution, and after she heard the clunk of the front door closing behind Mr. Wainwright, she climbed the stairs, two at a time, to his bedroom.

Time was of the essence, and as she opened the drawer and sifted through several boxes, she panicked that she wouldn't be able to find anything modest enough for her to hide away unnoticed—at least until she could find the money to buy it back.

Then she opened the slim, narrow box of rings, nine in all.

Surely he wouldn't miss one?

Quickly, she selected the smallest, most insignificant of them, and slipped it into her pocket.

And not a moment too soon.

The sound of a key in the front door came from downstairs. He was back too soon. He must have forgotten something, or even worse, he might have sensed what she was up to, that she couldn't be trusted.

Her fingers fumbling, she shoved the boxes back in the drawer, listening as the front door opened and his heavy feet trudged through the hallway and then, ominously, made their way up the stairs.

She barely had time to close the wardrobe before Mr. Wainwright was at the bedroom door, puffing as he bellowed, "What are you doing in here, girl?"

"Laundry, sir!" She bobbed her head, scooping up the clothes discarded onto the floor before scurrying out, almost tripping down the stairs as she dashed, so desperate was she to get away.

In the kitchen, she sank into a chair, trying to stop her racing pulse.

Deep inside, she heard a small voice: *How has it come to this?* She came from one of the finest families in Berlin. First a maid and now . . . a thief?

Gradually, she calmed herself down, focusing on the laundry, trying not to think about the stolen ring in her pocket.

It wasn't until after lunch that she managed to escape to the shops, claiming to need cleaning supplies, and as she tiptoed through the hallway, she could hear Mr. Wainwright's jagged snores coming from the living room. She would have an hour or more before he missed her, but she would have to hurry to squeeze in this extra errand.

She raced through the park to the high street, drawing to a halt outside the tatty pawnbroker, hesitating uneasily. Never would she have gone anywhere near a place like this in Berlin. It was a desolate, rundown shop, crammed quietly into the otherwise neat row of shops. "L.P. Mitchell" was painted in uneven capitals on a chipped black background. The dusty window displayed a dismal array of people's possessions: china pots with bead necklaces spilling out; medals from the last war; and a ballerina figurine pirouetting atop a grandmother clock, its time set permanently at midnight.

Pawnbrokers were flourishing with the war. Everyone needed money, from wives with their husbands away to people needing funds to flee the city. Then there were all the soldiers on leave, wanting to impress a girl with a special night out before facing the uncertainty of the front line. Like so many other necessities, money was in scant supply.

Worried that people would see her hovering, she pulled herself together before going into the shop. She had to be brave. She had to get a good deal.

The door made a dissonant jangle as she pushed it open, the smell of mildew and mothballs mixed with an unplaceable whiff of something decaying.

Along one side was a counter, behind which stood a stout, middle-aged man with thin, oiled hair plastered over his scalp. "How can I help you?"

His waistcoat bore the signs of age and negligence, and his rounded belly bespoke an appetite for good living. Meanwhile, his balding head threw an unfortunate light on his cauliflower ears and broken nose; this was a man who wouldn't hesitate to hold someone to their debt.

Sofie stiffened. "I need to have something appraised."

Mr. Mitchell's eyes traveled over her, taking in her meager maid's clothes and her thin frame, his face falling as he assessed how much money the deal was worth.

But then he smiled, and there was something predatory about the glint in his eyes. After all, a girl like Sofie appearing in his shop must be desperate. "It would be my pleasure to take your article off your hands—for the right price, of course."

She passed the ring across the counter, and he reached inside his breast pocket for a jeweler's loupe, which he jammed expertly into his left eye.

"Ah, yes," he muttered. "Just as I suspected. It isn't a perfect gemstone. There is a flaw, small but present nonetheless."

Impatience shot through her. "Where? Let me see it."

He handed her the ring. "I can't share my loupe as I'm prone to infections, I'm afraid."

Holding the ring to the light, she peered into it. "But I can't see anything. If I can't see the flaw, how can I make a deal?"

Again that smile. "Well, in that case I can only wish you a good day."

Frustration rattled her. This was her one chance. She didn't know of any other pawnbrokers, even if she had time to visit them.

Annoyed, she handed the ring back to him. "How much will you give me for it?"

He looked at the item again. "The gold is only nine carat and the garnet is small. Since you look like you're in need, though, I'll make you a deal and give you three pounds."

Disappointment flooded through her. Three pounds might not be enough to pay for even the most basic information. And what about her other expenses? If she was given an address, might she need to send things to Rachel? It seemed ludicrous to risk so much for only three pounds.

There was a fraction of a second where she weighed up her life, her future, her dear father and sister, and suddenly frightened, she took a hasty step back, shaking her head nervously. "That's not nearly what it's worth. Give me the ring. I'll take it somewhere else."

He stood, the smile still on his face, looking the ring over. "You seem a little scared, my dear. I hope this ring didn't come to you via improper means?"

She stood up taller, trying to keep calm. "Not at all. It's worth more money, that's all. Give it to me."

He eyed her, and then said, "I'll give you four pounds, and that's the lot." He pulled the notes out of his pocket and laid them on the counter, too tempting to ignore.

Wrestling inside with the unfairness, the injustice of life, and yet desperate to be out of there, suddenly she could bear it no longer. And almost with relief, she grabbed the money and pushed it into her pocket, the discordant bell jangling behind her as she ran down the street.

# KATIE

KATIE PUT HER HEAD DOWN AS SHE HURRIED THROUGH THE back alleys of Bethnal Green. If she was seen there, it could be the end of her reputation.

But what had to be done, had to be done.

Without Christopher there, how could she ever survive this pregnancy? However much she longed to keep the baby, she was too young, too naïve to get through it on her own.

And Mrs. Dempsey and her procedure was her ticket out.

She'd left the library after lunch, complaining of a headache, gathering her bag with her wad of savings hidden inside and setting a resolute frown onto her face. With luck, she could have the procedure and be home by evening. No one would ever have to know.

It was the only way.

The bustle of the main street and the tenements petered out as she took one of the shadier alleyways toward the old workhouse on the outskirts of town. The brick block looked more like a prison than a place where the destitute used to live and work. No wonder the government had closed them down in the last few decades.

"Want to earn a bit of money, dearie?" A middle-aged man in a long coat approached her lasciviously, his breath rank.

Frantically, she jumped away. "N-no, I just came to see someone."

"A young thing like you could make a pretty penny, you know."

Unsure what he meant, Katie hurried on, but as she caught sight of the women in the shadows, a few of them shuffling small children behind them, she registered the smell of desperation. Some, like Katie, used their hands and arms to cover their distended bellies while tugging their tops lower to show their wares.

"Wanna join us?" an older one jibed, her eyes looking Katie up and down. "You're new around here, aren't you?"

"I-I'm looking for Mrs. Dempsey," Katie stammered.

The woman started a laugh that grew into a great cackle. "Up the duff, are you?" She called over to another woman standing at the opposite corner. "This one wants Dempsey, wonder if she'll live to tell the tale."

Timidly, Katie asked, "Do you know her?"

"We all know her, and we all know what happens to girls like you." She nodded toward the back of the alley. "Some of them don't make it, get buried in the back." She gave her a wink. "You'd be better off joining us here in the workhouse."

"But I thought it wasn't a workhouse anymore."

The woman chuckled. "They changed it into a mental institution, even though a lot of us aren't mad. We just don't have nowhere else to go—and if you aren't mad when you get here, you soon will be." She let out a laugh. "But we get on fine, making a bit of money on the street."

A little girl, grubby and with a large open sore on her mouth, peered around the woman's legs.

Katie found herself blurting, "You have children here, too?"

The woman nodded. "People from the church or the council used to come to take the babies, but the war's stopped that now. There's already too many orphans. So we get to keep them."

The derelict place reeked of disease and decay, and Katie fought an instinctive urge to pull the little girl away, find some ointment for her sore, and just give her a jolly good bath.

"You should think about it," the woman went on. "A lot of the girls in trouble end up here, running away or kicked out of home, not having anywhere else to go." She grinned, baring a set of crooked, dirty teeth. "It drives you a bit balmy, but better than ending up dead on that woman's filthy kitchen table."

Gasping with horror, Katie reeled away, running around the building to the cold, dank Coalman Street beyond. It was deserted, a ghoulish emptiness as her footsteps echoed through the narrow passage. The number six was painted unevenly onto a black door, and cautiously, she knocked.

The middle-aged woman who opened the door wasn't at all what Katie had been expecting. With spectacles and scrawny, sinewy cheeks and neck, she had a royal blue church hat on, making her look strangely respectable in her surroundings. Her eyes didn't meet Katie's, darting behind her newcomer as if checking for someone else: the police perhaps, or an interfering parent?

Without a smile, she said, "Come in," rather mechanically, turning to lead her through a small, dark front room into a kitchen.

As soon as Katie entered, the stench of a butcher's shop swelled her stomach with nausea. Even though it was scrubbed clean, Katie's eyes were drawn to the long wooden table running down the center. She couldn't help but imagine herself lying on that table. . . .

How many young women like her had died there?

The woman turned to her as she pulled a brown, stained blanket over the table. "Do you have the money?"

Katie felt her breath stop. Was she really going to entrust her life to this woman? No one knew where she was, what she was doing. If she simply didn't arrive home that evening or to work the next day, who would even begin to know where to look?

A movement in her stomach made her hunch protectively forward, covering her precious baby, the only part of Christopher she had left. How could she do this to him—to herself? What kind of a world was this where such a choice had to be made?

And as she watched the woman open a cloth case filled with all kinds of knives and hooks, Katie's legs made the decision for her as she bolted back through the front room to the door, yanking it open and running out into the gloomy alley.

She made it to the gutter just in time for the contents of her stomach to be propelled out of her, hot and acidic.

Mrs. Dempsey called her back inside. "Good to get it out of your system before we begin."

But before she'd even straightened herself, Katie was sprinting as fast as she could away from the hovel, away from the strange woman, and away from the one thing that might have been her salvation.

Tears caught in her throat as she raced back past the workhouse, the prostitute calling out, "That's right, love! Run for your life! You know you can always come and join us."

She heard the words echoing around the side street as she sped through the busy tenements, only slowing as she reached the high street where she stopped to lean against a closed-down shop, bending over to catch her breath.

The more she regained herself, the more certain she was that she'd done the right thing.

However, with this relief came the awful new reality: Her predicament was here to stay.

A dread seared through her: Sooner or later, she would have to tell her mother.

# JULIET

THE FOLLOWING WEEK, AS JULIET HURRIED HOME FROM THE library, her mind whirred with uneasiness. Although the park was peaceful in the late afternoon sunshine, in only an hour or two the sirens would start, and then the planes would come.

Ever since the first air raids had struck London a week ago, waves of bombers had come every night. The toll of people injured and killed had tracked steadily upward, while more and more homes and businesses were destroyed. Everyone was petrified, and those who could had fled the city.

The sirens had been starting so regularly that people had begun to plan around them, grabbing extra naps during the day after sleepless nights in railway tunnels, basements, and public shelters.

Juliet was among the luckier ones. Before the war, a man came to the door offering Mrs. Ottley an Anderson shelter for her back garden, and she'd been talked into it.

"It's turned out to be quite a good idea, hasn't it?" Mrs. Ottley said every night, trying to make light of the narrow, short bunks and the puddle on the floor. And then there was the all-too-audible thump of bombs around them. Only a thin layer of corrugated metal existed between them and the planes, and Juliet didn't hold out much hope for their chances if it was struck.

Fortunately, they hadn't had to share the already cramped shelter with Sebastian yet. He was at home for the occasional evening, and they'd taken to cooking together—once they even embarked on a spot of housecleaning, her dusting the shelves in the living room while he swept the floor, making each other laugh with their easy banter. But then he'd always left before the sirens went off, either to the ARP or elsewhere. Sometimes she wondered if there was a girl he met; did they go dancing? Did they share a kiss at the end of the night?

His advice about experiencing life had lingered in her mind, and with a sense of great pride, she'd joined the Ambulance Service. Of course, the pride had quickly given way to worry that she wasn't up to the task, but with all the bombs, it was only right that she should set aside her own discomforts for the sake of others. She'd be starting training soon, and hopefully that would sort her out.

Juliet let herself in the front door and, sniffing another of Mrs. Ottley's concoctions emanating from the kitchen, she hurried through to help. There she met with the usual mayhem, graters and peelers strewn across the table, a mist of flour hanging in the air, while something that smelled a little too odd for comfort boiled noisily in a pot.

In the middle stood Mrs. Ottley, delighted by her arrival. "Oh, Juliet! Could you give me a hand?"

The usual routine ensued, Juliet working out what needed to be done while Mrs. Ottley chatted away. Only this time she began tentatively, "I wondered if we could try something other than the Anderson tonight, dear?"

"I've heard the public shelters are very cramped," Juliet said with a sigh. "If you can get into one at all."

But Mrs. Ottley leaned toward her and whispered, "Marigold told me she's been going down to the underground station to sleep. It's much safer, and probably less damp, too."

Unsure what she meant, Juliet said, "But didn't the government say that we're not allowed to use the tube stations?"

"Someone has organized a protest of sorts. Everyone's fed up, according to Marigold. There aren't enough public shelters, so they've all started going down to the station, buying the cheapest ticket, and simply staying put in the tunnels till morning. They reasoned that if enough people do it, they can't arrest them all, can they? It's been going on for a few days now, hundreds of people down there every night. Even the Miss Ridleys are going." Her eyes gleamed with hope. "I thought we might join them."

"But it's still illegal, isn't it?" Juliet, with her inherent law-abiding nature, wasn't as comfortable with the idea of minor acts of criminality as Mrs. Ottley evidently was.

"I see it as an act of public support. It's irresponsible of the authorities to leave us under flimsy bits of tin when we have the ideal shelter right on our doorstep—or rather, under our doorstep." She chuckled and gave Juliet a nudge. "Come on, dear. If Irene Ridley's doing it, it can't be that wrong, can it?"

Juliet sighed. "Well, I know we try to jolly along in the Anderson, but it is rather disheartening," she admitted. "So yes, maybe we should give it a try."

The sound of the front door opening came from the hallway, and they turned to see Sebastian coming to join them in the kitchen. Hastily, they pulled apart, focusing on the potatoes. Something told them Sebastian wouldn't approve of storming the underground station.

Tonight, he looked incredibly businesslike in a dark gray suit. If she hadn't known better, she would have thought he was one of those stiff bankers, betting against the war. But there was a weariness about him, his mouth clenched in a straight line. She remembered how he used to look, wearing his country suits, a healthy glow to his skin from cricket or sailing. Now he looked serious and wary.

As he came in, the side of his mouth flickered with a ghost of a smile. "I feel as though I've interrupted something. What are you two cooking up?" He looked from one to the other.

Mrs. Ottley was shuffling to the cooker with obvious guilt, which must have looked utterly out of place beside Juliet's indignant sense of righteousness.

"If you must know, we're going to join a protest to use the underground as a shelter this evening." Her decision had been made, and Sebastian Falconbury would not be able to change her mind.

But all he said was, "That's a good idea," and then his face scrunched up as he smelled Mrs. Ottley's cooking. "Is it whale meat again?"

"No, it's oxtail hash." She drained the boiled cabbage and sniffed disparagingly at it. "Perhaps not the best dish in the world."

But before she could mash the ingredients together, the sound of the air-raid siren filtered in through the window.

"Well, that puts paid to my oxtail then, doesn't it?" Mrs. Ottley said, taking off her apron with quiet elation to have been let off the task. "I expect we'll be able to buy sandwiches underground." Leaving the pots and pans, she ambled out and up the stairs. "We'll need to bring a few blankets and cushions, Juliet," she called as she went.

Juliet looked at Sebastian, who had come in to make himself a cup of tea. "I'd better go upstairs, get ready for the night ahead." But as she brushed past him to the door, he stopped her, his hand gently touching her arm, and she caught the scent of him, warm and masculine.

"You will take care of yourself and Mrs. Ottley, won't you?" he said.

She suddenly thought of how dangerous and grueling his ARP shifts must be with the bombing raids—what he must have seen. From what she could gather, it wasn't for the fainthearted.

She laughed, shrugging her arm from his hand. "That's why we're going to the underground. Hopefully, we'll be a bit safer down there."

"You're right to go, and Bethnal Green is a deep station, too." He grinned. "And you'll escape the oxtail hash."

"Thank heavens!" She smiled. "Are you on ARP duty again?"

"Yes, the early shift tonight. I don't suppose you've thought any more about driving ambulances? We're desperate for more volunteers."

"As a matter of fact, I already joined," she said primly, straightening her jacket. "I start first-aid training tomorrow. They're rushing us through so that we can get started."

"That's very decent of you." He brightened. "I'll see if we can get your first shift together. I can show you the ropes."

Never one to like feeling as though she needed help, she replied, "I'll be perfectly fine on my own, thank you."

"Very good." Amused, he chuckled a little at her confidence, his eyes challenging her to back down and accept his help. "I'll tell the ambulance team to make way for a very able new driver."

She nodded, unmoved. "You do that, Sebastian."

The sound of Mrs. Ottley coming back downstairs made them get back to the task of preparing for the night ahead, everything left half finished: the cabbage growing cold in the colander, her skirt suit left unironed, the shallow bath she'd been anticipating postponed.

Juliet dashed upstairs to her room to gather two blankets and a pillow, deciding to forgo her hat for the sake of practicality. Then she looked longingly at the handful of paperbacks beside her bed and, indecision getting the better of her, threw them all into her bag.

"Are you coming, Juliet?" Mrs. Ottley was already outside the front door waiting, but as Juliet came out of her bedroom, she saw Sebastian ahead of her hurrying down the stairs, pulling on his ARP jacket, his shoulders broad and muscular beneath his shirt.

"Do be careful now, Sebastian!" Mrs. Ottley called as he stopped in front of the hallway mirror to do up his buttons.

He looked up at that, but Mrs. Ottley had already hurried out, only Juliet left beside him, her eyes meeting his in the mirror as she quickly re-pinned her victory roll, wondering how dangerous the night ahead would be. And that sense of the closeness of death suddenly overwhelmed her, how casual it had become for someone to die, that this could be the last time she ever saw him.

He might have been thinking the same thing as their eyes locked a moment more than was polite, an unsettling solemnness exchanged between them, for the bombs, the night ahead, for what the world had become. But then it was gone, and they both quickly glanced back at their own reflections, him straightening his collar, her tidying her hair, as if it had never happened.

"Are you coming, dear?" Mrs. Ottley's voice came from outside, and Juliet darted off after her without another glance.

The evening was bright and clear, the wail of the siren like a nocturnal beast rising from slumber as the two women rushed down to the corner.

At the junction, a group of around thirty or forty had gathered around the entrance to the underground station, and Juliet and Mrs. Ottley joined the back. Soon they were wedged in by more coming from behind as they shuffled with the crowd down the steps into the station.

A voice called, "Juliet!" and there was Marigold, a large carpetbag in one hand and two fold-up deck chairs in the other. "Wait for us!"

Beside her were the two Miss Ridleys, their silver-white heads looking around in interest.

"Thank goodness Marigold's giving us a hand with our things," Dorothy said. "I don't know what we'd do without help."

Instead of the expected brawl with police or even soldiers stopping their entry, a single policeman blew his whistle loudly. "Anyone who doesn't have a genuine reason to travel has to go and find a proper shelter."

The crowd simply filed past him. Many were families from the poorer tenements who didn't have the money or space for an Anderson shelter, but Juliet spotted a few from the wealthier neighborhoods, too. Then there were the black-market runners, their coats bulky with sugar or alcohol as they glanced around for punters or the police.

"The underground station is becoming the best undercover rendezvous in town," Marigold whispered to her. "There's a proliferation of secret liaisons, especially in the service passages."

"Liaisons?" Juliet inquired. Marigold had the uncanny effect of making her feel incredibly sheltered.

"Mostly it's affairs," she whispered. "Everyone's at it with the war now in full swing. Husbands are away, everyone living for the moment in case a bomb has their name on it. I'm sure I saw that insurance agent who lives on Bethnal Green Park in a dark corner with someone. And then there are the crooks; the place is crawling with them. Talk about 'underground networks.'" She laughed. "It's certainly become a hub for dirty dealings!"

Curious, Juliet asked, "Marigold, how do you know all these people?"

Lowering her voice, Marigold leaned toward her. "If you grow up in the old tenement blocks, you get to know who's who." Her eyes hardened, as if a different woman were lurking beneath the flamboyant veneer. "I had to do everything I could to stay alive in that place, know the streets like no one else."

Down the single flight of concrete stairs from the street, they arrived in the vast underground ticket hall. Bright lights filled the bustling space, the ticket offices on one side, the turnstiles on the other. The shiny beige tiles coating the curved walls made it echoey, the cacophony rising as people funneled through and down the escalators.

They joined the line to buy the tuppenny tickets they needed to get through the turnstiles.

"Where do people sleep?" Mrs. Ottley asked Marigold. "Don't the trains get in the way?"

"Most people sleep in the connecting passages—the ones that passengers use to get to the platforms. There are several of them, some quite wide, and they get cleaned every day. After the last trains go at nine o'clock, they switch off the electricity in the lines and some people sleep on the tracks." Marigold grimaced. "I'd never go there, of course. It's filthy, and you have to make sure you're up early so that you don't get electrocuted when they switch the line back on." She chortled. "And I'd rather sleep on the stairs than come face-to-face with a rat in the middle of the night."

At the bottom of the escalator, the main concourse was tall and wide, with smaller passageways leading off to the platforms. Down here the mood was congenial, people settling down for the evening, laying down blankets, the bustle of the day over.

The place was busier than Juliet expected. Well over a hundred people were there, with more coming down. The aromas of different foods wafted in and out. The well-prepared brought baskets with cold pies and salads, while for others dinner was a heavy, whole-meal National Loaf, hastily cut into slices and handed around large families, sometimes with a scrape of margarine or dripping.

"Tuppenny meals," a woman called, walking up and down with a tray of sandwiches and pasties.

Mrs. Ottley rummaged in her handbag for her purse. "We'll need some of those," she muttered to Juliet. "I wish I'd made a pie and brought it along with us. Maybe we can try that tomorrow."

A makeshift canteen had been set up beside the escalator, three women with giant tin teapots behind a fold-up table. *Bring your own cup* was handwritten on a piece of cardboard.

Two underground guards were halfheartedly trying to break everything up, calling out, "If you're not here to travel, you must leave immediately," and, "The underground station is not an air-raid shelter. I repeat, no one is allowed to sleep here."

But everyone simply ignored them.

Music tempted Juliet to look down some of the smaller passages, of which there were several, some a hundred feet long or more, others down a few stairs to a lower level. In one, children swung a skipping rope. "Johnnie and Janey sitting in a tree, K-I-S-S-I-N-G."

There was so much to see: a raucous game of blackjack with piles of coins on a makeshift table, an old couple waltzing as an older boy played Strauss on a violin, a girl trying to contain her large cat who was desperate to hunt for mice. Women sat in groups gossiping and laughing while they knitted black socks and balaclavas for the troops. Men read newspapers in deck chairs, smoking pipes in clenched jaws, some with a bottle of beer by their side.

It was as if life had simply been transported under the ground.

At the end of one of the platforms, there was an old curtain cordoning off a small area, and if the large sign that said WC didn't indicate its use, the smell certainly did.

They found a spot to call their own for the night, far away from the WC, and laid down their blankets, helping the Miss Ridleys set up their deck chairs.

Irene Ridley watched as Juliet unpacked her paperbacks. "What a splendid array you have."

Juliet flicked open the first page of *Emma*, by Jane Austen. "This is one of my favorites."

"Read it out to me, won't you, dear?" Irene settled herself down. "There's something soothing about having a novel read aloud."

And so Juliet began. " 'Emma Woodhouse, handsome, clever and rich, with a comfortable home and happy disposition, seemed to unite some of the best blessings of existence; and had lived nearly twenty-one years in the world with very little to distress or vex her.' "

After the first few pages, Juliet drew to a halt, but a woman's cockney voice came from the other side of them. "Carry on, won't you, duck? It's nice to hear a story, and if you don't mind me saying, you've got a lovely reading voice, just like those people on the radio."

"Thank you," Juliet said. "But I don't want to disturb anyone who wants a little peace and quiet."

"Don't worry about us," a young mother with a baby in her arms muttered. "It might entertain the little ones for a while, keep them out of mischief."

Two little girls with blond curls came to stand in front of Juliet, side by side. They looked at her solemnly, too young to know not to stare. One of them had the buttons on her red coat done up wrongly, the triangle of the bottom edge sticking down her leg while the adjacent piece at the top came up over her chin.

"Oh, all right then." She smiled at the girls.

And she carried on, reading a bit louder this time, more like the readers on the radio.

" 'Mr. Knightly, a sensible man about seven- or eight-and-thirty, was not only a very old and intimate friend of the family, but particularly connected with it. . . .' "

And as she became absorbed with the story, she felt her self-consciousness melt away. Within minutes, she was barely aware of the many eyes resting upon her, the ears pricking up, the shuffling of possessions ceasing as the people around her began to listen. *Emma* wasn't perhaps everyone's cup of tea—it was far too old for the two little girls—but it seemed that if someone offered a story, whatever it might be, it provided a distraction, an escape from the boredom and fear.

Soon, a kind of peaceful corner had been created. People passing through began to slow or stop, a few taking a seat on the floor around her or leaning against the wall.

At the end of an hour, she finally said that she needed to stop, and everyone gathered to thank her, to ask her about the book.

The young mother, who was called Mary, asked, "Can you read us a bit more later?"

The loud cockney woman, Mrs. Patterson, joined in. "We need to know what happens next."

Quietly thrilled with how she could generate so much good feeling, Juliet nodded. "I'll read again tomorrow, if there's another air raid."

While some of the crowd drifted away, others lingered, Mary asking if she could take a look at the book.

Juliet passed it over. "It's a library copy. You're welcome to borrow it or one of these other ones." More women came over, eager to see what was on offer. "They're all library books, so you can either give them back to me in person or simply hand them in at Bethnal Green Library."

"I need a good distraction," Mary said. "I'm worried sick about my husband. He insisted on joining the fire service, and they're out there all night, dodging the bombs and the flames, trying to get people out of burning buildings. I keep thinking I'll come home at the end of the night and there'll be a policeman at the door telling me he's gone." She was only about twenty, a baby in her arms and the other two winding around her legs like shy little puppies.

"I know," Mrs. Patterson said. "The sooner they let people sleep in the underground the better. My daughter's in the ARP, and she says half her job is convincing people to find a proper shelter."

Mary had *Pride and Prejudice* in her hand. "This is by the same author. Is it any good?"

"I think that's her best. Why don't you borrow it? See for yourself." Juliet watched as the other women vied for the remaining novels. "Perhaps I should start a register, take your name if you want to borrow a book, just like a library." Mr. Pruitt wouldn't be happy if he found out, but Juliet couldn't ignore the simple joy the books seemed to bring.

As she took down the names, she pointed out the stamp inside the front that indicated when the book was due back. "And of course, you can always come to the library to take out other books. We have plenty to choose from, all free of charge."

Mary shuffled uncomfortably. "Libraries aren't for people like us, they're for the upper class."

"Of course not! They're for everyone."

"Not the one in Bethnal Green. I only went in there once, and a snooty librarian told me my children were making too much noise. He showed me the door straightaway."

"And there's nowhere to sit down and read comfortably," Mrs. Patterson said with feeling.

"I see," Juliet said. "Well, leave it to me. I'll see if I can make some changes."

"It's easier to borrow books from you down here," Mary said. "Besides, I never have time to get to the library, not with the little ones."

"Aren't they supposed to be out of the city?" Mrs. Ottley said, a little frostily. "The government says it's selfish to bring evacuated children home."

"They were too young to go by themselves, so I had to go with them, and the woman we were staying with was bossy and rude. In the end, we had to leave before someone was killed—and not by the bombs."

A ripple of laughter lifted the crowd, and the conversation turned to dreadful evacuation stories, which were rife. Many children had been brought home, either because their mothers missed them or because they begged to leave after being mistreated, starved, or overworked on farms. Down one of the passageways, Juliet had spotted a girl sitting alone, playing cat's cradle with some spare wool, an embattled look in her eyes, as if she'd already seen enough of life.

Once the last of the books had been distributed, the small gathering gently drifted apart. The lucky ones with Juliet's novels settled down to read, and Juliet watched with satisfaction as Mrs. Patterson opened *Vanity Fair.*

Around Juliet's huddled little group, discussions began about sending someone off to get tea for them all, and Juliet quickly volunteered, closely followed by Irene, who said she had some cups that they could use.

As they walked, the old lady said, "Have you any news about your young man, the one who's missing in France? You must be worried about him."

"I suppose I am," Juliet said. "Although I can't see how he could make it back, if he's even still alive." The thought of his death made her shudder hot and ice cold—*How could he have deserted? But should he deserve to die for it?*

"Were you together for a long time?" Irene's voice meandered through her thoughts, gentle and sympathetic.

"Yes," Juliet said quietly, her mind drifting back to those heady early days. "We met about four years ago. He came to the village library to speak about his new book." She smiled at the memory, a sudden yearning to talk about him. "I'd never met a real writer before, and he was so eloquent, so clever. He asked me to dinner, and I couldn't believe my luck. After that, he walked me to his hotel—" She broke off, adding, "Sorry, I probably shouldn't have told you that."

Gently, Irene said, "Don't worry, dear. I was a headmistress, and I've heard a lot worse. Go on! He sounds intriguing. What was he like?"

"Well, I'd never had much to do with men before, certainly not a man like Victor. He made me see that the boys my mother introduced to me were spoiled and arrogant, products of their privilege. Victor had made his own way to become a political writer, and well," she felt herself blushing, "he was good-looking, too, in that tall, dark, and mysterious way." She chuckled at herself, remembering the schoolgirlish fluttering she'd had for him.

"It seems like he won you over."

She felt the blood rush to her face. "It's just that he understood me so well, and he *loved* me—the first love I'd ever felt in my life." She remembered those clandestine meetings. How he would open his door and pull her inside his world. Slowly, carefully, he'd seduced her, showing her how to remove his clothes, where to touch his skin, while she felt the bonds of her own childhood slip away from her as he gently disrobed her.

"I'd been flattered he'd picked me, that someone had seen me for my intelligence at last. He'd talk about Huxley, Plato, the Spanish Civil War, and then there were his own writings, which he felt had the power to change the world. He was mesmerizing."

It was only later she could see there was also a darkness about him, a bleakness that attracted as much as it repelled her. He swung between intense conversation and deep contemplation, a true genius at work.

"What did your parents say about him?"

"We kept it secret for a while." A light laugh escaped her, then it dropped. "But eventually they found out and forced him to propose, which he did." She looked at her hands, touching the place where the ring used to be. "Only he said that the wedding would have to wait until he finished writing his book. I thought it romantic, that he couldn't compromise his writing by having a proper job." She paused. "But he never did finish it."

"Didn't you get tired of waiting?" Irene asked.

"Of course not. It would have been selfish to put myself above his writing. It was an important treatise, not only for us but for the world."

"You're a faithful person, my dear," Irene said gently. "A lot of women might not have stayed. It sounds as if he was very preoccupied with his work."

Juliet frowned, unsure about this. "But I could truly depend on him, you see. He saw how my parents had hurt me and promised to always cherish me. He said that he'd protect me from them, that without him I'd be trapped under my mother's thumb forever."

There was a pause as Irene took this in, a small frown forming on her face before she said, "But you don't seem lost without him at all. You should give yourself credit for finding your own way out so quickly, making a new home for yourself here in Bethnal Green."

Looking around the happy crowd, Juliet smiled. "It's been lovely here—apart from the bombs, that is. Funny, I'd never thought of coming to London before. I suppose it was Victor. I couldn't have left him to live somewhere else, especially for a library job. He always loathed my work in the village library."

"That doesn't sound very fair," Irene said.

But Juliet only shrugged. "That was just what he was like, single-minded and completely adoring. He needed me, you see, just as I needed him."

They'd reached the front of the canteen line, watching as the women behind the table bustled around, the sugar and milk already run out.

Irene turned to Juliet. "Well, I know that men who are Missing in Action sometimes make it home, and I hope he does, too."

"So do I," she murmured uneasily, the unspoken reality of Victor's desertion omnipresent at the back of her mind.

"And if he does return, will you have to move back to your village?"

Juliet's heart fell at the notion of leaving Bethnal Green, her new life. She realized how much she'd experienced, her home with Mrs. Ottley and Sebastian, the friendships she'd made. Despite the setbacks, she'd made changes at the library, and they were beginning to see more memberships. Until that moment, she hadn't registered the difference in herself, the energy with which she met every day, the pleasure she got from helping people.

But she was promised to Victor, and she found herself saying, "I suppose I would have to leave, but it would be so wonderful to have him safely home."

She tried to ignore the awful reality that had gradually dawned on her since she'd found out about his disappearance. Even if Victor were able to get back to Britain, he faced criminal charges. In all likelihood, if he was alive, he would remain in France, where he'd find another little cottage, and a beautiful French woman, too. Her heart ached at the thought of him with someone else, but she knew how he was, how he would need someone.

And she would be left here on her own, never knowing whether to hold on for him or if he was even alive.

Suddenly, she saw her life pass in front of her. She would be stuck, waiting. But for what? A letter, a message, for the small possibility that he might walk back into her life?

Was that really the life that she wanted?

# KATIE

E VEN THOUGH THE LIBRARY WAS BUSY, KATIE STILL FOUND A MOMENT to pull out the medical book, flicking through the pages to find the right section. It was the day after she'd fled Mrs. Dempsey, and Katie struggled with how to face the future. She only had a few days of her library job left to go—she was due to start college in a week's time—and she still had no idea what she was going to do. Frantically, she devoured the pages, desperate for some kind of answer.

Surely knowledge was power?

Now that she felt the baby moving inside her, the size of the bump swelling over the last few weeks, there must be some way to work out how long she had to go until the birth. How miserable were her options: having her name ruined by going to a young mother's home or running away and struggling through by herself.

Katie had never done anything on her own ever before.

And this was a mammoth task, with the responsibility of a fragile newborn. How could it possibly be left in her small, young hands?

She'd been there for half an hour already without finding anything, but as she turned the page, a shadow came over her, and she heard a sharp intake of breath.

With a gasp she turned, but even before she saw her, Katie knew.

It was her mother.

Frantically, Katie grappled to close the great volume, but not before her mother's eyes had taken in the page, where the words "fetus," "gestation," and, most alarmingly, "pregnancy" were there for all to see.

Suddenly, Katie felt her pulse race. "W-what are you doing here, Mum?" She wanted to sound casual, but it came out harried, accusatory.

Her mother's eyes were on her, going from her face to her soft, protruding belly. Her look of pained dismay morphed into one of repulsed horror, and she whispered furiously under her breath, "What have you done?"

"Mum, please," Katie whimpered. "I didn't know . . . you didn't tell me."

But her mother wasn't listening, her mouth aghast as she took in the situation. "Who knows about this?"

"No one," Katie promised.

She glared at Katie for a moment, her eyes packed with despair and then disappointment, followed by more anger than Katie had ever seen in them.

"We'll speak about this when you get home." There was an iciness to her voice that Katie had never heard before, and as she watched her mother storm out of the library, she felt panic well up inside her.

The walk home after work was a slow, reluctant one, and Katie stopped for a moment at the bench, the place where she and Christopher used to sit. The blooms from the magnolia tree had fallen away, only a few withering leaves moving in the wind, exposed and defenseless, vulnerable.

What would her mother do to her?

And what about her father? He would be insane with rage if anyone should find out.

After a moment collecting herself, she made her way to the house.

"Mum?" she called as she walked through the door. There was a tremor in her voice—although she was home, it was like she was stepping into enemy territory.

"Oh, there you are." Her mother seemed larger and more formidable as she strode into the hall, suddenly brisk and businesslike. "We'd better go upstairs."

Katie trailed behind to her bedroom and sat on the bed, as instructed by her mother's pointed finger.

"I will save us both the embarrassment of asking you what happened," her mother snapped, pacing the room. "I can only assume it was with Christopher, and now he isn't here to claim the child as his, nor to make a decent woman out of you." Hands on hips, she was livid, her lower-class accent no longer hidden behind the genteel vowels, a new grittiness about her.

"He would marry me if he could," Katie pleaded.

Her mother's face scrunched as she struggled to hold back her frustration. "Do you have any idea how much this is going to harm the family? We'll be lucky if your father doesn't disown us. His business is reliant on our respectability." Her voice cracked with tears. "Do you understand the full scale of what this means, the social disgrace? Our entire family will be cast out of the community, and all because of your stupidity!"

The deep grimace made her mother look older, craggier. It was as if she had taken off her mask, let Katie see the reality: the woman desperately protecting the respectability she had so carefully fostered. Katie's father had always accused her mother of marrying above her station, bringing lower-class habits into their family. Brought up in the tenements, she'd made it her mission to don the cloak of respectability— the pretense that Katie's pregnancy now threatened.

Throwing herself down on a chair, she snapped at Katie, "Now, let me tell you what we're going to do. First of all, you will conceal the pregnancy. I will lend you some dresses and coats, and you can use scarves and cardigans to cover the bump. You will stay at home as much as you can." Her eyes bored into her. "You are to tell no one. Do you understand?"

"Yes," Katie murmured.

"Meanwhile, I will pretend that it is me who is pregnant, so that when you give birth at home, we can pretend I'm the one having a baby. Everyone will think the child is mine, and we can bring it up as part of the family."

"But doesn't that mean . . ." Katie grappled with the plan in her mind. "That I will have to act as if the baby is my sibling?" Tears came unstoppably to her eyes. "Wouldn't it be better if I left home, fended for myself?"

Her mother scowled. "And let the gossips loose? Our family would never recover, and your father would leave us high and dry. Where would we be then?"

"I could go far away from here. No one would ever know."

Her mother shook her head as if she'd never heard anything as idiotic. "Do you have any idea how hard it is for an unmarried mother on her own? Landlords won't give you a place to live. You'd find it hard to get work, and then you'd have to take low wages, barely able to get by. That's why so many women like you fall into"—she gave her a meaningful look—"a certain way of life."

Katie looked out of the window, the birds soaring through the evening sky. How she longed to just soar away, too, go to a different world where having a baby was a joy, not a major disaster.

As if reading her mind, her mother grabbed her hand, forcing Katie to look at her. "My plan gets you off scot-free. You can hold your head up high, find a new boy, get married, start your own family with as many children as you'd like. No one need ever know the truth."

"When my younger brother or sister is actually my own child?" Katie was still trying to take it in.

"At least you'll still be close to it." Her tone was curt, clipped.

"But it'll be as if I'm denying my own child." A knot seemed to tie inside her stomach. "In any case, how will we get away with it, living a lie for the rest of our lives?"

Frustratedly, her mother got to her feet. "Where I grew up, it happened all the time, a mother pretending a daughter's child was her own. It goes on around here, too, if you know the signs."

Katie thought of the young woman opposite, the once flamboyant and fun-loving girl now standing behind the rest of the family, always silent, subservient.

Was that the role Katie was to play?

"What about a mother and baby home?" she asked. "That's what usually happens, isn't it?"

"People always find out. Every girl sent away is suspected. And since you're supposed to be going to college in London, everyone will realize there must be a good reason why you've suddenly left town."

"But—"

Her mother interrupted her. "And speaking of university, well, you've blown that, haven't you? Soon the bump will be too obvious for you to work or go to college. You'll have to stay at home, wait for the birth."

"I thought that maybe I could start college once all this is over." Katie felt her future slipping away from her.

"Not with a baby to look after. You're going to have to do all the hard work, you know. All the washing, the nappies, the midnight feeding, and heaven help you if it cries a lot." She let out a long groan. "This whole thing is going to cause so much trouble for us."

Katie's hands went to the unborn child, as if trying to protect the poor thing. What kind of a life would he or she have?

And what about Katie? Her mother would always look at her in the way she was right now, her eyes bulging with anger and disappointment.

Her lips trembling, Katie buried her face in her hands, swallowing back the nausea that burned acidic up her throat.

How had her life descended this low?

There was an ache in her chest, and although she knew it was indigestion, she couldn't help but feel her heart slowly decomposing inside her, darkening and collapsing as if her body were rejecting it, the desperate requirements of this bleak new reality.

CHAPTER

14

# SOFIE

THE MESSAGE FROM MARIGOLD'S CONTACT WAS DELIVERED WHILE Sofie was doing the morning shop, a simple, small envelope resting on the doorstep.

In a single, swift action, Sofie picked it up and hurried down to the kitchen.

*Miss Baumann*

*I have information that would be of value to you. Meet me in Bethnal Green Underground Station, Tuesday night 9 o'clock sharp, beside the main canteen. Wear something red.*

*Mac*

"But that's tonight!" Her hand shook as she pushed the note into her pocket. How would she get away?

With the bombers coming every night, the government had finally allowed tube stations to be used as shelters, and thankfully Mr. Wainwright had decided to join the throng. He would send Sofie down early to save them a spot in one of the more peaceful tunnels. To make time to meet with this Mac, all she had to do was make sure he was fed and content, and she could slip away for five or ten minutes.

Nothing would stop her from making that meeting. Every day, she walked past the pawn shop, and there in the window was the garnet ring, a reminder of her dirty deed. A plan to buy it back would come to her soon, but in the meantime, the only way she could assuage her guilt was by putting the money to good use, bringing her family back together.

By five minutes to nine, after she'd fed and pampered him, tidied their camping area, and provided him with a fresh newspaper, she prepared her getaway.

"Why don't I fetch some tea before the lights go out?" she said softly, avoiding his eyes. "There'll be a long line, and we might miss it if we leave it too late."

"Be quick about it!" he grunted without lifting his head.

Before he could change his mind, she dashed into the main concourse, tying a maroon napkin around her neck, the closest thing to red she could find.

But as she saw the crowd by the canteen, she felt a shiver of panic. Who was this "Mac"? How would he see her among all these people?

"Miss Baumann?" The voice came from behind her, and she spun around, startled to find herself only a foot away from a young man dressed in a cheap dark suit that was slightly too small for his wide shoulders. His face was narrow, gaunt even, and his dark hair neat, but there was a wariness about him, shadows beneath his eyes as he glanced over his shoulder. In the bright lights, his blue-gray eyes were unusually pale, piercing hers with trepidation.

"Mac?" she whispered anxiously.

He put a finger to his lips, and bent his head close to her ear to whisper, "Count to five and then follow me. We must not be seen together." He spoke with a foreign accent, but from where she couldn't tell.

Before she could ask, he peeled away, weaving through the crowd toward a narrow door at the back of the concourse.

*One, two, three* . . . she counted in her head and then she darted after him, hurrying through the crowd lest she lose sight of him.

He was already at the door, vanishing inside.

Quickly, she caught up, pulling open the door and glancing into the dark, dusty interior, hesitating, thinking of the danger. He could do anything to her and who would know?

*Where is your bravery, Sofie?* she said to herself, as if Rachel were there, goading her on.

She had already been through so much: the journey, the job, the broken ornament, and now the ring. How could she let it be for nothing? The danger, the threat of imprisonment, everything was worthwhile if it meant she could find her family.

With a deep breath, she slipped inside.

Although it wasn't completely dark, it took a moment for her eyes to adjust. Dingy, naked bulbs hung at irregular intervals down a narrow passage, the grimy black walls thick with cables, smaller passages connecting in different directions. Electrical boxes and gauges protruded sporadically, giving the place a shadowy feel. A whiff of cigarette smoke combined with stale alcohol, and the sound of low voices and scuffling echoed through the passages, the hum of electrical wires punctuated with a sporadic drip resonating eerily through the maze.

"Miss Baumann?" the man's voice whispered from the main passage ahead of her.

She looked into the darkness, and there was Mac ten yards ahead of her. She hastened after him, trying not to peer at the men tucked into passages and crevices, doing business or exchanging goods.

It wasn't long before Mac turned into a small gap in the passage wall.

Suddenly the low hum from the cables rose quickly, swelling to a massive whirr. She put her hands over her ears, as did Mac, and it built to a crescendo before stopping.

"It's a train, probably the last one of the night." He looked at his wristwatch as the noise built up again, the train leaving.

"I have to be quick," she said. "What news do you have for me?"

"Where is the money?" His tone was detached, a shade of urgency behind it.

"Did you find my family?" Papa always told her to make sure to get the goods before handing over the money.

He paused. "I have information, but no addresses yet. It was hard to get, and it'll cost you five pounds."

A wave of panic shot through her. "But I only have four." Struggling, she wrenched the money from her pocket, holding it out to him, scrunched in her hand. "It is all that I have—*more* than I have."

"Four will do," he said in his quiet monotone. He found her hand in the darkness, opening it, taking the notes.

"I have news about your sister." He paused and then added, "Although, I am not sure it is her."

"What do you mean?"

"There was a Rachel Hoffman who tried to get a Portuguese visa in Bordeaux, France, and I wondered if she might have married her traveling companion Frederick Hoffman?"

"Married Frederick?" she repeated. Could it be true? They were friends, nothing more. But still, she supposed, it could happen.

How incongruous to hear of her sister's marriage from a stranger in this dark tunnel.

Mac carried on speaking. "A lot of Jews fled into France, and now that it is occupied and Spain dangerous, Portugal is their only hope. The capital city, Lisbon, is packed with people trying to board ships to Britain or the Americas."

Her head spun with all this new information. "Is my father with them?"

"There was no mention of his name, but the sources are sporadic at best."

"Is there an address for Rachel, in Bordeaux?"

He shook his head. "The visa form is dated two months ago, so it is possible that she has moved on. There are signs that the Portuguese ambassador in Bordeaux has sympathy for the Jews and is handing out more visas than he is allowed, but we don't know whether your sister got one. I could try to find more information, but I would need more money." Desperation tremored in his voice—was he living on the very edge of existence, too?

Her breath caught in her throat. "But that is all I have." She thought of the box of rings. Could she risk it again?

Mac was taking a step back toward the passage. "In that case, Miss Baumann, I wish you good luck."

He walked away, leaving her alone, frightened and panicked. Quickly, she chased after him. "I will find the money. I promise I will." In her desperation, she grabbed the sleeve of his arm. "Can you find out more? An address maybe?"

"I will do what I can." He turned to her, and his face softened as he saw her tears. "The French Underground are getting what information they can, as are Jewish groups on the ground. If she got a Portuguese visa, the trip is hazardous. They have to walk over the Pyrenees and then get through northern Spain. I hope she is fit."

Sofie felt helpless, suddenly agitated. "Can nothing be easy? Haven't we suffered enough already?"

He peeled her hand gently from his sleeve. "It is the Nazis. They are the enemy. We Jews are just victims. There is nothing we can do except try to stay alive."

She shuffled, embarrassed at her outburst at this stranger. "Are you Jewish, too? Did you escape?"

With a sullen single nod, he said, "I had to leave my home in Poland soon after the invasion." His tone was straight, stoical, as if all emotions had been locked away.

Suddenly the door was pushed open from the outside, a burly man thrusting into the passage ahead. Hastily, Mac pulled her into a dark side passage, his breath heavy beside her as they watched the heavyset man stalk down the main passage.

Once he was gone, Mac whispered to her in Yiddish, "Look, I will be generous and give you the information for free next time."

Balking, she quickly tried to get a grip of herself. It had been such a long time since she had heard the language, and the words wove such a familiarity around her that she felt almost flattened by homesickness. Slowly, she whispered back to him in Yiddish. "Thank you, er, Mac? Is that your real name?"

"Does it matter?" And with that, he turned and left her, striding quickly through to the main passage and back toward the door.

Quickly, she followed him out, wanting to talk more to him, frightened to be on her own. As she crossed another passage, a movement caught her eye, and she turned to see a couple in the shadows, the woman pinned to the wall, her dress rucked around her hips.

*What kind of place is this?* she thought, darting for the door.

She yanked it open, and suddenly she was back in the busy, bright underground concourse, back in normality once again.

It took a moment to get her bearings, to catch her breath. She looked around the vast space, but Mac was already gone, lost in the crowd.

Leaning against the wall, she steadied herself. Her head swam with the new information about her family. Even though she didn't know Rachel's exact whereabouts, the fact she knew something poured into her like a warm, nourishing fuel.

But then her elation subsided.

Suddenly it hit her that without the money she had just given to Mac, she had nothing left with which to protect herself. She couldn't buy the ring back if need be.

In need of some kind of solace, she found herself taking a detour to where she'd seen Juliet and the others earlier, finding them sitting on rugs and fold-up chairs, listening to Juliet as she read aloud. And as Sofie made her way to the small group, something inside her unfolded, like a tightly wound spring being released.

Seeing her through the crowd, Juliet paused slightly, giving her a smile, and the group turned to her, beckoning her to join them, Mrs. Ottley moving over so that she could share the rug she'd spread over the floor.

Maybe she could stay for a few minutes, just to calm her nerves.

Gratefully, Sofie sat down, one of the old ladies beside her taking her hand. And as the words went in and out, trickling through her frantic mind like a cooling stream, she could only feel grateful for her new bookish friends.

# JULIET

THE NIGHT WAS ALMOST PITCH BLACK AS JULIET TROD CAREFULLY through the school playground to the door. It was her first night as an ambulance driver, scheduled for the graveyard shift from midnight to eight, and excitement mingled with nerves as she held herself up straight, eager to do her bit for the war.

The Ambulance Service was housed in the same evacuated school building as the local ARP team, the smell of chalk dust and gym shoes lingering in the hallway, the overhead lights bright after the dark of the blackout. Through the corridor, she could hear activity and shouts coming from the main hall, now used as a first-aid clinic, the ambulances bringing the walking wounded here instead of overcrowding the hospitals. There had been an air raid earlier in the evening, and the place was already busy.

A makeshift sign on a classroom door indicated that she'd found the ambulance section, and with a deep breath and her usual spirited smile, she opened the door.

But as she looked around, all she saw was two women knitting at the back, both looking a bit worse for wear in old slacks.

"Hello, you must be the new one! You'll have to excuse our trousers." A curvaceous brunette smiled over, looking at Juliet's smart skirt suit. "It can get a bit mucky if you're not careful. I'm Camilla, by the way, and this is Maureen." Judging by her accent, Camilla was very posh indeed.

"I'm Juliet. I moved to Bethnal Green last month to be the deputy in the library."

"Oh, are you the one who started the Underground Library, lending out books?" Maureen looked up from her knitting. She wasn't as upper-class as Camilla, but Juliet could see the two of them were friends, a tin of sandwiches on a desk between them.

Juliet laughed a little. "I haven't heard it called that before."

"You've made a lot of people very happy," Maureen went on. "I've caught a few of your book readings. Who'd have thought a library in an underground shelter could be just the thing we need?" Her eyes flickered back over Juliet's skirt. "Would you like to borrow some slacks?"

"I'll be fine, thank you." Juliet smoothed down her skirt.

But Camilla got up and pressed a pair into her hands. "You can get soaked from the fire hoses or"—she paused, reaching for a nice way to put it—"general grime. You'll thank me."

In a dingy toilet, Juliet quickly put them on, pulling the belt tight to keep them up. When she returned to the main room, an older man was there with a clipboard.

"Juliet, this is Mr. Moore." Camilla added with a grin, "He's just the coordinator, but he thinks he's in charge around here."

He laughed, obviously in on the joke. "Who'd want to be in charge of you lot!" He looked down at his list. "Now, here you are, Juliet Lansdown. You're to go along with Camilla tonight." He took off his glasses to look at her. "It's your first time, isn't it?"

"I did the first-aid course, but that's all so far."

"Well, there's two of you in each ambulance, one to drive and the other to navigate. It's impossible to know where you are in the blackout. Both of you help with the injured, carry out first aid on the spot, and drive those who need it to the hospital. We have single-driver cars to take the walking wounded back here for first aid—the ambulances are reserved for stretcher cases only." There was a pause before he added, "And leave the dead beside the road. A van will come round for them later."

Silently, Juliet shuddered.

After that, he ran through the evening's events. "The underground station at Bounds Green was hit in the earlier raid. A bomb went through the buildings above it and plunged down onto one of the platforms." He grimaced. "We like to think tube stations are invincible, but you can still get crushed down there."

"Were there many dead?" Camilla asked, trying to hide any emotion. If the underground wasn't safe, then where was?

"We don't know yet—the government might try to keep that close to their chests. . . ."

He was cut short by a messenger at the door, a lad of fifteen or so.

"ARP got the call. At least thirty bombers coming from the coast, should be over London in half an hour. Be on ready!"

"Well, that's all for now, then," Mr. Moore said. "Take her outside, Camilla. Show her how the ambulance works."

With that, they hurried out of a back door, pulling their coats around them. The darkness was so peaceful, it felt impossible that a team of bombers was already in the distance, bent on their deadly mission.

The two ambulances were housed under a corrugated metal canopy behind the school. Both were large civilian cars with their backs cut away and an off-white canvas-covered frame attached. There was room for two stretchers in the back, and the canvas "doors" could be rolled up or down as needed.

Camilla showed Juliet to their ambulance, opening the driver's door. "You can drive today. Get in and make yourself comfortable. I'll fetch the handbook, show you how the thing works."

As she turned to go back to the building, a handful of ARP wardens came out, and Camilla called out to one. "Sebastian, is that you? I didn't see you earlier."

Through the car window, Juliet saw him stop beside her. "On the same shift again, Camilla? How very convenient!" He was as charming as ever.

They stood chatting for a minute or so, Juliet catching only a few words, and she wondered if there was anything going on between them. Camilla was very pretty, and by the sound of it, she was just as capable a flirt as he was.

Suddenly deciding to make her presence known, Juliet stepped out of the car, walking over to say hello.

At once, he turned to smile at her. "Oh, there you are, Juliet! I thought I saw your name on the list. You're in good hands with Camilla here. She's one of our finest."

Camilla gave a mock bow. "At your service," she said before heading inside the building for the handbook.

After Camilla had gone, Sebastian raised an eyebrow. "I must say, Juliet, you're looking very fetching tonight," he mused, eyeing the trousers bunched up around her waist.

"They're far too big for me," she laughed. "But Camilla insisted. She said it'll get messy."

His smile fell a little. "It's not always a pleasant way to spend an evening."

"I'd have thought with your daytime work you wouldn't have time for this, too."

With a shrug, he said, "I suppose I'm not the kind of chap who can sit back and watch everyone else do it. In any case, I've already seen how unpleasant war can be on the front, so I probably find it easier than most."

It wasn't the first time he'd mentioned the front, and she gave him a close-lipped smile. "Underneath that rakish façade, you're actually quite decent, aren't you?"

He laughed and was about to reply, but then the air-raid siren began blaring, and they parted company, him to the ARP section and her back to the ambulance office to wait for her first call.

"Good luck!" he said. Their eyes met, suddenly serious, fearful, but then he smiled. "Maybe I'll see you along the way." And with that, he was gone.

Almost immediately, the messenger boy appeared at the door.

"Two high explosives on a tenement block on Bishops Way," he shouted above the noise—the anti-aircraft guns had started, thrumming from Victoria Park with increasing racket.

Hurrying back outside, Camilla pulled her to the ambulance. "You drive, Juliet! I'll show you the gauges on the way."

Juliet started the ignition, fumbling with the pedals, trying to ignore a great flash of light—a flare the bombers used to light the night sky, illuminating their targets.

The car stalled.

"Don't worry, darling," Camilla said. "Take a few breaths and try again. We won't get anywhere if you're all fingers and thumbs."

The next time, it started smoothly, and she drove onto the main road.

The city felt like a ghost town, dark and shadowy in the blackout. No cars or buses were on the street, only the occasional ARP car or heavy truck. They passed a pedestrian, a lone middle-aged man, walking on his own.

"Is he a looter?" Juliet whispered to Camilla.

She laughed. "Not at all. He's a firewatcher. They're volunteers who walk their neighborhoods every night to report bombs to the ARP and fire crews. It's probably where we got the call."

Soon enough, they were on Bishops Way, and Camilla pointed to the glow of fires coming from a side street to the left. "We're here before the fire crew. That's always useful—especially if you don't want to get wet."

Juliet marveled at the girl's nonchalance. "How long before I'll be as cavalier as you?"

"You'll soon see, it's the only way to cope." She drew a deep breath as they pulled the ambulance up and got out. "In a lot of ways, avoiding the bombs is the easy part."

How right she was.

Devastation surrounded them. The tenement had been blown to smithereens. A fire raged on the edge of an uneven mound of rubble, household objects everywhere: fragments of blue-patterned crockery, a ripped counterpane, the arm of a chair, a man's shoe, a rug sagging over a gaping hole in the ground, clothes strewn everywhere, a broken hand mirror, a smashed photograph frame, the portrait inside yellowed and warped by the heat of the flames.

Amid the crackle of the fire, the sounds of moans and cries could be heard.

"Over here," Camilla nudged her, flashing her light to a lump among the rubble.

As Juliet got closer, she saw what Camilla had spotted. Out of a dark green coat, half-hidden by bricks and debris, protruded an arm, straight and angular, as if twisted back from the person's body.

"It might not be one for us," Camilla said breezily, meaning that the body was already dead, "but let's make sure, shall we?"

Carefully, she crouched over the arm.

"Ambulance here," Camilla called loudly. "We'll have you out in a jiffy. Can you tell us if anything hurts?" She listened intently as she watched for movement. Then decisively, she turned to Juliet. "Let's uncover her."

With her gloved hands, Camilla began scooping away the debris and fragments of a ruined home, shreds of books and clothes, furniture and wallpaper.

Juliet joined her, brushing away particles from the coat until more of the body emerged.

Only it didn't. The coat was there, but it was empty, only the arm, now bent, the hand pale in the torchlight, protruding from one sleeve.

Bile surged up her throat and into her mouth. Just in time, Juliet turned to retch, quickly getting to her feet, hiding her reaction as Camilla pulled out the arm and coat and laid it down on the pavement, as if it were nothing but an object.

"I wonder where the rest of her is—we always have more limbs than anything else." Hands on hips, she looked around the rubble. "Hello-o!" she called out, again listening hard for any responses. "Ah, over here! Juliet!"

Quickly, she scrambled up the heap, Juliet pulling herself together and following, praying it wouldn't be another body part.

It wasn't.

A woman was lying on her front, her feet strangely twisted, pointing in different directions. A low moan came from her.

"We're the Ambulance Service. We're going to get the stretcher for you, all right?"

They returned a moment later, and carefully turned the body to see the woman's face. She was far younger than Juliet imagined, around her own age, her eyes closed tightly, her mouth open and filled with blood.

Swallowing hard, Juliet focused on her training. Never had she felt so completely out of her depth.

Two ARP cars arrived, and Juliet could see shadows of figures coming toward them, one of them Sebastian.

"Hurry," Camilla called over to him. "Get this one into the ambulance. I'll see if I can find any more."

As soon as he arrived, Sebastian began the checks, and Juliet couldn't help but watch as his hands worked gently over the body, as if he had done this a thousand times before.

"She has multiple breaks. I'll give her morphine," he said as he quickly administered the drug, dabbing his finger in the dirt to write the letter M on the woman's forehead. Juliet knew that was a message for the hospital: A patient could only be given one dose of morphine to prevent an overdose. These days, morphine was in every first aid kit; gone was the era of a few bandages and an aspirin. No one mentioned that morphine addiction was already becoming a problem. Under the circumstances, it seemed almost inhumane to withhold it.

Together they lifted the woman onto the stretcher and carried her to the ambulance, sliding her into the back.

As Juliet stood up, she felt a surge of nausea wash through her.

"Well done," he said, coming up beside her. "It's always hard at first."

"I d-didn't think it would be like this," she stammered.

"I don't think anyone does," he said.

The other ARP warden was calling him, and for a brief moment he paused, putting a reassuring hand on her upper arm, before striding away to help.

Debris from the explosion lay strewn across the road, and while she waited for Camilla, she picked up a long piece of cloth. It turned out to be a woman's coat, blue and stylish, a little like one she had herself. It must have been thrown a dozen yards from its wardrobe or coat stand. She folded it up and laid it on the pavement, just in case.

Camilla and the other warden were coming down to the ambulance with the other stretcher. "This one's an emergency," she called. "Better get going."

Before she got into the ambulance, Juliet turned to see Sebastian, now falling into conversation with another ARP warden, but just at that moment, he turned to her, their eyes meeting, and with a small, soft smile, he made a nod, as if to say, "You'll be just fine."

And as she started the engine and headed for the hospital, Camilla chatting away beside her, she was suddenly aware of belonging to a new team, a group of volunteers who did their best to keep going in this awful new reality.

CHAPTER

**16**

# KATIE

I T WAS KATIE'S LAST DAY OF WORK AT THE LIBRARY, AND SHE COULDN'T have felt more desolate, desperately trying to read as much as she could while she had the chance. As from today, her mother was insisting that she stay at home, hidden away lest anyone guess the truth. Already her stomach had become too big for her own clothes, and she'd been forced into an old dress of her mother's that hung off her like a tent, a symbol of her shame. Her mother, meanwhile, had a small cushion strapped beneath her clothes, and she announced her pregnancy to Mrs. Baxter and the church ladies with a feigned delight that dropped like a sledge-hammer as soon as the front door was closed.

Life at home had become a misery. Her father redirected all his anger toward her, while her mother vanished behind a wall of silence, her lips pursed with disappointment and loathing. Katie's dependable, loving ally had become her worst enemy.

She had never felt so alone.

Every time the baby turned, she felt a new protectiveness, a new nurturing, making the reality all the more hard to swallow.

Didn't her body know that she couldn't keep the child? Shouldn't it save her from the thousand tiny heartaches that happened throughout her day?

Juliet disturbed her in the history aisle. "Not long before you start college. You must be excited."

"Y-yes," Katie stammered, trying to look elated for an experience she knew would never happen. But she took the history books from under her arm. "I'm going to take out a few books before I start," she said, trying to keep up her act.

Even though she may not have her university place any longer, there was nothing to stop her from conducting her own studies. History books, journals, and encyclopedias beckoned, and she planned to make her own notes, forming timelines, extrapolating the past to take her mind off the present.

"What a good idea!" Juliet beamed, adding, "I hope you're coming to the book club later? We've decided to hold it in the underground while we shelter. Sofie's been helping me find something special for our discussion."

Katie's mind shifted uncomfortably to the interminable evenings now spent with her family beside the rail platform. "Mum likes me to stay with her, but I'll see if I can find an excuse to get away."

Quickly pulling the books back toward her, Katie didn't realize that they were caught on her dress, pulling it tightly across her bump. Hurriedly, she rearranged the fabric, praying that Juliet hadn't noticed.

But to Katie's utter dismay, she looked up to see Juliet's puzzled expression as she gazed first at Katie's stomach and then into her face. "I hope you don't mind me asking, but," she paused, trying to find a delicate way of putting it, "is there a chance you might be, well, expecting a baby?"

A tremor of panic raced through Katie, and she murmured, "Whatever do you mean?"

"It's all right." Juliet moved a little closer. "I won't tell anyone."

Katie's eyes began to brim with tears, and she gazed at Juliet wordlessly, clenching her mouth shut in case she started to cry so hard that she wouldn't be able to stop.

"I'm sure it's not all that bad." Juliet put an arm around her shoulders.

"It's the worst thing that could ever happen." The words came tumbling out, and Katie heard her own voice, brittle and desperate.

"My mother says that if anyone finds out, I may as well be dead. My reputation will be destroyed, and I'll have ruined the family as well. Mum's barely talking to me anymore."

"Isn't she trying to help you?"

Sucking in a great gulp of air, Katie explained her mother's plan to Juliet. "She says I should be grateful. But somehow it doesn't feel that way at all."

"Do you have long to go?" Juliet asked, struggling to take it in.

"About three or four months, or so Mum says. She won't let me see a doctor or a midwife to find out for sure." Katie wavered. "To be honest, I'm a bit worried about the birth. I've been reading about it, and it doesn't always go as well as it should."

"Why don't you ask her if you can have a midwife at the birth? I'm sure she'd be discreet—you certainly aren't the first woman to find herself in this position."

"Mum insists that no one can ever find out."

Juliet gave her a firm look. "You will let me know when it starts, won't you?"

"Thank you, but . . ." Katie looked at her hands. "But my mother says I have to trust her."

"Just remember that you have us here, in the library."

Suddenly fearful she'd said too much, Katie was already getting up, trying to get away.

What had she been thinking, telling someone about the baby?

But Juliet was a friend, a trustworthy person, wasn't she?

Her panic was interrupted by the familiar drone of the air-raid siren seeping in from outside, earlier than usual, the sound synonymous with an untidy mixture of exhaustion, tedium, and fear.

"Not again!" Juliet moaned, her eyes going to the clock on the wall, turning to Katie, "We'd better go straight to the underground." They hurried back to the main desk, joining the other staff who were collecting their coats, Juliet quickly racing to the fiction aisle to pick up a few more books to lend out in the underground.

It wasn't until they were outside, rushing to the underground entrance on the corner, that a thought occurred to Katie. "As I won't have time to go home, perhaps I can avoid sitting with my mother—well, I can try."

Juliet grinned. "You can come and camp with me and the Miss Ridleys, help us prepare for the book club." She linked her arm through Katie's as they went down into the station. "Funny how quickly you get used to sleeping underground every night." She laughed, trying to make light of it. "I've taken to carrying my toothbrush, a comb, lipstick, and a spare pair of stockings in my handbag. In my reckoning, that's the absolute minimum I need before work in the morning."

Katie fell into step beside her, glad of Juliet's warm chatter, her acceptance of the situation without too many questions. If only everyone else could be so understanding.

Crowds gathered at the turnstiles to the escalators. No one knew how many more nights of air raids they would have. The Nazis were trying to bring the nation to its knees, but Britain seemed only to dig her heels in more firmly. More and more of life was moving underground every night. Some factories had moved to cellars when there was an air raid, and one military equipment plant had relocated to one of the unused tube tunnels in East London, women working shifts around the clock.

As they descended into the underground, the two women let out a sigh of relief at being safe. People spoke about a bomb having someone's name on it, how a split-second decision to fetch a coat or go to a different shelter could mean life or death. Everyone had stories of their own near misses.

The dead, of course, did not.

The main concourse was teeming with life. Since the government had allowed undergrounds to open as shelters, an influx of services had come in to smooth their running. Equipped canteens were supplied by a morning underground train, and proper chemical toilets quickly came into being. Voluntary shelter marshals made sure order was kept.

Luckily, Bethnal Green was one of the larger stations with plenty of tunnels and passageways in which to sleep, read, or partake of any number of underground activities, illicit or otherwise. Some of the less busy connecting passages were permanently roped off for shelterers to sleep, while others had paths cordoned off for travelers trying to get to a platform. After the trains stopped running at nine o'clock, the platform space and tracks became available, but you had to be ready to pack up and leave before the trains began again at around six in the morning. Everyone else had to be out before seven.

At the end of one of the quieter passages, great white curtains cordoned off a makeshift first-aid clinic. Sometimes Katie caught sight of the nurse cleaning a burn or taking out fragments of shrapnel with tweezers, the injuries of a besieged city.

As they passed some of the smaller tunnels, Katie's eyes were drawn to a familiar-looking woman, a pretty brunette in a red coat. It was only as she saw who was with her that the penny dropped, his bald head glinting in the bright lights as they shared a joke, a little too close, a little too intimate.

Katie balked. Was her father having an affair?

But Juliet took her arm, hurrying them along, unaware of what she'd seen, what it could mean.

Finally, Juliet drew to a halt just inside one of the quieter passages. "This was the very first place that I camped, and now everyone knows where to find me if they want to borrow a book. Good company has been the one positive thing about the shelters. It's heartwarming for the bereaved and people with loved ones away. It can't be easy for them, by themselves. At least they're surrounded by people down here, feeling less alone."

As soon as they sat down, people began coming over to ask if Juliet had any books, the Miss Ridleys arriving with their deck chairs.

"You're becoming quite well known around here." A woman beside Juliet had a baby in her arms, two little blond girls watching them. "I hope you've brought more for us tonight."

"Oh, lovely to see you, Mary." Juliet began to set the books into three piles beside her. "Here are classics, then we have romances, and these are the ever-popular murders."

Soon they were swamped. Some people sat or knelt down on the floor beside her to look through the books, others stopping to chat.

But Katie found her eyes going to the young mother, Mary, holding her baby so close, smiling down into his face with such a soft, intense love it was disarming. The way she held the baby easily while smiling at the twin girls, telling them to keep still, it made it seem so simple, so natural.

Soon Katie, too, would be a mother, albeit one that would never be acknowledged, and the thought punctured her like a spear. Perhaps her mother was right. If it was the only way that Katie could keep her baby close to her, it was the best plan going.

"When you're free, Katie, Irene can show you how to register the loans in my notebook," Juliet was saying, bringing her back down to earth. "You and the Miss Ridleys can do it for me when I have a shift with the ambulances."

The book club members were already gathering, Mrs. Ottley plumping cushions on the floor to sit down beside Marigold.

Sofie arrived, treading through to join the Miss Ridleys. "Thank you for the food you gave me, and the book, too. It was in German," she told the others. "It reminded me of home." From inside her shopping bag, she brought out a box. "I baked a cake to keep Mr. Wainwright happy so that I can sneak away this evening, and I made extra for you, to say thank you." Beaming at them, she opened the box to reveal half of a Bundt cake, cut into slices.

"But you shouldn't have!" Dorothy said. "What with the rations, you should save it for yourself. You could do with a little fattening up!"

Sofie grinned, urging them to take a slice. "Yesterday was the Jewish New Year, so it's an apple cake. It's supposed to bring prosperity and sweetness for the coming year." She smiled at them. "And I wanted to share my appreciation. Everything was so bad that day you took me in for tea. You made me feel like I wasn't on my own."

Dorothy reached for her hand. "You're never on your own while we're here."

The apple cake was shared around, everyone wishing Sofie a happy new year, and then Juliet stood up to begin the book club.

"Welcome everybody. Tonight, we're having a poetry evening, prompted by one of our keen regulars, Sofie."

Everyone clapped, Marigold giving a little cheer.

"And Sofie has been kind enough to share her choice of poems for me to read out. The first is called 'Hope.' It's by an American poet, Emily Dickinson."

*"Hope" is the thing with feathers -*
*That perches in the soul -*
*And sings the tune without the words -*
*And never stops - at all -*

The poem had several verses, and at the end, the small group gave heartfelt applause.

Juliet stood, her gaze thoughtful. "I began learning about poetry by asking one question: How does it make me feel? Does anyone have any answers?"

"It's the metaphor," Dorothy said. "Hope is like the bird in the poem, singing in your heart. It makes you picture something, hear it, bring it to life. We all need hope, and it reminds us that we have it, there inside us, whatever is happening outside."

"Like this dreadful war," Mrs. Ottley said with a huff. "The idea is uplifting, isn't it, to think about a songbird in your chest piping away regardless of all the danger, our loved ones so far away."

"There's a truth in it, though," Irene said. "The poet recognizes that hope never dies."

"Unless we want to give up hope, but there's a reason why we can't." And Katie realized it was her own voice, suddenly gruff with tears. Something about the poem needled her, and as everyone turned to her, it became clear. "Sometimes hope has gone, but for someone else's sake we have to carry on, no bird singing in our hearts, just a plain, dull silence."

"But surely hope will always be there, if we are still alive," Sofie said quietly, her eyes piercing Katie's with understanding. "I have existed in a hole in that man's house this past year, and there were times when my body ached and my spirit was crushed, and then I remembered this poem, and I realized that the bird of hope inside me still sang. Its voice might be weak, its tune very changed, discordant and muddled, but I still had hope, hope to see my family again, hope for a new home, hope to be free. Now I need to do all I can to make that hope come true, no matter how difficult or painful or risky."

The words resonated through the small gathering, and it sunk in how much the poor girl had gone through, how much they all had with this war. Somehow, it seemed to bring them closer, nestling with each other protectively, building their resilience.

And suddenly Katie knew: She couldn't let her situation overwhelm her. It couldn't be the end of her story. She mustn't let this defeat her.

And as she took in a great lungful of air, she felt the small bird of hope inside her singing for all it was worth, while the small child lower in her abdomen settled into sleep, safe and sound, at least for now.

# SOFIE

AUTUMN WAS COMING, THE LEAVES IN THE PARK YELLOWING, the smell of bark and decay thick in the air as Sofie rushed home with the morning shopping, a spring in her step. The nights in the underground meant that she'd been able to spend more time with the book club ladies, and the poetry evening had really lifted her spirits. In addition to that, she'd managed to buy some lamb chops for lunch, which should keep Mr. Wainwright happy, at least for the rest of the day.

But as she opened the front door, she was met by Mr. Wainwright's almighty bellow.

"Baumann!" His voice boomed from upstairs, sending a vibration through the banisters as Sofie dashed up to find out what it was now.

But as soon as she entered his bedroom, she knew.

There he stood, glaring at her, a long, narrow box open in one hand.

Behind him, the wardrobe door stood open, the deep drawer with the false bottom standing empty, his precious jewelry boxes scattered over the bed.

"Where's my ring, you little thief?" His wet lips slobbered out the words as he thundered toward her. "Where is it?"

Sofie took a step back, thinking fast. If she stood a chance at all, she had to put on an act like she never had before. "I don't know what you mean." She gazed innocently over the boxes on the bed. "What ring? I'm not a thief, Mr. Wainwright!"

Careening forward, he shoved an angry finger at the open ring box. "There's one missing." He spat out the words. "What have you done with it?"

Panic rose inside her. "I d-don't know where it is. Maybe you misplaced it, took it out to clean it and didn't put it back in the same place." Hastily, she skirted around him and began to tidy up. "Did you search the other boxes?"

"I looked through them all, you stupid girl!" He snatched a box away from her, throwing it across the room. "You've got it hidden away, haven't you? Thought I wouldn't notice one small ring." And with that he stormed out and down the stairs. "Let's have a look, shall we?"

"But—" Sofie called, panic swelling up in her. What had she been thinking, taking the ring?

*Calm down,* she told herself. *You have to act innocent. You don't have the ring anymore. He can't prove a thing.*

She stood at the door of her room while he emptied her suitcase, searched every inch of the room. "What have you done with it?"

"I told you before. I don't even know what ring you're talking about. You can't come in here and accuse me of something I didn't do."

He stood for a moment, fuming under his labored breath, and then reluctantly, he went to the door, barging past her to the back stairs. "I'll find that damned ring, my girl, and when I do, your life won't be worth living."

Standing stock still, she tried to calm her breathing as she heard his footsteps heading up the stairs.

Slowly, she lowered herself onto her narrow bed. Would he guess that she might have taken it to the pawnbroker's? If he found it there, the vile man behind the counter would sell her out in a moment.

What was she going to do?

There was only one option: She had to get the ring back before Mr. Wainwright found it. She had to get the money from somewhere, and there was only one person she could ask: Juliet.

It would be too obvious if she left the house immediately. In any case, there was lunch to prepare. She gritted her teeth in frustration. It would have to wait.

Frantically, she threw the lamb chops into a pan, going over her options. Sofie could hardly bear to consider what her new friend might think of her crime, but it was too late for that. Even if Juliet never spoke to her again, she needed her to do this one, crucial favor.

As soon as lunch was cleared and washed up, she fetched her shopping bag and headed for the door.

"I need to buy flour for tonight's cake," she called, trying to keep the whine of fear out of her voice.

But Mr. Wainwright had already gone out, hopefully off to his club as usual, although a thin wedge of doubt crept in: Could he already be at the pawn shop?

As she sprinted through the park to the library, the first few drops of rain began to fall around her, and by the time she made it there, she was damp and breathless.

Juliet was at the main desk, and as Sofie hurried over, she looked up and smiled. "Hello, Sofie!" But then she saw her face, and her forehead furrowed. "Are you all right?"

Leaning over, Sofie whispered, "I've done something terrible." Unable to stop herself, Sofie put her head in her hands and sobbed. "I don't know what I'm going to do."

Quickly, Juliet guided her into the reading room, sitting her down. "What on earth happened?" she asked, pulling up a chair beside her.

"I made a mistake." Sofie heard her own voice, hushed and trembling, unsure whether her new friend would be so appalled she'd turn her back on her for good. "I didn't know what to do. I was desperate." She looked over her shoulder, then whispered hoarsely, "I stole a ring from Mr. Wainwright."

"What?" Juliet's eyes were wide with alarm, making Sofie even more anxious.

"After I broke an ornament, Mr. Wainwright stole my mother's gold bracelet to pay for it. But I'd needed the money from the bracelet to pay for the information about my family. So I thought I could pawn something of his, just temporarily, then buy it back later." She bit her lip, suddenly hot with terror. "And now he's found out it's missing. I have to find the money to buy the ring back from the pawn shop right now, and I don't have a penny."

"You already pawned it?'

As she watched Juliet's dismay, Sofie's heart beat faster. "You don't understand. I needed the money to find my family. I was desperate." Her eyes stung with unstoppable tears, and Juliet put her arm around her, pulling her close.

"You poor dear!" Her voice was soothing and kind, but she heaved a long sigh. "It isn't good though, is it?"

"If Mr. Wainwright finds out, he'll kill me."

Juliet frowned. "Well, every problem has an answer, if you just think long enough. First of all—and most pressing—is the ring. We need to buy it back before he finds it there. I can lend you some money, and you can pay me back when you have the means." She looked at her watch. "I'll tell Mr. Pruitt that I need to pop out for some stationery, if you have a few minutes now?"

With a gasp, Sofie threw her arms around her. "Thank you, Juliet. I'll pay you back as soon as I can."

Juliet got to her feet. "It's better to owe me than Mr. Wainwright." She made her way to the door, turning with a quick smile. "In any case, it's always good to help a friend in need, don't you think?"

Relief flooded through Sofie. It was so long since she'd had anyone who helped her, and this one large act of kindness was almost too much for her to bear. It was done so easily and with such practicality—almost like Rachel would have done it if she were there.

By the time Sofie met Juliet outside the library, the rain was coming down harder, and the two women dashed through the downpour to the shop.

"What's he like, the pawnbroker?" Juliet asked.

Sofie grimaced at the recollection. "He took advantage of me. He could see I was desperate. I loathed even having to set foot in the place." She looked at the ground. "I'm afraid I didn't get a good deal at all, only four pounds."

Juliet put a hand on her back as they reached the shop. "Don't worry. We'll soon sort this out." She looked through the grimy window. "Which ring is it?"

But as she scoured the shelf, Sofie's heart squeezed tightly in her chest.

The ring was gone.

"It was there, at the front with the other rings." Panic set in. "Where is it?"

"It must be inside." Juliet took her arm and led the way inside.

Behind the counter, Mr. Mitchell greeted the young women, his toadlike smile growing as Juliet explained the situation.

"Yes, I remember the young lady well," the man said, all false politeness, the glint of easy money in his eye. "It was a garnet ring, as I recall."

"We have the money you paid for it and would like to buy it back." Juliet's voice was crisp and no-nonsense, her hand reaching into her handbag for her purse in anticipation of a quick deal.

But he raised an eyebrow. "I'm afraid the ring has already been sold. Only an hour ago, a man saw it in the window. Quite a gentleman, he was. I'd put him at about sixty, wearing one of those tweed suits."

A wave of nausea came over Sofie. "That's Mr. Wainwright," she whispered.

The man hid a smirk. "Funny, he wanted to know where I'd got it. The thing is, I couldn't remember quite what you looked like." It was said slowly, carefully. "I told him I would think it over." His fingers came together in front of him, as if in conclusion. "Isn't it odd how the memory works? Sometimes all it needs is a bit of encouragement, one way or the other."

"What kind of encouragement do you mean?" Juliet said, annoyed.

"The monetary kind," was his even reply.

Sofie watched as her friend pulled some folded notes out of her handbag.

"I only have the four pounds." Juliet put them down on the counter.

It was more than Sofie earned in a month.

"Only four?" A restless growl came out of the man, but Juliet folded her arms, not budging, so he pocketed the notes. "Nice to do business with you, ladies."

Juliet politely said, "Likewise," and taking Sofie's arm, she headed for the door.

As they stood outside, not caring about the rain, Juliet whispered, "Thank heavens he took it."

"But we lost your money."

"I know how these people operate," Juliet said. "And frankly we got off lightly. It was as plain as the smirk on his face that he knew you'd be in trouble if he told Mr. Wainwright. Hopefully, he'll pocket the cash and say no more about it."

"But what about Mr. Wainwright?" Sofie was still trembling.

"He has no proof it was you. You have to carry on denying it, and soon he'll forget about it."

They'd reached the front of the library, where Sofie thanked Juliet again and dashed off through the rain. She had to buy flour, standing in a line at the grocery shop for half an hour, desperately trying to calm her nerves, telling herself that everything was going to be all right.

By the time she reached the house, the rain had cleared, and an autumn sunshine seeped through the sodden oaks. A chill shivered through her. She'd have to bake an especially good cake, that was the least she could do.

But as she took out the key, the front door opened from the inside.

There stood Mr. Wainwright, his mouth in a firm scowl. "There you are."

Behind him were two policemen.

Her bag fell to the floor. There, lurking behind them like a hiding ferret, was the pawnbroker.

"Is this the woman?" a policeman asked him.

"Yes, that's her." His eyes avoided hers, his hands wringing each other.

Even with Juliet's pound notes in his pocket, he had sold the information again.

Mr. Wainwright gave the policeman a tidy nod.

"Miss Sofie Baumann, you are under arrest for stealing a garnet ring belonging to the late Mrs. Eunice Wainwright of 26 Bethnal Green Park."

Sofie felt her throat dry up.

"Take her down to the police station," the older policeman ordered.

Handcuffs were clamped onto her wrists, and she was led out of the door, frog-marched down to the main road.

Hardly believing what was happening, Sofie felt her entire world crashing around her.

"Can I get something from my room, my shawl to keep me warm?" she begged.

"No."

A vision came to her of her photograph of her family, her book of poems.

"But I have important things, my own possessions. You can't let that man take them away from me—" She began to pull at her handcuffs, scraping her wrists.

The policeman muttered, "We'll tell Mr. Wainwright to put them in a box for you."

"Do you think he'll bother? He's treated me abysmally since I've been here, giving me only a fraction of what I should be paid, making me do three times as much work. Of course he's not going to pack my things for me."

All the way to the police station, she tried to persuade him how unfair the whole thing was, but there was always the same response. "You should have thought about that before you took the ring. The pawnbroker says it was you, and that's all the proof we need."

"But I needed to find my family." Her voice was hoarse with tears. "You can't lock me away!"

He eyed her as if she were a mere inconvenience. "Can't we?"

After taking down her details, he led her to a small, damp, windowless cell. Without another word, he banged the door shut and locked it, and she listened as his footsteps receded before another door closed, sealing her completely from the outside world.

She was alone.

But what was more, no one even knew she was there.

And as the complete horror of her situation became clear, she slid down onto the cold hard bench and began to cry.

# JULIET

THE LAST HOUR BEFORE THE LIBRARY CLOSED WAS ALWAYS A BUSY one, people getting off work to get a good book to see them through the night's bombings. Juliet sped around, helping people and reshelving the last pile of returns, hoping Sofie got home safely.

Never before had she plunged herself into a job with as much gusto. Ever since the night with the ambulances, she'd wanted to keep her mind busy. The awful vision of the young woman flashed behind her eyes whenever she closed them, that blue coat an inescapable reminder that it might have been her body, her life, her time on this earth gone.

She hadn't seen Sebastian since that night, although she'd found herself looking out for him, listening for him on the stairs only to find it was Mrs. Ottley. He'd seen her at her worst, frightened, trying to hold herself together, and he'd been so understanding, so patient and caring.

As if from nowhere, the building drone of the air-raid siren seeped in from outside, and the library assistants began the usual routine of helping people out, fetching their coats and gas masks, and heading to the doors.

In theory, you had ten minutes or more to get to a shelter before the bombers came, but in reality it could be a matter of seconds before you heard the roar of the planes, the whistle of the bombs.

As she grabbed her bag, Juliet remembered the novels she'd promised for her underground readers, and darting into the fiction row, she began pulling out book after book, pushing them into her bag.

"Juliet!" Mr. Pruitt's voice rang out from the main entrance. "Hurry up! I have to lock up. I hope you're not taking books to lend out in the underground. What on earth—"

His voice was engulfed by the thunder of bombers, vibrating the panes in the windows and the dome. Already they were above them.

She had to hurry, her heels skidding amid the chaos. As she darted back through the aisle, the sound of an explosion outside made her jump out of her skin. Then came another, this time almost on top of them.

The books slid from her hands, falling onto the floor.

And that was when it happened.

A colossal crash roared through the atrium as cascades of glass and plaster showered down like icicle shards. The world seemed to slow as the air swirled around her, smoke and broken fragments whirling in the great gusts. Through the haze, she watched in frozen dread as the black, bulletlike bomb came down onto the dark rows on the far side.

An intense flash of bright white came before a roaring explosion, sucking the air out of her lungs as she was thrown back through the air. The blast sent a massive thrust of shards and debris through the open space, forcing the shelves down, each cascading onto the next, as brittle as dominoes. Landing hard on her side, Juliet scrambled away in time to avoid a heaving, emptying shelf crashing onto the floor beside her.

Billows of smoke flooded into her lungs, and as a rain of debris came down, a high-pitched buzz seared into her brain. In a daze, she looked up to see a thousand paper fragments speeding through the amber whirl, loose pages and burnt embers all held in the air, as if the books had come to life in the moment of their death, words and phrases, ideas and other worlds all tumbling through the dusk before returning up into the sky.

"Juliet!"

Was someone calling her?

Coming to her senses, she looked around her, scrambling to her feet. Where she had been standing in the fiction aisle, the shelves were now thrown to the floor, books everywhere.

The throng of more planes above made her hunch her shoulders against another hit, and she clambered to her feet and ran as fast as she could, her head reeling with the lack of air, her ears ringing from the explosion.

She stumbled out onto the pavement, dizzy, unsure what to do. Even outside, the air was dense with dust and a murky chemical smoke. People were running down the middle of the street to the underground, covering their heads as best they could. Debris from the library and parts of other buildings coated the ground. A child screamed as his mother pulled him as she ran, shouting at him to keep up, *keep up!*

Juliet's lungs wheezed with the dust and acrid smoke as she ran to get underground. There was a stabbing pain in her leg, but she couldn't worry about that now. She had to take cover.

Suddenly, another blast from behind thrust her forward, and her feet tripped over a jagged chunk of roofing, hurling her down onto the sharp debris coating the road.

Hearing a long, shrill cry, she realized with incredulity that it was her own.

And then a hand clutched her arm, pulling her up.

"Argh," she yelled as the agony in her leg shot through her, but the hand only yanked her harder. Then, without another moment, her hand was caught in his, and she was forced into a broken run behind the man, down into the hectic, dark steps of the underground station.

She stumbled trying to keep up, but he carried on, down the steep steps, not stopping until they came into the bright, chaotic ticket hall.

Her lungs heavy with smoke, she bent over, choking.

"Are you all right, Juliet?"

"Sebastian?" she murmured, but the shock and the chaos had made everything shift and turn in front of her. "Is that you?"

"Your leg," he said. "It's bleeding."

A thick stream of blood, fresh and bright, spilled down her shin.

"Oh," she muttered, a slight dizziness overcoming her as she tried to pull herself together.

He put a hand under her elbow and guided her to the wall, where she slumped down onto a bench.

He crouched beside her so that he could check her pulse. "You probably have shock, so try to keep still." He dug out a roll of bandage. "It was quite a blast. A lucky escape."

"W-what are you doing here?" She wondered if she was hallucinating.

"I was on my way to ARP, the early shift. I saw the bomb hit the library and ran over to make sure you were all right." His voice was kind, his hands firm but gentle as he wound a length of gauze around her leg. "How are you feeling? You seem dazed."

"Everything's a bit hazy, and there's a loud ringing in my ears."

"That's the aftershock. It's normal after an explosion. What about your lungs? Can you breathe well?"

A hazy memory of her ambulance training came back to her. Blasts could suck the air out of your lungs if you were close enough. She felt her chest, wheezy and hoarse with dust, but still functioning. "I'll live," she tried to joke, but then she began to cough, and he was forced to put down the bandage to pat her back.

"You're quite in the wars," he said with a smile. "But I think you'll fight on for another day." There was something calming about his way, suddenly reminding her of his father, the village doctor.

In her daze, she muttered, "What happened to you, Sebastian? You're so different now."

"I suppose the war makes you see a different side of life. I was responsible for my unit, some hardly more than boys. I had to grow up, make good decisions, safeguard them as best I could, even when I couldn't." He focused on the bandage.

Tentatively, she asked, "How were you injured?"

"It was a shell," he replied evenly, not looking up. "I was unconscious for a while, woke up in a hospital in Kent. All I wanted to do was to go back, help save my men, but they told me it was over. The Nazis had taken Dunkirk. Three hundred thousand soldiers picked up off the beaches, or like me, rowed out on stretchers." He shook his head. "I was more of a hindrance than a help that day."

"I'm sure you did your best. Just because you were injured . . ."

But he stopped her. "It's not something I like to talk about, better in the past."

"I'm sure that . . ." she began.

But he was already tying up her bandage, saying more brightly, "You'll be right as rain in no time." He took her hands to pull her to her feet. "I have to get back, report for ARP duty."

Through the furor in the ticket hall and the sharp ringing in her ears, she could hear the aircraft outside, the blasts in the distance. Going back onto the street was insane, like a suicide mission, and she found herself catching his arm. "You will take care, won't you?"

He gave her a close-lipped smile and a quick nod, and then he was gone, vanishing up the steps through the crowds heading down.

"Juliet! There you are!"

She turned to see Mr. Pruitt, unsteady and unkempt. "Juliet! Why didn't you leave when I told you?" But before she could answer, his face crumpled. "I can't believe it! We all might have been killed. And the library, bombed!"

As he went on, a heavy breathlessness came over her. How thick the air had been inside the library, choking her with smoke and dust. There was still a sharp ringing in her ears, a fogging in her vision, and she felt herself sinking back down onto the bench, exhausted and shaking.

She tried not to think how she might have been dead if the bomb had fallen just a short while earlier, when she'd been putting a biography of Joan of Arc back in its place. Her life could have been so casually blown apart, so carelessly lost, as if she were nothing. And a sudden sense of all that she had yet to do flickered through her brain, the fun she'd yet to have, the adventures, the family . . .

She couldn't stop trembling, the blast still resonating through her, and as if by instinct, her hand slipped into her bag for some kind of comfort, her fingers reaching for a book, pulling one out, opening it.

Mr. Pruitt slid down beside her onto the bench, looking over her shoulder. "Read it out for me, Juliet. Read it for both of us."

And with a sudden kinship for their lost library, she began to read.

It was the best of times, it was the worst of times, it was the age of wisdom, it was the age of foolishness, it was the epoch of belief, it was the epoch of incredulity, it was the season of Light, it was the season of Darkness, it was the spring of hope, it was the winter of despair.

And as the opening lines of Charles Dickens's *A Tale of Two Cities* swam in front of her eyes, she grasped the true and immense power of books. How they could transcend time and speak to an inner voice. How much they needed them. And that no matter what the Nazis did, they could never take that away.

# SOFIE

IT WAS A LONG, LONELY NIGHT IN THE POLICE CELL, AND SOFIE'S fears of what might happen to her were only intensified by the heaving explosions of the air raids outside. After only a few hours of fitful sleep, she was finally woken at dawn by a guard putting handcuffs on her. Again she was marched through the police station, this time out to the street corner, where the back of a police van was opened for her to get inside.

"But where are you taking me?" she asked frantically.

As the policeman handcuffed her to the short bench in the back of the van, he grunted, "You're going to an internment camp."

"W-what?" she cried.

But the door was slammed shut, and the van began to move.

Foreboding surged through her as she tried to loosen her hands, sobbing, "What's going to happen to me!"

Had she escaped the Nazis and their work camps only to be locked up by the British?

The bench in the van was cold and hard, and as she looked around the dim space, trying to see a way out, she realized she wasn't alone. Another prisoner sat at the end, and as his head lifted, she recognized him.

"Mac? Is that you?"

He looked over to her, startled. "Sofie? What are you doing here?"

Swallowing, she wondered what story to make up for him. But then she remembered that he himself was a criminal, just like her. "I stole a ring from my employer and pawned it to get the money to pay you." It sounded pathetic, pointless.

"You stole?"

Blood surged to her cheeks. "I'm sure you think I'm terrible, don't you?"

"No, of course not, I just . . ." He reached for the right words. "I just wouldn't expect you to do anything so"—again the pause—"so desperate."

Her fists clenched with sudden fury. "But I *am* desperate! You were my one chance to find out something—anything!—about my family." She cried hot, exasperated sobs.

Mac was silent for a moment, and then murmured, "This war has made criminals of both of us."

"What happened to you?"

He drew a fragmented breath. "I knew it would happen one day. The police swept through the underground service passages last night and picked up a handful of black-market runners. They couldn't pin anything on me, so they did the next best thing: They're sending me away." He glared ahead, stoical.

But fear and anger raged inside her. "And now we're both being taken to a prison?"

"Calm down, Sofie. It's not a prison. We're going to the main internment camp on the Isle of Man."

"Internment camp?" Her heart tightened. "Isn't that a workhouse or a prison of sorts?"

"No, it's a camp where they put people who might try to help the Nazis. At the beginning of the war, it was just the fascists and political objectors, but now every German and Italian has been ordered there, even if they've lived in Britain for years."

"But that's insane."

He shrugged. "It's because of what happened in Rotterdam last May. To make the invasion easy, the Nazis sent in spies pretending to be

Jewish refugees and pacifists. They came out of hiding before the invasion, sabotaging Dutch defenses from the inside. That's why no one's taking refugees anymore."

"But we're Jewish. We're the enemy of the Nazis. We'd never help them in any way."

"I know that, and you know that," he said. "But no one trusts anyone with a foreign accent—which is why I am here. I'm Polish, so they shouldn't imprison me. We're on the same side. But they are accusing me of being a Nazi pretending to be Polish, and I have no passport or identity papers to prove otherwise. But the internment camp is better than prison, so I'll take it."

In a smaller voice, she asked, "Do you know what it's like?"

"The Isle of Man is a tourist island between Britain and Ireland, so most of the Category C interns are given rooms in hotels or boarding houses."

"What is Category C?"

"The ones who don't pose any real risk—that's people like us. They just want to keep us out of the way. With the threat of invasion, Churchill decided to simply haul anyone risky to the Isle of Man."

Exasperated, Sofie clenched her teeth. "I can't believe it! If Britain is invaded we'll already be in a work camp, nicely rounded up for the Nazis." Then she began to fidget, exasperated. "And now I won't be able to search for my family. Even if they make it to Britain, they won't be able to find me."

With this, she began to cry in earnest, and through her tears, she felt a warmth along her side as the quiet young man shuffled closer to her. With his wrists handcuffed, he couldn't put an arm around her, but just the sensation of him being there, the sides of their bodies touching, soothed her. She leaned her head down onto his shoulder, suddenly desperate for human contact.

"You'll find them, I'm sure of it," he whispered.

She didn't move, just stared into the darkness. "But my employer's address is the only one my family has for me. What if Rachel tries to send a message?" She sat up with a sudden determination. "I have to

escape, get back to London. I can't just wait for them to release me."
Frustrated, she turned to him. "And what about you? You must have a
plan to get out."

He shrugged. "They will release me after a few days, once they realize I'm not German, and then I'll go back to London, back to work."

"Why don't you get a proper job, join the military? Surely it's safer."

"I lost my papers after I left Poland, and I have no visa. I am here
illegally," he said stiffly. "But I prefer to work on my own. If the Nazis
invade, it's better to be out of the system, underground."

She knew it couldn't be easy. If he had no papers, he had to stay hidden.

There was a long, uncomfortable pause, and then she asked, "Is that
where you live, underground?"

"I have a room behind the high street. It's not much, but it's something."

"Aren't you scared they'll deport you, when they find out you're
Polish and have no visa—and a criminal, too?"

He drew a defensive breath. "They can't pin anything on me. In
any case, they don't deport illegal refugees back to the continent anymore, they put us on a ship to Canada or Australia, where we would
have to sit in a camp until the war is settled one way or another." His
hands fidgeted restlessly.

"At least you'd be safe over there, far away from the Nazis."

Suddenly tense, his eyes glared stonily ahead. "I have reasons to
stay in Europe."

"Do you?"

There was a pause, and then he quietly said, "My brother, Uri, is in
the resistance in Poland. There was a petition for his arrest when I left.
I have to know he is alive. He is the only family I have."

"Is that why you do your job, finding people's families?"

He didn't reply, and it felt as if he'd vanished into his own world.

And she, too, let her thoughts wander back to her home in Berlin. In
her mind, she could hear the familiar sound of Rachel's piano playing
drifting through the corridors, the poignant cadences of Beethoven's
"Moonlight Sonata" repeating over and over again.

She wondered if Mac's thoughts, too, were dwelling on his old home.

After a moment of silence, she ventured: "Did you escape through Portugal, like Rachel is trying to do?"

For a long time, there was nothing, but then, almost inaudibly, he said, "No."

That appeared to be the end of the conversation, but then he cleared his throat. "Ever since the war began, it has been hard to get out of mainland Europe."

"How did you escape, then?"

His face fell, and he looked down at his hands. "I was in the Polish Army and had just been trained as a radio operator when the Nazis invaded. The country was overtaken quickly. It was like our army was nothing but ants, marched over by the great German platoons. Our unit was one of the last to be taken, and we were ordered to deliver our radio equipment to our allies in Hungary. As soon as we arrived, we realized that the Hungarians were ready to turn on us, petrified of the Nazis. We scattered, and a few of us escaped over the border into Yugoslavia and then across the sea to Italy. From there we got into France."

"Was France still free then?"

"Yes, it was. Boats were leaving from every port, with thousands of Jewish refugees crowding onto ships for Argentina or Brazil— anywhere that didn't need a visa. Anyone like me who had no money for the fare had to stow away on whatever vessel we could. I made it onto a boat to Britain, and I've been in hiding here ever since."

The statement was said matter-of-factly, as if it were commonplace, normal.

"Then you made your way to London, making money on the black market?"

"I don't like it," he said defensively. "But my papers were stolen in Hungary, and I have no passport, no visa, and no work permit. I have no other way to survive."

Quietly, she said, "Why don't you join up? If you're a radio operator, I'm sure they'll want you, papers or not."

"I won't go back to the front." His voice was sharp as ice, putting a barrier between them. She wondered what had happened to him.

They sat in silence for a while.

"Do you think my family will be able to escape?" she said at last.

"It depends. If they are clever and good at changing plans, thinking on their feet, then perhaps. If they get to Lisbon, they will be fine, provided they still have money to pay the boat fare. I have heard of people who make that mistake. They use their money and jewels bribing border police and people along the way, and then they don't have enough at the end."

"Rachel has a good head on her shoulders. She'll be fine," Sofie said with more confidence than she felt.

"Luck plays a part, too. It's a toss of a coin whether you meet someone who will help you or have you arrested. You might find yourself on a train that doesn't stop, or one that is searched."

Sofie felt her heart racing as she remembered her own harrowing journey. "I was hidden by a nun on the train through Germany," she said. "I don't know why she did it, but I wouldn't be here if she hadn't."

"I wouldn't be here if not for a French lorry driver who worked for the underground. We talked all the way about the French novelists Voltaire and Victor Hugo."

"Voltaire? Where in Poland did you grow up?" Sofie couldn't help wondering if he, too, had been living a different life, one with books and libraries.

"Krakow. It's an old university city, beautiful, with turrets and squares. The Nazis didn't bomb it like they are destroying London, but they found other ways to ruin it. They arrived with tanks and troops, established fear, and then they began to remove the Jews. 'Racial cleansing' they called it. First they asked for Jews to move into a ghetto, saying that if they did so they could take their belongings with them. Then the others were hounded out without their possessions. But it made no difference; those with were soon the same as those without. The young men, some of them boys, were taken to forced labor camps, and the others, well, there are stories about camps where they let people starve."

They sat in silence for a moment, and then she said, "It must have been dreadful."

"It was. I am lucky to have escaped, but I feel guilty, too, for not being there to fight like Uri." He drew a long breath. "But I suppose you do what you can to stay alive, to stay free."

They fell into silence, Sofie wondering who he had been before this war. How young he seemed, like her, both of them out on their own, struggling and failing to even stand still.

And as the police van rattled through unknown cities and towns, she let her mind drift back to the "Moonlight Sonata," gently lulling herself as she started to hum the quiet piano music.

Slowly, beneath the sound of her own, she detected the sound of another voice, Mac's. Did he, like her, have a place to go inside his mind, an old home full of books and music and light? She shuffled a little closer to him. They were both fish out of water, barely able to survive.

He began to take on the lower part of the "Moonlight Sonata," the slowly ascending notes harmonizing with her melody, and at the end, they simply began again, and then again, as if their voices somehow drowned out their reality, neutralized it. The beauty of the music, entwining and weaving together—it was a respite, a comfort, an alliance against the enemy.

And there they sat as they wove through the British countryside to the coast, bound together by a piece of piano music that reminded each of who they were: They may have been incarcerated as criminals, but they still had the memory, the knowledge, of another, better world.

# JULIET

OWN IN THE UNDERGROUND, THE LIGHTS WENT ON AT SIX o'clock in the morning precisely, the rumbles of the first trains coming soon after. Juliet stirred, the groggy underground sleepers coming to life around her. People were standing up, folding blankets, slipping on shoes, and combing their hair. A few had the luxury of going home for a nap, while most would head straight to work where they would take turns in the lavatory for a makeshift wash and brushup.

War work had to be done. Bombs had to be made, uniforms sewn, accounts balanced. Government buildings had to be opened, army centers prepared for operation, volunteer services put to the task of clearing the night's carnage. The shelter wardens had been told to get the population up early. The Blitz had driven people to flee the capital, and now there were fewer people to do the work. Already the war had forced more work hours out of everybody, often nine or ten hours a day, more if they volunteered, too. But the city had to keep going.

For Juliet, it was the end of a fraught night. Her library was destroyed, her leg was in bandages, and that ringing in her ears simply wouldn't go away. Her body ached, not only from the blast but from the whole wretched war—the horrific devastation that was her life. Her calling to run a great library in London felt like a charade, a futile, infantile attempt to give her life meaning. Even though she loved the library, she knew it represented a haven away from her parents, away from the mess of Victor, a place where she could exist in a world of books without having to touch reality.

Well, reality had now come to her.

Shutting her eyes tightly, she tried to untangle the present, unsure what the future would hold.

Bethnal Green Library would surely have to close.

Then what was she going to do?

In the cold, stark light of day, Juliet carefully got to her feet. Through routine rather than thought, she combed her hair and folded her blankets, heading up the escalators onto the street.

It was the smell that struck her first. Spent cordite and leaking gas gave the air a disconcerting incongruity, and as she reached the last few steps, the fumes became mixed with dust and smoke, and she choked, taken back to the moment the library was bombed, that stifling catch in her lungs.

She began to walk down the main road, looking for the great library through the gray-yellow haze.

As she saw its shape develop through the fog, her pulse jittered into life.

"It's still standing!" she gasped.

The place looked strangely ethereal in the settling dust, and as she walked closer, she could see daylight streaming in through the great roof, the insides collapsed, a wooden beam at an angle across one of the large front casements. The two double doors were ajar, one of them off-kilter, hanging from its upper hinge, and she gingerly crept through to the atrium, holding her breath at what she might see.

The entire dome had fallen through, the windows shattered, and over the chaos, a shower of autumn leaves had blown in, scattering yellow and gold over the jumble of broken wood, glass, and the thousand fragments of pages and book covers.

The far end of the room bore the brunt of the bombs, the remains of shelves like whale ribs looming over the chaos.

Books lay everywhere, open, face-down, piled up, torn apart.

Instinctively, Juliet bent down to pick up a large atlas that had landed on its edges like an alpine roof. She closed it, carefully dusting it down, looking for a space to put it, for the shelf where it belonged. But it was gone, of course.

"What are we going to do?" she asked herself bleakly.

A scuffle behind her made her turn to see Mr. Pruitt, taking off his spectacles to survey the scene. As he looked, he cleaned his glasses with a handkerchief, quickly using it to wipe any unnecessary moisture from beneath his eyes.

"It'll take months to fix this—years even," he muttered, and instead of the curmudgeon who stood in her way, she saw only an aging man, as broken by the war as the library itself.

There was a battered copy of *The Age of Innocence* on the floor, and she picked it up, thinking that it would be a good one to hand out in the underground before realizing that, now that the library would be closing, she wouldn't be able to take books to hand out.

Without thinking, she began to collect more of the intact books in her arms, as if they were lost children she was desperate to save, and as they built up, she realized how many were left, how many could be rescued.

"Mr. Pruitt," she began tentatively. "Do you remember that I suggested that we take some of the books down to lend out in the underground?" She showed him the books in her arms. "Well, why don't we take the whole library underground—well, what's left of it? You know that I've already been handing around books down there, and it's been very popular. Why don't we set up a proper desk, do it on a larger scale?"

"What on earth are you thinking?"

"Can't you see, Mr. Pruitt? We can keep our library alive, save our books, and give the community something everybody wants."

"I don't think you understand how a library works, Juliet."

"On the contrary, if you give me the chance to show you, I will help Bethnal Green Library survive the war."

With a shake of his head, he muttered a quick "No, no. Absolutely not. Libraries aren't simply a collection of books that can be shunted from one place to another."

A sense of desperation came over her. "But, Mr. Pruitt, the library will be closed otherwise. You will no longer have a job."

"It's a terrible tragedy—I've put so much into this place—but they'll move me on to that position in Suffolk, I dare say," he said, perking up somewhat. "This could be a blessing in disguise."

"But this is about the future of the library, the community. All our readers are underground. We can bring the library to new people, show the authorities how much it's needed."

"I can't begin to imagine how it would work. How can we protect our stocks without a closed building with a proper door?"

"We could bring some bookcases down into one of the connecting passages, set them up with a desk to register withdrawals and returns. Anyone can come into our library, can't they? We always have one or two go missing, more since the war began, so why should we start worrying now? We can put up some barriers, trust people to follow the rules. Just think what it will do to your reputation! You'll be the first head librarian to offer books to bomb shelterers, a real help for the war effort. It'll be all over the newspapers."

Sensing a potential public dispute, he deliberated fast. "I will telephone my superior. That will settle the matter once and for all. In the meantime, we should continue our efforts to stack the books. I imagine they'll be sent to library storage in Wales—that's where they've put stocks from all the big libraries."

With a frenetic fervor, Juliet darted about collecting books, keeping aside the ones she deemed as useful reads for the new Underground Library. The chiefs at central office had to agree to it. They simply *had* to!

As she put *The Sun Also Rises* onto her underground pile, she turned to notice that first one and then more locals had come into the building.

"We're here to commiserate," said one. "And to help, if we can," said another.

Overwhelmed with gratitude, Juliet felt a lump rise in her throat. "Th-thank you," she said, trying to pull herself together.

And then she saw the Miss Ridleys and Marigold there with a few cardboard boxes.

"What are we going to do with all these books then?" Irene asked crisply. "I hope you're not going to let them fester away in storage for the rest of the war?"

With a grateful smile, Juliet shook her head. "No," she said. "We're going to take them down to the underground."

"What a splendid idea!" Irene said, adding quietly, "I'm surprised Mr. Pruitt came around."

"Well, he hasn't yet," Juliet whispered. "He agreed to ask head office. But it'll take so long for them to decide, so I say we set it up and show them how good it can be." She grinned. "They can hardly object to it after that, can they?"

Everyone got to work, sorting the books, carrying shelves and tables to the underground, praying that it would all come together.

Juliet kept an eye open for Sofie, worrying that she hadn't seen her. She asked the Miss Ridleys to look out for her, but otherwise there didn't seem a lot she could do.

Meanwhile, Marigold and Dorothy went to have a word with the stationmaster about moving the library underground, reporting back that he was very much in favor of the idea, saying, "Anything to keep people busy and out of trouble." He allocated one of the quieter passages, directing some staff to help them set it up.

Juliet remained in the library, sorting through the books, Irene Ridley helping her. "I hope you're feeling all right, my dear, after such a horrific night?"

"Yes, I think so." Juliet looked abashed. "I was lucky to make it out—silly, really, I was gathering books for the underground when I should have been running for the shelter. Then I was blasted down the road as well. Fortunately, Sebastian was there to help me up, pull me along to the underground." She paused, unsure how to go on.

"Why the consternation?" Irene asked, lowering herself onto a chair as she went through a pile on the newspaper table.

Juliet shrugged. "He was just so very kind, that's all."

She picked up a few more books, deep in thought, but then Irene began to cough, and when Juliet turned around to look, the old lady had gone quite pale. Juliet rushed over to her, drawing up a chair beside hers. "Shall I get you a glass of water?"

It took a minute or more for Irene to recover herself enough to speak. "I'll be all right, but don't tell Dorothy about my cough. I don't want her to fuss." She gave a weary smile. "She's a worrier, you see."

Juliet's brow knit, and she sat in silence for a moment before asking, "At least let me take you to the clinic when we go down to the underground tonight. There's a doctor there these days, and you never know how serious a nasty cough like that could be."

The old lady gave her a fragile smile. "Let me sit for a while and catch my breath. I'm usually as right as rain before long." She seemed to relax into the chair, her breath disconcertingly raspy. "Tell me about Sebastian, my dear. I have a feeling you think far more about him than you're letting on."

"Not at all," Juliet said quickly. "It's just that he was so kind, even though he never used to be. We've become friends, doing the housework and cooking, making jokes and telling stories."

"Are you sure that's all you want from him, friendship?"

Juliet felt herself blushing. "It doesn't feel right to get involved with anyone, not since Victor went missing in France." She took a deep breath, remembering what she always told herself. "I've been through too much, and even though it's unlikely he will ever be back, I can't imagine getting close to someone again." Then she added with a smile. "And definitely not with a charmer like Sebastian."

"Life isn't always straightforward, though," Irene said, her pale blue eyes glistening. "Sometimes we have to find the courage to try something new, not worry about how it might turn out."

Juliet paused in thought, her fingers fiddling with a sooty copy of *Persuasion*. "But what would happen if Sebastian didn't like me in the same way?" A sudden horror struck her. "And what if he got himself killed? Where would I be then?"

"Have faith that you'll be able to pick yourself up, Juliet." The old lady looked into her eyes. "That is the crux of the matter, my dear. You have friends here now. Mrs. Ottley talks about you as if you're her long-lost daughter, and the book club are all with you no matter what happens. You can't stop living life just in case you get hurt." She took Juliet's hand in hers. "You have to let yourself go, get back to the business of being alive."

The old lady began to cough again, and Juliet patted her back.

"I really should take you to see the doctor. That cough doesn't sound good at all." Juliet pressed her, but the old lady recovered herself, looking back down at the books.

"I'll be fine. It was just something going down the wrong way. Not a word to Dorothy," she said with a smile.

And making a mental note of it, Juliet resumed the difficult task of deciding which books to keep and which to send into storage, the helpers drifting down to set up the new Underground Library. It wasn't until late afternoon, long after the others had gone, that a voice came from behind her.

"Nice to see you back on your feet." Sebastian, spruce in a Westminster suit, wore a half smile on his lips as she spun around.

Juliet straightened her skirt awkwardly. "Thank you for helping last night. It was good of you to stop for me, and dangerous, too, with all the bombs."

"Heaven knows what Mrs. Ottley would have done to me if I'd left you there." He grinned, but his eyes strayed to her calf, the long gash now covered with a white bandage visible beneath her stocking. "How is it?"

"It's fine." She shuffled nervously. "I went to the first-aid clinic, and they put a few stitches in it."

"That's good." He surveyed the chaos. "I wondered if you needed a little help here, putting things to rights?"

"We still need to pack these books into boxes, if you could help?"

Virtually the entire contents of the nonfiction bookshelves would be going into storage, and together, she and Sebastian began at the end of the collapsed aisle.

"You have a lot to get through," he said. "I'm glad I dropped in, although I'm afraid I have to leave for ARP duty in an hour or so."

"Oh, I'm quite happy, organizing the library. Books are my favorite things." She smiled as she stacked them neatly into the box. "And what about you, Sebastian? There must be something you like to do when you're not working?"

He picked up a couple of encyclopedias. "I sometimes meet up with some old college chums working in Whitehall, but I don't have a lot of spare time these days. Before the war, I used to go fishing a lot, but you can't do that in London." He nodded, half to himself. "I've always preferred being outside, rambling up hills, sailing on the lake. That's what I miss about Upper Beeding, the freedom to ramble through the countryside, the views from the hills. They're like old friends to me. Did you ever go up Beeding Hill?"

"I've never managed to get to the top." She shrugged. "My parents didn't like me getting dirty so I was never encouraged to go outside. It's funny that I've never thought about it before, but Upper Beeding is a pretty little place, isn't it?"

"I'd like to live there one day, whenever this war finishes." He looked up through the broken dome into the dusky sky. "After I qualified, I took a position in the local lawyers' office there, so I'll go back if they'll have me. It's nice to be close to my family." Blushing slightly, he stood back and looked at her. "I know it might sound silly, but if I have any children, I'd like them to grow up where I did. I can walk the hills with them, show them how to build a dam, spot herons, swim in the lake. It was a happy time for me, and it probably sounds a bit sentimental, but I'd like them to have that, too."

She thought about the hills she'd never climbed, the wild birds and animals she'd never seen, the fact that he'd had such a wonderful childhood that he'd want to replicate it. Suddenly, she was filled with the idea of what it might be like to be someone else, living in a different kind of family, one with streams and hills and pleasure, the sheer joy of being alive.

He watched her, smiling. "I imagine you would prefer to stay in London, now that you have a taste for it."

"Sometimes I don't know what I want," she said uneasily. "What are your family like?"

"Ah, my family." He laughed, his eyes flickering with light. "Well,

I have two older sisters, both of whom tease me. They're both married now, and I have," he counted on his fingers, "three nephews and one niece." He leaned forward and confessed in a whisper, "She's my favorite. And you probably know my father."

She did. Dr. Falconbury was a jovial sort, legendary for his winning bedside manner. "I know your mother a little, too."

"To be honest, she's a bit like our dear landlady, only Mrs. Ottley is quite a bit younger than Mum and far more scatterbrained. But they both have the same sense of humor, the same kindheartedness."

"I adore that about Mrs. Ottley," Juliet declared. "I've only been here a few months and she's welcomed me like a family member." Her smile dropped. "It's a far cry from my own mother, who's perpetually cross."

"That must have been hard. What about your father?"

"He never really had a lot to do with me, except when I got in his way. I think having a child was difficult for him, and for my mother, too. They were older, and it must have been complicated for them to share their lives unexpectedly with an energetic, chaotic child."

"I'm sure you were never chaotic, Juliet." He raised an eyebrow.

"If I was, it was ironed out of me as soon as the governess could manage it." She laughed, and suddenly those frosty dinners seemed a long time ago. She was an adult now, with a library and a community to help. Not only was it up to her to decide how she would live her life, but also it was her responsibility—she couldn't blame her parents or anyone else for her own decisions.

"It doesn't sound like you had much of a childhood. No wonder you buried yourself in books." He smiled, as he picked up a book. "This was one of my favorites, *Winnie-the-Pooh*. We used to play Poohsticks on the little stone bridge past the church."

"Perhaps you can teach me how to play it when Jake and little Ivy come home."

He smiled. "Then you can play it with your own children one day."

As usual, she pushed away the thought. Children had never been on Victor's agenda; his writing was too important.

She looked up to find him watching her, and she flushed, quickly moving the conversation safely back to books, and she found herself telling him about her favorite authors.

They'd become so absorbed, there by themselves, talking as they cleared the books, that they'd forgotten the time; and so, when Mrs. Ottley trundled in to drop off a homity pie for dinner, Sebastian hastily took his leave for his ARP shift.

As he pulled on his jacket, he said, "I was just thinking how I ought to take you dancing, show you a bit of life outside of the library, as I promised. Maybe on Friday? We could try one of the new clubs in the West End?" A little too hastily, he added, "As friends, of course."

"Of c-course," she stammered. "I think I'm free on Friday."

Then that half smile crept back. "It'll be good for you to see a bit of real life."

And with that, he headed outside, leaving her wondering if he felt the same flurry of excitement inside. How fresh it suddenly felt, how new and yet how terrifying. And as she went back to the boxes, her mind was now busy with questions, wondering what she should wear, how she should act, and what, if anything, might happen.

CHAPTER

**21**

# SOFIE

—————

THEY'D BEEN ON THE BOAT FOR OVER AN HOUR BEFORE THE ISLE of Man appeared on the horizon, larger than Sofie had expected and perhaps a little less desolate, too. Around thirty or forty miles long, the coast was pocked with little towns, often surrounding small quays and beaches, the church spires nestling amid clutches of houses.

Other than a few barbed wire fences and the usual beach defenses to prevent enemy landings, it didn't look like a prison at all. As the boat came closer, Sofie saw a few soldiers lingering at the quay, but mostly there only seemed to be local people going about their business. It looked peaceful, as if the war were a thousand miles away.

The journey had been a long one. After a few hours in the police van, Sofie and Mac had been dropped at a railway station where they'd joined a party of others bound for internment. Herded onto one train and then another, they finally reached a port and were put onto a large old fishing vessel.

"All the usual passenger ships have been taken by the navy," a friendly young soldier told them. They'd had an army escort throughout the train journey, but the men were relaxed, evidently not too worried about escapees.

"We've had a few jumping off the boats on the way, scared they're heading for the kind of camps the Germans have, but most of the interns know it's just a place to keep them out of trouble." He leaned forward and said in a lower tone, "It's the fascists that are the biggest problem. They can be violent, and we have a full armed escort for them." Quickly, he added, "But don't worry, they'll be on a different part of the island to you." He smiled at Sofie keenly, and she blushed. It had been a long time since she'd even considered such things, and she swept a hand over her hair, wondering what a sight she must look.

Mac eyed him coldly. "You must be busy with the new prisoners."

But any hostility went over the young soldier's head. "Not so much anymore. We've got twenty thousand interns on the island now, but most are Category Cs, mainly foreigners and refugees. There are only a few hundred dangerous ones. They're in high-security areas with a full guard."

The boat arrived at a dock beside a picturesque little tourist resort, and they were led into a building where they were registered. The women were to go to the southern tip of the island, while the men were spread among smaller camps in different locations.

A female soldier ushered the women to a van, but Sofie stalled, turning to look for Mac through the crowd. "Can I see someone before I go?" Sofie asked.

This seemed to strike a chord with the woman, who asked, "Is he your husband?"

Quickly concealing her left hand, Sofie nodded. "Just let me find him and say goodbye. I don't know when I'll see him again."

"All right," she said, "but be quick."

Sofie darted into the group of men, looking this way and that, before she felt a hand on her arm.

"Sofie?"

"Mac!" Knowing that the female soldier was watching, she put her arms around his neck, and hesitantly, he pulled her in. "I told the guard you're my husband," she whispered. "If you figure out a way off this island, can you try to tell me?"

Pulling away from her, he looked at her, uncertain. "I'll try, but it might be too hard to get a note to you." He took a breath. "You're resourceful though, Sofie. You'll find your own way out if you put your mind to it."

"I'm not good at things like that . . ." she began.

But the female soldier was coming toward her, gently pulling her away. "Everyone's waiting. We have to go. One last goodbye, that's all I can give you."

The woman watched, expecting a keen embrace, so Sofie pulled him close, slightly hesitating before pressing her lips to his. She felt him shudder with the sensation, at first pulling away but then leaning in, savoring it, just as she was, too. The softness of his lips, the warm tang of his breath, the sensation of his arms around her suddenly gave a short, sharp reminder of a former, freer world.

As they drew apart, her eyes met his, wide and alive, and she was pulled away by the woman soldier, glancing back at him over her shoulder, wondering when or if she would ever see him again.

Hastily, she was put into a van with the other women, and soon it began its journey, the town turning into the countryside, until it stopped at a barbed wire boundary and then continued down to the coast.

"This is Rushen, the women's camp," the female soldier told them. "They've closed off the southern tip of the island along with the two towns inside it. There's a checkpoint on the road to make sure only the locals come and go. The women are trusted to stay put in the area." Then she added, "You'll be free to go around town as you like."

When they reached a beach promenade, the doors were opened for them to get out. A row of elegant Victorian townhouses stood behind them, the sea stretching out to the horizon.

"Sofie Baumann," the woman soldier repeated. She was holding a clipboard, directing the women to their lodgings. "You're to go to Mrs. Ackerman in number 14. She'll look after you." The woman pointed with her pen to the mansions behind her, and Sofie walked hesitantly across the road.

The Trevelyan Hotel, number 14, was painted cream, displaying the elegance of an older, more genteel era.

Cautiously, Sofie pressed the bell.

Before long, a woman of around forty opened the door. Wearing a blue floral housecoat, she spoke with the cockney accent of a Londoner, lightly traced with a German accent. "Are you the new one?"

"I'm Sofie Baumann."

For a split second, the woman looked her up and down, but then a welcoming smile came over her face. "Well, come in! I'm Mrs. Ackerman." And as she began telling her about the place, she switched to Yiddish, and suddenly she sounded just like Sofie's aunt back in Berlin. It was so heart-wrenchingly familiar that it was as if a great wave had just washed Sofie back to her grandparents' house.

"Most of the residents are Jewish here," she said as she showed Sofie through the lobby to a large reception room with armchairs. "So we're like one big happy family, organizing our own cooking and upkeep."

A once-smart hotel, the Trevelyan was showing signs of wear, its embossed gold wallpaper peeling at the seams, the edges of the maroon Persian rug gently fraying.

Quite the opposite of the bare cells Sofie had imagined, the place was comfortable, friendly. It took a moment for the reality to settle in, the tranquil gentility of her surroundings, the woody scent of a fire, the sound of chatter—laughter even—coming from one of the reception rooms, where four ladies played cards at a table.

A radio was on in the background, the newscaster relaying details of the previous night's bombing in London. Juliet and the book club came to mind; she knew they'd be worried about her. She'd have to write if she could.

"You're just in time for dinner," Mrs. Ackerman said. "Let me show you to your room, and then you can go straight through to the dining room."

"Are you the owner?" Sofie asked.

She laughed. "No, I'm an intern here like you." She led her up three flights to the small servants' rooms at the top of the house. "They decided it was easier for each house to have its own head so that we can organize our food rations and make our own rules." Down a narrow corridor of doors, she stopped and opened one, allowing Sofie to go inside first. "This one's yours."

The room had a large dormer window looking over the sea. A single bed down one side left plenty of space for a rug, a small chest of drawers, and a chair. It was much brighter than the dark cupboard of a room in Mr. Wainwright's, larger, too.

"It's lovely," Sofie stammered, hardly able to believe it.

"Do you have any clothes with you?" Mrs. Ackerman looked around Sofie for a hidden bag, and then said, "We have a few spares. You wouldn't be the first to walk in here with nothing but the clothes you stand in. If you go to the glove factory later, you'll find some fabric to run up a few things."

With that, Mrs. Ackerman hurried out, leaving Sofie alone.

After feeling the smooth bedcovers, she went to the window and budged it open, a cool sweep of sea air swirling inside, making her feel paradoxically free—here she was in supposed captivity, and yet she had no cleaning, no cooking, no one shouting at her, and no bombs coming down.

A hand bell was rung downstairs, reminding her oddly of school, and someone called, "Dinner!"

Much like the living room, the dining hall had the air of a polite hotel of yesteryear. The ladies from the card table were already seated, as well as other younger residents, some removing headscarves and work aprons. A few women brought in large dishes of some kind of pie followed by smaller dishes of vegetables and potatoes. It was the most food she'd seen in over a year, and her mouth watered at the smell of fish pie and carrots, prepared as if they were still in Germany. Sofie followed Mrs. Ackerman's lead in taking a plate and helping herself.

"We're allocated food deliveries to cover our rations," Mrs. Ackerman explained. "And some of the residents have volunteered as chefs." She smiled. "We're a working community. We all volunteer for something. Do you know how to sew by any chance?"

"Not very well. Why?"

"Some of the women have set up a glove factory, using offcuts of fabric and wool. They're shipped to the mainland to sell. It's a good way to earn a little money to supplement your allowance."

"Allowance?" Sofie wasn't sure she'd heard properly.

"The government gives us twenty-one shillings a day. Our board and food is taken from that, but there's still a little left. There are a few clothes shops in town, so you can buy some once you've saved up."

But Sofie was barely listening. "They give us money?"

"Yes, and some of the locals aren't too happy about it. The servicemen's wives only get seventeen shillings, but I suppose they also have their husbands' pay and they don't have such high rent and so forth. But most of the islanders are happy to have us here. We bring them extra income, you see, filling the hotels and guesthouses that would otherwise be left empty with the war. Anyone with a spare bedroom is renting it out, and most of us are getting on well—at least we are in the women's camp."

"Are the men's camps different from this one?" Sofie's mind went to Mac. Perhaps he wasn't faring quite as well.

"It depends which camp you're in. They're dotted around, most of them in requisitioned homes, whole streets surrounded by barbed wire and high fences."

"Do they work there, too?"

"Men with craft skills make things to sell. There's one camp with only Jewish men, Hutchinson, where there are a lot of artists and academics, and they've set up a series of courses, people who know things teaching others who want to learn. There are classes on everything from art history to astronomy. They call it the Hutchinson University. The women do things like that here, but it's usually only useful things like languages and sewing."

Sofie looked around the room. "Is there somewhere I can get some books?"

"There's a small library in the town, but new books are scarce these days because of the paper shortages. We have a few here, in the living room. You can read any you like."

"That would be so wonderful." Sofie beamed. "What an extraordinary place this is!"

Mrs. Ackerman smiled. "It's not for everyone, but for me it's far better than being stuck in the Blitz."

"Were you in London, too?"

"I was in East London. They interned half my neighborhood back in July because we're all Jewish immigrant families who moved from

Germany in the twenties—my mother saw how things might become difficult for Jews over there and got us over to London in 1927. We thought she was mad at the time, but look at what's happening now."

Sofie bit her lip. "My older sister talked about leaving Germany after Hitler came to power, but it was too much of a shift for our father." She pursed her lips with frustration. "I'd always hated the idea, but now I wish we'd done it. If we had, we would have still been together."

Little by little, Mrs. Ackerman got Sofie's story out of her. Unsure of how the older woman would react to having a thief in their midst, Sofie approached that part tentatively, but the older woman only shrugged and said, "You poor love! At least you're safe now. You'll like it here. If you ask me, it's like being on holiday, and my daughter's just down the road with her little ones. They've started a school for them."

"But don't you feel like a prisoner?"

She shook her head. "Especially since the government has started making it easier to leave. It's too impractical holding us all here, never mind the expense and soldiers and so on."

Sofie's ears pricked up. "You can get out? How?"

"If you join the military or find some kind of official war work where your skills are needed, they'll give you a special pass." She nodded thoughtfully. "Your English is good, so you could probably find work as a translator. That's very common for Jewish Germans as they need native speakers, what with all the German messages and codes they're trying to intercept." She paused before adding, "And a job like that would grant you a proper visa—you wouldn't be bound to your domestic work anymore."

Sofie could hardly take in what she was saying. "I would be free?"

But Mrs. Ackerman was still talking. "You could apply to the women's army, or maybe someone you know in London might be able to help you get a desk job in Westminster."

"I'll write to them today," Sofie said with determination, but then her face fell. "Although I don't have paper or a pen, and no money to buy any either."

The woman smiled. "I have some spare, and you'll get your allowance soon, so you can pay me back." She bustled out of the room, returning with a few pages and a pen as well as a small stack of battered paperbacks. "I'll lend you a few pennies to post it in the morning." Mrs. Ackerman took in the dark shadows under her eyes, the slightness of her form. "But maybe you should rest for a while before you rush back. You look like you need a bit of a break, and a week or two here will do you the world of good."

After dinner, Sofie went up to her room. Although her body was aching to lie down, she kept herself awake to compose a letter to Juliet. She knew she would worry about her, and perhaps she could help her find a war job, get her back to London.

After finishing it and addressing the envelope, Sofie lay down on the soft little bed with its floral cotton counterpane.

She felt herself relax, her bones melting into the soft sheets and mattress, the sweet scent of fresh laundry mingling with the salty sea air. How peaceful it was, she thought as she drifted to sleep. And how much she needed a rest.

# KATIE

---

## THE UNDERGROUND LIBRARY
## NEWSLETTER

---

**OCTOBER 1940**

**WELCOME TO OUR NEW
UNDERGROUND LIBRARY**

---

*While our usual building is repaired,
we will be in the tube station.*

*Please spread the word!*

**THE UNDERGROUND READING HOUR**

---

*Every evening at 7 o'clock, Juliet reads one
of the classics aloud.*

**THE BOMBS WON'T STOP OUR BOOK CLUB . . .**

---

*We are meeting in the
underground station instead!*

*Please join us on Saturday evening
at 8 o'clock.*

"LEFT A BIT," KATIE CALLED OUT AS MRS. OTTLEY AND MARIGOLD
stood on chairs to hang the banner above the main desk.

## THE BETHNAL GREEN
## UNDERGROUND LIBRARY

*Grand Opening*
*Thursday 7 o'clock*
*All welcome*

The new library was in a wide connecting passage around thirty feet wide and fifty feet long. The front desk sat along the far wall, and a maze of tall bookshelves hid a small, cleared area for the newspaper table. Around three thousand books had been moved there, mostly by locals with wheelbarrows, while the rest were on their way to storage in a mine shaft in Wales.

While Katie had been devastated to see the library bombed, now that it was underground, she could visit more often, slipping away from her family on the pretext of visiting the WC.

The situation with her mother had worsened, especially as her father was increasingly absent. Every evening in the underground he'd vanish, arriving back at the house in the morning, demanding a cooked breakfast and clean clothes like the place was a hotel. Whenever her mother tentatively asked where he went, he'd sneer back, "Well, if you didn't bother to keep track of your daughter, why are you bothering to keep track of me?"

Once or twice, Katie had spotted him in town with the pretty brunette, buying her a perfume, taking her out to a restaurant. Precisely what this meant for the family was as yet unclear, but it had made her mother all the more fanatical about hiding the pregnancy.

"Once this charade is over, we can finally get back to normal," she'd mutter under her breath. "It'll be a miracle if you haven't ruined everything, you silly girl."

Setting up the new Underground Library had given Katie an escape, and tonight was the grand opening, Juliet and the others bustling around making sure everything was ready.

A crowd of shelterers waited in the area in front of the main desk, mostly the regulars from Juliet's reading hour and the book club, which had been steadily growing.

On one side, suited men from the council library board stood, arms folded, wondering how many of their precious books were about to go missing. They hadn't granted the Underground Library full permission yet, giving it a chance before they made a decision.

Beside them, local journalists took notes, a photographer poised with his camera. Cheerful news stories had become few and far between since the bombs began, and this was one that captured it all: Blitz spirit at its very finest.

Mr. Pruitt, who had arrived after all the work had been done, smiled at the photographer as he took center stage, ringing his little brass bell until the crowd fell silent.

"Thank you for coming, everyone." His voice was loud but gracious, as if he had been asked to accept a noble honor from the king himself. "It is my duty today to open this, the underground department of our library, which will be our central location until our magnificent building is restored." For a moment, it looked as if it was all too much for him to bear, but thankfully, he swallowed a few times and bore on. "So it is in the spirit of determination that we are opening the Bethnal Green Underground Library."

A round of applause rippled through the throng. More people had come in at the back, wondering what was happening, and a smattering of children surged forward, racing into the tight aisles, desperate for some kind of fun.

The women and men rushed in behind them, eager to find the best books or trying to collar their children.

"Try not to crowd the aisles," Katie called out, threading her way through to make sure no one was hurt.

But it wasn't until she was at the very back of the library that Katie found a girl, sitting on the floor in a tight ball. As Katie approached her, she looked up and Katie could see tears streaking down her face through the dust.

"Are you lost? Shall I find your mum?" Katie asked, crouching beside her. She must have been about eleven or twelve.

Her eyes wide with fear, the girl glanced over her shoulder. "I don't have a mum, and Dad would get cross if he found me here."

Katie frowned. "But he must be worried about you. Did you come to the shelter with him?"

She shook her head. "He's at work, down at the docks." She got up, putting on a brave face. "But I'm old enough to come down here on my own, honest I am."

It was hard to tell her age. Small and slight, she was dressed in the old gray school pinafore, too small and with stains and marks from a lack of care—and washing, too, by the aroma. Her dark hair was growing out of its practical, short cut, and she tucked it behind her ears, aware that she was being scrutinized.

Putting on a bright smile, Katie offered to shake her hand. "I'm Katie, and I used to be a librarian here. What's your name?"

"Meg," she said, but her eyes were on the books. "I'll be allowed to come here on my own, won't I, to read?"

Katie smiled. "Of course you can! What do you like to read best?"

She shrugged. "I'll read anything. My dad doesn't like me coming to the library, but old Mr. Burnley next door lends me books sometimes."

"That's nice of him," Katie said, dubious. "What kind of books?"

"There was one about a man who brings a monster to life, and the other was called *The Scarlet Pimpernel*, which was a bit confusing."

"The first one sounds like *Frankenstein*." Katie frowned. "Haven't you ever read any children's books?"

"No." The girl scratched her head, most probably the result of head lice.

"Not even *Alice in Wonderland* or *Wind in the Willows*?"

The girl shook her head.

"Wait here." Without another moment, Katie took off to collect some books. *The Scarlet Pimpernel* indeed! She trod carefully through the bookshelves, spotting one that was indelibly marked on her heart.

Scooping it up, she hurried back, but when she got there, the place where the girl had sat was empty.

Where had she gone?

For one moment, she stood, looking at where the girl might have slipped through the crowd, suddenly remembering the girl she herself had been, intrigued and unsure of the world.

How much had changed.

How much naïve anticipation had been extinguished.

"Did you find something?" The small voice came from behind her, and she turned to see Meg standing there, her hand outstretched for the book.

And as Katie offered it forward, she felt something warm and glowing inside her, that sense of sharing, of helping, of forming a new bond.

"*Little Women,*" the girl read out loud, dubious.

But a laugh suddenly spilled out of Katie, delighted to be giving this one precious gift. And with a lift in her heart, she found herself telling her, "You'll enjoy every word, I promise. It's one of the best books that I have ever read."

And she realized what a simple joy it was to share a much treasured story, and wherever her life was headed, any joy she could get was there to be cherished.

# JULIET

JULIET STOOD IN MRS. OTTLEY'S BEDROOM LOOKING AT HER REFLEC-
tion in the full-length mirror. The first week of the new Underground
Library had been hectic but successful, and now she was preparing for
a celebratory evening out with Sebastian.

The pale lilac silk gown belonged to Mrs. Ottley and was hastily
taken in last night, and it now clung to her curves elegantly, ending just
below the knee. She wore matching shoes, and Mrs. Ottley had insisted
on her leaving her hair down for once, curling it around her shoulders.
It had been a long time since she'd worn an evening dress. Victor
hadn't approved of frivolity or evenings out, preferring to stay inside
to write. Then after he'd left for war, she'd just forgotten about it, like
so many other things, such as going for walks, chatting to friends,
laughing.

"You look like one of those movie stars," Mrs. Ottley said as she
came back in with a gold necklace. "And far better without that victory
roll. Sebastian won't be able to keep his eyes off you."

Ignoring Mrs. Ottley's gleeful grin, she found herself smiling.
"Your lovely dress would make anyone look beautiful." She turned this
way and that, gazing at her reflection. "Speaking of Sebastian, did you
ask him about finding a job for Sofie yet?" she asked. Her letter had
arrived a few days ago, but Sebastian had been away.

"Don't worry about a thing, dear," Mrs. Ottley said, attaching the
necklace at the back. "Sebastian said there were plenty of translation

jobs and he'd forward a job offer to her as soon as he has one. I told the Miss Ridleys what happened, and they've managed to coerce Mr. Wainwright into dropping charges, too, although they didn't tell me precisely how." She chuckled as she stood back to look at her. "Oh, you do look lovely," Mrs. Ottley said. "You'll have to be my substitute daughter until Ivy gets back."

"Only if you'll be my substitute mother. I could do with a kind one, like you." Juliet made a small laugh. "My own mother would never have helped me dress."

"Well, it's my pleasure." Mrs. Ottley began plucking at the fabric. "I don't know why you don't show yourself off more." She smiled. "Who knows, Sebastian might be keener than you think."

That made Juliet's head turn. "What do you mean?"

"He told me he's taking you somewhere special." Mrs. Ottley chuckled.

"Really?" A spark of excitement flickered inside her and she found herself putting a little extra effort into her makeup.

By the time she came down, Sebastian was waiting at the bottom of the stairs, raising an eyebrow in surprise that she looked so different, so glamorous. "You turn out rather well when you put your mind to it, don't you, Juliet?"

A nervous laugh spilled out of her. "It's Mrs. Ottley's doing. She's been preening and fussing over me since teatime."

"Well, it's nice to see you getting into the spirit of things." He grinned, and she slapped his arm playfully.

"You don't look bad yourself," she said. He wore a pristine dinner suit with ease, reminding her of the gallivanting younger man he'd been when she'd met him before, cautioning her to tread carefully.

The air-raid siren began as he opened the door, and they ventured out into a misty evening, hurrying down to the underground.

"It's safer to travel by tube rather than take a taxi," Sebastian said. "Although we'll probably have to take our chances on the way home as the trains will have stopped by then."

"I don't mind. It's what everyone does from time to time, isn't it? Taking a chance, enjoying life while you can." She laughed, snuggling into her coat. "In any case, I'm sure we take more risks volunteering in the ARP and ambulances than a simple night out dancing."

The journey went quickly, and soon they were walking up Piccadilly side by side. In spite of the planes now moving over the horizon, the streets were still busy. Soldiers on leave laughed with girls, kissing on street corners or hurrying into bars and clubs, desperate for as much fun as they could have before heading back to the horrors of the front.

The air was fresh, Juliet's high heels echoing through the street.

"It's heavenly to be out," she said, feeling elegant in her dress, enjoying the appreciative looks from passing men in uniforms. "It's funny, I'd forgotten how jolly it can be."

"With the right company, of course!" Sebastian laughed, stopping in front of an iconic arch of one of the most opulent hotels in London. "And here we are!"

"The Ritz?" she gasped.

"They've opened a special dance club." Taking her arm, he led her through the grand revolving door. "Come on, I'll show you."

Inside, the hall was glittering with chandeliers, guests mingling through the colonnades.

Sebastian took her down first one and then a second flight of stairs into what must have been the service cellars, and the farther they went through the maze of corridors, the more unfinished it became, the walls open brickwork, the floor bare stone.

Then she heard music coming from somewhere, and as Sebastian turned a corner and then opened a door, the din of chatter and jazz spilled out, along with dimmed, moving lights, the scent of perfume mixed with cigar smoke, the heady warmth of excitement.

"All the big hotels are doing up their cellars," Sebastian said as a waiter led them to a table. "Just like everything else, London's nightlife has moved underground."

Far from the expansive refinement of the Ritz ballroom upstairs, the low-ceilinged vault was cozy and buzzing, the bare brick walls dotted with iconic photographs of musicians. A small jazz ensemble pelted out "It Don't Mean a Thing If It Ain't Got That Swing," while couples sat at candlelit tables, some holding hands, others kissing. The club had the air of secrecy, as if they were in a private, clandestine hideaway, suspended in time.

In front of the band, couples twirled each other around with abandon. Women in uniform outnumbered those in colorful cocktail dresses these days—it was de rigueur to show off what you were doing for the war. For the first time in history, frumpy khaki uniforms and brown lace-up brogues were deemed more fashionable than the finest Paris gowns.

"Shall we sit down?" Sebastian pulled out a chair for her. "The place will fill up later—there's always a surge in the early hours, after the restaurants and theaters close. What would you like to drink?"

"A pink gin, please," she said demurely, trying to conceal her nerves. She'd never been out with a man like this before.

Sensing her discomfort, he looked over to her. "Look, why don't we both have a break tonight, stop trying to behave as we ought? Let's take some time away from the world, just be ourselves."

She laughed nervously. "I'm not very good at letting myself go."

"How do you know unless you give it a try?"

She smiled, feeling the ease of the place seep into her. "I confess, it does feel nice to be shut off from it all, forget about everything for a while."

"You certainly deserve a night off after all the work you've been doing lately. You should be proud of yourself, Juliet." He sat back in his chair. "I've always known you were someone who gets things done, that there's far more to you than just a pretty face."

She laughed. "Flattery will get you nowhere. I bet you use lines like that with all the girls."

"Oh, I used to have far better lines than that." He grinned, leaning forward and rather surprisingly taking her hand in his. "I'd thread my fingers through theirs, like this." She felt the softness of his fingers intertwining with hers. "And then I'd look into their eyes like this." Then his eyes, shining in the candlelight, intensified as he seemed to look straight into her, and something inside her shifted, opened up.

Disarmed, she let out a nervous laugh, letting go of his hand, saying, "Oh, that's very clever! No wonder you're so popular with the ambulance girls. I gather that Camilla finds you rather dashing."

He raised his eyebrows in surprise. "Didn't Camilla tell you that she's already taken? Engaged to a lieutenant in Malta. We just flirt for the fun of it, try to make the night a little lighter." He looked at his hands. "I don't have a lot of time for romance these days."

"But what about your former belles? Weren't you a great hit at the debutantes' ball in '38? Or was that '37?"

"Both!" He grinned before adding, "But a lot of those girls are married now, and the others aren't as interested in a man who was sent home injured and then discharged." He shrugged. "In any case, I think it's easier to be on my own for now."

The sassy lull of the jazz music was loosening her up, and before she knew it, she asked, "Were you ever in love with any of them?"

Looking at the dance floor, he shook his head. "I know it's a bit old-fashioned, but I think love should last forever, like it is with my parents. They always got on so well together. It's as if they fit around each other perfectly, and I suppose that's what I want, too." He glanced at her. "And what about you, fair Juliet? Have you ever been in love?"

She took another sip of her cocktail. "Well, there was only Victor really."

"I'm sorry about what happened to him. You were engaged for quite a while, weren't you?" he asked gently.

"Three years." She tried to make light of it. "I know I should have pressed him to marry me, but there was a bohemian charm about not being conventional. When Victor came along and loved me for my mind, I was smitten."

"Did you go to the dances in Brighton with him? They were quite the thing before the war."

She faltered. "Victor was too studious for things like that. He said it was only hedonists and the privileged who went dancing." She laughed nervously, hearing herself sound a bit pompous and stuffy. "Not that he was overly serious, of course. We just somehow skipped over the dinners and dancing."

"It sounds like you went from being a bookworm to acting like an author's wife in a matter of months, only without the wedding."

Juliet laughed. "You never did take to Victor, did you?"

"Seriously, though, what was it that drew you to him, apart from the fact that he was handsome, a known writer, well-read . . ." he counted things off on his fingers, as they both chuckled.

"I suppose it was all of those things. He had moments of great romance, writing a love poem or leaving roses for me." She smiled, but then her eyes shifted as she remembered other times, when he could be so tumultuous. "There was something enigmatic about him, like a puzzle that I couldn't quite grasp." Then she let out a small self-conscious laugh. "It sometimes felt like I was chasing a ghost or a vision."

"Goodness, he sounds very intense."

Trying to lighten it up, she said jokingly, "I like to think of him as dark and mysterious, like Mr. Rochester."

Sebastian sat up straight, grinning. "Well, if we're comparing people to literary heroes, then I should definitely be Mr. Darcy."

Patting his arm, she countered, "More like Bingley!"

They laughed for a while, but Sebastian brought the subject back to Victor. "It must have been hard for you, him going missing." He carefully refrained from using the word "deserted," though it was clear that he knew. "It must be strange, not knowing where he is."

"You have to get on with life, I suppose." She gave a half-hearted smile. "Even though I don't know whether I'll ever see him again—if he's still alive."

"Well, at least you're in London. It's the best place to be if you want to live for the day." There was a pause, and then he said, "There must be a lot of other chaps interested in you."

And he moved his hand across the table so that it was closer to hers, although not quite touching. It conveyed something more than the friendship that had been building between them, and she swallowed, nervously pulling her hand back and casting her face down, worried that it would give too much away.

"Not that I know about." She felt herself blushing. "In any case, I'm far too busy for all that."

"Sometimes I feel like that as well, that it's too complicated to get involved with anyone properly."

"Why not? I'd have thought you'd be keen to plunge in."

But he avoided her gaze, looking onto the dance floor. "Well, to tell the truth, I didn't come back from the front in a very good state. It was hard out there, and I'm not sure I can act as if everything's all right, pretend to be someone that I'm not." His hand smoothed down the tablecloth as he spoke, embarrassed, trying to push the thought away. "I don't sleep all that well, and sometimes I have dreams, about the front."

Gently, she said, "I hear that happens."

With a half nod, he carried on, more briskly this time. "Well, I don't want to put the burden of that onto someone else. Hopefully, it'll improve with time, but I think it's better to stay single for now."

"It sounds a bit like you might have shell shock."

He shrugged and put on a smile. "I'm not sure about that, but I can understand how it feels to want to focus on work, to occupy yourself with something else."

Quietly, she said, "Just like me."

For a moment, their eyes met, a connection between them. And suddenly, embarrassed and self-conscious, they both began to laugh.

"I can't believe that I'm telling you this," he said. "I'm glad we've become friends. When I first heard that you were coming, I confess that I met the news with mixed feelings."

"That's not terribly flattering."

"Well, if I'm honest I remembered you as being incredibly beautiful and clever."

"But?"

His eyes leveled with hers. "I think we both recall that garden party." He began to laugh. "I was trying my best lines with you, and all you could do was brag about Victor and how intelligent he was."

She slapped his arm playfully. "You criticized him insufferably. I can only thank heavens you're no longer so scurrilous."

"And I can only be pleased you've stopped being so uptight and let your hair down a little. You know, Juliet, you can be quite fun when you stop trying to show everyone how prim and clever you are."

"And you can be quite civilized when you're not too busy keeping up your bravado."

Laughing, he reached across the table and took her hand. "I don't suppose you'd care to dance?"

With a flutter of trepidation, she let him lead her to the dance floor, and while the band played "Dream a Little Dream of Me," he put his arms around her with that half smile of his as he caught her eye. After a few minutes, he pulled her in closer, and gently, almost naturally, she put her head on his shoulder. Only the dim flickers of candles glimmered amber around them, the smell of his body detectable through the scent of soap and musk. Couples around them had their bodies clenched together, their mouths pressed to each other's, and Juliet wondered if Sebastian was also wondering how it might feel.

As the song went on, he drew back slightly so that he could look at her, and she could tell that the thought was there by the way he looked at her. And they swayed there for a while, both looking into each other's eyes, tantalizingly close as the music wove itself around them.

The evening went by quickly, the last dance arriving too soon, and their newfound closeness dissipated as they parted to clap for the band. Together, they watched the singer take his bows on the small stage, suddenly distant once again.

The lights flickered on, and they gathered their coats to leave, following the other revelers upstairs. As they spilled out onto the street, the air was laced with that familiar smell of spent explosives and smoke, but there was no sign of aircraft.

"We must be in a lull," she said, looking into the dark, clear sky, a few stars peering through, watching on from afar.

The street was almost deserted as they walked toward Trafalgar Square, the occasional sight of a couple in a doorway enjoying a last kiss, a drunken soldier lurching as he walked, singing a song for which he'd forgotten the words.

"We'll find a taxi, if we're lucky," Sebastian said, but his pace was unhurried, and when they'd reached the Strand without seeing any, he asked, "Shall we start to walk home, see if we can find a taxi on the way? It's a bit of a way, but at least we'll be heading in the right direction."

"Well, we're not ducking bombs yet." She laughed, falling into step with him, and with a familiar ease, he took her hand in his. Something about them, walking hand in hand down the moonlit empty London street, made her feel younger, lighter, like they were starting afresh, giddy with the thrill of togetherness. His hand was firm and warm, and she had to remind herself how precious his friendship was to her, desperately ignoring the tingling thrill she felt inside.

When they reached Holborn, an ARP car stopped for them, taking them as far as Shoreditch, and from there it wasn't long until they were opening the front door of Mrs. Ottley's house, Juliet taking off her coat, turning to see him watching her.

"It was a lovely evening, thank you, Sebastian." She moved closer to him. "Just what I needed."

"You really do look wonderful, Juliet," he said, his eyes on her dress.

And for a moment, they stood there, and she wasn't sure whether he was going to kiss her, but then he turned his head very slightly to one side and kissed her cheek.

"Goodnight, fair Juliet," he whispered. "I know I'll sleep well."

"As will I," she murmured, not wanting it to come to an end.

But the clock in the living room chimed three o'clock, the wretched thing, and slowly she stepped toward the staircase. "Goodnight," she whispered.

And softly he whispered back, "Sleep well."

Soundlessly, she slipped up the stairs, listening to him as he went up after her, getting ready in the attic room above hers. Like her, he must be slowly undressing, sliding into bed, and as she pulled the blankets up, she wondered if he was thinking of her, too.

How perfect the evening had been, yet how differently she wanted it to end! And as she closed her eyes, she let her imagination go, reliving the night in her mind, only this time with a few, added embellishments, for once allowing herself to dream a little dream.

# SOFIE

THE GLOVE FACTORY WAS IN AN OLD HALL AT THE BACK OF THE town, filled with sewing machines, glove patterns, materials, and rabbit furs. Dozens of women of all ages had their heads down as they sewed, crocheted, and knitted amid loud chatter in English, Yiddish, and Italian.

A wireless played piano music in the background, and Sofie thought of Mac, wondering where he was, whether he'd managed to get back to London. There was no communication among the camps or indeed with the mainland. It felt isolated, far away from everyday life, like a strange kind of holiday camp. Even though she wanted to get back to London, it was comforting to be among her own people. In the short space she'd been there, Mrs. Ackerman had made sure she ate properly, and she'd had time for reading and sleep, too.

Taking a seat at one of the large busy tables, she selected a crochet hook and twine and got started. Since her arrival, she'd become proficient at crocheting gloves. Every week, they were shipped to sell in a department store in Manchester, and Sofie had already earned a few shillings, money she saved to pay back to Juliet when she returned.

"The weather is good today," she said in English. "Can anyone describe it for me?"

When she'd first started working in the factory, she'd endured a barrage of questions to discover if she had any skills that she could share. Quickly, the women had designated her as their English teacher, and she happily took on the role, chatting to the women while one of them taught her to crochet, another explained nutrition, and one of them shared an analysis of the day's news. If they were stuck on an island, they were going to make the best of it.

Sitting beside her was Monika, a lively girl of seventeen who'd come over on Kindertransport and was desperate to improve her English.

"It's my aim to go to America. My cousin's family live in New York. They say it's the best place on earth. I applied for a family visa, but it might take awhile now that so many people are applying for them."

"There are rumors that the government is going to send some of the internees to Canada," another woman said. "Anywhere far from Germany, that's all I want!" she added with feeling.

Sofie sighed. "I know what you mean, but I would love to spend just one more day at home in Berlin with my family. Sometimes I imagine being there again, sitting with a book in the window seat." She blushed, embarrassed she was saying it out loud.

But the woman only said, "We all do what we can to get through this war."

In the evening, the household cooks had made matzo soup, the taste reminding Sofie of Berlin. She felt closer to her family here than in London. The familiarity of the food, the weekly Shabbat, and being part of a Jewish community all brought her heart back to the home she'd lost.

And now she missed her family more than ever, which was why, after dinner, she asked Mrs. Ackerman if she might know a way to find them.

Much to her surprise, her landlady asked, "Where were they when last you heard from them?"

"My father was still in Berlin, and my sister left through France last year. Someone told me that she tried to get a Portuguese visa in Bordeaux, but I don't know how to find out if she got there." She looked hopefully into Mrs. Ackerman's eyes. "Can you help me?"

"There is a group of Jewish women in East London. They're in touch with the Jewish underground network throughout occupied Europe. Write to Mrs. Bloom. Tell her that I gave you her details. She will do what she can to find your sister." She went to the sideboard and took out a sheet of writing paper. "I'll give you the address when you've finished."

Immediately, Sofie sat down and began to write, every word ladened with a silent prayer that Rachel and her father were safe—a prayer that they were still alive and free.

"Is everyone ready?" a voice called from the door, and Sofie looked up to see Monika, spruced up in a dress for the evening.

Seeing Sofie, Monika trotted over. "Oh, come on, Sofie, get changed! There's a special event in the hall."

Sofie looked at her own floral dress—she'd bought it with her weekly stipend, the first new item of clothing she'd had for years. "I don't have anything else to wear."

"You look perfect as you are!" And gathering her hands, Monika pulled her to her feet, turning to Mrs. Ackerman. "You'll come, too, won't you? We don't want to be late."

Mrs. Ackerman smiled. "I wouldn't miss it for the world."

It was a short, chilly walk, weaving through the narrow streets until they arrived at a hall beside a church. Inside, the place was teeming with life, amber lights from the walls illuminating a stage with the heavy maroon curtains closed. Rows of chairs were already half-filled with chattering women.

"A show?" Sofie murmured. It seemed unbelievable. As they took their seats, Sofie felt that warm glow as the performance prepared to begin.

A dramatic-looking middle-aged woman walked in front of the curtain to the middle of the stage to present the evening, and Monika turned to Sofie.

"That's the actress Dora Diamant. She organizes the performances."

The crowd hushed, the eager expectation for the evening palpable in the air.

And then, in deep, languorous Yiddish, Dora Diamant began. "It is with the greatest of honors that I proudly welcome you to An Evening of Acts, beginning with Otelia and Catrine."

With a sweep of the curtain, the whole stage became visible. In the center were two women, both sitting on chairs, both cleaning vases. The play—evidently written by the two performers—was a comedy, parodying the life of a domestic servant, like Sofie, escaping from the Nazis in Europe. Sofie could hardly believe her ears! Other women had been through the same as her, the negligent employers, the lack of cleaning experience, the holes they used for bedrooms, and the extraordinarily bland food they had to cook. By the end, she was in tears with laughter.

Next, Dora Diamant herself took to the stage, her hat at a jaunty angle. As the applause quieted, she waited, watching the audience, an air of drama, of anticipation, of connection with everyone in the room.

And then she began to speak, a dramatic and forthright short story, one from before the war about a picnic on a beach, a man whom she loved, a world that had been lost. Her eyes flickered over the women, and she seemed to pause on Sofie, who felt herself flutter with excitement.

At the end of the story, the woman bowed and left the stage to mighty applause.

The curtain closed briefly before opening again for a violinist playing a beautiful old Jewish ballad, and then a piano was moved onto the stage, the player performing Debussy's "Clair de Lune" perfectly.

The next act was the final one of the evening. The curtains once again opened, and there was a woman in the center of the stage, preparing to sing.

"Nina used to be an opera singer before she was married," Monika told her. "Isn't her voice magnificent?"

It truly was, and she was evidently a favorite with the audience, who began to call out songs, which she duly sang. She finished with a rousing chorus of "Hava Nagila," and everyone got to their feet to join in.

And as Sofie clapped and sang, she felt a shiver of inspiration course through her. It was time to stand up and speak for herself, for her family, to make the most of what she had and use it to better the world around her.

# JULIET

THE ONE PROBLEM WITH BEING AN AMBULANCE DRIVER, JULIET found, was that you invariably staggered home in the cold morning light hungry, exhausted, and incredibly dirty, and there was only one question in your mind: which of these issues to tackle first?

And as she huffed up the stairs after a particularly wet and grimy night, she couldn't decide. If she took a bath, she'd be too hungry to enjoy it, and she was almost too tired to do anything except collapse into bed—but then that would dirty her bedclothes.

With a sigh, she decided that the only thing for it was to have a wash before she did anything else.

She looked down at herself: Her trousers were caked in mud and her skin was splattered accordingly. A downpour early in the shift had made every bombsight into a mudslide, coating them with everything from debris and dirt to blood and gore. What was worse, her clothes were still wet, clinging coldly to her skin.

Never had she been so pleased to close her bedroom door and peel her jacket off, trying to contain the offending article and the caked mud that fell off it in a corner of the room. After that, she wriggled off her trousers and blouse. How grim it all was, standing shivering in her damp camisole, and suddenly she couldn't wait to get into a nice, hot bath.

Of course, with fuel rations, it would have to be only five inches in depth—Mrs. Ottley had diligently painted a line around the tub at the beginning of the war—but at least it would be warm.

The clock on her bedside table told her it was already nine o'clock, which meant that Mrs. Ottley would already be at the WVS and Sebastian would probably be at work. Since the library had moved underground, her work didn't begin until the afternoon, giving her time to catch up on a little sleep after her ambulance shift. Goodness knows how Sebastian would be at work today, having to go straight from his shift with all that mud.

Quickly, she pulled her bath cap over her hair, grabbed her towel, and darted down the landing to the bathroom.

But it wasn't until she was there that she saw that the bath already had its regulation five inches filled with lovely steaming hot water. Tempted to simply slip straight into it, she resisted, bending over to dip her fingers into the water, feeling how warm it was: the perfect temperature.

Before she could think how the bath came to be drawn already, the door opened, and there was Sebastian, wearing nothing but his underwear, looking at her in surprise.

Briskly, she stood up straight, fumbling with her towel to cover herself up, watching as he began to laugh, his eyes going from her damp camisole to her legs.

"Goodness, Juliet, you're a sight for sore eyes." He strolled in and put his hand in to test the water. "We should meet like this more often." He stood up, only feet away from her. "Would you like to take my bath?"

"I thought you would be at work by now," she said, wavering between indignation and utter humiliation at being caught, in her wet underwear, trying to pinch his bath. But then she found her eyes lingering on his shoulders, his chest, something about the closeness of him so tantalizing.

He also seemed distracted, as it took him a moment to reply. "I'm too dirty to go to work without a quick wash." He laughed, showing her a long, muscular leg splattered with mud.

"Well, if you have to go to work, I suppose you should take the bath." She sniffed. "I'll have one later."

But his eyes were on her camisole. "I hate to say it, but I think you should take it. Your undergarments are completely drenched. At least I'm not as wet as you are."

She looked at his underpants, and quickly glanced away, suddenly laughing with embarrassment. "We're just as wet and dirty as each other."

And at that moment, he took a step toward her, and she wondered chaotically if he was going to kiss her, a blush surging through her entire body as she felt his eyes on her.

But abruptly he stopped himself, awkwardly bending down to feel the water again. "It's getting cold, so you'd better go first."

"But what if there isn't any hot water left afterward? You know how Mrs. Ottley tries to keep it low for the rations."

He gave her his half smile. "Leave your water in for me. I'm sure it'll be fine."

She grimaced. "But I can't do that. It's far too—" she reached for the right word, but could only come up with "familiar," or worse, "intimate," both of which revealed more about her current thoughts than she liked.

"Practical?" he ventured as he backed out of the room with that half smile of his. "I insist, even though I loathe to leave you like this, fair Juliet. I've always said that you should get out of your skirt suits sometimes, but I wasn't quite expecting silk underwear."

With a parting grin, he left, sweeping the door closed behind him.

And as she peeled off her damp undergarments and stepped into the warm, soothing water, she couldn't help but smile to herself.

# KATIE

KATIE SAT ON HER SMALL BED, THE PINK CHILDHOOD COUNTER-pane now horribly out of place with her swift move from schoolgirl to mother-to-be. She was waiting for her mother, who had left a note on her door that she'd be coming in "to make sure you have what is needed."

A succinct, businesslike knock came, and then her mother entered.

"Nice to see the place tidy." Her eyes swept around the room. "Well, did you get everything?"

She was referring to the list she'd left in Katie's room a few days before, along with the names of a few secondhand shops and jumble sales. She knew that Katie's small savings wouldn't be enough for anything new, even if she had the rationing coupons.

Tentatively, Katie pulled out a box from under the bed.

Her mother strode over, ticking off each item as she unpacked them. "Four clean towels, an old sheet, extra monthly rags—you'll need those for a few days. Four newspapers: two for putting under the sheet so that the mattress isn't ruined and two for the afterbirth—we'll have to bury that in the garden. Some terry napkins and pins, disinfectant, and a small, very sharp pair of scissors for cutting the cord."

Katie winced. "I read that it's easy to get an infection from cutting your own umbilical cord."

"That's why we have the disinfectant." Her mother was grimacing as she took out the next item. "What's this?"

"I knitted a few clothes for the baby."

Her mother unfolded the small white cardigan, the small pearlized buttons taken from one of Katie's old dresses. Hastily throwing it onto the bed, she picked up matching trousers and booties, a little hat, all in the same white wool. It had been Katie's salvation, the one thing she could do for her child.

Her mother tossed them aside. "I'll get some clothes for it after the birth."

"The baby is a he or a she, not an it." Katie felt a throb in her throat, and before she could stop herself, she blurted out, "I read a few things about childbirth in the library. It can be dangerous, you know, if things don't go as they should."

"You can't learn everything from a book," she snapped dismissively. "Perhaps you should have read more about how *not* to get pregnant."

Katie ignored her and carried on. "Maybe we could find a midwife to help out. I'm sure she'd be discreet."

For the first time since she entered the room, her mother's eyes met hers, and there was a hardness in them that Katie had never seen before. "I thought I told you. We can't tell anyone."

"But what if the cord is around the neck or the baby's the wrong way around?" She knew her voice was rising with panic, but she couldn't do anything to stop it. "What if I bleed so much that I die?"

Her mother's mouth firmed into an uncompromising frown. "That's very unusual. If it should happen, we'll deal with it then."

But Katie could only remember her mother going to pieces when that first stream of Nazi bombers came over London, not knowing which public shelter to go to, nothing planned at all. It was Katie herself who took charge under pressure.

"Have you thought this through properly?" she heard herself ask.

But her mother was already at the door. "You watch your tone, young lady." And with an angry yank, she pulled the door open. "This is the only way you'll get through this unscathed and get to look after your baby, too—in fact, you'll jolly well have to. I didn't sign up to have another child."

The door slammed behind her, and Katie was alone.

Her hands went to her enlarged belly. How tight it must be in there, she thought. How safe and warm.

Unlike the outside world, which seemed cold and hostile.

If Katie's mother had developed such a hatred for Katie, how much loathing would she have for the new baby?

She barely had time to put everything away before the wail of the air-raid siren seeped in from outside, and Katie grabbed her small bag for the underground. With her father progressively more absent, it was up to her to carry the bags for her mother, who was supposedly the pregnant one.

Wordlessly, the family trooped outside, Rupert running ahead to save a spot. Without their father, her brother had become more detached. It was as if the whole family had split apart into free entities, moving away from one another like a star system slowly exploding into its four distinct parts, spinning silently off into the universe.

The underground was busier these days, and Katie was relieved to see that Rupert had managed to save their usual, quiet space. Even though her exhausted body yearned to sink to the floor in the corner, her mother made Katie set up the cushions and blankets for everyone.

"I'm too tired to get the tea today." Her mother propped herself up, picking up a magazine. "You can go to the canteen, but keep your coat buttoned up and be quick about it!"

Only too grateful for the time away, Katie rushed off, seizing the chance to drop into the Underground Library. As she went into the passage, she heard a small, young voice come from behind her. "Excuse me, Miss, but you said you'd help me get a library card."

Katie turned to see the girl she'd met at the opening. "It's Meg, isn't it? Did you like the book?"

The girl's face lit up, her front teeth protruding as she smiled, making her look different, full of life. "I finished it in two days," she said with pride. "It was the best book I ever read. Is there another one?"

Katie laughed. "*Little Women* is a tough act to follow, but let's see what we can do."

She led Meg to the children's section, perusing the shelves until she found what she was looking for, pulling it out and handing it to her. "This is your next one."

Meg read it. "*Anne of Green Gables.* Well, if you think so?"

"Oh, I do!" Katie pulled her over to the main desk, telling Juliet, "Our new bookworm here would like her very own library card."

And Juliet leaned across the desk to take the girl's details. "Would your mum or dad like to join, too?" she asked.

Meg shook her head decisively. "I'm allowed to come on my own." She stood up taller, and Katie exchanged a glance with Juliet. It was clear the poor girl had been allowed to do a lot of things on her own for a long time.

Juliet came around the desk. "Now why don't you let me show you how to check books out with library cards." She walked her down the aisle to the children's section. "We're very particular about it, you know, but I can already see you're a clever young lady."

Smiling as she watched them go, Katie retreated to the Miss Ridleys, sitting in their deck chairs ready for the reading hour.

"Your protégé has returned," Irene said, beckoning her to sit with them. "You look like you could do with a rest. Dorothy's back is playing up again, so you're in good company."

"It's sleeping on the floor that does it." Dorothy's face winced in pain.

Katie went over to her. "Why don't you go to the first-aid clinic, see if they can give you something to ease the pain?" She bent over to help her up. "I'll come with you, if you'd like."

With only a little pressing, Dorothy agreed, and the two of them left the others preparing for reading hour, weaving slowly through the passages to the cordoned-off clinic. Money had gone into making the first-aid posts into proper medical centers, and the unit now had a few beds and a partitioned room in the back.

One of the two nurses bustled around Dorothy. "Sit down and the doctor will see you soon." Then, to Katie's horror, she appeared to register Katie's bump. "Oh, do we have our first birth?" she cried, barely able to contain her excitement. "Oval Station had one last week, but we can still be the second!"

Blushing hotly, Katie rearranged her coat, which had pulled around her stomach as they'd sat down. "No, I'm not pregnant," she whispered, panicked. "Not at all! I've put on a bit of weight, that's all." She prayed that her mother wasn't nearby. That was all she needed; the local nurse knowing she was pregnant.

The young nurse leaned forward. "Sorry, love. Your big coat made me think—oh, never mind," she said, but her eyes were still on Katie's stomach. "If you happen to know anyone who's expecting, you can tell them we're set up to deal with births now. We can handle all of the common difficulties: breach, umbilical cord problems . . ." To Katie's dismay, the nurse proceeded to count them off on her fingers. "Ruptures, toxemia spasms, internal bleeding, and even some of the more unusual ones." Unaware of Katie's pallor at so many "common difficulties," the nurse went on, delighted to be advertising the clinic as the best place to have a baby. "I don't suppose you know anyone who's having twins, do you? We'd be in all the newspapers!"

"I don't think so," Katie said nervously, her hands going to her stomach. How would she even know if there were two babies inside her? She'd never been examined by a doctor or midwife. Her mother had insisted that it was very straightforward, no difficulties at all. But was that truly the case?

There was nothing like a list of things that could go wrong to put her mother's birth plan into an even more dismal light.

"Do you have long to go?" Dorothy's voice was soft, concerned.

Inwardly, Katie winced. Of course the old lady knew; she and her sister were sharp as tacks. Quietly, she said, "I'm not supposed to talk about it." She kept her eyes on the floor. "No one's supposed to know." But after Dorothy persisted in asking, Katie briefly communicated her mother's plan in a hushed voice. "I'm not sure how we'll get away with it—how it will feel. You won't tell anyone, will you?"

Dorothy drew a deep breath. "My mother didn't want anyone to know when it happened to me."

A stillness fell over them. Had Katie heard correctly?

Then quietly, Dorothy went on. "I was packed off to a secret house in Wales without a clue what was going on, separated from my family for the first time. I just cried and cried. I've never felt so desolate, that anything so horrific could make my parents send me away to such a dreadful place. My son was handed over to a childless couple. I still wonder where he is today." The skin on her hands was paper-thin as they moved anxiously against each other, as if she were still that young woman, still outcast.

"Before you ask, the father was a friend of my brother who I rather liked. I was too innocent to know what we were doing. My mother took charge after she found out. I'd never thought of her as callous, but she was—or rather fear forced her to be like that." She swallowed, pursing her lips.

"That's how it is with my mother. She absolutely loathes me."

With her face pale and her frown suddenly pronounced, Dorothy looked older. "That's why Irene took me under her wing. She was never the marrying kind, always so academic and ambitious—in those days a woman couldn't have both a marriage and a career." But then she brightened slightly. "And she's looked after me ever since."

"You're lucky to have a sister like her."

Dorothy's eyes gleamed at her. "Remember, Katie. Whatever happens, you're not alone. There's Irene and me, and Juliet and the rest of the book club. We're all on your side, you know. Always will be."

And as the old lady reached for her hand, Katie felt the truth of this, like a warm, soft blanket on a cold, bitter day. "Thank you."

# SOFIE

OUTSIDE THE TREVELYAN HOTEL, MRS. ACKERMAN WAS THERE TO
wish Sofie a bon voyage, the wind biting under a blue autumn sky as the
van pulled up. The fishing boat that had brought her to the island was to
take her back, her release papers clutched in her hand ready for inspec-
tion.

The letter from Juliet had arrived only three days ago, along with
the translation job offer that Sebastian had organized with a war ministry. With it was a beautifully handwritten letter from Irene telling her
that Mr. Wainwright was dropping charges. The details of these were
passed to the authorities on the Isle of Man to organize her release.
She'd be staying with Juliet for the time being, until she could find a
room of her own.

"Good luck with the search for your family." Mrs. Ackerman
opened the van door for her.

"Thank you for everything!" Sofie gave her a hug before climbing
inside. "Stay in touch, and I'll see you when you're back in London."

As the van pulled away, she waved farewell to the Trevelyan Hotel,
the place where she'd been able to reconnect with her Jewish heritage
and recuperate her energies.

In her hands, a handmade cloth bag carried the clothes she'd made
at the factory, plus two pairs of gloves for the Miss Ridleys. She'd come
to the Isle of Man with nothing, and now she was leaving with a few
skills, some new friends, and a fresh determination. She was going to

stop dwelling on everything that had gone wrong and start doing all she could to find her family.

As the boat set sail, she looked over the railings as the quiet little island dwindled to a mound on the horizon, and then she pulled out the letter from Mrs. Bloom, even though she'd read it a dozen times.

*Dear Sofie,*

*I have asked the network in Bordeaux and Lisbon to see if they can trace your sister, Rachel. From your letter, we know she most likely tried to get to Lisbon, so we will start with that.*

*In your letter, you stated that you intend to return to London. Let me know your new address, and when I have more information, it would be useful if you came to visit me here in East London. My address is 37 Alderney Road, Stepney.*

*Yours faithfully,*
*Lena Bloom*

If Mrs. Bloom didn't have any answers, Sofie would find someone else who could help her.

After the crossing, the train to London was interrupted by waits and diversions, lines closed due to bombs or military needs. As the halts became longer, she became hungry, the autumn chill stealing into the carriage whenever they stopped.

By the time the train pulled into London, it was already dusk, but through the dying daylight, she saw the devastation of the bombs, her forgotten fear reemerging with the acrid smell of cordite. The Blitz was still raging, bombs raining down night after night, the crags and half-demolished buildings showing the impact.

Paddington Station was chaotic. The air-raid sirens had just started, and people were rushing in different directions, either trying to get home before the bombs began or heading down into the shelters. The tube was packed, people with blankets and pillows bedding down or traveling to one of the larger stations to shelter. After changing once, Sofie heaved a sigh of relief as the train finally pulled into Bethnal Green Station.

The place was busier than it had been before she left, and she carefully avoided the passage where she used to sleep with Mr. Wainwright, thanking heavens—and the Miss Ridleys—that she wouldn't have to deal with him any longer.

Hurriedly, she made her way to the place where Juliet always set up her readings, praying she was still there.

But as she turned the corner into the passage, all she saw was a great mass of people.

They were standing around, some talking, some of them seated on the floor, others joining at the back.

And that's when she noticed the bookshelves and the main desk. Many of the people had books in their hands, some even reading as they stood, one bending the cover back in a way that Irene Ridley would certainly not condone.

Through the crowd, she spotted some of the book club, and there at the front was Juliet, everyone watching as she opened a book and flipped through to find the right page.

A voice came from beside her. "Sofie, you're back!" And before she knew what was happening, Marigold's fur-coated arms swept around her to give her a tight squeeze. "We were so worried about you."

"Oh, you needn't have been!" Sofie said as Marigold pulled her through the crowd. "It turns out an internment camp is far better than living with Mr. Wainwright."

They wove through until Sofie saw the two white-haired old ladies, waving their hands to greet her, shifting their chairs along to make space for her to sit beside them.

"So lovely to see you, my dear," Irene said.

Sofie beamed at them, taking out the crocheted gloves and explaining that she'd made them herself. "I hope they fit," she said eagerly.

"They're perfect!" Dorothy exclaimed, trying them on. "What a fine treat! You didn't have to bring us anything as special as these."

With a meaningful look, Sofie said, "I have you to thank for clearing my name."

"The way that man was treating you, he deserved it," Dorothy said with feeling.

Irene nodded. "We only did what we thought was fair." Then she added, "Juliet told us you were looking for somewhere to live, and you must feel free to stay with us."

Dorothy stretched out a hand and covered hers. "We would love to have you, and it would be a real help for us to have a spring chicken like you in the house."

Without hesitation, Sofie reached over and gave Dorothy a hug. "What a lovely offer! Thank you both! I'll be able to help with the housework, now that I'm an expert, and I can pay rent, too, as soon as my job starts."

"No need for that, dear," Irene said, and as they began to plan which room she would take, more people began to take their places on the floor around them. Blankets and coats were being laid down, books placed in small stacks, and a girl introduced as Meg came to sit cross-legged beside Katie.

The crowd hushed as Juliet began to speak. "Thank you for coming, everyone! Tonight we're on chapter eight of *The Great Gatsby* by F. Scott Fitzgerald."

Juliet began, her warm, characterful voice carrying through the passage.

Beside Sofie, Dorothy found her hand and gripped it, and Sofie felt overwhelmed with gratitude. The ladies were giving her somewhere to live, but more than that, they were giving her somewhere to call home. In return, she would do all she could to make their lives easier. The Blitz was hard for older people, and she wanted to repay their generosity with kindness.

As the reading continued, a movement at the back of the crowd caught Sofie's eye. There, standing at the very edge, was Mac.

Looking a little tidier than the last time she'd seen him, he was gazing over the crowd, trying to find her.

She waited patiently until his eyes lit upon hers, feeling them connect as a small smile crept onto his lips.

"Could you look after my bag for a few minutes?" she whispered to

Dorothy as she got to her feet and carefully slipped through the crowd to the back of the passage.

"I wondered if you'd be here." She came to stand beside him, letting him lead her away from the crowd and into the maze of bookshelves that made up the Underground Library.

"I come here every night if I can," he whispered. "I knew this would be the first place you'd come. I wanted to know you were all right, that you found a way out."

She explained how Juliet helped her to get a release, how she had a new job. "What about you?"

"It was as I said, once they realized that I truly was Polish, I was put on the next ship back." He shrugged. "The only trouble was they found out that I don't have a visa, and so I've had to take war work. They wanted me to join the army, but I convinced them I was too valuable as a criminal mastermind." He made a small, self-conscious laugh. "I'm not allowed to tell you what I'm doing, but let me just say that since our armies can't compete with the Nazis, Churchill has set up a ministry to cook up all kinds of cheap, clever ways to undermine them."

A group of children pushed past them, forcing them together, and she was just beginning to feel awkward when he said, "Are you still looking for your family? I can help, if you'd like. I work long hours, but sometimes I have a day or two off."

"Why don't you come with me to meet Mrs. Bloom? She's part of a Jewish network trying to trace people in Europe. My landlady on the Isle of Man put me in touch with her. She might be able to help you find your brother."

His face lit up. "That would be wonderful. Maybe she could help some of the other people I know searching for their families, too."

Without knowing why, she moved a little closer to him, and his eyes met hers.

For a moment that felt like both a split second and a thousand years, they stood there, looking at each other, and she bit her lip, wondering if he, too, remembered that kiss, the one on the docks when she pretended he was her husband. How insane it seemed now, yet she wouldn't take it back for the world.

Then the group of children threaded back through the aisle, one of them pushing between Sofie and Mac, and they were separated again, as if their moment had all been nothing.

"Shall we sit down?" Sofie whispered, and they made their way back to the book club. When she reached her space beside Dorothy, she shifted over a little to make room for Mac beside her, and as he sat down, he smiled at her, and she felt the warmth of his body beside hers.

# JULIET

T HE AMBULANCE SERVICE HAD ALREADY HAD A BUSY EVENING BY the time Juliet's shift started. She was on duty with Camilla again, and it wasn't long before they were pulling up beside a row of bombed houses.

A small group of ARP workers stood in the rubble, shovels in hand, looking down a hole, and as the two women hurried to join them they began to take in the situation.

From beneath the rubble came loud, piercing cries, a high-pitched yell of utter distress that made Juliet desperate to help.

"What's that?"

"It's a young man, trapped by the debris." One of the ARPs turned to them, an older man who was clearly fraught.

Amid the wails, Juliet heard whimpered words, calls for his mum, for God.

"Can't you do anything to help him?" Camilla asked.

"We can't get down there. There are too many beams blocking the way. It's only a narrow passage, too tight for any of us."

Juliet became aware that their eyes were on her, looking up and down her slim figure.

"You'd be the only one who could fit, Miss," a middle-aged man said urgently, another adding more kindly, "It's the only way."

The wails of pain were rising into full-throated shouts.

"What are you asking me to do?"

"Someone's gone to get a medic. He'll have something to alleviate the poor man's pain. But we need someone narrow to go down there and administer it to him."

Blood drained from her face, and she flashed her beam down the hole, which appeared to be a deep, craggy, vertical channel filled with debris. "But how? There's no space down there."

"We can hold your legs, and you can go down head first, see if you can reach him and give him the chloroform. It'll sedate him, make things easier as we dig him out. . . ." His words petered out, their meaning clear. The man was dying. It was the only kindness they could offer.

A tremble shot through her as she looked at the narrow opening, the man's screams gruesome, a frightening reminder of her own mortality. "I don't know if I can," she muttered uncontrollably. "I've never done anything like this before."

Another ARP car had pulled up, and she glanced behind, hoping another woman would appear, only to see two more men hurrying toward them. One of them was taller than the other, and Juliet recognized his gait: Sebastian.

His eyes met hers in the dim moonlight. He must have known of the situation already, as no one apprised him. The older man with him was a doctor, and he quickly opened his medical bag and pulled out a bottle and a thick dressing, looking up at them. "Who's going down?"

All eyes went to Juliet.

"Oh, all right then," she said, briskly taking off her coat and handing it to Camilla, thanking heavens she was wearing trousers.

The medic handed her a face mask. "You need to put this on first, just to make sure you don't get asphyxiated with the chloroform fumes."

Camilla tied it around Juliet's head as the medic poured a good dose from the bottle onto the dressing and handed it to her.

"We're sending someone down, just hang on another minute," Camilla called down to the man, a tension to her voice that hadn't been there before.

Sebastian turned to Juliet. "Are you sure you're all right for this?"

"I'll have to be," was all she said, gesturing for the men to lift her. "Just make sure you hold on to me," she called back with more bravado than she felt.

Kneeling on the rubble, she felt her legs being picked up, lifting her upside down and slowly lowering her through the hole. The sides of the narrow channel were jagged and uneven, and every so often she had to twist herself to wriggle through.

Louder and louder, the shouts of the man cut through her, and she suddenly felt alone with him in the close chaos. The stench of something putrid filled her nostrils, making her want to vomit, and she quickly began to breathe through her mouth, praying the face mask would absorb the pungent air.

Down she went, unsure how deep it was, feeling the men's grip on her legs move from around her knees to her calves and then her ankles and feet.

"Are you down there yet?" Through the man's screams, she could hear Camilla's voice, now distant from above.

Taking the light in her hand, she flashed it around, seeing that the channel was opening up. "Almost, I think."

That's when she saw him. First the mangled legs, trapped by a heavy, metal beam, then the rest of him, a mess of intestines and fluids, and finally his face, his features so distorted and bloody they were virtually indistinguishable. The smell was intense, the stench of his insides, the blood and bodily fluids around him.

Bile flooded her throat and mouth, and she quickly swallowed it back down. She had to get a grip. She had to forget herself and her own feelings. She had to think only of how she could help this young man in unimaginable pain.

Taking out the dressing, she brought it close to his mouth. "Shh, take a deep breath. You've been so brave."

His cries dropped as he heard her voice, sobbing as he cried out, "Mum, help me!"

Tears sprang to her eyes. "It's going to be all right. Take a deep breath."

"Mum!" his voice had mellowed, dropping in volume and intensity, and she saw the whites of his eyes gaze up at her, the fear slipping away as the chloroform took hold.

"You're safe now," she murmured gently, wishing she could take him in her arms, wishing she could make this moment warmer, more gentle.

For a while, she stayed there, wondering how to comfort him, and without knowing why, she began to softly speak, "The Lord's my Shepherd, I'll not want. He makes me lie down in green pastures, beside still waters . . ."

And as the words filled the void around them, she watched him fall into unconsciousness, and only then a sudden choke of tears made her call, "You can bring me up now!"

Immediately, the hands began to pull her up, her body scraping against the sides, tearing her clothes, but she didn't care.

As soon as she was up, she felt strong arms haul the top part of her out, and there was Sebastian, guiding her to the ground.

"Are you all right?" he said.

She let out an uncontrollable sob for the poor young man. He would have been so fit and able, a life in front of him wiped out in a single moment. Then she was engulfed by nausea, pulling away to retch again and again, sliding down onto the ground, her head in her hands, desperately trying to remove the image from her mind—the stench, the mangled body, the screams.

An arm came and pulled her close, Sebastian sitting down beside her on the rubble.

Quietly, he said, "A lot of people wouldn't have been able to do that."

She found herself shivering with horror. "It was unimaginable. The poor man—his body . . ."

Soothingly, he said, "I know," pulling her closer. "I've seen it all, too."

Remembering what he'd said about bad dreams, she whispered, "Dunkirk?"

Into the silence, he murmured, "Yes."

His hand rubbed her back, and she welcomed it, her throat raw and her body exhausted, as if she herself had been through a fight. And slowly, she found herself asking, "What happened out there?"

He took a deep breath. "It was horrific, the brutality and sheer chaos, the knowledge that you could be killed at any moment, or the man beside you could be. The fragility of it all—the futility."

Tentatively, she whispered, "Did Victor see the same kind of things?" After what she'd just gone through, she wanted to understand what had happened, how Sebastian and Victor could have reacted so differently to the same situation—one diving in, one running away.

After a slight pause, he said, "Yes, he would have. I only know the bare facts about what happened to him, but I gather things hadn't gone well for him from the beginning. He joined as a regular soldier rather than an officer, and the other men thought him too high-minded. You need friends in war to survive. Then the unit was sent ahead of the platoon to capture a small town, and half were mown down by the approaching Nazis. The other half fled. He may have been injured or trying to escape capture, we don't know, but we do know that Victor was one of the ones who didn't return to his unit." He paused for a moment before adding, "The irony is that a week before, his unit was commended for their bravery, Victor included. Men unravel in bad situations. Victor and the others who deserted had probably reached the end of their tether."

"It must have been terrifying. No wonder they fled," she muttered, the idea of all he must have gone through muddied with her own guilt for denying it. "Do you think he's still in hiding in France?"

Sebastian shrugged. "If he's injured, it might be hard for him to survive. A lot of deserters don't make it, especially if they contract gangrene or an infection. Some are captured or killed by the enemy, and others are imprisoned in France for the petty theft they commit in order to stay alive. Some might make it to a city where they can stay underground, live off crime."

"Do you think Victor might be able to get back to Britain?"

"I don't know. I imagine a few deserters make it home, especially those who feel that they're wrongly accused and want to clear their names."

"I'm sure he was wrongly convicted," she said quickly. "He couldn't possibly have deserted. He's far too moral for that."

"The front line is a chaotic place, Juliet. Nothing would surprise me of even the most honorable of men. I saw hardy soldiers on the brink of madness. What they were asking of us was often too much—the Nazis were coming so fast that our orders were out-of-date before we'd even received them. Sometimes we were commanded to go on suicide missions, straight into enemy lines, just because the orders were based on yesterday's battle map." His voice was becoming gravelly with emotion. "The injuries were grotesque, the men you knew—the men looking to you for guidance—exploded by bombs and grenades while you watched."

Glancing up at him, she met his gaze, for the first time realizing how much Sebastian must have been through.

As if to answer her unspoken question, he said, "Desertion crossed everyone's mind out there, either that or insanity. It was no wonder it took me so long to recover once I was back."

"It sounds horrendous," she said gently. "I imagine it'll take a long time for you to come to terms with it."

He rubbed his face with his hands. "I've never spoken about it before. No one deserves to go through that, or even to hear about it." He paused, closing his eyes. "You can't blame the men who couldn't face any more, Juliet. Do you have any idea of the men I've seen crying, the brave souls who think they're cowards when really they're heroes, the number of disparate remains I've had to identify as my own men? Every day is a new bombardment of horror, and every day I silently thanked the men I was with for sticking with it, and together we forgave those who didn't or couldn't."

And without a word, she turned and put her arms around him, suddenly understanding why he was so different than he had been before the war. A strange sense of disconcertment came over her that this war was changing more than just the way people lived—it was changing them on the inside, too. As she heard him take a deep breath, she pulled him closer, as if their physical connection could somehow protect them, shut out this incomprehensible world of chaos and brutality.

# KATIE

KATIE HAD BEEN INSTRUCTED TO MEET IRENE RIDLEY IN THE UNderground Library at two P.M. sharp, necessitating her to sneak out of the house while her mother was at the WVS, darting through the park to get to the station on time. These days she escaped whenever she could, desperation and loneliness making her ready to break rules. No longer was she the dutiful daughter doing as she was told. Now she knew she had to think for herself.

During the daytime, when the Underground Library was technically closed, the Miss Ridleys could still be found there, sorting books and preparing for the busy evening ahead. Today, as Katie pushed aside the barrier, she heard the two old sisters bickering at the newspaper table. And that's where she found them, Irene at the head of the table in full, determined headmistress mode, Dorothy at her side.

"Ah, Katie! There you are." Irene adjusted her spectacles, gesturing for her to take a seat.

"This is very intriguing." Katie laughed nervously.

Unable to stop herself, Dorothy sat forward excitedly. "We're going to start an Underground School."

With a despairing look at her sister's lack of restraint, Irene then gave Katie her professional smile. "That's right. When the local junior school was evacuated to Wiltshire, teachers and all, the school buildings were taken over by the ARP. Now that some of the younger children have come home early, they're left with no education whatsoever."

Dorothy cut in. "And so we're organizing a school of sorts, here in the Underground Library."

"Well, that sounds like a marvelous idea!" Katie said.

"I'm glad you think so," Irene said. "Because you're to be their teacher."

"Me?" Dismay overwhelmed her. How could she do it with her situation as it was?

But there was that determined glint in Irene's eyes. "Since all the usual teaching staff are still in Wiltshire, and we are in need of one or two here, it seemed only natural that I should think of you, one of the top students in your class."

Through her turmoil, Katie couldn't help but feel a swell of pride: Someone had remembered that she still had at least this one redeeming quality.

Her heart expanded as she looked gratefully at Irene. "Well, I'm very flattered, of course, only I'm not sure I'll be able to help very often." She grappled for an excuse. "My mother likes me to stay with her now that she's pregnant."

Irene nodded sagely. "Yes, I gathered as much. But the way I see it, she'll be giving birth in the next few months, and after that you might be more available." Katie could only feel grateful that although Irene knew about her pregnancy, at least she was keeping up the charade.

Interrupting again, Dorothy added, "And you won't be needed for long. The school will only run for two or three hours every afternoon, before the library opens at five o'clock."

Irene's eyes bored into Katie's. "I think you have the makings of a very talented teacher, Katie. You have a sharp mind and a great deal of common sense."

"Goodness, do you think so? I have a little experience, but only helping school friends with difficult subjects. I'm not sure I'd be good with discipline."

"You can leave that to me," Irene said brusquely. "They'll be a little undisciplined at first, no doubt, but I'll have them in shape for you to step in once you have more time." Her eyes gleamed, reminding Katie that Irene Ridley was renowned for running a tight ship. "I have every faith in you, Katie. With a brain like yours, you can achieve anything you want."

Katie felt herself blush.

"That's the ticket," Dorothy grinned. "We knew you'd say yes, didn't we? And it's a good thing, too, as our first students are coming this afternoon."

"Today?" Katie gasped. "But I would need to prepare. . . ."

Irene put up a hand to stop her. "I'll be here to organize it for now. I just wanted to involve you from the beginning, to give everyone a sense of continuity. Then you can pop in when you have time."

"That sounds marvelous," Katie said, quietly thrilled at the prospect of a new challenge. It might be hard to find time after the baby was born, but it would be good for her to be involved in something else, especially if she was valued. "What would you like me to do today?"

Irene passed a sheet of paper across the table. "I'd like you and Dorothy to set up the classroom. Young Meg is going to join you as a special helper, too. I think it'll be just what she needs, all that time on her own isn't good for her. The details are on the list." Readjusting her glasses, she returned to her notebook, as if that was that.

"When does it need to be ready?" Katie asked.

"The parents have been told to meet Mrs. Ottley in the main concourse at three, and she'll bring the children straight over." Irene looked at her watch. "So if I were you, I'd get a move on."

Katie and Dorothy made their way up to the ticket office, perusing Irene's list as they went.

"How many children do we have coming?" Dorothy asked as they took the escalator.

"Twelve of them, so not too many." Katie was busy reading. "It says we're to check with the stationmaster, and he can organize some benches to be brought down."

Fortunately, the stationmaster was eager to help. "It'll keep the young rascals out of mischief," he said with much feeling, making Katie wonder what they were up against. "The ones who came back from evacuation seem to be the troublemakers who couldn't get on in the countryside." He drew a long, exasperated breath. "And if the countryside can't keep them occupied, I don't know how we're supposed to in a train tunnel."

A couple of station workers brought down some benches, and after deciding on a good place beside one of the walls, Katie directed the men to set the benches in rows, a blackboard on a wooden stand at the front.

"Are we ready yet?" Meg appeared eagerly behind Katie's shoulder, looking a little sprucer than usual, her hair neatly combed and wearing a clean dress. She'd become a familiar face in the Underground Library, starting to lose her shyness with Juliet and the others. Katie had seen Irene talking to her the week before, and now she understood why. If there was one thing that Katie knew, it was that if Irene Ridley decided you were going to do something, there would be little you could do to resist her.

"Could you make sure the benches are clean and ready?" Katie said with a smile, happy to have at least one pupil doing what she was told.

Dorothy was checking the list. "It says here that every child is supposed to bring a small chalkboard or notepad and something interesting that they can show the class."

"Let's hope they remembered," Katie said with a chuckle.

Just as everything was becoming shipshape, a turbulent sound came down the passageway, and as it drew closer, it became more identifiable as a pack of marauding children.

"No running!" Mrs. Ottley's singsong voice resonated above the throng, nobody paying the slightest attention as the wild children surged past Katie into the library.

Just in time, Katie drew Dorothy back against the wall. "There's a lot more than twelve, isn't there?"

"There's twenty-eight," Meg said, diligently counting.

Dorothy looked worried. "Let's hope Mrs. Ottley knows how to control them."

She didn't.

After a lot of her high-pitched calls to "Put that away!" and "Settle down!" she retreated back to join them. "I'm not terribly good at being cross. What are we going to do?"

The horde of children zoomed around, pretending to be fighter pilots, shooting each other with "*Ack-ack-ack-ack!*" issuing loudly into the fray. Some of them began dropping "bombs," which comprised throwing chalkboards and notepads at other children, and Dorothy was called upon to administer first aid to at least two minor injuries within minutes.

Mrs. Ottley had been drawn into splitting up a fight between two of the pilots, only to find that a trio of girls was using someone's skipping rope to tie her up.

A small boy of only two or three had burst into tears, and Katie scooped him up, balancing him on one hip while she tried to pry the girls off Mrs. Ottley, getting everyone to sit down.

But as soon as they sat they were restless, looking around for the next excitement. So Katie called above the din, "Did anyone bring something interesting to show the class?"

A sweet-looking girl with a cage-like contraption put up her hand, and with relief, Katie walked over to her.

"What have you brought us today?" she asked, taking a closer look to see a small brown nose poking out of a box. "Is it a mouse?"

Smiling prettily, the girl opened the cage, putting a hand inside to bring it out. "That's right. He's called Harry. I caught him last week on the westbound tracks."

But as she pulled Harry out of his cage, Katie shrank back with a screech. "It's not a mouse. It's a rat!"

Before the girl could put him back into his cage, Harry utilized the commotion to make a bid for freedom, jumping onto the floor and darting under one of the benches, the girl crawling after him, distraught. "Harry! Harry!"

Mayhem ensued, and Katie was just about to tiptoe out and see what on earth was keeping Irene, when a stern, booming voice came from the end of the tunnel.

"What is the meaning of this?"

Come to bring order to the chaos, Irene strode into the tunnel, separating boys, sitting people down, and treating a few to her more intimidating stares.

Within moments the volume had gone down, as the children nervously took a seat while they assessed how much of a threat this new lady could be.

"This is a schoolroom, not a playground." She glared at them. "I am Miss Ridley, and everyone in this area—your parents included—knows that I am not to be crossed, am I clear?"

They nodded, unsure.

"Right, let's begin, shall we?" Irene announced loudly, completely in control as she walked to and fro: "This is our reserve teacher, Miss Upwood," she said, gesturing at Katie. "She'll be stepping in full time in a few months once we're set up and running."

Katie went to stand by Irene's side. Like the children, she knew what was expected of her. Trying to don Irene's bearing, Katie gave the class a brusque nod. If she was to be their teacher, she needed to instill authority from the beginning.

Irene gestured for Meg to come to the front. "And Meg here is going to help anyone who is struggling. If you need her, just hold up your hand, quietly."

Delighted, Meg stood up straighter and eyed the younger children as if she meant business.

There was a steeliness in Irene's eye and a renewed energy about her as she regained the children's attention. "Right, the first person who tells me what seven plus eight equals will not have to stay late."

The children began to vie for early release, a few at the front determinedly reaching up hands, desperate to be chosen.

"Come up and show me on the blackboard, Stanley," Irene instructed one of the boys at the back, who reluctantly obeyed. "I remember your father, such a good student of mine. Let's see if you're like him, shall we?"

As the boy took the chalk, Irene looked across at Katie and Dorothy and gave them a small nod. They knew they were dismissed and gratefully retreated.

"How does she do that?" Mrs. Ottley marveled.

Dorothy shrugged. "I have no idea, but thank heavens she came when she did."

"If my Jake were here, he'd be right in the middle of the mayhem, that's for sure," said Mrs. Ottley with a grin. "Such a high-spirited boy."

And as they watched the class now doing sums on their chalkboards, Katie couldn't help but think of what Mrs. Ottley must be going through. How life goes on, for her and all the other broken hearts here in the underground. Over time, maybe ten or twenty years from now, everything would be different again for all of them, and Katie, too. Maybe she would be a teacher, or even a principal, like Irene. Maybe life would give her a second chance at love, at having a family of her own.

And the child growing inside her would be an adult. Would he or she know the truth about her by then? Would she ever be called "Mum"?

And she knew right there and then, that if and when she did have a family of her own, she would neither take it for granted nor let it slip out of her fingers. To have control over her own life, over any children she brought into the world, was surely the only goal she could ever really have.

Her heart fell.

If only she had that control now.

She was still carrying the little boy, who had fallen asleep, his head on her shoulder, and she felt the warmth of him, the strange pleasure of being responsible for another life—of having someone count on you. It had never crossed her mind how warming it might be, how easy and somehow natural. Looking after a child had always seemed so difficult, so alien, but now, as she took in his sleeping face squashed against her collar, listening to his gentle breathing, she was suddenly aware of how simple it was.

That beneath all the struggles and unspoken rules, life was about these inborn connections, as easy and instinctive as nature itself.

# JULIET

THERE WERE ONLY A FEW REMAINING BOOKS TO RESTOCK BEFORE the Underground Library closed for the evening, and Juliet left Sofie and Dorothy behind the main desk while she went to put them back.

At the newspaper table, she found Irene, who sat with the *Times* open in front of her even though she was leaning back in the chair, her eyes closed. The new school was bound to be exhausting, but Juliet knew that the old lady wasn't as well as she wanted to appear.

"Are you all right?" Juliet said, gently waking Irene only for her to break into a bout of coughing. "Shall I get your sister for you?" She looked around for Dorothy, relieved that she was already on her way over.

Irene's breathing was becoming more labored. "Perhaps I'll go and lie down for a while," she said, reaching for Dorothy's hand. "I'm sure I'll be fine after a little rest."

Juliet helped her to her feet, walking her to their usual sleeping quarters, down a short staircase in a lower passage. There, she laid an extra blanket on the floor to make it more comfortable, easing her down, watching worriedly as the usually spritely old lady turned onto her side and quickly fell asleep.

"I'll come and check on her later," she whispered to Dorothy before leaving.

By the time she returned to the library, people were filtering out for the evening, only a dozen people were left. Sofie was manning the main desk, so Juliet went through the aisles letting people know that it was closing time.

Katie put away her medical book.

"Reading up for the big day?" Juliet said. "It can't be long now."

The girl's eyes shone frightened and youthful in the bright lights. "Mum said it'll be in a month or so. She pretends she knows everything, but I don't think she has a clue."

"Maybe you should go to the medical center here instead?"

"I know, but—" Katie broke off as a strange rumble came from above. "What was that?"

They listened as a muffled boom and a crack emanated through the echoey passages. Then Juliet felt the floor shudder beneath them, wondering if she was imagining it. The underground was deep enough that they rarely heard the bombs from above, and they almost never felt them.

Then came an almighty crash.

The ground shook, and a series of thumps emanated through the tunnels. The ceiling ripped apart in one place, plaster and rubble raining down over them. On the walls, tiles began to crack, dust and debris plunging down, crashing to the ground, filling the passages with a thick, noxious dust.

Everyone began to run for the main concourse, where pandemonium had taken hold, people panicking and shouting, blankets and bags left strewn as people rushed for the escalators. An old man fell to the ground in the turmoil, a woman stopping to haul him up, dragging him along with her.

The ground shifted as if the entire passage was about to cave in, and Juliet felt a surge of fear as she told Katie to go upstairs, get herself out of danger. The noise was cacophonous, people screaming, children crying as they were dragged by the hand of a terrified mother, pushing through the crowds to get them to safety.

Suddenly, the great crack above Juliet opened up and the ceiling caved in, sending the crowd into paroxysms of terror, desperate to get out. Juliet could only watch in horror as the bookshelves cascaded down, the books falling from their shelves, tumbling into everything in their path.

Then the lights went out.

Screams echoed ferociously through the black space, people shouting, an increased desperation to get to the surface, to get outside. One of the escalators had broken, and someone had tripped on the stairs, leading to a pile-up of frantic people, dying to get out.

Then suddenly, out of nowhere, came the sound of water, gushing, gurgling, spilling into the lower chambers as if released from a great reservoir.

"Juliet!" A voice screamed through the din. Was Sofie calling her? She looked around but couldn't see.

With a flicker, the dim emergency lights came on, sending a shadowy amber haze through the chaos.

"Juliet! Watch out!" the voice called through the chamber.

And as she looked back into the empty passage, she saw a great river of water hurtling down the tunnel toward her. A bomb must have blasted through a water main, releasing a great torrent into the train tunnels.

Instantly, the force almost knocked her down to the ground. She grabbed hold of the nearest bookshelf, but as she did, it toppled away from her, smashing into the water as the books dislodged and were carried into the wake.

Another colossal wave pushed her down, and suddenly she was in the water, stumbling on the uneven ground with debris and books surrounding her. She couldn't get a foothold. How was she going to get out?

Then she felt it. A hand clutched her upper arm, yanking her hard, the fingers pressing in with a painful grip.

She felt herself being pulled forward, then slowly but firmly dragged up out of the water. She gasped for air, her heart pounding, as the water rushed and pooled around them.

It was only then that she turned to thank her rescuer, gasping as she saw that it was Sofie.

"Thank you," she called out, but Sofie was already gone, trying to prize a fallen shelf unit off a woman who yelled with pain on the floor.

"Juliet! Help me!" Sofie panted as she struggled with the moaning woman.

Quickly catching her breath, Juliet took the other side of the bookcase and heaved it off, getting the woman to her feet and leaving Sofie to help her to the stairs.

Meanwhile, Juliet set off, her heart pumping fast as she dashed through the tunnels, taking the steps down to the lower level that was now already three feet deep with water. Shelterers were staggering up the stairs in wet clothes, a boy telling her that there were a couple of old ladies straggling behind him.

"It's the Ridley sisters!" Juliet yelled, plunging forward through the water.

Through the amber haze, she saw a frail, thin figure desperately trying to help someone from the ground. It was Dorothy, her white hair flattened and gray with debris and water. Juliet dashed forward quickly.

But as soon as she was there, she froze as she saw Irene in the water. She was unconscious and her head seemed twisted in a strange angle. Blood oozed red into the water surrounding her.

"The water took her down and she hit her head," Dorothy sobbed. "She won't get up!"

Mustering herself, Juliet plunged into the water and lifted Irene out. Her body was limp and lifeless, light in spite of her water-logged clothes, and Juliet gritted her teeth as she waded through to the stairs up to the higher ground, to get out of the fast-moving water.

"Juliet?" The sound of Sofie's voice carried through the tunnel, and soon she was beside her, carrying Irene out of the water, lying her down on the dry mid-landing. "We need to get her to a hospital. She's losing blood fast."

Crouching beside the body, Juliet quickly tried to find the old lady's pulse, gently feeling her neck, pallid with the chill of the water. "Her pulse is still there. I'm sure I can feel it."

Desperately, she began to blow air into the old lady's mouth, but after a few minutes she slowed down, her hand feeling her neck for a pulse, her chest for a heartbeat. Slowly, she realized that Irene's breathing had stopped—perhaps it hadn't been there all along. Juliet had been willing her to be alive, unable to believe the truth, wanting desperately not to lose her.

She looked at Sofie, whose face crumpled into despair. "She can't be gone! She just can't be!"

And there beside her was Dorothy, her head bent over her sister's body, unable to grasp the death of the woman, sister, and friend who had always been by her side.

# SOFIE

A FAINT AUTUMN SUNLIGHT SEEPED THROUGH THE RED-LEAVED oaks as Sofie walked through the park, Dorothy Ridley slow on her arm.

"Have you had time to think about the readings for the funeral?" Sofie asked gently, trying to engage Dorothy in conversation. The poor woman had barely spoken a word since her older sister's body was carried out of the underground, and Sofie was frightened for her. Inevitably, memories of her mother's death came back to Sofie; at least she'd had her sister and her father.

Dorothy had no other family at all.

And she was becoming frailer by the minute.

As they passed the bench, Sofie walked Dorothy over, and the old woman lowered herself down in a daze.

"Dorothy, it isn't right for you to lock yourself away like this. You need to talk. We're here to help you, to support you."

Slowly, Dorothy's dried lips opened, and quietly, calmly, she said, "I don't know what the point is anymore."

Silence hung around them, only the sound of the breeze rustling the brown-gold leaves on the path.

"I remember when my mother died," Sofie began, almost to herself. "It felt like the end of the world. How could anything go on without her—she was the one who had given us life, after all. Without her life-force, we would wilt and perish."

A light rain began to fall, gently, and soft tiny droplets slid from the sky onto their heads and faces, their hands and coats.

"And yet I still exist, and she still does not," Sofie said.

Stirring, Dorothy looked around at her. "I thought you were going to give me some prophetic tale about healing from grief. I won't be able to, you know."

"Probably not," Sofie said, taking her hand and resting it on her own lap. "But Irene would be very cross with you if you gave up on life as easily as that."

That brought a smile to Dorothy's face. "She would, wouldn't she? And even though I would disagree, she would still insist. You know what she's like—was like."

Her mouth fell, and she bent her face forward and slowly, quietly began to cry.

And Sofie could only put her arm around her and whisper, "She will always be here, in our hearts and in our home, everywhere you look. Her spirit will always be around us, sharing all she has to give."

They sat there, on the bench, for a long time, Dorothy beginning to talk about her sister, the woman she was, her strength, her pragmatism, and her utter and unstoppable kindness.

The community had been devastated by the havoc wreaked that night. A bomb had struck a water main under the high street, leading to the underground deluge that killed and injured a number of people. To make matters worse, more people were hurt in the crush as the thousands of shelterers rushed up the stairs to the streets. A woman with a small child had tripped, leading to a pile-up of bodies as people stumbled into her. The tragedy could not have been more heart wrenching.

An exhausted medley of station staff and locals had cleared the station, and it was open again the following evening, even though many people, including Sofie and Dorothy, preferred to remain at home. The underground, the one place they'd been told was safe, had been struck, and that unnerved them to the core.

And Irene Ridley—a woman who had become Sofie's dear, trusted friend—had been brutally killed there. Her death came as a shocking blow to the whole neighborhood. The old lady had been at the very core of the Bethnal Green community, and anger welled up in Sofie: How could the Nazis randomly drop bombs on civilians? They knew the air raids would mean thousands of innocent deaths, and yet every night, special people like Irene were killed by the relentless bombardments. How dare they?

Once they were back at home, Sofie began to prepare a simple supper for them. She helped Dorothy to a chair in the kitchen so that she wasn't on her own, bringing in the radio from the living room. *It's That Man Again* was on, and the jokes about how everyone was getting tied in knots because of the war were strangely soothing. It served as a reminder that it wasn't just them in this horrific reality, it was a whole nation, everyone sacrificing something or someone, trying their best to carry on.

"It's a good thing I moved in," Sofie said as the program came to an end. "I wouldn't like to think of you here on your own." She was making chicken soup, and the scent of fresh herbs and chicken filled the room with warmth. "Isn't it strange how the smell of food can transport you back to a different time and place? My sister Rachel used to make this after our mother died, and the smell brings it all back to me." She brought the bowls to the table.

"I hope you find her, Sofie. Or that she finds you. Sisters are special." There was a wistfulness to Dorothy's voice, and her eyes strayed to the window, where dusk was gathering pace, sending a pink-red hue from beneath a thin layer of white-gray cloud. "Irene was the last one in my family. Our parents died a long time ago, but that never seemed so terrible when I had her." She looked down into her lap. "And now it's just me."

Sofie reached out and put her hand on Dorothy's. "We'll have to be our own family, you and I. We may come from different places, and we have different religions, too, but we don't need to be related to rely on each other, do we?" She pressed her hand. "You helped me, took me in when I needed a home, and now I want to be a family to you." She reached her hand over. "When you need someone, you can count on me."

Dorothy's eyes slowly came back to hers, and she gave her a weak smile, tears nestling in the corner of her eyes like gems glowing in the dim kitchen. "I'd like that, too."

They ate in companionable silence, which was sporadically broken by thoughts about the funeral. As Sofie cleared the plates, the gradual whirr of the siren began, and they gathered their belongings.

Tonight, Sofie was going to try to take Dorothy back to the underground. She was only too aware that it would be difficult for her, but it was better to face it now, to be surrounded by other people who cared for her.

The walk took longer than usual, and as they reached the main road, they saw the new bomb craters from that terrible raid. Half-collapsed buildings were exposed like doll's houses, private rooms laid bare for all the world to see.

But neither of them paid much attention. Dorothy was lost in her own world, her mind still catching up with the reality, and she kept stopping and looking over her shoulder, something missing. It was as if she were trying to spot Irene coming up behind them as usual, but instead she only saw the gap where Irene should have been.

"Only a few more minutes." Sofie urged her on, worrying about how she would get Dorothy to go underground. The poor woman seemed ready to give up on life, and the closer they got, the slower her pace.

But as they turned into the main road, Sofie knew that she needn't have worried.

There on the corner waiting for them was Marigold, clutching her fur coat around her as she hurried over to greet them.

"I knew it would be hard," she said, "so I decided to show my support, make sure you don't feel alone."

Lost in her own thoughts, Dorothy stood still for a minute or two, and then, weakly, she heaved a great sigh as Marigold took her other arm and led her to the entrance.

Slowly, they made their way down to the Underground Library. A team of volunteers had cleaned the place up, returning it to normal as best they could, but there was still a smell of damp, piles of books too damaged to save stacked in a corner. But the bookcases were back up, the banner once again hanging defiantly above them, and Sofie felt the warmth of the books, the familiarity of the place envelop her.

They were greeted by the other book club regulars, who had gathered for a special memorial evening.

Juliet quickly came forward, followed by Mrs. Ottley, Katie, and Mac. Even Mr. Pruitt was there, grimly looking on, hands behind his back.

After they'd taken their seats, Juliet took her usual position at the front and began. "Tonight is a special, sacred time for us, when we remember our dear friend Miss Irene Ridley. Books were her world, and education was her life, and where better to celebrate her vibrant, energetic soul than here, in a library, and in her Underground School, where she was most at home."

And together, they settled down to talk about Irene. They shared memories and stories of her life, of the ways she'd helped them, of her stern schoolmistress voice, but that glint in her eye that showed the fun that lurked inside. And they talked about her energy in spite of her illness, her spirit in setting up the school.

Then Katie pulled out the books that Irene had loved, the Shakespeares and the Brontës, offering them as a tribute to her spirit, which seemed to thread through and around them.

"How momentous a loss," Juliet said through her tears. "How greatly she changed the world she left behind."

# KATIE

I T WAS ONE OF THOSE SHARP, BRIGHT MORNINGS, THE BOUGHS OF the trees bare against the intense blue of the sky. A single thrush sang plaintively on the green as Katie joined the small group outside the Ridleys' house. It was Irene's funeral, and the original book club members were there to mourn her death and support Dorothy as best they could.

The women glanced nervously at one another as they waited for Dorothy and Sofie to emerge from the house.

"I worry about her," Mrs. Ottley said quietly. "Irene was always the one in charge, the one who looked after her. They did everything together."

Slowly, the front door opened, and Sofie led the way out. Behind her came Dorothy, taking her arm to be helped down the steps. Katie hurried forward to take her other arm, sensing how slight the old lady felt, weightless and untethered without her sister.

It was a distraught little group who walked down to the main road, quiet except for Sofie softly explaining how the funeral was to proceed. A local funeral parlor, Tadwells, had stepped forward to organize it, a succession of Tadwells having been taught by Miss Ridley, and the service would take place in the large Victorian church on the main road, her body interred in the graveyard behind. Afterward, the small group would go to Marigold's for tea and sandwiches, although with Marigold, there would probably be sherry, too, at the very least.

But nothing prepared them for what they saw when they reached the main road.

Crowds of people lined the pavements, and as Katie wondered what they were doing there, it soon became clear.

As Dorothy emerged from the lane, a reverent silence fell over them. Hundreds of faces gazed in her direction, everyone there in deference to the much-loved community leader.

On the road was a horse-drawn funeral carriage. A dozen men in black suits with top hats stood before and around the hearse, and in front of it, six black horses stood still, plumes of deep purple rising from their heads into the sky.

"It's a traditional East End funeral," Mrs. Ottley gasped. "They're doing the old lady proud. I bet everyone here was a student of hers once."

The crowd stood, heads bowed, for this one dynamic woman, for what she meant to the neighborhood, for what she had imparted to each and every child who passed through her school.

Then in the center, the tall, dignified funeral director at the front of the hearse brought down his silver-tipped staff twice, and called for silence as the procession began.

A smaller man dressed in black led Dorothy and the group down to take their place walking behind the procession, and it slowly made its way down to the church.

Around them, people lined the procession route. On the other side of the main road, the older girls and boys from the high school, wearing full school uniform, stood by respectfully. After them, a group watched on, and Katie realized that she recognized each and every one. It was the crowd that gathered every night for the reading hour, the people brought together by the Underground Library.

The church was packed, people standing in the aisles and at the back, spilling out into the street. Katie saw Juliet looking around the congregation until she spotted Sebastian, smart in his Westminster suit, their eyes meeting with sadness through the throng.

It was a traditional service, the vicar giving the eulogy. "Miss Irene Ridley built our local high school from virtually nothing, advocating for the creation of the junior school for younger children. Even in her old age she was still busy, setting up an Underground School that would continue after her death. She made our locals literate. She made them value education. She encouraged them to be brave, to be bold."

After the emotional tribute, the school choir sang a powerful rendition of "Amazing Grace." A girl of only twelve or thirteen stood at the front with large, scared eyes as she sang the verse as a solo, the sound echoing through the massive interior, the crowd so still it was as if the place were empty.

After the service, they watched the coffin being lowered down onto the soft autumn leaves. Dorothy turned into the group's warm embrace, and Katie could only think of how good it was that she had friends.

After all, what is life without the knowledge that you are not alone?

When the service was finished, a long line of locals formed, waiting to speak to Dorothy, to shake her hand. They wanted to convey their sympathies, to share stories of Irene's strength and indomitability, to explain how greatly she had touched their lives.

The group stayed for a long time, greeting people and talking, and it was over an hour before the somber party walked slowly back to Marigold's house for a quiet gathering.

And as they sat, numbly trying to accept their old friend's death, Sofie stood to share a poem by Clare Harner.

> *Do not stand*
> *By my grave, and weep.*
> *I am not there,*
> *I do not sleep—*
> *I am the thousand winds that blow*
> *I am the diamond glints in snow*
> *I am the sunlight on ripened grain,*
> *I am the gentle, autumn rain.*
> *As you awake with morning's hush,*
> *I am the swift, up-flinging rush*
> *Of quiet birds in circling flight,*

*I am the day transcending night.*
*Do not stand*
*By my grave, and cry—*
*I am not there,*
*I did not die.*

# JULIET

### THE UNDERGROUND LIBRARY
### NEWSLETTER

#### NOVEMBER 1940

#### THANK YOU FOR HELPING WITH
#### THE FLOOD DAMAGE

*With your help, we were able to reopen*
*a few days after the flood.*

#### HELP WITH THE RATIONS

*A new library section is filled with handy books and*
*government leaflets on cooking with rations, growing*
*vegetables, and Make Do and Mend for clothes.*

AS JULIET BUSTLED AROUND, RELIEVED TO SEE THE LIBRARY OPEN once again, she felt a surge of gratitude. Together, the sheltering community had helped them, the regulars showing up with brooms and mops, determined to have their library up and running.

But the reality was that, with the flood damage, the Underground Library was in trouble. The stock of books had been reduced by over a third, and two of the larger bookcases were looking very fragile, even after they'd been mended. Juliet had suggested getting more stock out of storage, but it was impossible to tell if Mr. Pruitt had even inquired about it.

There seemed little she could do except keep it going until the inevitable end. But what would she do then?

And all the while, in the back of Juliet's mind was Sebastian. How close they'd become—and yet he'd always pulled back. She remembered the kiss on the cheek at the end of their evening at the jazz club. Although they seemed to be getting closer, it was clear he wasn't prepared to take that step.

She'd barely seen him recently. Either his long hours or his work trips had kept him away, and even at Irene's funeral, their eyes had only met solemnly through the rows. Quickly, she reminded herself that they were nothing more than friends, brushing her hands together as if to banish him from her mind. Hadn't he himself told her that he didn't want anything more serious at the moment?

It was opening time, and when she moved the barrier, a waiting crowd spilled inside to peruse the aisles.

But as she went back to join Mrs. Ottley and Dorothy at the main desk, something made her stop and look back.

Between the flow of people, standing completely still by the entrance, she saw a tall man with dark hair, his eyes piercing hers through the crowd.

"Victor?" she gasped, paralyzed to the spot, wavering momentarily with doubt before shaking herself.

Was it really him?

"Victor!" she said, louder, people turning to see, watching as she darted through the crowd, jolting to a stop a few feet away from him, suddenly shy, anxious. "What are you doing here? The army sent a telegram saying that you'd, well, that you'd gone missing."

He laughed, stepping forward to take her in his arms, squeezing her tightly, and she felt the powerful heat of his body. "Those idiots mixed it up, got the wrong man. I was injured, unconscious for a while. By the time I came to, I found that my unit had withdrawn to Dunkirk, along with the rest of the British forces—most of them had left France completely. I had to trek across the countryside and finally got a boat from Brittany." Suddenly he looked tired, and she could see the shadows under his eyes, the strain behind his striking features. "I almost died out there, darling."

"But—they said you were a . . ." She didn't want to say the word. How could she ever have thought it of him?

"I got an honorable discharge once they realized their mix-up." He smiled, and she felt that familiar rush, that sense of togetherness. "You should have seen their faces, groveling with apologies."

"You must have been furious."

He nodded. "I knew it would be sorted out quickly once I was home, and it was, thank heavens."

She gazed at him, still not quite taking it in. "And now you're back."

"And I want you to come home and be my wife!" And before she could say another word, he stepped forward, took her in his arms, and kissed her, his lips warm and hungry for her. She found herself kissing him back, feeling those familiar sensations, but her mind reeled.

"It's incredible to see you—I can hardly believe it!" she said when he finally drew away, only too aware that her smile was wavering.

"It's marvelous, isn't it, darling. I've been looking forward to this moment for such a long time." He put his arm around her shoulder, turning her toward the main concourse. "I saw a canteen on the way. Let's get some tea, and I'll tell you all about my journey here."

Tentatively, she gazed back at the main desk. "But I can't leave the library yet. I'm in charge here. It's my new job," she added, gesturing to the place with pride.

He spun her toward him. "But I've only just come back! Don't you want to see me, with all I've been through? In any case, as soon as we're married you won't need this job anymore. What does it matter if you leave a bit early today?" He beamed at her, his eyes glistening with emotion. "Once you're back in Upper Beeding, I'll book the church. I've waited far too long, been through so much, and now I know exactly what I want—what I need." He gazed into her eyes. "It's only ever been you, my darling."

Everyone was watching the spectacle. Dorothy's mouth had fallen open slightly, and Mrs. Ottley eyed Victor with curiosity, probably realizing that her matchmaking scheme with Sebastian was now clearly off.

And that's when Juliet remembered Sebastian. A shiver went through her. If Victor ever found out that she'd been to a dance with another man, that they'd become as close as they had, she would never hear the end of it. Even though nothing had happened between them, Victor would sense a connection. She knew from before that Victor's jealousy was best avoided.

Victor took hold of her hand and pulled her out of the Underground Library, and she laughed lightly. "But Victor! I can't just leave."

"Oh, come on, darling. The women behind the desk can do anything that needs to be done."

Everything felt uncertain, slipping away from her. "Can you look after the desk for me?" she hollered to the others.

"All right, dear," Mrs. Ottley called back. And for a moment, her eyes met Juliet's with an almost imperceptible question mark—what was she doing?

The line for the canteen was short for once, and after Victor treated them to tea and scones, they went to sit down in a quieter passage, easing themselves down onto a bench.

"I can't tell you how good it is to see you, Juliet," he said, gathering her hands in his. "I came as soon as I had a new home for us, somewhere we can move straightaway." He smiled. "There's a small garden of sorts, and the kitchen is a little old, but I know how you enjoy a challenge, darling." He grinned. "I can't wait to give you everything you always wanted. I was wrong to hold back before, to put our wedding off until the book was finished. Now I know that all I want is you."

Juliet felt the last six months fade away. As she looked at Victor's manly face, his dark eyes looking intensely into hers, she felt herself being pulled back into his orbit. The dream she'd eradicated when he went missing quickly resurrected itself in her mind. How much she'd longed for a proper home, a proper future for them.

"Is it large—I mean, I wondered if there might be room for children, if we have any," she said it hurriedly, without thinking, and as she saw him recoil, she wished she'd never said a word.

Then he seemed to think about it, nodding. "Of course we can have a child, if you'd like." He smiled at her, putting an arm around her, and suddenly she felt that familiar sense that she was special, loved—only Victor seemed able to give that to her. "We'll have the perfect life! You reading with a little one beside you, and me writing my books. I have some terrific new ideas—just wait until I tell you about them!"

As if in a dream, she murmured, "And we'll be married?"

He pulled her in close. "Yes, let's get married as soon as we can. A small, intimate ceremony, just you and me and a few friends as witnesses. Our love is so deep, who needs more than that?" He kissed her again, muttering into her hair, "I've missed you so much, my darling."

Her mind spinning, she found it hard to keep up with what was happening. "I still can't quite believe you're here—that you're alive, that they acquitted you. How did they manage to mix you up?"

He chuckled. "Before a big push, some of us men would swap identity tags for good luck, and the chap who deserted must have had mine."

"How horrid for you," she said. "At least the Nazis didn't take you prisoner."

"They didn't have enough men to search every house and quickly passed through to take the next town. Once I realized what had happened, I went into hiding from them, making my way through the countryside back to base. But it was gone. They'd already started evacuating men from Dunkirk."

"You must have been terrified, stuck in France surrounded by Nazis."

He drew a long, broken breath as she pulled him close. "I struggled on, finding some civilian clothes so that I wasn't a walking target, living on scraps and anything the French could give me. Once I reached the coast, a fisherman gave me and a few other stranded soldiers a lift over to the south coast of England. You can only imagine how happy I was to be on home soil."

"Did you even know that you'd been mistaken as a deserter?"

He shook his head. "Not until I reported for duty." He smirked. "They were surprised to see me, but it was sorted out quickly. Then I was discharged on medical grounds." He indicated his right arm—

thank heavens there were no visible signs of a lasting injury. "I went straight back to Upper Beeding to see you. When I heard you'd moved to London, I couldn't believe it. I knew I needed to come and find you, bring you home with me."

Suddenly, Juliet realized the full extent of what he was asking of her.

"But I'm not sure I can go to Upper Beeding right away, Victor. My life is in London now, and I have the Underground Library to look after."

He pulled away with an inquiring smile. "The Underground Library?"

"After the main library was bombed, I pressed for it to be moved underground, to help the people sheltering pass the time. It's brought the whole station together."

"That's just like you to be so caring. It's a shame you'll have to give up work—especially if you want to have a child."

"Well, why don't you move to London?" she said brightly. "Then I could keep my new job. We could both be happy."

He heaved a momentous sigh. "My next book is going to be an important one, not only for me—for us—but for the country, too. I need the quiet of the countryside in order to write." He took her arm, looping it through his own. "And you should see the lovely house I rented, surrounded by all the beauty of the land. You'll love it there, darling. I promise you."

"But what about my life here—"

She was cut off by Victor's sudden gasp of dismay as he looked down at her hand. "But where's your engagement ring?"

Guilt flashed through her, and she pulled her hand away. "It was a little too big, and I was worried I'd lose it," she lied, trying to appease him.

But he saw through it, his face hurt. "Did you really believe I would desert?"

"Of course I didn't. It was just, well, what was I to think? I spoke to your parents, and they told me they'd checked with the officials. . . ." Her voice petered out as his eyes bored into her with hurt and disappointment.

"I thought you knew me, Juliet." He shook his head sadly. "I thought we were truly made for each other, you and I, but now, now . . ." He glanced toward the exit. "I've come all this way, staggered through France, roughed the sea crossing while injured, only to find that my fiancée didn't have the loyalty, the love, to stand by me."

The hurt in his voice made her wince, and she quickly took his hands back in hers. "Of course I stood by you," she said through tears. "And now you're home, it's just so marvelous. And your new book sounds wonderful. What do you have in mind for this work?"

He eyed her moodily for a moment, and then, thankfully, began to elaborate on his next tome.

While he spoke, her mind tried to unravel this strange new reality. Could she really just leave? Without her, Mr. Pruitt would be sure to close the library down. But then, she admitted to herself with a heavy sigh, the chances of the library staying open were slim, what with the flood damage and the stock so low.

And if it closed, she would have to find a new job anyway. Perhaps she could take up her old position in the library in Upper Beeding, she thought.

"Shall I help you pack then, darling?" Victor said, getting to his feet.

"W-what, now?" He couldn't possibly expect her to leave immediately. "I can't go yet."

"Why not?" There was an impatience about him, an impulsiveness that she realized she'd forgotten. "Don't you want to be with me?" He looked into her eyes as if he could see straight through to her soul, a wild passion about him that never failed to draw her in. "I've been through so much, and now all I want is to be with you again, to be married. I thought our love was above everyday things, a truly spiritual connection. I thought you felt the same way, too."

"Of course I want to, Victor. But I need to tie a few things up here before I leave, organize someone to look after the library. I owe it to the people here."

He paused, but slowly he nodded, patting her arm as if letting her off. "All right, why don't you stay for another few days, say your farewells, and come down on the train. I can meet you at the station." He moved his head closer to hers to add, "And don't tell your parents yet. It can be a surprise after we're home and married."

Her smile faltered. She'd always pictured her parents being there at her and Victor's wedding. She wanted to show them she was capable of finding her own husband without their help—although somehow that didn't seem to matter to her anymore. But it would be fine without them there, she supposed, better most likely.

She smiled. "I'll come as soon as I can. It's wonderful you're back." She threw her arms around him.

And so the evening went on, Victor talking about his time at war, how it had changed his writing. He couldn't stay the night, and so as the time for the last train approached, they walked slowly to the platform.

"At least it will only be for a few days this time," he said, pulling her toward him. "Write and tell me which train you'll be catching, and I'll meet you at the station, take you to our new home," he said, adding, "And I'll see if we can be married next week."

She heard herself laugh, tinkling with delight, as if it were a crazy dream.

"I can't wait for you to be Mrs. Manning." He took her hand and kissed it. "It'll be just you and me, Juliet. No one will be able to touch us. We'll hide away from everything."

It was the kind of thing he'd always say, sheltering her from her heartless parents. She hugged him tightly as the train roared through the tunnel and onto the platform.

As the doors opened and he got on board, he turned back to her. "I love you, Juliet, my darling."

"I love you, too," she said, their eyes meeting as the doors closed and the train pulled away, vanishing into the tunnel.

And he was gone.

Numbly, Juliet walked back to the Underground Library. It was closed, the dimmed light casting shadows through it, and guilt threaded through her as she noticed how tidy it was, all the books reshelved, the cushions and blankets put away by someone else's hand.

It wasn't until she went behind the main desk that she realized she wasn't alone. Dorothy was there, sitting at the newspaper table, reading *Jane Eyre*. As Juliet approached, the old lady looked up. "How nice to have your young man back," she said, an eyebrow raising slightly.

Juliet pulled out a chair and sat down beside her, leaning her elbows on the table with a long sigh. "He wants me to move to Upper Beeding, to marry him."

"You don't seem very enthusiastic, my dear."

Juliet laughed. "It's what I've always wanted." Then her face fell. "But it means that I'll have to leave London, leave my job, leave everyone." She looked at her hands. "Since I've been here, I've realized how good it is to have created a place like this, somewhere that really feels like home. It'll seem a bit empty without it."

"It'll seem a bit empty without you, too." Dorothy looked at her. "It must be strange, that he's alive and not missing after all."

"It's wonderful to see him," Juliet said hesitantly. "But he wants me to move so quickly. He doesn't seem to understand what I've done here, how much it means to me."

"And how much it means to everyone else."

They sat in silence for a while, and then, tentatively, Dorothy asked, "What are you going to do about Sebastian?"

Juliet lowered her head into her hands. "I don't want to think about it. I feel so disloyal to Victor, going to a dance with another man." A blush came over her. "And I'm worried I'll hurt Sebastian's feelings by leaving—well, if he likes me, that is."

"I think he does," the old lady said quietly. "And I think you like him, too."

Suddenly agitated, Juliet said, "But he hasn't said anything, has he? He hasn't done anything. He talks about everything except love. He hugs me and takes my hand, and when we danced together it was like heaven, but then his goodnight kiss was a peck on the cheek."

"Maybe he wants to make sure everything's right first," Dorothy said gently. "You can't blame him that Victor's shown up to take you away before he's had time to declare himself."

"But you don't know Sebastian. He's having fun with me, like he does with half the ambulance girls. At least with Victor I have someone who will marry me."

Dorothy patted her hand. "Remember, if Victor truly loves you, he'll want you to be happy." Her eyes softened. "There's a great spark inside you, Juliet. Don't let him smother it by hiding you away behind him and his career."

A twist of discomfort stole through Juliet, but she quickly put a smile onto her face. "I'll do my best."

How Juliet wished that Dorothy could know Victor as well as she did. But at the same time, Juliet could feel that a gap had grown between her old life and her new one. She feared that she'd leave and all of this world would simply fall away. Dorothy, Sofie, Katie, Marigold, and dear Mrs. Ottley, they were all part of her new life, the life Juliet would have to abandon forever.

CHAPTER

**34**

## SOFIE

 HE EVENING AFTER VICTOR'S UNEXPECTED ARRIVAL, SOFIE ARRIVED
early for the reading hour as she often did, helping Dorothy mend the
books damaged in the flood. Juliet was leaving in a few days, and Sofie
and the other volunteers were set to staff the library, at least for as long
as the council kept it open.

In the wake of Irene's loss, Sofie and Dorothy had become closer
than ever, and she found herself depending on the maverick old lady as
much as the other way around, both of them muddling through together. As the war progressed and the Blitz had worsened, Sofie was
encountering more and more vitriol when people heard her accent, and
she was more grateful than ever to Dorothy for standing up for her.

Sofie's war job had turned out to be in an unmarked ministry building in Westminster. After signing the Official Secrets Act, she was told
to translate German newspapers, checking the facts against interviews
with German POWs. The idea was to find the parts not being told to
the German public: a U-boat bombed through confused communication, a shipment of food for Nazi soldiers captured by the enemy, Luft-
waffe bombers running out of fuel and crashing into the North Sea.
These blunders were then broadcast through a German radio station,
exposing the Nazis' lies to their own people.

Everything about the work appealed to her. It used her knowledge
of the German psyche and her yearning to tell the population the truth
about their leader. With every broadcast, she saw an opportunity, a

chance to change another person's mind, a chance to undermine the Germans' confidence in Hitler.

The reading hour was her favorite time of day, and she'd hurry back after work, putting her bag beside Dorothy's deck chair and pulling up a cushion. These days, people from all walks of life came along to listen, especially now that the station was busier, shelterers coming from other areas to take advantage of the only underground library in London.

The place was filling up by the time Juliet began, the crowd hushing as she stepped forward to speak.

"And for tonight's reading hour, I want to ask a new reader to step forward. Can you all welcome Sofie Baumann."

Applause went around the passage, while Sofie looked frantically around. Had she heard right?

But everyone was looking at her expectantly.

Quickly, she went over, whispering to Juliet, "I can't do it, not with my German accent. Someone will think I'm a Nazi and they'll cause a scene before I have a chance to explain that I'm Jewish, that I hate the Nazis even more than they do." She balled her fists in frustration.

"But that's the point," Juliet said. "I'll explain who you are at the beginning. It'll be our way of showing our solidarity with you and all the refugees from Europe. No one who witnesses you reading here in the underground will ever call you names again. You shouldn't have to bear anyone's ire at the shops when you are doing more than most to help the war."

"But my reading voice isn't so good." She squirmed uncomfortably.

Juliet pressed the book into her hands. "I've been thinking more and more about your underground libraries in occupied Europe, and it's made me realize that our library isn't only about us. It's about the whole community. It's about changing perceptions, broadening minds, supporting and nurturing all of us, wherever we come from, whoever we are."

Sofie looked at the book in her hands, begging Juliet, "Can't I practice and do it next week?"

But Juliet gave her a confident smile. "Do the best you can, Sofie. We're all here to support you."

And without giving her a chance to back out of it, Juliet addressed the crowd.

"Sofie is a Jewish refugee from Germany, and although you might find it hard to listen to her accent at first, once you know her story, of how her family has been forced to flee Berlin, and that she now works as a translator for our side, you will embrace her as one of us. She and other refugees like her are part of our robust and diverse Underground Library, part of a community that helps all of our allies."

The crowd looked expectantly from Juliet to Sofie, who stood nervously fidgeting with the book, grateful that Juliet had picked one of her favorites.

"And now I want you to give a wholehearted welcome to Sofie."

Claps and cheers went through the crowd, some people taking to their feet in support of the girl.

As the crowd hushed, she began, her voice trembling and self-conscious. "Today we are starting a new book, *Anna Karenina,* by Leo Tolstoy. Chapter One . . ." And as she read, the people around her moved their heads forward to hear, and she raised her voice a little, speaking slowly and clearly. No one mentioned her accent, no one said a word; there were only the small whispers of newcomers as more and more people came to hear what the strange foreigner was reading.

At the end, there was a quiet appreciation, and then one by one, people began to clap, showing their unity and support for the Jewish refugee in their midst. Some came forward to thank her, to find out where she was from, what she had been through. And she bit her lip as she listened to them, her eyes meeting Juliet's with gratitude, friendship, and a renewed sense of belonging.

It was awhile before the crowd began to clear, people hanging around to talk to her and one another, a new energy in the air, a new interest in what was happening in Europe.

Then a familiar figure made his way forward. Smart in a suit, his hands casually in his pockets, Mac sauntered up.

"Wasn't anyone else available to read?" he joked, a cheeky grin on his face.

Nudging him playfully, she laughed, "I don't know what Juliet was thinking! I was so nervous."

He leaned forward and said quietly, "You were my favorite reader so far."

"Well, maybe you should have a turn next time." She thought of Juliet telling Mac's story, too.

But Mac had his mind on other matters. "I have a surprise for you."

"Oh?"

With a smile, he slipped his hand into his inside pocket and pulled out a small dark blue cloth bag, the type that contains some kind of jewelry.

With an intake of breath, she stepped back. "What is it?"

But then he opened the ribbon and tipped the bag into his palm, a heavy gold chain slipping out.

She recognized it immediately. "My mother's bracelet!"

As she put her hand forward to take it, he motioned for her to hold her wrist out, and then, gently, he put the bracelet around it and attached the clasp.

Something about its cool, smooth weight felt heartbreakingly familiar. A lump formed in her throat as she remembered herself as she had been before the war, trying on her mother's jewels, pretending to be grown-up.

Well, now she *was* an adult. There was no doubt about that!

She looked at the precious object that was packed with memories and meaning. "How did you get it?"

"I knocked on Mr. Wainwright's door and told him I was a merchant paying good money for gold by weight, should he have anything he'd like to sell. He brought down a few items, and I said the quality wasn't good enough for any except for this one bracelet." He grinned. "Then I bought it from him."

Immediately, she pressed him. "How much was it? You have to let me pay you back. I earn money now. I can afford it."

He put up a hand to stop her. "I took your four pounds when I first met you, and that will cover it."

"But that was for the information. . . ."

But he wasn't listening, taking her arm and heading for the main concourse. "Friends don't charge money for information. In any case, we have to hurry. We're going to be late as it is."

"Late for what?"

"For your other surprise, of course."

Pulled along behind him, she felt a buzz of excitement as he wove through the crowds, around the canteen, then down a short staircase, and into a quieter passage, stopping suddenly in one of the quieter passages.

"What . . ." she began, falling silent as she looked around her.

There, in front of her, were a few lines of chairs, people sitting in silence, waiting. At the front stood a string quintet, dressed in black tie, a woman in a long black dress, their music stands before them with crisp music, their bows poised to begin.

"Ladies and gentlemen," one of the violinists announced. "Please welcome the Royal College of Music Quintet."

As the crowd gave a reserved applause, Mac stepped through to find two spaces in the middle, their shoulders squashed together as they squeezed in.

The passage fell into a hush, waiting for the music to begin.

And slowly it came, the sound bringing a smile to her face. "Beethoven's 'Moonlight Sonata,'" she whispered. "They're playing it for us."

"I read a poster about them," Mac whispered back. "They're touring the larger tube stations, and after hearing you hum it on our way to the camp . . ."

And as the magnetic rhythm of the trios began, she whispered, "Thank you." Finding his hand, she pressed it in gratitude; only then, instead of pulling it away, she let it rest there, his hand between her fingers, the soft warmth of him, the stirring sound of the music twisting between and around them.

On her other hand, her mother's bracelet hung heavily from her wrist, and she turned it, letting it catch the light in the soft glow of the passage. And in that one moment, with Mac by her side and the magic of the "Moonlight Sonata" swirling around them, there wasn't anywhere else on earth that she would rather be.

# KATIE

KATIE GRIPPED THE DESK IN HER BEDROOM, HOLDING HER BREATH to stop herself letting out a terrific scream. The pain was almost unbearable, crippling her in great waves and then leaving her almost as fast as it had come. She hadn't been expecting the baby to come for another few weeks or more. Was it too early? Would that put the birth in even more peril?

The room was almost dark. Dusk had descended quickly, and she was in too much pain to put up the blackout blinds, which meant that she couldn't switch on the light. As the contraction subsided, she looked at her bedside clock. It had been seven minutes since the last one.

The books had been clear. A first birth could take a whole day and night. The contractions would begin gradually and then come closer together. When they were five minutes apart, the birth would become imminent. After that, it could come quickly or take a number of hours.

Katie hoped it would be the latter.

After her mother's little talk about getting everything in order, Katie had begun to worry in earnest. She'd remembered only too clearly what the nurse had told her in the medical clinic, how many things could go wrong.

She couldn't simply sit back any longer.

She was going to have to take control. This was *her* baby, *her* birth, and regardless of what her mother said, she needed a medical professional. It was too risky to do it without. Katie could die, or the baby. Or both.

So she'd made her own plan.

The air-raid sirens began between six and eight every evening, at which point the Upwood family went to the underground shelter. All that Katie had to do was to pretend all was as usual until the sirens sounded, and then once they were in the underground shelter, no one would be able to stop her from going to the clinic.

Once the birth was over, she would be able to call her baby her own and look after the child herself. Who was to say that Katie couldn't brave it out in the world on her own? These days it was easier for unwed mothers to get by alone with all the husbands on the front. War work had led to a proliferation of nurseries. No one needed to know she wasn't married—she could always move away and say her husband had died fighting. Why would anyone single her out?

And there were better jobs for women now, too. Mothers were expected to work in wartime, even if they had young children, so there would be no stigma attached to it. Her mother's fears for her reputation were quickly becoming baseless in this new wartime culture of getting through each day.

Weren't they?

She wasn't completely sure, but there was one thing she was certain about, and that was she wanted to keep her baby, to bring him or her up in a world of love.

Another wave of pain rose up, growing into a massive clench in her stomach. She tried to steady her breathing, counting in the way she'd read about in the books, grabbing the desk, trying to get a grip on herself.

Was it right that it was so painful?

Slowly, it began to subside, and she felt a cool wash of relief come over her. How was she going to get through this?

She looked at the clock. It was only four minutes since the last one. Dread shot through her.

The contractions were coming too quickly.

The time was just after seven o'clock. Where were the sirens? How she longed for that awful, familiar wail to come now.

She couldn't let her mother find out she was in labor until they were in the underground, otherwise her mother would insist on both of them staying at home.

Then suddenly, as if the universe had heard her plea, the noise of the air-raid siren seeped in through the window, gaining power and strength like an angel come to save her.

Relief made her slump down on the bed. All she had to do was pretend everything was normal until she was down underground.

Hasty footsteps came from the corridor, and Katie quickly pulled herself together. By the time her mother entered the room, she had her bag for the shelter on the bed and was busy putting up the blackout blinds.

Her mother moved about the room, organizing things. "Hurry now! And we won't need our pillows and blankets anymore as I've made a contingency plan. We're not going to go to the underground station."

"What?" Reality seemed to slide from beneath her. "What do you mean?"

The siren was rising, but her mother wasn't moving, and Katie felt the dreadful clamp of another contraction coming.

"A while ago, I asked Dorothy Ridley if I could use the Anderson shelter behind her house when my time came." She patted the cushion under her dress. "She was kind enough to say I could have it any time I wanted." She gave a small smile. "So I took the precaution of putting some supplies inside, and we'll be sheltering there until the baby comes." And as she watched Katie's hand go to her head, her jaw clenching with the pain, she added, "It could happen at any time, and now that we'll have some privacy in the Anderson shelter, no one ever needs to know."

Katie tried desperately to keep control of herself. Spasms gripped her abdomen, a pain so sharp she felt like curling up in a ball, screaming in agony. She tried to even her breathing, but it came either in fits and starts or in great gulps of air.

*I have to stay calm,* she thought, getting up and striding to the door, gasping out the words with more difficulty than she'd have liked, "It's not coming tonight, so why don't we just go down to the station as usual? It'll be far more comfortable down there."

But her mother had taken her wrist.

"Not for us," she hissed, inspecting Katie's grimacing face. "It looks like your baby's coming sooner than expected. I think it's time to go to the Anderson, isn't it?" There was a determined iciness in her eyes. "And on the way, you can tell me how long you've been having those contractions."

Katie thought about trying to run, but her head was pounding and she felt dizzy from the pain. How would she be able to get herself to the station in this state?

Grabbing her handbag, her mother led Katie down the stairs and out of the front door, calling to Rupert to go ahead without them.

Oh yes, she had it all planned out this time, so neatly sewn up.

She pulled Katie down the road to the side gate into Dorothy's back garden. The lights in the house were already out, no one to witness her mother dragging her through to the Anderson.

Even in the dark, Katie could make out the small corrugated metal hut sitting among the bushes. It was dug into the ground, only the entrance visible through the shrubs, branches straying across the bottom of the door.

Her mother trod over the undergrowth and pushed open the loose wooden door, and Katie was propelled down into the dark, damp gloom. An oil lamp displayed the tight underground space, a narrow metal bunk on each side.

The place was filthy. The ground was compacted soil going muddy in the corners, and the smell of dampness and cabbage compost was overpowering.

"It's not very clean." Katie grimaced with uncertainty. "What if I get an infection?"

"We'll be fine." Mrs. Upwood began to organize the blankets.

Katie perched on the opposite bunk, her head in her hands, barely able to think. What was she going to do? She couldn't have her child here, the risk was too great. If anything went wrong, it would take an hour at the least to get help, and that was far too long to wait if she or the baby was in danger.

Her mother pulled out a suitcase and set it on the bed. "I have all our supplies in here." Hastily, she began to unpack: the extra blankets, a basin with some glass bottles of water, the scissors for cutting the cord, nothing boiled nor sterilized.

The hut was cramped even with just the two of them, the smell churning Katie's stomach. She eyed the door, but another strong contraction took hold of her, and she curled her body onto the bunk, giving in to the sharp wrench with a loud shriek of pain, something inside her snapping, tearing, wrenching.

Finally, the contraction subsided, and Katie collapsed onto her back, watching as her mother refolded towels and counted the monthly rags. Katie knew she was killing time, trying to look busy, trying to look as if she knew what she was doing.

And that's when it struck her. Katie was the one who had read the books, understood the principles of sterilization and infection. She alone knew the risks. Her mother only had her own experience of two births, both of which had been carried out by trained and experienced midwives.

Katie glanced at the door.

All she had to do was walk out and get to the underground clinic.

But Katie had never defied her mother—she'd never defied authority at all. A tremor went through her. It wasn't in her nature to go against the grain. She couldn't do this on her own.

Could she?

Her mother was busy emptying a bottle of water into an enamel bowl, and Katie winced. The flickering light from the oil lantern cast shadows over the uneven dirt floor, and the door was budged closed to stop the cold night air seeping inside.

She watched her mother's hands tremble as she pulled out the scissors, which rattled between her fingers, the pivot screw loose.

Something about the noise unhinged Katie to her core—she needed more than the woman beside her to make it through this.

And after a new wave of contractions began to subside, she found herself pushing her body to the side of the bunk, putting her feet on the ground, and pulling herself up.

A rush of energy flooded through her, and she knew what she had to do.

"What are you doing?" The scissors clattered out of her mother's hands onto the damp ground with a metallic thud. "Get back onto that bed."

But Katie was suddenly unstoppable, pushing through the door, scrambling to get through the undergrowth around her feet.

Her mother rushed after her, tugging at her hand and her sleeve. "Get back down here," she yelled, the sound echoing around the gardens.

Katie felt herself being yanked back, a hand grabbing her arm, dragging her down into the shelter.

"You need to come back inside!" her mother barked at her as if she were a child, and something in her tone made Katie suddenly beside herself with rage.

"You used to love me, Mum! You'd do anything for me, and now you're forcing me to give birth in this pit of a place, risking me and my baby's lives for the sake of your reputation!"

"I told you before." Her mother held back a sob. "I'm doing what's best for you."

But Katie was heading back out. "This isn't what's best for me, this is what's best for you. I'm going to find somewhere safe."

With that, she threw her mother's hand off her and made her way outside.

"You can't leave!" Her mother's voice had an edge of fear, of panic. "You can't do this to me, Katie! You can't just ruin everything!"

But Katie was already pushing through the bracken to the path up the side of the house.

"Come back!" her mother cried, scrambling up out of the shelter behind her. "You don't understand anything." And through her tears she cried, "We can still do it, you and I, here together! We can do it for our family!"

Katie began to cry as she made for the gate, unable to see if her mother was following her through the darkness.

But then the almighty drone of enemy planes came from overhead, loud and urgent. Katie knew that she had to take cover. She looked into the road and thought of the walk to the underground—would she make it in time?

Then her eyes went back in the direction of the dark shelter. She could faintly hear her mother's voice, now distant, still pleading with her.

And as the noise of the planes became deafening, she knew she had to run.

Off she sped through the park, stumbling over the grass, her heavy belly unbalancing her as she battled on. A plane roared overhead, followed by others, and then suddenly, the whole park and houses were alight with flares dropped from the sky for the bombers to see their targets.

The next contraction came on hard, a ruthless pain cramping her insides, and no matter how much she told herself to keep going, she had to stop, clutching onto a tree, letting herself scream out with pain, free to cry as deeply as her body demanded.

As it subsided, she set back off, the planes circling overhead like vultures after their prey, great explosions sounding from the tenements at the top end of the park.

Reaching the underground, Katie grasped the handrail and plunged down into the light.

She neither knew nor cared if her mother would follow her there.

Without a moment to lose, she hurried down the escalator to the medical clinic.

On the way, she met Juliet. "Katie! Thank goodness you're here! I was so worried. But now I see . . ." Her words petered out as she saw the pained anguish on Katie's face, and quickly, she put her arm around the girl and helped her along.

Katie sobbed with pain. "My mother wanted me to give birth in the Anderson, but I just couldn't."

"You'll be safe here," Juliet said. "Let's put that to the back of your mind for now. You have a bigger job to do."

Luckily, the clinic wasn't busy, and the young nurse leaped up to help her inside. "Dr. Jacobs, we've got one! We've got a birth!" She turned to Katie, taking her pulse. "Have your waters broken yet?"

Katie shook her head as another contraction took hold. Trying her utmost not to cry out, she let the nurse guide her to the cordoned off room at the back. Katie had never been so relieved to see a proper, clean bed. And in that moment, it all made sense. She knew she'd done the right thing for her child.

"I can't believe we've got one at last!" the nurse said with elation, checking her watch to time the contractions. "Stockwell had a baby girl last night, the lucky things!" She took out a clipboard and wrote something down. "Not long to go by the look of you."

The doctor was a kindly man, too old to go to the front line, and he bustled in and peered over her. "Don't mind Nurse Preston, she's been waiting for a baby for weeks. Now, make sure you tell me if things get too much. If need be, we can get you out and to a hospital in ten minutes flat." He nodded, checking his watch. "Right, let's see how you're doing."

As Juliet took her leave and Katie was left alone with the medical staff, she felt a curious sense of freedom: She was on her own now, for better or for worse.

CHAPTER

**36**

# JULIET

THE NEXT DAY THE UNDERGROUND LIBRARY WAS FILLED WITH THE news: Katie had given birth to a lovely baby boy. A great cheer had echoed through the entire underground community: The birth was living proof that Londoners were thriving, regardless how much Hitler bombed them. In the morning, Katie and her new son were whisked away to a maternity home in the countryside.

It was heartbreaking that Juliet had to leave before Katie would return. And as she stood surveying the Underground Library that evening—the final night before her departure—a sadness twisted through her, for the library, for the good times she'd spent there, and for the friends she would miss.

Even with the reduced stock and battered bookcases from the flood, women and men filtered in and out of the aisles, children sat cross-legged on the floor with picture books, Meg busily trying to tidy up around them. Nearby, Dorothy perched on a chair at the newspaper table like a slim silver-white dove; beside her, Marigold flipped through *Vogue*, as flamboyant as a flamingo in a cerise-pink dress. Sofie arrived from work, Mac joining her, sharing a joke or two as they chatted about their day.

It was four days since Victor had come to find her, and tomorrow afternoon, she would be boarding a train for Upper Beeding. All of this, the bustle of her job, the cheery camaraderie of the people, the books and the meetings and the friends, would be a memory.

A quiet excitement spread through her as she thought of her and Victor's future: a pretty cottage, him at his typewriter, her gardening in the sunshine. She'd go back to working in the library, maybe now as a deputy there, too, perhaps with a child on the way.

But Juliet felt her heart breaking that she had to leave the Underground Library behind, especially when its existence was so very precarious. People were already starting to arrive for the reading hour, and ever since Sofie had done the reading, Juliet had realized that it was a good way to show how the war was changing outlooks, how attitudes were shifting.

As Sofie began to read aloud, Juliet remained at the back, leaning against the wall, her mind elsewhere.

Even though she tried to block Sebastian out of her mind, she couldn't stop thinking about him. He'd been away on a work trip for the past week, and she longed to see him before she went, to explain.

But what would she say? It was uncomfortable at best; downright awkward, if she was honest.

Sebastian was a friend—a dear, dear friend—but no more than that, except for inside her mind. He hadn't made any attempts to take it further, or even to kiss her, so why did she feel so uneasy about leaving with Victor? He was her fiancé, promising her marriage, a future. Meanwhile, Sebastian had told her he didn't want anyone special in his life. She thought of Camilla and the other girls at the ARP, how Juliet was probably just another one of his lighthearted flirts. When he'd invited her to the dance, hadn't he added the words "just as friends"?

Deep down, however, remorse coursed through her. No matter how much she denied it to herself, she knew she was leaving Sebastian just as their burgeoning feelings for each other could be growing into something far more than just friends.

But it was too late.

Promises had been made to Victor, who'd come all this way back for her—and she was doing the right thing, wasn't she?

And so when she saw Sebastian coming into the library, she felt a flush come over her. Had he heard the news? What would he say? And how on earth was she to respond?

He was wearing his ARP uniform, probably on his way to the early shift, and as she watched him, a sudden yearning caught her breath, and it was all she could do to stop herself from running over to him and throwing her arms around him.

When he spotted her, he steadily walked through the throng, pausing slightly before he leaned against the wall beside her. "How are you?" he asked.

"I'm fine," she replied. "And you?"

For a moment, he looked at her. "I didn't know if you'd still be here."

"I take it you heard about Victor, that I'm leaving?" Her eyes darted back to the front, unable to meet his.

"I did." He gave her a twisted smile. "Our dear landlady gave me the details."

She looked at the floor. Briefly, she pictured his face as Mrs. Ottley elaborated on Victor's appearance, the lengthy kisses, the professions of love, the plans for the wedding. She felt herself redden under his gaze.

"I've told Mr. Pruitt I'll be leaving tomorrow, and he said he'd make do with the volunteers," she said stiltedly. "I hope it doesn't mean the end for the place. Katie and Sofie are determined to try to keep it going."

"I'm sure you'll be missed." He was distracted, looking around the Underground Library as if trying to gather his thoughts, and then, as if he couldn't hold it in any longer, he said, "Are you sure you're making the right decision, going off with Victor?"

She swallowed. "That's an odd thing to say to a friend who's about to be married."

"Friend?" he murmured, his face serious. "I hope we're friends, Juliet, more than anything else."

Cautiously, she asked, "What do you mean, 'anything else?'"

"Well, I sometimes wondered if . . . But I suppose it doesn't matter anymore. In any case, you were still getting over Victor, and I didn't want to—"

Interrupting him, she murmured, "Perhaps it should have been up to me to decide that."

His eyes softened as he looked at her. "You know that I've always liked you, Juliet. No, more than liked: I've adored you. But the war has taught me that to care for someone is to risk losing them."

Their eyes met, the softness transforming quickly into something else, something disarming, as if he were looking right into her, seeing the confusion, the hurt she carried inside.

He took a step toward her, and she felt her body relax toward his, desperate for his arms around her.

But then his eyes spotted her narrow silver engagement ring, and he stopped. "Juliet, what are we doing?"

Briskly, she shook herself, stepping back. "I don't think either of us know."

"You're getting married, moving to a different place."

She looked at the ground with the truth of it. "And you'll be flirting with the next ambulance driver, I expect."

And there they stood for a moment, and the times they'd had together flickered through her mind, the cooking, the dancing, the laughing, all combined with what might have been, the lovemaking, the togetherness, the family. She had chosen a different path, and he wasn't willing to stop her.

Instead, he put his hand forward to shake hers. "You've been a good friend, Juliet, I'll give you that. We've had fun together, and I've shared things that I would never have told anyone else—I think you have, too?"

Unsure, she nodded. And then, because it felt so natural to do so, she stepped forward and put her arms around him, and together they stood like that, in a bond of friendship, of what they had meant to each other, to mark the end.

Finally, they broke apart, Sebastian taking his leave for his ARP shift. As he left, he turned one last time to her, his eyes intense. "One last thing, Juliet. As your friend, I want you to know that you deserve the very best. You will remember that, won't you?"

Nodding, she swallowed back her tears, determined not to let Sebastian see her cry. As she waved to him and he vanished out of sight, she felt her whole body heave with anguish that she was leaving him, the dashing man who'd become the best friend she'd ever had.

How she wished things could have been different.

And it was with this in mind that later that evening, when everyone had left the library, she lit the lantern she kept under the main desk and slid out a single book from one of the bookcases, *Goodbye to All That*, by Robert Graves, checking it out in her own name.

She would leave it in Mrs. Ottley's house, just outside his bedroom door.

Then she took out a sheet of paper to write a note to slip inside. And in the glow of the lamp, she sat at the desk, her pen poised, ready to wish him well and to ask him to look after Mrs. Ottley for her.

But then she paused. This would be the last chance she would ever have to say anything to him. She owed it to herself—and to him—to be honest.

And so she took a deep breath and began.

*Dear Sebastian,*

*I wondered if this book might help you come to terms with what happened on the front. Please see it as a gesture rather than a remedy, an encouragement to try to get beyond it. The best way through these things, I think, is to talk to others, and I hope that by telling me what you did, you might have begun to make things better. Maybe one day, you'll be ready to start living in earnest again.*

*You once told me that I shouldn't bury my head in the pages of a book, that life is for living. Now I would like to level the same to you. You worry that you've been through too much, that no one will understand. But how will you ever know—how will you ever begin to heal—unless you let love in?*

*Getting to know you has been one of the great pleasures of my life here in London. I neither expected nor encouraged more than just a friendship, but now that I'm leaving, I can admit that*

*there were nights when I dreamed about you, hoping for some-
thing closer, more intimate. I will always remember the night we
went dancing, the fun, the easiness between us, the closeness.
It will remain in my heart forever.*

    *Now I have a different life to begin. I know that I shall miss
you. This war has a long way to go yet, but maybe when it's
over, in years to come, our paths will cross again. Perhaps I will
be on Beeding Hill, and you will be there with your children,
showing them where the badgers live. And when our eyes meet,
I hope that it is with friendship, the bond that carries on even
after we have gone on to live different lives.*

                                  *With love,
Juliet*

# SOFIE

DUSK WAS FALLING AS SOFIE STOOD ON THE QUIET STEPNEY street corner, pulling her scarf close as she took in the heavy bomb damage on the street opposite. The letter from Mrs. Bloom had arrived that morning, and Sofie couldn't wait to visit her, bombs or no bombs.

On the corner of the road opposite a shadow appeared, and she took a step back before recognizing the approaching figure.

"Mac," she whispered, dashing across to meet him. "I was thinking of going without you."

His dark eyes glinted in the dusk as he smiled at her. "Thank you for waiting for me. I couldn't ask for a better job, but they always need me to stay late."

She linked his arm in hers, like they were old friends, and together they scurried down the lane. "Quick, we don't want to miss her."

Mrs. Bloom's was in a long terrace of small two-story houses. The narrow lane became busier as they went, women bustling in and out of each other's houses with shopping bags, pots filled with stews or cooking oils, or with children attached to each hand, looked after by a neighbor for the day. Violin practice was coming from one house, while from another came the voice of an old man singing a Hebrew chant, the inflection so familiar that it jerked Sofie back to her childhood as if it were yesterday.

The young woman who opened the door put a finger to her lips. Pale, she looked them both over without so much as a smile, whispered, "Miss Baumann?" and then beckoned them to follow her through the house to the small, dimly lit back room.

"Mama, she's here."

Around an old dining table sat five middle-aged women, three of them in headscarves, a healthy fire burning in a small fireplace.

The woman at the head of the table gestured for Sofie to take a seat, looking askance at Mac.

Courteously, he bowed his head. "My name is Malachi Perec, from Poland. I've spent the war trying to help people find relatives in Britain and Europe, although I was not able to find Sofie's family."

Sofie watched him, suddenly seeing the upright young man he must have been before he fled Poland.

After seeming to weigh him up, Mrs. Bloom nodded. "All right, you can stay."

There were no other chairs, and he shuffled behind Sofie, leaning against the doorframe as the daughter quietly left.

Mrs. Bloom's eyes met Sofie's. "We have news of your sister Rachel. She was lucky to get one of the visas to Portugal given out in Bordeaux. The Portuguese ambassador there is great friends with the local rabbi and has been bravely defying orders and handing out visas. Luckily, we have access to the list, so we could trace her to Lisbon. We are hoping that her husband is with her." She quietly closed her notebook. "It will be hard to know much more until they move again. Like many others trapped in Lisbon, they can't board a ship to Britain without a visa, and the ships to North and South America are few and costly."

"How can I help her?" Sofie sat forward in her seat. "Can I send food, money? Do you have an address for her?"

Another of the women pushed a square of paper across the table. "They were last known to be in a boarding house in Tejo, a town just outside Lisbon. There are a lot of Jews there, hoping to get passage before the fascists arrive. Portugal is a neutral country, but in Spain, Franco has been eyeing Portugal for a while and may seize his chance to invade."

"Are the Portuguese desperate to be rid of the Jewish refugees?" It was Mac who spoke up.

"Not at all. They're very generous, taking in as many as they can. We owe them a great thanks."

Sofie looked at the address scribbled onto the thin paper, her sister's new married name, Rachel Hoffman, so curious that she found herself mouthing it to herself, as if to test it out.

"You will need to get them British work visas." It was the voice of another of the women, a smaller one, a dark brown headscarf affixed tightly under her chin. "The domestic servant's visa is easiest."

"I could ask a friend to offer them work." She was thinking of Dorothy.

"Have them write an offer of employment for each of them, setting out terms and dates, and send it to your sister. She can use these to get visas at the British Embassy, and that will allow them to get onto a ship. Buy and send a ticket for them, in their names, and for a sailing in a few weeks' time. Money tends to go missing along the way, so only send that as a last resort."

The women looked at their lists and then at Sofie. "Is there anything else?"

With a low cough, Mac stepped forward. "I wanted to know if you could help me find my brother. His name is Uri Perec. When Poland was invaded, he joined the resistance in Krakow." His face had flushed, revealing a desperation. "I have money," he added, bringing a roll of notes from his pocket, putting it on the table with a small square of paper with Uri's name and last known whereabouts.

The women looked at Mrs. Bloom, who slowly looked at the small sheet, ignoring the money.

"Mr. Perec, we use our networks where we can, but it is not easy for us to get behind enemy lines. Vichy France, Spain, and Portugal are quite well documented, and even the low countries have people willing to send details, but Poland is impenetrable."

An older woman who had so far remained silent added, "What little contact we have we are using to try and find out where they are sending the Jews. A Polish officer has infiltrated one of the workhouses, Auschwitz, and he is forming a resistance. I must warn you the messages we've received are gruesome. He reports that many are being systematically worked until they die, and there are indications that some are being killed outright, too. But we need more evidence before the British Government can get involved."

From the other room, a telephone rang, the noise sharp and modern in the humble surroundings. Two of the women rose, guiding their visitors out while someone in the next room answered the phone.

The woman in the brown headscarf handed the roll of money back to Mac. "We will do what we can to find your brother, Mr. Perec, but we can make no promises."

At the door and after a hasty goodbye, Sofie led Mac away. "At least you know you've done what you can."

He swallowed, murmuring under his breath, "Uri is all I have left."

She knew how he felt, that raw anger of not knowing what had happened to his sibling—how lucky she was to have an address for Rachel. Threading her arm through his, she pulled him toward the underground station. "We have each other now. I know that you don't like to rely on anyone, and I was like that, too, but the people at the library have given me so much help. Dorothy has taken me in, made me feel at home, and Juliet, well, I don't know what I'd have done without her."

And then there was Mac, she thought to herself.

And before she could help herself, she was speaking out loud. "Can you imagine if we'd met in a different time, in Berlin or Krakow? It might have been at a music festival, you dressed in a suit and me in one of my evening dresses, my hair properly put up. Papa would have been there, discussing the orchestra with friends, and Rachel, dear Rachel, dancing. Everything would be as it should be"—her face fell—"or rather as it had been."

"It feels like it was a different world."

"It's as if everything's changed and we can't go back—we have been through so much that we can never be the people we were before this stupid war began." She kicked a small stone along the pavement. "I had to grow up fast, and so did you." She glanced up at him, seeing his jaw clench with the thought of how tough and resilient he'd had to become.

But then, out of the blue, he said with a smile, "But let's imagine your dream a bit longer. Perhaps we would have been introduced, spoken awhile, and then maybe I would have asked you for a waltz." He took her hand in his and made a mock bow.

She smiled. "And I would have said, 'Why certainly, Mr. Perec.'"

"Call me Malachi, please!" He smiled back. "And I would hold your hand like this, and put my other hand on your waist." And she felt his hands, warm and firm, on her. "And then the music would begin."

Carefully, slowly, he began to hum under his breath, and together they began to dance, down and around the empty lane, their speed building until they were turning so fast they could have been anywhere else in the whole world.

# JULIET

ON THE DAY OF HER DEPARTURE, JULIET STOOD IN THE UNDER-ground Library, taking a last look around her. It was empty, of course, it being early in the afternoon. She set her suitcase on the floor, tears in her eyes. The book-ladened tunnel had become a haven of peace in a world of chaos, and as she turned, the memories of friendship and merriment warmed her and then melted away.

It had been a few weeks since the floods had devastated the Underground Library, and it looked as if Mr. Pruitt might have finally won his case to close the library down. The councilors were coming soon to decide its fate, and then he could retreat to his safe new job in Suffolk.

"I bought you one of these for the trip, knowing how hungry you always get." Mrs. Ottley came up beside her, handing over a brown paper bag.

She opened it to see a Cornish pasty from the canteen. "My favorite!" she declared, although for once her appetite seemed to have deserted her. Flinging her arms around Mrs. Ottley, she said, "Thank you for everything. You have no idea how much I'll miss you."

"We'll miss you, too, my dear." She took out a handkerchief and blew her nose loudly. "I'm quite sure Sebastian won't be his usual self for a while either."

Juliet flushed. That morning, before she left, she'd slipped the book for Sebastian with the note beside his door. She wondered what he would think when he read it, and a pang of loss wound through her for all they'd become to each other.

Sofie, Dorothy, and Meg were also there to see her off, and the sad little group made their way to the platform.

The tube would take her to Paddington, where she'd catch the one o'clock train. Victor would meet her at the station in Upper Beeding, and as she thought about her new home, her spirit lifted a little.

Victor had written to say that he had booked a time for their wedding next week. There would be a whirlwind of preparations to make, even though it would be a small one, just two of his friends as witnesses.

The westbound platform looked completely different in the daytime, people bustling on and off the trains. The only sign that it was swarming with shelterers every night was the handwritten posters on the walls: *No Saving Places* and *Pick Up Your Litter*.

She gave Meg a hug, pulling away to look earnestly into the girl's eyes. "Now, I'm trusting you to look after Dorothy. If the Underground Library's closed, you know where to find her, don't you?" The girl nodded, giving her another hug.

Dorothy tried to keep a smile on her face as she put her arms around Juliet. "Too many people leaving," she murmured. "You will come back when you can, won't you? Remember, you'll always have a home with us here in Bethnal Green."

Then Mrs. Ottley threw her arms around her. "Oh, I'll miss you, my dear! It's been so lovely to have you with me, and I just want the best for you. I hope your Victor can give you that," she said, blowing her nose loudly.

The lump in Juliet's throat grew, and she couldn't trust herself to speak, pressing her lips together to stop herself from crying. In the end, she gathered herself and said, "Oh, Mrs. Ottley! You're the first person who ever made me feel really at home. I'll miss you so much."

Next it was Sofie's turn. "You're the very best librarian," she said through her tears. "And the best of friends. Thank you for saving my life—and remember, if you're ever in trouble, I am ready to return that favor."

Juliet hugged them for all she was worth, but the train was already coming into the station, the doors opening, beckoning her to her new future.

Pulling herself away, she got on board, watching as they stood together waving, her little world blurring before her eyes.

And then the doors closed and the train shunted forward, plunging into a tunnel, and as quickly as that, Bethnal Green Station and her beloved friends waving on the platform became a thing of the past.

Dolefully, she found a seat and numbly watched the stations go by, mechanically getting off at Paddington and boarding her train. She watched out of the window as the city—battered by the bombs—passed into the suburbs and then into the green fields and gold-brown woodlands dotting the countryside.

It was the same as her journey to London, except in reverse. Now, instead of trying to put Victor out of her mind, she could hardly believe he was alive, not a deserter after all. He had come back home to marry her.

Now, instead of feeling worthless and put down by her parents, she knew she'd accomplished something worthwhile. Even if the Underground Library had to close, it had been a success, and there was a new swing in her step, a new confidence in her abilities. It no longer mattered what her parents thought of her; in her own mind, she had achieved what she'd set out to do. She didn't even care how much they'd disapprove of her marrying Victor. After her months away, their opinions had become irrelevant. Her decisions were now her own responsibility.

The rest of the journey went swiftly, and when the train pulled into the little station at Upper Beeding, she couldn't have been more relieved to see Victor, coming out from the shadows, as handsome as ever.

Hastily greeting her and taking her suitcase, he led her out of a small side gate into the pasture that ran next to the track.

"It's easier to go this way," he said jauntily as he hurried her along, cutting through the field and onto a woodland path. "And it's far more scenic, too."

Once they were in the wood, his pace slowed, and he turned to kiss her properly. "That's better, away from prying eyes," he said as he put down her suitcase and pulled her close. "You know me, I prefer to steer clear of the village."

She laughed. "I remember. But don't worry, I can do the shopping from now on."

"Oh, we won't need to bother with shops. The farm down the road gives us food without using our rations, and it's much fresher." He grinned. "We have fresh eggs every morning, and the meat is incredible. I'm lucky to have found such a place."

"But isn't it illegal to get food off the ration?" As soon as she said it, she wished she hadn't.

He turned to her, a withering look on his face. "Nobody around here sticks to that, and the cottage is on the farmer's land, so officially we're part of the farm."

She changed the subject. "I hope your writing's going well. It must be nice to have your own place again, away from the mayhem."

He smiled, taking her hand in his. "I'd like you to read it when we're back." His eyes strayed down her body. "After we've reacquainted ourselves, that is." He took her face between his hands and gazed into her eyes. "I've missed you so much, my beautiful girl!"

As he kissed her cheeks, her forehead, she felt that charisma that had magnetized her all those years ago. But her smile faltered, a sudden shyness coming over her. So much had happened since she'd seen him—it had been well over a year ago that he'd gone to war—and suddenly it felt as if everything was happening too fast, out of her control.

After quite a walk, they came out of the wood, and Victor pointed at a building on the side of the bare grassy hill. "There it is, our new home!"

Her heart plummeted. The place looked drab and rundown, as if it had been left for derelict. The dark blocks of stone were haphazardly thrown together, probably centuries ago, and since then had been weathered out of shape. The roof was wooden, the timber battered and frayed at the edges.

The wind picked up as they walked to the exposed building. "Isn't it a little far away from the village?" she said quietly, not wanting to state the obvious, that the place seemed no more than a disused hovel.

"As I said, we don't need to go to the village. That's the beauty of it, the romance." He clasped her hand. "It's just us two, here among the elements, like Cathy and Heathcliff."

It was the right thing to say, and she had to smile. "How like you to think of *Wuthering Heights*! But if we're going to have children, it would be better to be closer to the school and the shops, wouldn't it? And I was thinking of taking up my old position in the library, too."

But Victor brought her hand to his lips and kissed it. "Oh, you won't have time for that. I have a pile of articles I need you to read for research. We'll be our own little team again!" He grinned down at her. "And then there'll be meals to cook, a proper home to make. I know you'll have it clean and comfortable in no time."

He led her through the decrepit front door and into a small, low room. "Well, this is it!'" he said, opening his hands.

Two small square windows with cracked, dirty panes shed a mottled light over the stone floor and bare walls. In the middle of the room, a typewriter sat on a table with two chairs. Beside it was an old sofa, empty of cushions. On the far wall, a simple fireplace sat ready with a few logs to burn, some pots beside it.

A worrying thought crossed her mind. "Is there a kitchen?"

"Well," he nodded at the pans. "We do the cooking over the fire, just like they did in the olden days."

She looked around the room. "There is running water, though, isn't there?"

"Of course there is! The tap's outside, and the lavatory's there, too."

Crestfallen, she couldn't help but murmur, "I have to say, I'm a little surprised. You made it sound so lovely, but it's barely habitable."

A shadow crossed Victor's face. "There was nowhere else around, and we can get food here, too. It will be fine for now." He picked up her hand, and she let it fall loosely into his. "Come on, darling. Let me show you around."

His tour of the building entailed leading her into the only other room. "This is the bedroom," he announced portentously.

Juliet looked at the small double bed, nicely made with a new-looking blanket.

And as he sat her down and began to unbutton her coat, she knew why the bedroom had been the next stop. But Juliet was so dismayed by everything around her that she couldn't bring herself to go along with what Victor so clearly wanted.

"Later, my darling. We only have a few hours of daylight left, and there's so much to do. I'd better get started." She walked briskly into the living room. "Why don't you pop down to the farm and get something for dinner, and I'll unpack, light the fire, and put the water on to boil." She smiled, willing him to fall in with her plans.

"All right," he said, although his eyes were on her warily. "But no sneaking off to the village while I'm gone." He said it as a joke, but there was a seriousness lurking behind the façade that didn't seem right to Juliet. Then he turned, and with a nod, he left.

From the window, she watched as he took long strides down the hill, and it wasn't until he was safely out of sight that she sank down onto the moth-eaten sofa, put her face into her hands, and burst into tears.

Why on earth had she agreed to come here?

Her mind went to Mrs. Ottley's house—how far away it seemed, how long ago! The cozy bedroom, the smell of cooking in the air, the sound of Mrs. Ottley pottering around, of Sebastian, too. How she missed them both. And her mind paused as she thought about Sebastian, all the wonderful times they'd had together, the night at the dance, how he'd walked her home. How mesmerizing he was, and how close she had been to falling in love with him. . . .

She let her thoughts trickle away. Why was she thinking of Sebastian? She'd made her bed here with Victor, and now she had to sleep in it. Tomorrow, regardless of whether Victor liked it or not, she would walk to the village, pick up some things for the house, and some food, for heaven's sake. And then she'd pop into the library, too. After all, there's nothing like a good book to settle the nerves.

# KATIE

THE ROYAL LONDON HOSPITAL'S MATERNITY DEPARTMENT HAD BEEN evacuated to an old rectory just outside London, and Katie's ward was a large, airy drawing room, converted for the purpose. After the birth, an ambulance had driven Katie and her new baby there. Now, only a few days later, she was sitting up in bed, her new son in her arms, with two friends up from London for visiting hour.

"What a lovely place to have a baby!" Sofie said. It was her day off, and she and Dorothy had come to make sure Katie was doing alright.

"It's just what I needed—what *we* needed." Katie leaned her head forward to smell the soft, sweet head of the baby. "Most of the people here are lovely, but I've had a few remarks about not being married. It's to be expected, I suppose."

"You can't let what people say bother you," Dorothy said. And she added, "In any case, not everyone is so judgmental. The regulars in the Underground Library want to know how you are." She leaned forward to stroke the baby's fluffy dark hair. "Little Johnny already has plenty of fans. He's been dubbed the 'underground baby.' Word went around as soon as you went into labor, with updates every hour, people crowding into the library waiting for the big news. When the nurse announced that you'd given birth, the whole place erupted in cheers."

Katie looked down into the little face, his eyes tight shut in sleep. "Did you hear that, Johnny? You're famous in Bethnal Green!"

Sofie passed across a small package wrapped in newspaper. "Meg asked me to give you this."

Unwrapping it, Katie pulled out a handmade puppet made from an old gray sock with sewn-on green fabric circles for eyes and a red tongue. She slipped it on to show Johnny, even though he was still fast asleep.

Dorothy continued, "Meg's especially eager for your return. The Underground School won't reopen until you're there to head it. And that leads me to another thing." She reached into her handbag. "Irene wanted you to have this."

It was a book. "*School Discipline and the New Psychology.* How intriguing," Katie said, flicking open the thick tome. "Just like Irene to keep up-to-date with all the new ideas."

"I think she had you earmarked as her successor." Dorothy grinned. "Although I'm sure she wouldn't mean for you to start teaching as soon as you're back."

"And obviously you shouldn't worry about helping in the Underground Library either," Sofie added quickly. "We have that in hand for now, although it won't be the same without Juliet."

They glanced despondently at each other. Juliet's departure was both sudden and sad, and in the midst of her own events, Katie struggled to come to terms with not being able to say goodbye.

Dorothy dug into her handbag and pulled out a knitted baby blanket. "And Mrs. Ottley made this for you. She said that once you're ready to come home, she would be happy to have you and Johnny stay with her."

Sofie smiled encouragingly. "She adores babies, and now that Juliet's gone, she'd love the company."

But Katie let out a deep sigh, shaking her head. "That's very generous of her, but I'm not sure. It's too close to my mother. I just want to be as far from her as possible—and I'm sure that she feels likewise."

Cautiously, Sofie asked, "Did you know that she had a bad fall? They think it's a fractured hip."

Aghast, Katie sat forward. "What? No, I didn't know. I haven't heard anything from her since the birth."

"It happened on the night of Johnny's birth," Sofie continued. "The ambulance crew picked her up during the air raid after she'd struggled home from the Anderson shelter."

Letting out a gasp of dismay, Katie murmured, "I suppose that explains why she didn't follow me to the underground." She felt her breath quicken. "I thought she didn't come because she was too angry with me. It never crossed my mind that she didn't come because she couldn't." Tears began to course down her face as her pulse raced. "I should have gone back to check on her."

"You can't blame yourself, Katie," Sofie said. "It was an accident."

"But Mum will blame me!" She leaned her head forward, crushed. "What have I done?"

On the other side of her, Dorothy took her hand. "You can't think like that now. You have your lovely baby, and you have to focus on him."

Tentatively, Sofie asked, "Maybe when you're back and she's out of the hospital, you can go to see her?"

Katie hesitated. "I don't know if I can. How can I ever trust her again? And how will she ever forgive me for ruining the family?"

"Maybe she feels differently about it now that the deed is done."

"I doubt it, not now that it's common knowledge that I had a baby outside of marriage." She heaved a great sigh. "Even though I'd never regret what I did to keep Johnny, I do wish it had been done better."

Putting an arm around her, Dorothy said, "Perhaps you'll be able to settle everything once you're back in London."

"I don't know if I can ever trust her. Now that I have Johnny, I have to think of what's best for him." As she pulled her baby closer, all Katie knew was that she would do anything in the world for him, and whatever her mother wanted from her, she couldn't risk going down that path again. She had far too much to lose.

The sound of a bell announced the end of visiting hour, and after a sad farewell, Sofie and Dorothy left. As they reached the door, Sofie turned one last time as if to double-check, smiling as she saw Katie watching, trying to wipe the worry from her face.

And then her two friends were gone, the ward going back to its usual business as the nurses began to scurry about, checking charts and taking temperatures.

It was only as the last of the visitors left that someone caught Katie's eye. It was a slender, older woman, spruce in her WVS skirt suit, striding for the door, and Katie found herself cowering lower in her bed.

Mrs. Baxter was the very last person Katie wanted to see. The woman must have come to see one of the other new mothers, no doubt one with a legitimate child.

Katie's heart sank. She knew Mrs. Baxter well enough to imagine her scorn—the woman could smell immorality from fifty yards, for heaven's sake—so she dipped her head down into the soft sweet baby in her arms, hoping she wouldn't see her.

But as Mrs. Baxter's footsteps paused and then headed in her direction, Katie knew it was too late.

"Is that you, Katie Upwood?" Mrs. Baxter said, her incomprehension making her even more abrupt than usual. "What on earth are *you* doing here?"

Katie took a deep breath and said as proudly as she could, "I have a beautiful baby boy, Mrs. Baxter."

Immediately, the woman's beady eyes narrowed. "But you're not married! Isn't it your mother who was pregnant? I heard she's in the hospital. . . ."

Katie held herself back from explaining that her mother was actually *pretending* she was pregnant—surely that would only make matters worse, wouldn't it?

And in that instant, she found herself suddenly on the same side as her mother against this new, greater enemy: Mrs. Baxter and the people like her. After all, it was their old-fashioned notions that had ended up endangering her life—and the life of her child.

Trying to hold her head high, Katie said, "No, I am not married, Mrs. Baxter. My fiancé went to war, and he didn't make it home."

"So the child is illegitimate?" Mrs. Baxter demanded as if this were the only reasonable and natural response—commiserations for her loss nor congratulations for her birth weren't even considered.

Suddenly, Katie realized how unkind and uneducated this woman must be to think that this was the only rational thing to say. And instead of reaching for excuses, trying to placate Mrs. Baxter, she began to use her head. "I think you'll find that society's views of birth outside of marriage have fluctuated greatly over the past centuries, and to come to such a narrow conclusion is very shortsighted in the larger historical context. Legitimacy only became an issue in the Middle Ages, I think you'll find."

The woman frowned, confused for a moment before sneering, "But none of that will save your family name, nor your mother's place in the women's groups, will it?"

"Surely if the purpose of the women's groups is to raise funds for those in need, then my mother deserves a place if she can raise money? Or are you willing to take money away from the needy simply to prove a point?"

But Mrs. Baxter was shaking her head. "The needy don't want money from a woman with an illegitimate grandchild." The woman's lips twitched as she watched Katie's reaction. "And of course we all know she's heading for divorce, too."

"Divorce?" Katie let out a gasp. "I didn't think it had come to that."

But Mrs. Baxter wasn't paying attention. "Once she's divorced, she won't be welcome anywhere. Our local organizations are respectable ones, and we couldn't possibly welcome divorcees or," she glanced disgustedly at poor Johnny, "illegitimates."

Instinctively, Katie pulled Johnny to her.

"Most clubs and employers won't have divorced women for fear they'll spread their immorality." She eyed the baby with disparagement. "Neither of you will be wanted anywhere." And with a sneering, "Well, good luck to you—you'll need it," she strode out.

Katie's mind reeled. *Were her parents really getting a divorce?*

And it suddenly dawned on her: Was this why her mother had been so adamant about hiding her pregnancy—was there far more on the line than Katie had ever realized?

Had she been thinking about this the wrong way around?

CHAPTER

**40**

# JULIET

A THIN MORNING MIST COVERED THE REMOTE, GRASSY HILL, THE smell of decaying leaves and spent fires in the air, as if the place itself were already rotting. As Juliet half walked, half ran through the wood to the village, she couldn't help worrying that Victor might be home before her.

She'd forgotten how easily his temper could be triggered, and now that she'd had a taste of independence, having to tiptoe around him was exhausting.

Her first evening in the cottage had been a fraught one. After she'd made a vegetable soup for dinner—no fresh eggs or meat to be seen—they had spent the evening discussing Victor's book. At the end of the evening, she'd told him that she needed a few nights on her own to "get used to things," appealing to his gentlemanliness, and he'd reluctantly agreed, vanishing into the bedroom with a hurt silence.

She'd hardly slept a wink, her mind too busy. Why was she so reluctant to sleep with him? He would be her husband soon, after all. She shouldn't be holding herself back. Maybe it was tied to her disappointment about the cottage, or had they simply been apart too long? It was bound to feel a lot more normal once she got into the swing of things.

The morning seemed better. Once breakfast was out of the way, Victor plunged into his writing for an hour or two, and then he got up and stretched, his body lean and taught. "What I need is a good walk to think through this new chapter." He looked at her as she cleaned one of the windows. "Will you join me?"

Wiping her brow with the back of her wrist, she slowly shook her head. "I'd better get on with this. I've got the other one to do, too." She looked around the room with a smile. "I'm sure we'll both feel better once it's nice and clean," she added, to make sure he left her to carry on by herself.

She went back to cleaning, watching through the cracked glass until he was out of sight. Then, without a second to lose, she put the cloth down and found her coat. She knew that if she'd asked him, Victor would never have allowed her to go to the village, and in situations like this, it was better to act as if she thought he wouldn't mind.

Hastily, she'd leafed through the papers on the table for his ration book—whatever Victor said, she needed to buy some food. She loathed going through anyone's personal belongings, but Victor's documents were muddled together, research papers nestling with the military papers of another man, probably the source of the identity confusion in France. Finally, she spotted his ration book under the bed, scooping it up and dashing out.

It was surprisingly comforting to see the village again, and as she walked down the main road, she glanced into the shops. Nothing seemed to have changed at all since she'd been away. A few people waved to her, and she waved back and hurried on.

When she spotted the library on the corner, her spirits lifted. She opened the door and took a great, calming breath of the book-scented air, basking in the friendly buzz of the place as people drifted in and out.

"Juliet Lansdown, is that you?" The voice behind her sounded familiar.

And as Juliet turned, her heart exploded with joy. "Mrs. Ottley!"

But as the woman began to laugh, Juliet quickly realized that it wasn't her dear old landlady, but her older sister, Mrs. Falconbury—Sebastian's mother. "No, but it's very flattering to be mistaken for her. She's quite a few years younger than me, you know." She chuckled, reminding Juliet once again of her London home, and she held back an urge to throw her arms around her and burst into tears.

"I didn't know that you were home," Mrs. Falconbury said. "Did you move back in with your parents?"

Juliet blanched. "No, actually. I'm getting married to Victor Manning next week." She carefully refrained from saying precisely where she was living.

But a frown came over Mrs. Falconbury's face. "Victor Manning? I thought he'd vanished."

Juliet smiled, not really wanting to discuss it. "He was honorably discharged, and now he's back to his writing, renting a house up behind the big farm beyond the wood."

But Mrs. Falconbury only looked more baffled. "Discharged? I wonder when that happened? The police were in the village looking for him only last week." She put a kind hand on Juliet's arm. "I hope he isn't wanted for anything serious, my dear."

Juliet's stomach tightened. What was the woman saying?

Perturbed, she gathered her wits enough to put on a polite smile, bidding Mrs. Falconbury goodbye before rushing out. Wrenching open her bag, she sifted through it for Victor's ration book. At last, she dug it out and opened it.

A jolt of alarm shot through her as she read the name: Percy Foreman.

Shaking, she shoved the ration book into her bag and began to stride back to the cottage, her pace speeding into a run.

Suddenly, everything fell into place: Why Victor was living in an unused hovel in the middle of nowhere, why he was avoiding the village, getting food illegally from the farm, and why he had refused to buy anything for their home.

It was clear as the new day: Victor was in hiding.

And as she came out of the wood and looked at the building so far from civilization, she realized just how dangerous the situation was for her.

She had to pack her things quickly, escape before he got back and realized she'd found out about him.

The moment she reached the house, she yanked her suitcase from under the bed and began throwing her things into it. Fortunately, she hadn't unpacked a great deal for want of any cupboards or drawers, and it was mere minutes before she was reaching for the front door.

But as she went to grab the handle, it was pushed open from the other side.

And there was Victor, his smile becoming a scowl as he took in the suitcase, the coat.

"What's going on?" he growled, stepping into the doorway and forcing her back into the house. "Where do you think you're going?"

She couldn't pretend she wasn't leaving, so she turned around and pulled out the military papers she'd seen earlier. "Why do you have someone else's papers, Victor?"

"You shouldn't be going through my things," he snapped, adding, "But if you must know, it's the man who deserted, the one they thought was me."

She looked at the name, half expecting it to be Percy Foreman, but it wasn't. It was Mark Brinton. "How many different people are you, Victor?"

He grabbed her arm and tugged her toward him until their faces were almost touching. "You think yourself so high and mighty, don't you? How dare you judge me! You don't understand anything about this war."

Juliet knew she had to calm him down. "Victor," she said gently. "I want to understand, truly I do. You have to tell me what happened. The truth this time."

He released her and fell back onto the sofa, raking his hands through his hair.

"Even though I was injured—not a deserter at all!—the army seems to think otherwise. The military police found out I'd managed to get back into the country. They're determined to lock me up, take me to court." He clenched his jaw with annoyance. "It's a conspiracy."

Unsure that it was, but deciding to use caution, she replied, "But how did you get back to England without anyone noticing? Surely your papers would have given you away."

"Look, I'm not proud of it, but it was hell out there on the front. Then when I was left on my own, I knew I had to get to the coast.

France was in chaos after the surrender, and it was easy to slip through the country unnoticed. A couple of us stowed away on a fishing boat and overpowered the fisherman once we were at sea. We got him to drop us on the south coast of England in the dead of night." He slumped back in the chair, lowering his face into his hands. "I don't deserve this. All I did was survive."

"But you can't hide away forever."

He looked at his hands. "Now that you're here, it'll be easier. I'll have some company, and you'll be able to go to the shops in the next town where no one would recognize you."

Suddenly, it struck her that he hadn't realized that she'd been to the village. Then with a shudder, she remembered that she'd told Mrs. Falconbury where Victor was living. She had to leave before he realized what she'd done.

Petrified, she abandoned her suitcase and leaped to her feet. "I need some fresh air." She grabbed her coat. "There's a lot to think about."

In a flash, he was in front of her, standing between her and the door. "I know you're trying to leave me, but you can't! What about getting married, having children, our life together?"

Trying to stay patient, she said, "But how can this possibly work out, Victor?"

"They'll drop all charges at the end of the war, or the Nazis will invade and it'll be forgotten."

He tried to put his arms around her, but she struggled free, moving around him to the door. Turning, he caught her arm, his grip suddenly strong, his fingernails digging into her. "No, you don't!"

He dragged her back down onto the sofa with a violence she'd never seen in him before.

"Let me go back to London," Juliet pleaded with him. "No one needs to know that you're here." She was ready to tell him anything to get away. "I could send you money, food. It'll help you stay here, make sure you don't get caught."

"But how can I trust you if you aren't willing to be with me?" he said through gritted teeth. "You're just like all the rest of them."

Quietly, she said, "But it's not your fault, Victor. Surely it's better to hand yourself in, explain what happened to you? I think you'll find them more understanding than you imagine."

He put his head in his hands. "I can't believe this is happening," he said. "My name will be ruined, all my work, everything I've ever done."

"But you're not a military man, Victor. They'll take that into consideration, and then there's the fact that you joined up as soon as war was declared. That's not cowardly. That proves you had good intentions." She put an arm around his shoulders, trying to calm him, and then she heard something outside.

He must have registered it, too, as he looked up at the door. "What's that?"

Voices became distinct, men coming up from the lane. "It's probably just farmworkers," she said, trying to pacify him.

But then a knock came on the door. "Is anyone in there?" said a man's voice.

Victor's eyes were on hers, questioning her, and then he got up, creeping toward the door.

The knock came again. "Anyone there?"

And then, all of a sudden, the door was kicked in and three policemen pushed their way into the room. Victor pulled back a hand to throw a punch, but one of them wrestled his arm down while another pulled out his handcuffs.

It was over in seconds, Victor quickly subdued, a frown on his face as they led him outside and marched him down the lane. He didn't look back at her, only at the ground in front of him.

The remaining policeman searched the small room, taking the papers.

"I bet you're glad that's over," he said, guiding her to the door. "We'll need a statement from you, Miss Lansdown, if you'll come with me."

And it struck her that he knew her name without her mentioning it.

By the time they reached the police station, Victor was out of sight, locked up in a cell behind the building awaiting the military police. Juliet was taken to a small room, where the policeman took down a statement.

"I need an address for you, if you have one?" he asked her at the end.

Without hesitation, she said, "41 Bethnal Green Park, in London." And suddenly, through all the fear, she felt a tremendous wave of relief. She would be able to go back to her friends, back to Mrs. Ottley's house, back to the Underground Library.

Once the police had finished with her, she made her way outside. Alone and rather shaken, she walked ponderously up the main road to the station, her small suitcase in her hand. Life was going on as usual in the bustling little place, and it wasn't until she was passing the shops that a voice came from beside her.

"Oh thank goodness you're all right." It was Mrs. Falconbury, coming out of the doctor's office as she saw Juliet passing. "I hope I didn't step out of line, but I felt compelled to tell someone about Victor. You looked so fraught when you hurried away." She lowered her voice. "My sister would have my guts for garters if I didn't keep an eye out for you."

Juliet's eyes went to hers. "I wondered if I had you to thank for the very timely police escort." She made a small, self-conscious sigh, feeling a sense of normality start to settle back in. "I was relieved to have it brought to an end."

"I'm sorry dear, it must have been quite a shock."

But Juliet only nodded. "Yes, but it's also made me realize what's important, Mrs. Falconbury." And then, in spite of all that had happened, she smiled. "And now if you'll excuse me, I have an Underground Library to save."

With that, Juliet darted away to catch the next train to London, Mrs. Falconbury calling, "Good luck with your library!" to her down the small high street.

After a short wait, the train arrived, and in the hours that followed, Juliet went over all that had happened, concluding that Victor, his temperament, and his character had never been right for her. He had praised her to draw her into his orbit, only to make her world smaller. No one would ever be able to do that again.

The journey was interminable. Troop trains held her up twice, and it was early evening by the time the tube train pulled into Bethnal Green Station. As the doors opened and she stepped out, she saw the familiar signs on the wall, and a flutter of comfort washed through her. How lucky she was to have Bethnal Green to welcome her, and how good it felt to be back.

Her pace quickened as she walked through the tunnels, suitcase in hand, but it wasn't until she turned the corner into the Underground Library that she broke into a run, putting down her suitcase and dashing through the crowd, pulling Mrs. Ottley into her arms, unable to hold back the tears of relief.

"I was wondering when you'd arrive," Mrs. Ottley said.

"Did your sister tell you I was on my way home?"

Mrs. Ottley gave her a sympathetic nod. "She told me the whole story. What a dreadful time you've had! I'm only sorry I can't take you home right now and make you a good hearty pie." She sniffed plaintively. "Although it might have to be whale meat again."

In only a few moments, a small crowd was forming to welcome Juliet back.

"Thank goodness you've returned!" Dorothy said. "We tried everything we could to persuade Mr. Pruitt to stop the library closure, but since you left he's become determined—something about him taking a new post in Suffolk. You're the only one who has a chance of saving it."

Juliet sighed. "I'll do my best, but I might not be in Mr. Pruitt's good graces after leaving so recklessly."

Grabbing her arm, Sofie begged, "But you have to do what you can." She gestured to the throng that was gathering for reading hour. "It's not just for us, Juliet. It's for all these people, too."

Around them was a great crowd of faces, people sitting on the floor and on chairs, a growing contingent standing at the back, all waiting for the book reading to begin.

"Why don't we get on with the reading," Juliet said, "and we'll discuss what we can do later."

She went to take a seat, looking forward to a rest after her travels.

But Sofie pulled her to the front, announcing to the crowd, "Good evening, everyone! We have great news—we're absolutely thrilled to have our dear deputy librarian home, Miss Juliet Lansdown."

Applause echoed through the passageway, accompanied by some whistles and cheers, and as Juliet saw the beaming faces looking up at her, she knew she could never have stayed away.

And as the crowd settled for the reading to begin, Sofie grinned as she passed her a battered copy of *Death on the Nile*, whispering, "We're on chapter two."

# SOFIE

By THE TIME SOFIE AND DOROTHY WERE MAKING THEIR BEDS ON
the hard underground floor, it was already approaching lights-out. It
had been a busy day, but tonight Sofie had something very special to
ask Dorothy, and as they began to settle down on the blankets, Sofie
seized the chance.

"I know you have been so very good to me already," she began as
she lit the candle between them. "But I have a great favor to ask." She
pulled out the slip of paper that Mrs. Bloom had given her. "This is an
address for my sister Rachel and her husband Frederick. A Jewish network in Stepney found them, and now we've discovered that they've
made it to Lisbon, which is wonderful"—she paused, unsure how to
put it—"only they can't get passage to Britain without a work visa."

She waited for Dorothy to make the connection, to offer some help,
but she only looked expectantly at Sofie, waiting for the next part.

Shifting, Sofie said, "I wondered if you might consider taking in a
housekeeper and a gardener. You don't have to pay them—I can cover
their costs—just get them the visas so that they can stay in the country.
It would only be for a little while, until they can find war work—I'm
sure with her language skills, Rachel will get a government job like
mine; Frederick, too."

"Of course they must come!" Dorothy beamed. "We could always
do with extra help, and you're too busy with your job and these wretched
air raids to look after the house. A gardener would be very useful, too.

We could have a proper vegetable garden to make up for the food rations." Her eyes glistened as she looked into Sofie's. "I'm glad you found them! There's nothing like having your sister beside you."

A tear ran chaotically down one cheek, and Sofie couldn't help but reach over and give the old lady a hug. "You truly are the best friend a person could ever have."

"Oh, it'll be lovely to have another one just like you coming to stay!" Dorothy gave Sofie a great smile.

That made Sofie laugh. "She's far better a cook than I'll ever be."

The conversation went on, Dorothy asking Sofie about her family, deciding which bedroom they could have ready, what she could do to make them feel more at home when they arrived. All the while that Sofie chatted, her mind imagined Rachel there. It seemed so incredible—she could barely even let herself believe it.

A movement at the end of the passage revealed Mac, walking carefully toward them balancing three cups in his hands.

"Hello again," he said, his eyes meeting Sofie's before handing one of the cups to Dorothy. "I had a bit of time, so I thought I'd get you some tea. I was going to ask if you'd like me to set up your beds for you, but I see you've done it already."

"What a capable young man!" Dorothy said. "Won't you introduce us?"

Sofie knew that Dorothy had seen Mac with her—they spent quite a few evenings together and Mac was always in the Underground Library—but she made a formal introduction, nonetheless. "Mac is from Poland. He's a friend helping me find my family," she said, wondering if that was enough—do you talk as much with a friend? Do you waltz down the middle of a road with one, half hoping he'd take you into his arms?

Carefully, she pulled herself together, busying herself plumping up some cushions.

"Is he your young man?" Dorothy whispered, her eyes gleaming in a way Sofie hadn't seen since Irene's death.

"Don't be silly," she whispered back, but she could feel herself blush.

"Well, we're very grateful for the tea, Mac," Dorothy said to him, warming her hands around the cup. "Do you sleep in the underground yourself?"

He sat down on the floor beside Sofie. "Sometimes, but I work long hours."

"Whenever you shelter down here, you must camp with us, if you'd like. Do you live far from here?" Dorothy asked, waiting for his answer with an expectant smile. How she could ease information out of him so cleverly was quite a spectacle, Sofie thought, as he expanded on how he now rented a room in a larger mansion, how he felt he could sleep anywhere after his escape across Europe.

Before long, his full story came out, followed by numerous questions to ensure that Dorothy had left no detail unexplored. Parts of his tale were new to Sofie, and she listened intently as the difficulties, injuries, and terrors of his flight were gradually unraveled.

Dorothy watched as he glanced at her small pile of paperbacks. "Would you like to borrow one of them?" she asked him. "There's nothing like a good read before going to sleep, don't you think?"

But Mac was busy picking up the one on the top, *The Metamorphosis*. "The Nazis banned Kafka in Poland," he said. "There's something rather otherworldly about seeing it here, as if there is still hope, a place where all the books continue to exist, whether their authors are Jewish or, well, whoever they are."

"I read that there's a library in New York where they're keeping a copy of every Jewish book banned by the Nazis to make sure at least one of each is left in the world." Dorothy watched him flicking through the book. "But perhaps you should read *The Metamorphosis* again, just in case. A book isn't just a physical object; once you've read it, it becomes a thought, a story, a memory that is alive inside you forever. Whatever the Nazis take from us, they can't take that."

"After the invasion, one of the first things they did was burn our books," Mac said. "Every Polish-language book was destroyed, every publisher burned to the ground, and every bookshop containing anything in Polish was demolished. They wanted to eradicate every part of Polish culture. We were part of their *Lebensraum* campaign—the expansion of Germany—and completely obliterating our language, our ideals, and our past was part of their Germanification program."

"That's what I heard," Sofie said. "The Nazis are destroying the traditions and values of every country they occupy, a kind of cultural eradication."

"It sounds as if the Nazis want you to forget what it's like to be Polish," Dorothy said.

Mac nodded, his jaw tightening. "But the more they try, the more we cling to it, the more we talk about stories from the past, share our own memories. I helped an underground publisher for a while in Krakow before I had to flee. He hid his printing presses and put them to good use churning out newsletters from the resistance and the exiled government in London. It was the only way we had to circulate the truth." He took a deep breath. "I can only hope they're still going."

They fell into silence, looking at the small pile of books beside the bags, suddenly realizing how precious they were—how much worse things could be.

The threat of a Nazi invasion onto the south coast of England was growing by the week. British defenses were being crushed by the Blitz and the sheer size and strength of the Nazi force. They seemed unstoppable, as if they could march into any country they chose.

By the time the lights went out at ten o'clock, Mac had become part of the little circle, with Dorothy insisting that he bed down on their "patch" for the night, and he thanked her, leaving the candle flickering to read his book long after they'd fallen asleep.

And so it was with a strange shudder that Sofie awoke in the middle of the night, opening her eyes to see Mac, lying on his side, his face toward hers. In the dim light of the candle, she saw that his eyes were closed, the even rhythm of his breathing indicating that he was asleep.

A soft smile touched her lips as she watched him, and she found herself studying his features. In sleep, he looked younger. She could see the boy he'd been, so different from the hardened man he'd had to become. That he had worn a uniform and fought for his army at such a young age seemed incongruous. It was as if the world were backward, asking the young to fight when they had so much life ahead of them.

Instinctively, she put out her fingers to touch the skin on his face, to feel the softness of his neck; but a few inches away, she held herself back, scared that he'd wake up and see her watching him, that he'd guess how she felt, that it might bring their friendship to an end.

She liked him far too much for that.

He stirred. Hurriedly, she pulled her hand away, but his eyes flickered open, alighting on her. Uneasily, she bit her lip, sensing her breath speeding, willing it to slow down. Without making any sound, she mouthed, "How are you?"

"Good," he mouthed in reply, a smile on his lips.

Silence hung in the air. They were less than a foot apart from each other, both on their sides. She was left grappling for something to say, anything to fill the void, to make this overly familiar situation more normal.

He must have felt the same, as he shifted onto his back, crossing one ankle over the other, his hands behind his head as if this were an everyday occurrence, nothing to worry about at all.

"I hope I didn't wake you up, me being here when it's normally just you and Dorothy?" He turned his head to whisper to her.

"It's all right. I woke up by myself. Sometimes the floor is too hard."

"You were fast asleep by the time I stopped reading," he said, and she wondered if he, too, had been watching her as she slept.

Cautiously, she put her hand up to tidy her hair. Had he?

"I only wanted to make sure I wasn't disturbing you," he whispered. "You look so peaceful when you sleep," he said, following hastily with "and doing your job, you must need plenty of rest."

"And you must, too," she replied.

The silence was left a little longer this time, only disrupted by Dorothy turning in her sleep.

Sofie put her finger to her lips so as not to disturb her, although she acknowledged guiltily that it was more because she didn't want this moment to be interrupted.

He slid back over onto his side, slightly closer to her. "We should get some sleep, too," he mouthed, smiling as their eyes met.

"Yes, we should," she mouthed back, suddenly unable to think of anything to prolong their chat. "Goodnight."

"Goodnight" he whispered, his voice soft in the flickering dimness.

Unsure what else she could do, she closed her eyes, wondering if he was watching her, using this opportunity to take in her face, her features, her lips—was he, too, wondering what it would feel like to kiss her?

There was a heat that came from him, if she thought about it hard enough, although perhaps it was her imagination willing it to be there, just his presence making her feel cozy, peaceful. The feeling was so welcome, calming yet exhilarating, that she vowed to stay awake all night, reveling in his closeness.

And that was the last thing she remembered until she woke up the next morning, the bright underground lights coming on as usual at six.

*Had it been a dream?*

Her eyes flashed open, but he was gone.

She sat up, straightening her hair, her clothes, looking at the place where he'd been.

His blankets were gone. The cushion was back by the wall. There was nothing to indicate that he had been there at all only the copy of *The Metamorphosis* beside her.

Slowly, she got up, leaning over to gently shake Dorothy and say good morning, wishing she'd been able to say it to Mac, too, and hoping he might come to sleep with her again some night soon.

# KATIE

H ER SMALL SUITCASE PACKED AND JOHNNY IN HER ARMS, KATIE stood at the door of her ward in the maternity home, not wanting to leave. She'd become accustomed to the routine, the nurses' care for her and the baby, for their shared responsibility for him.

"You'll be absolutely fine." The matron had come to see her off. "You're a good learner. Johnny couldn't be in better hands." Although he was getting stronger, he was still such a tiny thing. It felt like he might break or she might drop him if she wasn't careful. The nurses had taught her how to bathe and feed him, to check his health. But was she ready to do it all on her own?

"H-he seems so fragile." Her hands felt trembly and clumsy.

"Take him to your doctor when you get home. Don't you have a mum nearby, or a husband coming home from the front?"

"N-no," she stammered uneasily. "My fiancé was killed."

Sympathetically, the matron took something small from her pocket. "Well, you'd better have this for now. Might make things easier."

She didn't say any more, and as Katie looked at the plain metal ring the woman held out in her hand, she understood. Embarrassed, she slid it onto her finger, muttering her thanks to the matron, who gave her a brief nod, as if to say, "You'll need all the luck you can get."

With a heavy heart, she bid her farewells to the other women in the ward and slowly made her way to the front door. Outside, a car was waiting to take her the short ride to the station, and before long she was standing on the platform, clutching the baby, waiting for the one-thirty to London.

There was no one else there, only a bad-tempered stationmaster and a few magpies pecking up crumbs on the opposite side of the tracks.

She was alone.

A cold wind blew through her coat and around her legs, and she couldn't wait to get home . . . but she wasn't going home, was she? Unwilling to burden anyone and wanting to be as far from her mother as possible, she'd decided to rent a room on the other side of Bethnal Green. It would be better if she was on her own, focusing on Johnny, not having to be cheerful for anyone.

As she looked down the empty platform, a vision went through her mind of how this day might have been in better circumstances. Her mother would have come to collect her, delightedly parading her through the park, hoping for the neighbors to pop out and coo over her beautiful new grandson. The Upwood home would be filled with toys and gifts, new baby blankets, and the best pram money could buy. There'd be cards and flowers, maybe even a cake to welcome her home.

But none of that was going to happen. Her mother was probably still in the hospital with her fractured hip, oblivious to her departure from the maternity home, unaware of the fact that her daughter and new grandson were to be living on the other side of town. She would have heard about the birth, no doubt—who could miss hearing about the underground baby—but did she even think about Katie?

The sound of the engine came from the distance, and soon the train drew into the station.

As she looked at the carriage door in front of her, Katie felt like running back up the platform stairs, stopping a car and begging to be taken back to the safety of the maternity home. What were they thinking, leaving her alone with such a small baby? She'd only just stopped being a schoolgirl, for heaven's sake, and now she was to be a mother?

"Are you getting in, Miss?" It was the stationmaster, eyes glowering, holding his whistle two inches from his pursed mouth.

Not trusting herself to speak, she nodded, and he opened the door for her.

Struggling with the baby and her bags, she clambered onto the train. Johnny's blankets were so cumbersome that she felt like she was going to drop him, and she tried to pull herself together as the station-master slammed the door shut behind her.

The carriage was full. Eventually, she found a place to stand in the corridor, clutching hold of Johnny and gazing out of the window as the train chugged out of the station.

She watched the haze of brown fields and green woodlands, thinking about the look on the nurses' faces when she'd told them, "My fiancé was killed."

She felt a breath catch in her throat. What had happened to Christopher? There had been no further explanation, no recovery of his body, only his personal items returned from the army base: a photograph of his family, a slim volume of Plato's *Symposium*, and a crossword book, finished and rubbed out again. He must have had her photograph with him when he vanished, and a sense of relief that he'd truly loved her mixed inexorably with dismay as she realized that it must have been his most treasured possession.

Her face fell. Whenever she'd thought of their future, their family, she'd always thought he'd be there beside her.

In her arms, little Johnny began to stir. His eyes flickered up at her before his mouth opened wide, pausing for a heartbeat before he let out an almighty cry.

She began to panic, pulling him into her and jiggling to try to calm him. He might be hungry by now, but how could she breastfeed him without someone seeing? She couldn't just expose herself like that, but did she have an option?

She should have thought of that before she left—someone should have told her, someone should have prepared her.

Johnny's cries became louder, more agitated, and she began to worry that maybe it wasn't just hunger. Perhaps he wasn't well. He'd been born too early, and he'd always had trouble holding milk down. The nurses were experts, making it look so easy. But she hadn't a clue.

A lump grew in her throat as she wrestled with Johnny, now bellowing louder and louder, as if sensing that she was falling apart.

Without being able to stop herself, she began to cry, her sobs echoing through the train. A man down the corridor ruffled his newspaper with annoyance, but she couldn't stop herself. Rocking the child, she gripped him to her as he bellowed louder and louder. Unable to cover her stricken face, the tears came thickly down her cheeks as she cried with him, gulping for breath.

She pulled Johnny into her, desperate for some kind of comfort from the little thing, but he just wailed all the more, and she suddenly felt like giving up, her wails growing alongside his. Maybe their shared horror at reality would expand through the air, calling to Christopher through the universe, wherever those lost in the desert go when the very life has been crushed out of them.

After a while, a sense of self-preservation came over her. It was her duty alone to look after her baby, however impossible that felt. And she shoved aside her coat, opening her blouse and pulling the child to her breast, hoping that no one was watching, judging her. She didn't look over to the man with the newspaper, but she heard it rustle again in a crisp reprimand.

Thankfully, Johnny fell silent, and she felt a vague lightheadedness as the intensity of the moment dropped. Through the noise of chattering, the soldiers singing in the next compartment, and the cigarette smoke hanging in the air, she focused on the rhythmic movement of the wheels on the track, the inevitable onward thrust of the journey, *her* journey, whether she was ready for it or not.

Eventually, the train arrived in London and she struggled through the crowds with her bags and Johnny, who was thankfully now sleeping. She had to take the tube to Bethnal Green, and after a fraught underground journey, she climbed the stairs toward daylight, just as Johnny woke up again.

"Please Johnny! Please don't cry!" Katie whimpered as they mounted the last few steps, fresh tears in her eyes. She could hardly bear it as it was, returning to the place where Christopher and her had shared their first kiss.

"Coo-ee! Over here, Katie!"

Spinning around in surprise, Katie dropped her bag on the pavement.

Then she saw who was calling to her.

It was Mrs. Ottley, standing behind a pram, waving frantically. "I thought I'd come to meet you with the pram. It's a good thing I remembered I had it in the cellar. It's perfect for little Johnny, isn't it?"

Suddenly, she felt her legs give way.

But Mrs. Ottley was already taking Johnny off her, giving him a little hug before putting him into the pram. "He likes it in there already, don't you, duck!" She grinned at Katie, either ignoring or oblivious to her red eyes and blocked-up nose. "Juliet gave the blankets a wash for him. They're little Ivy's, but I'm sure he won't mind, will he?" She peeked into the little face, delighted.

Before Katie could say a word, Mrs. Ottley led the way into the park, pushing the pram and talking non-stop about the excitement of having a new baby in the house. Katie couldn't bear to tell her that she was renting another room elsewhere, but perhaps it would be better to stay for the evening at least.

Mrs. Ottley's musings were followed by updates on the Underground Library and Juliet's return.

"It's wonderful to have her back." She leaned across to add under her breath, "He's been away on a long work trip, but I'm sure Sebastian will be thrilled as well." And then she gave Katie a smile. "And now you and little Johnny have come to liven the place up, too. We'll be our own family of sorts. I can't wait to show him Jake's toys. You will be staying, won't you, dear?"

Looking into her kindly face, Katie found herself smiling. "Well, if you're sure?"

Mrs. Ottley beamed at her. "Of course, you must stay!"

Parking the pram in front of Mrs. Ottley's, Katie took Johnny out. Covertly, she glanced over to her old house across the park, wondering when her mother would be back, thinking of how she could avoid her. It was strange to be looking at her house from here, from the outside. Even though it was inevitable that her mother would find out that she was staying with Mrs. Ottley sooner or later, she'd rather keep it to herself, at least for now.

"Let's take you to your new room, and you can get settled in while I make us both a nice cup of tea." Mrs. Ottley led the way up to a large bedroom, lifting her suitcase onto the green-quilted bed. "It's my son's room. We pushed the bed to the side to make space for his train tracks."

In the center of the room stood a crib. "That's Ivy's, too." Mrs. Ottley gazed at it, her mouth curving into a sad smile. "All those days I'd just sit and look at her, such a pretty little thing she was."

Katie set Johnny down inside, pulling the little blanket around him. "Johnny likes it, too. Look, he's falling back to sleep."

Leaning her head to one side as she gazed at the child, Mrs. Ottley said, "We'll have a lovely time with you here, Katie. I can't wait to babysit. It'll be just like old times." Softly, she put a hand into the crib and gave Johnny's head a gentle rub.

A wet sheen came to Mrs. Ottley's eyes, and Katie put an arm around her shoulders. "I'm sure both of your children are having fun in the countryside."

"I thought the war would be over by now, and they'd be home." She waved her hand at the window. "But what with the bombs, half of London devastated and the other half living underground, I couldn't bring them back."

"Did you write to ask if you could visit them some time?"

Mrs. Ottley shrugged. "I haven't heard back yet, but it would be nice." She smoothed the bedcovers, her eyes softening as they went back to the baby, now fast asleep.

"I don't know how to thank you, Mrs. Ottley. I promise I'll get a job as soon as I can find someone to look after the baby. I'll be able to pay you rent in no time."

"Well, you need look no further for someone to mind the baby during the day."

"What about your WVS work, the ladies at the mobile canteen?"

She smiled. "I can take him along in the pram. My canteen helper takes her grandson everywhere, and he's a naughty two-year-old, so a lovely little one like Johnny will be no trouble at all." Reluctantly drawing herself away from the child, she went to the door. "Why don't you unpack your things, and I'll pop on the kettle."

The sound of Mrs. Ottley's footsteps on the stairs echoed into the room as Katie wandered to the window, looking out over the park, which was bleak and dull in the fading light.

She spotted the bench beneath the magnolia tree, and it somehow looked emptier from this angle, as if she and Christopher might never have been there, kissing, talking about love. It felt like a bygone era, and she imagined herself in her gray school uniform, books in her arms, a different universe, a different girl.

Katie lowered herself into the bedside chair, listening to the sound of her new landlady making the tea, letting the ease of the place creep into her bones. Never had she been so grateful—so utterly relieved—for the help of this loving, caring friend.

# JULIET

THE UNDERGROUND LIBRARY
NEWSLETTER

**DECEMBER 1940**

**HELP SAVE OUR LIBRARY!**

*After the flood devastated our stocks,
the council wants to close us down.*

*Please support us by encouraging friends
and family to register.*

**JOIN OUR TEAM OF VOLUNTEERS AND HELPERS**

*It's fun and helps the community!*

**BOOK DONATIONS**

*With our stocks damaged,
all secondhand donations are welcome!*

LONG AFTER EVERYONE HAD LEFT FOR THE NIGHT, JULIET STAYED in the Underground Library, making plans for the meeting with the men from the council. The main lights had been turned out, and she'd brought the lantern to the newspaper table, hidden between the rows.

"It's good to be back," she murmured to the shelves, to the books, and a soft smile came over her face as she gave a little nod. "And in the nick of time, too."

After a hearty welcome from the regulars, Mr. Pruitt had arrived, grumpily agreeing that Juliet could return to her position for what was likely to be the library's final week.

"The councilors are coming on Thursday, and in all probability they'll order the place to close." He looked at her shrewdly. "You'll be needed to organize the packing, especially as I might be away in Suffolk by then."

There was no doubt that the registrations were up, but the shelves looked so battered after the flood, the stocks so meager. It would be easy for Mr. Pruitt to argue that keeping it open was more trouble than it was worth.

First things first, she would make a list of all the reasons why the place should be kept open, but as she gazed around for inspiration, all she could think about was the people it had brought together.

Mrs. Ottley and Sofie sat behind the main desk most evenings, filling registrations and chatting to those who needed support: the grieving, those anxious about loved ones abroad, the older people facing difficulties, those with marital problems, those whose homes had been bombed. The library was a place they could come and talk about things, find a book to help, or find someone to listen, even if the only thing anyone could do was to offer kind words and a brave smile.

Katie had restarted the Underground School, and she'd evidently taken advice from Irene's book as she handled the class admirably. The role had stopped her feeling trapped and besieged by her situation, and now that she was a respected teacher, people seemed to overlook her circumstances.

And then there were helpers like Dorothy and Meg. Would they go back into their shells without the Underground Library offering them something to keep them busy and engaged?

At first Juliet didn't realize he was there, but then a footstep echoed through the aisle.

She looked around to see Sebastian walking leisurely up from the end of the row, the dim light catching his eyes. It was the first time she'd seen him since her return, and he looked as dapper as ever, wearing a casual light-colored jacket, the one he'd been wearing that first evening in Mrs. Ottley's house, his hands in his pockets and that half smile on his face. She couldn't believe how her heart melted at the sight of him, quickly changing to a deep shudder. The embarrassment of it was too painful, that she had left like that, thrown everything they had away so easily.

And then there was the note she'd left for him. Blood rushed to her face as she wondered what had possessed her to say such things. Had she really told him that she dreamed about him? What had she been thinking?

"Sebastian," she said, getting to her feet. She knew she'd see him eventually, but she still felt the flutter of nerves.

"It's good to see you back," he said, stopping a few feet away. "I gather you had quite a time of it."

She looked at the floor between them. "You've spoken to your mother, I take it." The humiliation of it!

"She was only glad she'd been at the library and seen you. Who knows what could have happened otherwise."

"Well, I couldn't be more grateful to her for telling the police as promptly as she did." She let out an embarrassed laugh. "Let's just say that I've never been so thrilled to see three policemen barge into a room."

He went to take a step toward her, but then thought better of it. "It must have been frightening."

Again, the nervous laugh. "With all my ambulance work, I've become quite the expert in holding it together."

There was a pause, and then he said, "I should have told you not to go. Something didn't feel quite right. I was worried about you."

"But you *did* warn me, Sebastian. I just wasn't listening to you." She took a deep, frustrated breath. "I was too busy living out a past dream, doing what I felt that I had to do." Sinking back down onto her chair, she looked numbly ahead. "I was so stupid, believing I had to be loyal to him when all he wanted was someone to help keep him hidden."

Sebastian came to sit beside her. "You can't blame yourself, Juliet."

She shook her head in annoyance. "When I first met him, I was so desperate to get away from my parents that I just went along with everything he told me, basking in his high praise, researching for his books, tiptoeing around his tempers." She took a deep, calming breath. "This time I could see what he was doing. I'm not that naïve anymore. London and the library have made me independent, and living with Mrs. Ottley has shown me how a family should look. Victor couldn't pull the wool over my eyes anymore." She hung her head.

He put his arm around her shoulders. "At least you're back safely. It could have ended much worse."

"I should have listened to you, Sebastian. I trusted the wrong person." She huffed at her own idiocy.

"It wasn't easy to see what he was like underneath."

"But do you remember what you said all those years ago at the garden party? Even back then you had doubts about him."

He shook his head, laughing a little. "No, I didn't see it at the garden party. I just didn't like his political rhetoric aimed at people like me and, well, I thought you could do a lot better. . . ."

"With someone like you." She finished his sentence, smiling in spite of herself.

He shuffled his chair closer to hers, grinning. "With someone like me," he repeated.

"Always the charmer, aren't you, Sebastian?"

"I think you know that there's more to me than that." He glanced away at the bookshelves. "But I confess, I do put on a lighthearted front to cover up the fact that I'm, well, a bit of a softy, to be honest."

And when she looked up at him, now so close to her, she saw that his boyish look had vanished, replaced by a disarming openness, as if he'd dropped his façade and she was seeing the real Sebastian, the vulnerable, kind man underneath.

"I thought you knew that, Juliet." His eyes went over her face.

"I did, but you kept telling me that you weren't interested in anything serious, that life was too short." She paused. "You seemed so far away, always backing off, politely taking your leave of me, talking about what good friends we were."

Something in what she'd said made him sit forward. "I didn't want to rush things." He made a big sigh. "Oh, Juliet! When you want something to be right, you don't want to ruin it by rushing things. I was unsure of you, unsure of myself, too, whether I was what you needed—if I'll ever be what someone needs. I wanted to make sure you were over Victor, and just as I was starting to hope that you were, the man himself showed up and whisked you away."

"I can't think what you must have thought of me, running off with him like I did." She looked down at her hands.

"At first, I thought you hadn't really cared about me." He hesitated for a moment, and then said. "But then I saw the book you left for me—how you'd listened and helped—and I couldn't believe that I was losing you."

"I worried you might feel it was too forward of me to leave the book for you." She wondered if he'd read her note—or perhaps it had fallen out.

"Well, I'm very grateful. I started the book, and although I haven't got very far, something about it—or perhaps it is simply the fact of it, and the fact that you gave it to me—has made me see that there are people who can make me feel better."

"I hope we're still friends enough that I can be one of those people," she said. "You must know how hard it was for me to leave, and to leave you especially."

"I know," he said simply, reaching for her hand. "You wrote it in your letter."

She swallowed hard. "You read the note."

Almost imperceptibly, he smiled.

Humiliation flooded through her, and she pulled her hand out of his, speaking quickly. "Well, I didn't mean it the way it came out, you know. I was upset. You have to realize that I was leaving everything behind, and I was very emotional, and confused. . . ." Her words ran to a halt, not knowing what else to say, and then she stammered, "W-well, say something, will you?"

He lifted her face so that she was looking at him, and she saw that he was smiling, a softness in his eyes that she'd never seen. "I've been

dreaming about you, too. That evening when we were cooking together, and we danced a little, that was when I first felt something between us, a kind of friction that I couldn't forget. And then that evening,
when our eyes met in the hall mirror, I just wanted to pull you into my
arms, tell you how much I worried about you. And the night we came
home from dancing? It took everything I had not to kiss you."

On the word kiss, his eyes flickered to her lips and then to her eyes,
and then, hesitantly, he leaned his head forward and gently touched his
lips on hers, letting them linger, barely moving as she let the sensation
go through her, at once warm and all-encompassing, her blood flowing
thicker and faster through her veins.

And slowly, he pulled away, his eyes searching hers. "Are you sure
about this, about us?" he whispered. "I don't want to do anything if
you're not completely on board."

As she drew a long, deep breath, she looked at him. "I couldn't be
more sure of anything," she said. "You're the one who makes me laugh,
the one who I can talk to all day and all night. You're the one who
makes my heart turn over and open so wide I can barely contain it."

He beamed. "I know exactly how that feels. When you wrote in
your letter that we would meet on Beeding Hill when we're older, I
realized that when I told you how I wanted to show my children the
badgers, I had meant for them to be your children, too, Juliet."

She let out a small laugh. "I was secretly hoping that as well, for us
all to be together, one family, going in search of badgers." She found
herself grinning. "But it felt like a dream that couldn't possibly come
true."

And with that, he took her into his arms and kissed her.

They stayed in the Underground Library all night, and at some
point, Juliet reached for the blankets under the main desk and spread
them on the floor between the aisles, and they lay down beside each
other.

"I can't tell you how relieved I was to hear you were coming home,"
he murmured. "After I read your note, I was all set to come down to
Upper Beeding and drag you away myself." Slowly, he ran his fingertips through her hair, his eyes soft in the light of the dying lantern.

And she entwined her hand in his. "I wish you had! You're truly the best friend I've ever had, and now you're, well . . ."

"I'm yours forever," he said with that smile of his. "I hope that's what you have in mind?"

She laughed, reaching her arms around him. "Oh yes, that would be perfect."

# KATIE

THIRTY CHILDREN NOW ATTENDED THE UNDERGROUND SCHOOL, Katie at the helm with Mrs. Ottley, Dorothy, and Meg helping. She tried to time Johnny's naps to coincide, but he seemed to revel in the children's company—and they adored him, too.

Teaching seemed easier now that she knew the children better, and Irene's book about the psychology of discipline had helped immensely. No wonder the old headmistress was ahead of her game.

Running the Underground School was definitely a joint effort. Katie might be the one at the front, but Dorothy was invaluable, and Meg was put to the task of helping those who needed it. Meanwhile, Mrs. Ottley spent her time with Johnny and a few other little ones. At Katie's insistence, they'd handed out some notices in the old workhouse, helping those on the fringes of society get an education for their children as well.

"Irene always said that no one should be denied a place in school," Dorothy said after the class had finished. "She'd be proud of you for standing up for them."

"Now I've seen how easy it is to end up in difficult situations, it feels right," Katie said, adding with a grin, "And it's my secret way of getting my own back on Mrs. Baxter."

Mrs. Ottley had vanished to get some well-deserved tea, leaving Katie to gather little Johnny in her arms as she and Dorothy watched Meg picking up the mislaid scarves and dropped pencils.

"Funny how it all fits into place," Katie said to Dorothy. "Irene knew precisely what she was doing when she asked us to set it up, didn't she?"

"Well, she spotted that you'd make a jolly good teacher, my dear."

Katie remembered the day Irene had asked her to help with the school, now realizing that her friend had seen that it wasn't only the school that was in need of a new teacher, but Katie who could do with a new challenge. It was just what she needed: something to remind her how capable she was. "Irene always managed to bring out the best in people, didn't she?"

With a chuckle, Dorothy nodded toward Meg. "You're not the only one she helped. The children's section in the library is now meticulous, and I can't go anywhere without Meg appearing beside me asking whether I need anything."

Katie laughed, looking down at Johnny as he began to move a little, finding the right spot before drifting back to sleep, as if nothing else mattered in the world.

"What a little treasure he is!" Dorothy said. "Looking after the babies was always my favorite part of being a nurse."

Together they watched him stretch his hand out, splaying it, his tiny fingers tipped with paper-thin nails.

"He looks like his father." Katie's smile faded. "I took him to see Christopher's parents yesterday. They could barely hold back their tears, of course. Can you imagine how overjoyed they were to see Johnny?" She shook her head slowly. "Who cares about society's rules if you have a part of your son still here on earth? I can't believe I let my mother convince me not to tell them before."

There was a pause, and then Dorothy said, "Have you seen your mother yet? I heard that she's coming out of the hospital tomorrow. If she's sheltering down in the underground, maybe you can find a time to speak to her."

Katie pursed her lips, then said under her breath, "After what happened, I don't know how we could ever make up."

"But I think you should try."

"I'm not sure," Katie said uncomfortably. "I know that she had little choice in hiding the pregnancy, with Dad threatening divorce if she didn't, but it's hard for me to forget."

"Divorce means ruin for most women, unless they have family money." Dorothy let out a long sigh. "I heard about it from a woman here in the Underground Library. Now that there are fewer men, especially here in London, certain younger, fancier women are grabbing men who aren't actually available. It's not fair, but as Irene always said, it's our job to support divorced women, not join the Mrs. Baxters of the world."

Katie thought of the brunette in the red coat, her cloying perfume—had her father found a younger, prettier wife-to-be? "Dad was always putting Mum down—and he blamed my pregnancy on her tenement background, too." She felt blood rush to her face. "And now the birth is out, she might well lose him—lose everything that means anything to her."

Dorothy heaved a heavy sigh. "The odds are against her with the war. People like your mother are bearing the brunt of other people's impulsiveness." Dorothy put a hand on Katie's arm. "Why don't you go and talk to her?"

"I'll think about it," Katie murmured under her breath.

But Dorothy's hand didn't move as she looked into Katie's eyes. "These days you never know if someone's going to be alive or dead tomorrow. Wouldn't it be better to have her know that you love and care about her?" Dorothy looked at the ground. "At least Irene knew that I loved her as we told each other every evening before bed, just to be on the safe side." She nodded sadly. "I know that however much we disagreed, we were always on each other's side, always together." She looked at Katie sadly. "We start and we end life with our family, and the connection between a child and a mother is the strongest there is. Look at you and Johnny—can you imagine how your mother feels now she's lost you?"

Katie looked down at her beloved baby, fast asleep in her arms, and swallowed hard as she felt that bond so powerfully, it was as if a thick gauze of golden threads were pulling them together, connecting them forever to each other. There was a new place in her heart, a new depth of love she felt for him that she had never even known was there. And as she gazed at him, she knew that those same cords bound her and her mother, tarnished and worn over the years, but still there, if she looked hard enough.

"You're right, I should see her," she murmured, a sudden chill coming over her.

Dorothy nodded warmly. "That's the spirit! You're stronger now, Katie, and my feeling is that now she's seen that you're an adult, she won't want to treat you like a child."

And with a weak smile, Katie nodded. "I am more sure of myself, aren't I?"

"You're robust enough to make peace with her, Katie." The old lady gazed at her intently. "Even if you're too old for someone to hold your hand, you have to realize that your mother is still the person who would do anything for you."

Katie nodded, as if suddenly the whole picture was sliding into place: the uneven marriage, the affair, her unwanted pregnancy, the divorce. The more she thought about it, the more she knew: She had to see her mother, to make things right.

CHAPTER

**45**

# SOFIE

A MIXTURE OF TREPIDATION AND EAGERNESS SEEPED THROUGH
Sofie as she pushed open the small door into the service passage, slipping inside as she had all those months ago when she'd first met Mac.
The bare amber bulbs were the same, lighting the same dank, dingy
maze of passages, and the smell of alcohol and smoke was, unfortunately, still lurking there as well.

But Sofie herself was different. She was neither a downtrodden servant nor as lonely and helpless as she had been before. First her new
friends from the library had helped, then her break on the Isle of Man,
and now her new job, her independence.

And maybe soon she would have another family member here, too.
She'd sent the employment offers and tickets to Rachel, with a hope
and a prayer they'd reach her. All of these things made her into the
Sofie she was today; not quite like the Sofie of Berlin, but more dynamic, more spirited, able to get on by herself.

As she retraced her steps through the service passage, she remembered how afraid she'd been, how nervous. Now she was more sure of
herself, although some of that, she confessed to herself, was because she
knew that Mac was there, just around the next corner, waiting for her.

He'd been there at the library when she came in after work, leaning
against the wall by the entrance, waiting for her.

"Come and find me in the service passage after the reading hour. I have a surprise for you," he whispered, giving her a secretive smile before vanishing off into the crowds.

Since that first night with her and Dorothy, he'd spent most nights camping with them, whispering to Sofie and laughing like they were children spending the night in a secret cave. Sometimes they'd read out different parts in plays or they'd find out more about the war in Poland from embassy leaflets and newspapers, starting a noticeboard in the Underground Library for refugees like them.

Deeper into the passageway she trod, then suddenly a hand touched her arm, making her jump, a laugh spilling out of her as she saw that it was Mac, coming to find her.

"Follow me," he whispered, beckoning her on, taking her hand as his walk sped up, becoming a trot and then a run as they dashed, laughing, through the maze of passages, ignoring the punters and the black marketeers, ignoring the smells and the sounds.

Suddenly, they turned a corner, and he drew abruptly to a halt.

"For my dear Sofie," Mac said, taking a bow like a waiter in a top-class hotel and pulling out her chair.

And there in front of her was a small, arched opening in the passage, half-hidden and cozy. Two chairs and a small, circular table sat in the center, covered with a crisp white tablecloth. The flickering glow of a single candle threw a dappled golden light over the hidden nook. The table was laid for a simple dinner, with two plates, each with a knife and fork, a covered dish in the middle.

"Did you cook for me?" she asked as he pulled out a chair for her to sit down.

"Don't get too excited." He laughed, lifting off the top to reveal two Cornish pasties.

"Let me guess, from the canteen?" she mused.

"Everyone's favorite," he joked, taking a seat himself and dishing one onto each of their plates. "Well, they're better than the carrot sandwiches."

As she began to eat, he pulled out a bottle of Bordeaux from beneath the table, pouring it into two glasses and handing her one.

"Oh, I see you still keep up with your old black-market contacts."
She chuckled, reveling in the pungent scent of the wine, the deep, spicy
flavors. "This is such a lovely surprise." Her eyes pierced his. "Is there
a reason?"

He blushed, looking at his plate. "Well, I do have something to tell
you." He pulled a folded sheet of paper from his pocket and handed it
to her. "Mrs. Bloom found Uri."

"That's wonderful!" Sofie cried. "Where is he?"

His eyes gleamed in the soft light. "He crossed into the Russian side
of Poland and joined some others in Lviv in the south of the country. A
lot of Jews are getting out of Europe southeastward through the Black
Sea to Palestine."

She grabbed his hands across the table. "What a relief, to know he's
alive!"

"I'm so relieved. Mrs. Bloom's contacts have heard that any Jews
caught working for the underground movement are being shot, so he
would have needed to get out of the country fast." He frowned. "I
hope he reaches safety soon. I know what it's like, traveling alone,
sleeping rough, keeping your ears and eyes open all the time, but at
least he is not being hunted down by the Nazis. There is nothing like
that feeling that you are the prey."

"Can you find out where he might be heading? I read in the German
newspapers at work that Turkey might turn their back on the Allies,
join forces with the Nazis. It will make it difficult for ships to leave
through the Black Sea."

"Mrs. Bloom said we can't be sure of anything now he's in Soviet-
occupied territory. The Russians are moving a lot of Jews to Siberia,
which is hard living. But the way things are going, it might offer better
odds than staying in Europe." Slowly, he shook his head. "I can only
hope he is safe. Uri is my only family."

Sofie said softly, "You have me, too, you know."

His eyes met hers. "I know," he smiled gently, "that's why we have
to be careful, look after each other."

Silence fell over them for a while, both so comfortable with each
other that they didn't feel the need to fill it. For Sofie, the dinner felt

special, even though it was just the same old pasties. The wine was exquisite, the flavors rich and mellow, making the evening almost magical.

At the end of the meal, Mac raised his glass for a toast. "To us both and our families, may they find us one day soon."

She let her glass tap his. "And to good friends."

For a moment, they both said nothing, looking at their glasses, and then Sofie looked up to see Mac's eyes meeting hers, an apprehension in them she hadn't seen for a while.

Quietly, he said, "I don't think I can bear to be just good friends with you any longer, Sofie." Then he gave her a tentative smile. "Not when I want to be so much more."

A tingle shivered down her spine as she felt her pulse quicken. Biting her lip to stop the smile spreading over her face too eagerly, she whispered, "I think I might feel the same way."

Cautiously, he put down his glass and got to his feet, moving around the table, and as he took her hands and pulled her to her feet, he folded her into his arms and gently, hesitantly touched his lips on hers. At first, he seemed reticent, restrained, but then, as she began to kiss him back, he relaxed, their kisses becoming more ardent as their bodies melded into each other's.

When she pulled away, he gazed at her. "I've been dreaming of this moment ever since you pretended I was your husband back in the Isle of Man."

Their eyes met, and suddenly, they both began to laugh.

"You made a very capable husband, Mac," she mused. "Not backing away or messing things up."

"I could hardly believe my luck." He grinned, taking her back into his arms.

Without another word, he pulled her toward him and buried his face in her neck, her hair, whispering into her ear, "I love you, Sofie. I never dreamed that I'd ever feel this way about anyone. I've hardly been able to stop myself from telling you. I love you so very much."

And as her heart melted inside her, she whispered, "I love you, too, my darling, darling Mac."

CHAPTER

**46**

# KATIE

WATCHING FROM MRS. OTTLEY'S FRONT WINDOW, KATIE GAZED over at the big house on the corner, wondering when her mother would arrive home from the hospital.

"I'm glad you're going to see her." Mrs. Ottley bustled in and out, trying to find her house keys, lost again in the chaos. "I don't know how she'll cope with the stairs. Do you think your father might help her, or your brother maybe?"

Katie's first reaction was to laugh at the absurdity of the idea. "It looks like my father's hardly there these days, and in any case, it was Mum who always cared for them. The men in the house were always cosseted—actually, before I became pregnant, we'd all been to some extent."

A frown came over Katie's face as she remembered the lovely mum her mother had been. Ever since her chat with Dorothy, the old woman's words had remained in Katie's mind, how life was too short to let such a crucial bond break.

Katie was just beginning to wonder if her mother wasn't getting out today when a taxi pulled up outside her old childhood home.

At first, she could hardly believe it was her mother, carefully getting out, propping herself against the gatepost to dig into her handbag for the money to pay the driver. Her hair hung limply from her head, and her clothes looked too big for her, sagging on her usually upright frame. She held a walking stick, evidently necessary as she hobbled forward.

Something inside Katie's heart lurched, and without stopping to think, she put Johnny into his pram and darted out of the door.

By the time Katie reached the house, her mother was still leaning on the gatepost, gathering her energy to get up the front steps.

"Let me help you," Katie called as she rushed forward.

With a start, her mother turned around, a look of exhaustion quickly changing to an indefinable expression that quivered with emotion.

Not waiting for an answer, Katie went to hug her, feeling her form now diminished, trembling beneath her hands. Instead of the energy passing from her mother into her, it was now the other way around, Katie helping *her.*

But even so, that raw sensation of having her arms around her mother was overwhelming, and Katie found herself clinging to her, unable to hold back her sobs.

Her mother's eyes, now glistening with tears, gazed at her and then moved down to the child in the pram.

Katie moved the pram toward her. "This is Johnny, Mum."

Her mother bent down to see his little face, now awake, his eyes on hers.

"He's beautiful." She looked up at Katie. "Well done for getting through it. I know it couldn't have been easy."

But then weariness made her look toward the front door, and Katie guided her up the steps, finding the spare key under the doormat, helping her inside.

Too busy struggling with her hip, Mrs. Upwood didn't speak, limping into the living room.

It was strange to be home, Katie thought as she wheeled the pram inside. The place looked the same as when Katie had last been there, but now it seemed so very cold and ornate—the actualization of the show they'd had to orchestrate for the rest of the world.

Pulling her coat closed, Mrs. Upwood seemed to collapse onto the chintz sofa, for once not worrying about dirtying the place as she put her feet up onto the coffee table.

"I'm so sorry about what happened to you that night, Mum," Katie said, sitting down beside her. "I didn't realize you were hurt, and needed to—I needed to protect my child, the way I see now that you were trying to protect me."

Her mother's face creased with emotion. "It's all right. I don't blame you, after what I put you through. It's me who should be apologizing. The Anderson wasn't fit to sleep in, let alone give birth in. I can't believe I was so desperate to think it would work."

As she began to weep, Katie put her arms around her. "It's all right, Mum. We both made mistakes, but it all worked out in the end."

She pulled away as Johnny began to fidget, and as she looked around the room, she realized how dusty it had become. The place looked unlived in, as if no one had set foot inside for weeks.

"Is there anyone who can help you around the house, Mum?" she asked. "I don't know how you'll cope with your hip. Could Rupert do anything, and what about Dad? Maybe it's his turn to show some compassion for a change?"

Mrs. Upwood stared ahead, as if it were all too much to contemplate—or perhaps it simply felt impossible.

"He's gone. After he heard everyone talking about you and the baby, he upped and left." She looked up. "I blame myself—blame him—for letting you down, because we did let you down, Katie." She picked up Katie's hand and squeezed it. "I should have listened to you. I knew deep inside that it wasn't right. The families I knew who'd hidden a baby like that always struggled. Nothing fell into place for them."

"I know you were only trying to do what you thought was best, Mum."

"I should have had more faith in you, Katie. It was only when I was in the hospital, hearing about Johnny's birth in the underground clinic, that I realized that I'd been looking at things the wrong way. It's not our reputations that should define us, but the other way around—we should be telling the Mrs. Baxters of the world who we are ourselves, not letting them be the judge. That's what truly matters, after all." She ⸱ ⸱ ⸱ie's hand in hers. "Sometimes we need to stop the cacophony ⸱ ⸱ ⸱ telling us who we are and how we should live. We need to be ⸱ ⸱ ⸱ oice proclaiming to the world who we are. And I realized that ⸱ ⸱ ⸱tters to me is you."

Katie drew her into a hug, not the type a child might give a parent, but one of two individuals supporting each other, building their connection anew.

As she drew away, Katie asked, "Have you heard anything from Dad?"

Her eyes fell. "He came to see me in the hospital, appalled by the spectacle of my behavior and our inability to keep the pregnancy undercover. He told me he wouldn't have his name tarnished by association and that he would be staying elsewhere and seeking a divorce. I haven't seen him since, and I'm assuming he went to stay with his new woman. No doubt I'll be served with the divorce papers soon."

Katie looked into her mother's exhausted eyes. Dorothy had been right. How devastating and humiliating for her mother. "What are you going to do?"

"Well, he can't throw me out of the house for now, although I have no idea how I'll get by without his income. I can't even get a job with my hip like this."

And then a thought occurred to Katie. "If Dad's gone, why don't I move back in to help you? It's too difficult for you to keep everything going with the bombs and your leg in plaster, and Rupert's not likely to be of much use."

Her mother slowly shook her head. "I don't deserve your help, not after all I put you through."

"Stop talking like that, Mum! I'm just happy for us to be together again. In any case, now it's my turn to look after you. If I can help you by coming home, then I would like nothing better."

"But we'll still need money."

"I can work," Katie said defiantly. "If you give Mrs. Ottley a hand looking after little Johnny, I'm sure I can find a good job."

"But what would you do?"

She smiled. "Well, I'm a capable teacher as it turns out, and not a bad librarian either."

"But a lot of places would never take on an unwed mother, Katie."

"People aren't so prejudiced now the war's on. If I've got skills that they need, they'll put up with it. I could do something that I enjoy, something that will make us money. We'll show Dad we're better off without him, and as for Mrs. Baxter and the ladies, we'll leave them to waste their own lives keeping up appearances."

"I should never have doubted you, Katie," her mother said. "Which reminds me . . ." She pulled a small brown paper package from her handbag. "I wondered if you might want these."

And as Katie peeled back the side of the paper, she saw a glimpse of white wool with the familiar white pearl buttons. Carefully, she pulled out the little clothes she'd knitted so long ago.

"You kept them!" she said, reminded of how awful she'd felt, how this had been her one small chance to do something for her child. Katie could only feel proud of herself at the sight of them, that she'd stood up for Johnny and found her own way out.

"I'm sorry for everything, Katie," her mother murmured. "I don't know how you'll ever be able to forgive me."

But Katie just put her arms around her. "All I care about is that we're back together. If you and I stick together, we can survive anything."

# JULIET

THE COUNCILORS COMING TO INSPECT THE UNDERGROUND LIBRARY were due just before opening time, and Juliet was at her wit's end, dashing about with a dustpan and brush.

They would be using their report to decide whether to keep the place open.

"It's no use, we still haven't recovered from the flood," she moaned. "No matter how much I tidy it up, it still looks like a few rows of bookshelves that have been randomly left in the corner of an underground station tunnel."

Thank goodness Katie had come to help her, little Johnny fast asleep in his pram.

"I don't understand why the councilors would want to close such a popular place," Katie said as she gave the main desk another polish. "Membership has never been higher, and the reading hour and book club are getting too crowded for the space. People need places like this for the company as well as the books."

Juliet sighed. "But with Mr. Pruitt telling the councilors otherwise, we won't stand a chance of being heard, will we?" She spread some books along a row so that it didn't look so empty. "If Mr. Pruitt didn't want to move to Suffolk, he wouldn't be so eager to close the place down."

"But surely a new position for him doesn't mean the whole library has to close?"

Juliet felt a ball of frustration rising up inside her. "He says that they wouldn't be able to find a replacement head librarian for somewhere this small."

"Well, can't you be the head librarian?" Katie frowned in confusion. "You do his job as it is."

"But I'm not a man, am I?"

And that was the crux of it.

Juliet rearranged the newspapers for the thousandth time. "They've made such a tremendous concession by allowing me to be a deputy, but to let a woman run the place?" She mimicked Mr. Pruitt's nasal voice. "That would be tantamount to madness."

"It's up to us, then, isn't it?" Katie said, determined to stay positive. "Things don't change by themselves." She straightened the already straight noticeboard behind the desk. "By the way, where's Dorothy?"

The old lady had become a permanent fixture, volunteering most days behind the main desk.

"She hasn't been in today, and I haven't seen Mrs. Ottley either. I was hoping they'd be here so that the councilors could see how many volunteers we have, how it keeps costs down and helps with community spirit."

The sound of male voices came from the library entrance, and the two women exchanged glances, straightening themselves and putting on keen smiles as they stepped forward to greet them.

Two gray-suited men entered, while beside them, Mr. Pruitt ran a commentary about the place, a new unctuousness about him.

"You see, it's terribly makeshift, isn't it?" Mr. Pruitt showed them through to the main desk. "We brought down the bookshelves that survived the library bombing, but frankly it's awfully dusty and damp for our precious stock."

"Hello, Mr. Pruitt," Juliet said, an edge to her usual cheeriness. "Won't you introduce us?"

"Well, these gentlemen are incredibly busy. I'm not sure they came all this way to meet the understaff."

"Understaff?" Juliet muttered, but she quickly drew herself up, addressing the board members directly. "I'm Miss Juliet Lansdown, the deputy librarian."

"Pleased to meet you." The men looked at their watches, eyeing each other as if they'd expected the meeting to be over by now. It crossed Juliet's mind that the bulk of the meeting had already taken place, probably in the councilors' office, where she wouldn't be invited.

"As you can see," Mr. Pruitt resumed, turning his back on Juliet, "the place is mayhem without the proper staff and organization. I would have thought that you of all people would agree, Mr. Grant?"

A broad middle-aged man with a thick mustache was evidently the one in charge. "Yes, yes, very makeshift. Just look at those big gaps on the shelves."

"A lot of the books have been taken out by our keen members," Juliet said quickly. "And the recent flood damaged quite a few, too. We wanted more of our stock in Wales to be delivered, but the message doesn't seem to have reached them." She looked pointedly at Mr. Pruitt.

Mr. Grant went to the shelf and pulled out a battered copy of *Bleak House*. "The books look rather tatty. Not the sign of a good library."

"On the contrary, it's the sign of an excellent library. They're worn because they've been borrowed so often," Juliet said, frowning defensively. "Our book turnover has increased hugely since we came underground. Everyone wants a book to while away the time." But the man didn't seem to be listening, looking at the exit as if he'd just remembered something more important.

Mr. Pruitt began to speak loudly, the last authority on the matter. "People can find everything they need in the Shoreditch Library."

"It's only a few miles from here, isn't it?" Mr. Grant nodded.

"But a few miles is no small feat when bombs are raining down overhead." Juliet grappled to quell her exasperation.

Mr. Pruitt blustered over her. "Only think of the saved money. How much does the council have to pay for the upkeep of this ramshackle place? How could you justify that expense to the minister?"

"Well, that's a salient point," Mr. Grant agreed.

Juliet's voice was rising in exasperation. "Actually it hardly costs a penny. We use the tunnel for free, we already have the books, and it's only our two salaries that need to be paid. The volunteers help with the rest."

Mr. Pruitt merely smiled. "Haven't we been told to cut costs where we can with the war?" He had prepared his case well, determined to take the position in Suffolk, and these men were unlikely to listen to a young female deputy instead.

"Well, there seem no good reasons to keep the place going. I'm surprised you're so very keen, Miss Lansdown." Mr. Grant turned to Mr. Pruitt. "Perhaps you're right. She wasn't such a good choice after all."

The older, balding councilor chimed in, "I don't see the use in taking on women for these more senior roles. They're simply not capable of taking on that level of organization." He looked pointedly at Juliet. "The trouble with women is that they're always so emotional."

Feeling a lump of anger build in her throat, she quashed her feelings. The last thing she wanted to do was to get upset, to be the emotional woman they assumed her to be.

Meanwhile, the men turned toward one another, Mr. Pruitt shaking hands with Mr. Grant, discussing the Suffolk position.

The deal had been done.

And no one had listened to Juliet's opinion at all.

She sank down onto a chair. That was it. That was the end of her path, the end of the Underground Library. After everything she'd survived, the bombs, the flood, then Victor—couldn't she keep this one bright spot?

"I suppose I've been living in a fantasy world," she murmured to Katie, "thinking I could make this work, make them see that women can be more than assistants."

"Juliet!" Katie tapped her elbow, her voice urgent. "Look!"

"They're not even giving me a chance. . . ." Juliet continued until Katie gave her a sharp nudge and she looked up and saw.

A crowd of people were streaming through the library entrance. Some of the faces she recognized from the reading hour or the book club, others were regulars, but all of them had one thing in common: Every one of them was carrying a book.

At the head was Marigold, larger than life in her fur coat and jewels, armed with a large hardback tucked under one arm. She was quickly followed by Mrs. Ottley, looking delighted with their efforts, accompanied by young Meg. Next to her was Sofie, straight from work in a smart jacket, Mac beside her.

The crowd, easily a few hundred, squeezed into the Underground Library, filling the space in front of the main desk and between the rows, trying not to crush the men in suits at the front.

In full spirit, Marigold came behind the main desk, pried the chair off a stunned Juliet, and stepped onto it.

Rallying the crowd, she called, "We can't let them close down our precious Underground Library. This place is at the very heart of our sheltering community. When we had to move underground, the library followed us, giving us books, groups, readings, and of course," she opened her arms wide as if to embrace the crowd, "friends."

A great cheer went up.

"The absolute and unmitigated success of the Underground Library is due to the hard work and perseverance of one individual."

Mr. Pruitt stepped forward, his smile wavering as he said, "Well, I'm not sure you can call it an *unmitigated* success. . . ."

But Marigold stood firm. "Juliet Lansdown is the one who made this happen. It was her idea, her hard work, and her determination that made it into the thriving hub that it is."

Everyone had turned to Juliet, a mass of faces, smiling, beckoning for her to get up and say a few words.

"Come on, Juliet!" Marigold called, stepping down and helping her up onto the chair to the sound of cheers and applause.

From there, she could see that the crowd spread farther than she imagined, packed around the entrance and spilling into the main concourse.

"Well," she began. "What can I say but thank you everyone for showing your support for the Underground Library."

A murmur through the crowd was quickly hushed.

"Books give us so many things." She paused, looking at the councilors. "They give us a world to imagine, a cozy corner to lull us to sleep on a hard cold stone floor. They give us facts and figures to guide us, a knitting pattern or a recipe to help us with the rations, a map of the world or a history of Europe, the poets from the last war, and the news of this war, too. They give us joy, hope, and inspiration. They help us to see inside someone else's world, empathize with people we've never met—and if there is one thing the world needs right now, it is the willingness to understand and connect."

A ripple of agreement went through the throng.

"These days people work too many hours to let them get to a normal library. The air raids have made every day busier, having to get ready to shelter, getting shopping, laundry, and chores done, finding extra sleep. Some have children or family depending on them." Her eyes flickered over to Mrs. Ottley, who now held little Johnny in her arms. "But when the air raids sound, we all know we can come underground and find our library where we have the time to use it. When there's little to look forward to out there, there's always something to look forward to right here."

A round of applause echoed through the passage.

"Today, standing here in a free, uncontrolled library is a true gift that we can't take for granted. Around Europe, the Nazis are burning books, restricting what people read. Our Underground Library isn't a propaganda exercise, nor is it a museum. It is a reflection of who we are. It brings us together, a place where we can all come, forming a bridge between us, a common ground. It has something for everyone, even those who can't read. It belongs to all of us—to every one of us."

A roar of assent went through the crowd.

Then Marigold's voice carried over the throng. "These books"— she raised the large hardback in her hand— "These books were taken out of this library. Where would we be without them? Books define us as a culture. They are symbols of our traditions, our values, and our freedom." She gazed around the crowd exultantly. "Everyone who has a book from the Underground Library, raise it into the air."

All at once, a multitude of books came into sight, held above the crowd. Large tomes to slim novellas, they waved chaotically like a great flock of birds taking flight, a hundred different colors, a hundred different messages.

"Save the Underground Library!" someone called from the back, and then another voice echoed the same message, and soon a whole host of voices called, "Save the Underground Library!"

Blood gushed to Juliet's cheeks as she looked around, quite unable to believe her eyes. All these people had come to save her dear library. She grinned as she took in the scene, brimming over with gratitude and solidarity.

"Look over there," Katie said, and Juliet followed her eyes to the two councilors, now conferring at the side. Left outside their discussion, Mr. Pruitt frantically tapped Mr. Grant's shoulder, desperate to be heard.

But it was too late.

After a nod of agreement, Mr. Grant came to the front, making a loud cough to get everyone's attention.

Shushes echoed through the space until the crowd had fallen silent.

"I have to say that it is unprecedented that a small meeting such as ours should cause this kind of protest, but although some of my colleagues think it is unnecessary to keep a library in the underground, I feel that current situations demand a change in outlook. Therefore, we have decided to keep the Underground Library open."

An almighty cheer erupted, several books tossed into the air.

"But, but, Mr. Grant . . ." Mr. Pruitt couldn't help raising his voice. "It is *untenable*. . . ."

Exhausted, Mr. Grant turned to him. "Well, according to this crowd, it sounds as if it's your deputy who's running the place. So I suggest you jolly well take the position in Suffolk and leave the place to her to carry on without you."

Juliet had come around the desk to join them. "But who will be head librarian?"

He smiled, his mustache twitching. "It seems only rightful that it should be you, Miss Lansdown."

"Really?" she gasped in utter astonishment.

"That's right," he said, putting his hat back on as if the matter was concluded.

Mr. Pruitt darted up to him, saying in a low voice, "We can't have a *female* head librarian, Mr. Grant. It's not policy."

But the man was already looking at his wristwatch. "Then we'll make it policy," he said and began to head through the crowd to the entrance, Mr. Pruitt scurrying behind.

Juliet watched in amazement as the crowd began to celebrate as they realized what had just happened.

"We did it!" Juliet said under her breath. Then, flinging her arms around Katie, she cried out, "We did it!"

"No, Juliet," Katie replied in delight. "*You* did it."

And as they stood arm in arm, Sofie came over, jumping in the air with glee. Marigold joined them, too, a great beaming smile on her face.

"Thank you, Marigold," Juliet told her. "What a terrific protest you led!"

"Well, someone had to let those toffee-nosed idiots see how much our library means to us, and especially when it's being run by such a resourceful woman."

"Or should we call you the head librarian now?" Sofie added with a grin.

Juliet's heart soared. How much she'd longed for some kind of recognition that she wasn't just a deputy, or the daughter or wife of a gentleman for that matter either. She was a force in her own right, not just a woman, but an individual who could have good ideas, put them into action, and run something that made hundreds of people's lives that much better.

Beside her, Marigold addressed the crowd, pulling Juliet's hand up high into the air. "Ladies and Gentlemen, may I present to you your new head librarian."

A colossal cheer went up, hundreds of faces beaming as people clapped and waved.

And there, through the crowd, Juliet spotted Dorothy, trying to make her way forward, a great smile on her face. She seemed to be mouthing something to her, congratulations no doubt, but then she turned to speak to someone behind her, someone following her through the throng.

Then Juliet saw them. And as soon as she made out the young woman with a striking resemblance to her friend, her dark hair loose over her shoulders, she knew.

"It's your sister!" she murmured with astonishment, turning to Sofie.

But Sofie had already spotted her, going pale as if she'd seen a ghost. "Rachel?"

And then, with tears in her eyes, Sofie plunged into the crowd, threading her way through to her dear, dear sister.

# SOFIE

I T SEEMED SIMPLY UNREAL. RACHEL WAS HERE. WITH AN EXPLOSION OF emotion, Sofie threw her arms around her beloved sister, drinking up her presence, her essence. She was alive, and she was in London with her. It was as if everything Sofie had been hoping and dreaming was suddenly, almost impossibly, becoming real.

At first, a reticent pause hung in the air, as if the swell of all that had happened in the last year was almost too much to bear, but then, without restraint, Rachel pulled her close as they both began to cry. The sensation of her embrace, so familiar and comforting, was like a blanket she wanted to submerge herself into, enveloping herself in its protection.

When they finally drew apart, Sofie took her arm and pulled her out of the crowd toward the main concourse. From time to time, she glanced across to her, just to make sure she really was there, taking in her thin hair, her tanned skin, her gauntness. She'd imagined this moment, the excitement of showing her around, introducing her to her friends, telling her what she'd done in spite of the odds. But now that Rachel was here, that fell away, and it was all she could do to stop herself breaking into a flood of tears.

Calmly taking everything in, Rachel was quieter than usual, more cautious and restrained. Beside her, Frederick seemed much older than the boy Sofie had known back in Berlin. His usual cheeriness was replaced with a watchful vigilance.

"I can't believe you're here," Sofie murmured, her tears unstoppable. "I've been dreaming of this moment since I left you at Friedrichstrasse Station so long ago."

"It is the same for me," Rachel said, but then her face dissolved into fresh tears. "If only Papa were here, too. I begged him to come, but he only said that he would hold us back, that he wanted to stay close to Mama's grave—who else would look after it without him there." She clamped her lips together with emotion. "We can only pray that the Nazis carry on being lenient with the Jews in Berlin—at least he is there and not in Frankfurt or Munich."

"I knew he wouldn't leave," Sofie said quietly. "Berlin has always been his home, the place where he met Mama, built his business, his home." She took her sister's hand. "But now that you're here, we're one step closer to being together again. Have you been to the house yet?" She led the way to the escalator. "We'll have to go back and get ready. When the air-raid siren starts, we have to come back down here for the night."

"You sleep in the underground?" Rachel laughed.

Sofie gestured for them to see the profusion of people coming down the stairs with cushions and blankets. "Life carries on as usual down here every night—you'll get used to it."

Mac had joined them, falling into step with Frederick, and Sofie met his eyes with gratitude, and then she grasped her sister's arm, alone at last.

All the way home, Sofie talked an inexhaustible stream of whatever came into her mind. "Dorothy's house is lovely and big, so there's lots of room for us, and can you believe it, there's a piano, too. I'm a bit rusty, not much time for practicing . . ."

The words seemed to go in and out for Rachel, the occasional smile or nod to show she was listening, when it must have felt like an extraordinary new reality.

As they entered into the park, their pace slowed, and with emotion in her voice, Rachel began to speak. "It was terrible, Sofie. We were almost caught, almost killed, almost starved to death. We got across Germany mile by mile, sometimes on foot, walking through forests and fields, sleeping rough or finding a barn or outhouse. I dyed my hair blond to pretend to be Aryan, but it didn't work after we became very thin; everyone in Germany is hungry, but we in hiding had a special boniness about us. We weren't the only Jews trying to leave, but it was safer to travel alone, to keep hidden. Some of the Germans helped us, giving us food and shelter, but they risked imprisonment or even death, so we only sought help in the more remote areas. One kind farmer hid us on his cart, carrying us for hours, saving us days of walking."

Sofie told her about her own journey over, how the old nun protected her, the young woman in the fur coat being marched off the platform, everything gone just like that.

"A soldier helped us once," Rachel said. "We were hiding in a forest when the hounds found us. It wasn't just refugees fleeing, the countryside was filled with deserters, men who could never return home. The Nazis were hunting down anyone they could find."

"Were you caught?"

She shook her head. "For some reason, the Nazi soldier who came to see what the dogs had found looked right through us, pulling them away, calling to his colleague that it was only a dead bird, nothing at all."

"He saved you?"

She nodded. "He wasn't the only one. In Germany, there were many people who overlooked us, didn't call the authorities when they found us in a barn or on a trail. I know we were lucky, but it made us realize that many German people don't agree with what the Nazis are doing."

Sofie thought about her work, how she longed for the whole nation to see what was happening.

"But there were also people who wanted to gain from handing us in," Rachel continued. "A woman at the border held us but we managed to escape before the Gestapo arrived, and another time an old couple locked us in their shed, trying to trap us inside. We had to break down the door and run for our lives."

Sofie put her arm around her. "Were things better in France?"

"Yes and no," Rachel replied. "The locals wouldn't hand you in, so it was easier to buy food, but there were German soldiers in every town and on every road." She drew a long breath. "It was easy to tell we weren't native French speakers, so we had to stay even more hidden, trust people to help us."

"How did you get to Portugal?"

"After a month in Bordeaux, we finally got visas, and joined a group trekking over the Pyrenees into Spain. It was a hard climb, and the cold was bitter. There wasn't enough food, making it slower, harder. We were in a group, mostly refugees like us, but there were some British people trying to get home, a few underground agents and a pilot who had parachuted down when his plane was struck.

"By the time we reached Spain, we were starving and exhausted, but we had to move fast to get into Portugal. From there we joined other refugees on the road to Lisbon. We had no money, and until the letter from you came, dear Sofie, we were trying to think of schemes to make enough for a fare to Argentina." She looked into Sofie's eyes. "But you found us. You helped us get here."

The two sisters gazed at each other, tears in their eyes, drinking up the relief of being together again.

And with a sudden outburst of a laugh, Rachel said, "And look at you, Sofie! Your smart clothes and your hair! You're looking very well indeed. I'm so proud of you."

"I have a translation job now, helping the Allies." Sofie grinned. "But it hasn't been easy. I had to learn to cope on my own without you here. I had to step into your shoes, to be my own Rachel." She smiled into her sister's eyes. "But there was one thing you never explained. What happened with you and Frederick? You're married now?"

Rachel glanced down, her face reddening. "I suppose I've always liked him. But there's something about being in hiding, sleeping beside him in caves or forests, huddling up for warmth, clinging on for fear." Memories must have shot through her head, as her eyes drifted into the middle distance, the blood draining from her face.

"It must have pulled you together?" Sofie prompted.

"Yes, well," she looked at Sofie. "Sometimes you have to do something to remember who you are, remember that you're alive—a kind of secret retaliation, the power of knowing that you're still free inside your heart. It makes everything seem so precious: living, breathing, eating, making love, when your freedom could be ripped away at any moment."

Sofie bit her lip, trying to work through her memories, how Frederick had always popped over to their house in Berlin, how he'd asked to borrow books from Papa's library, how he'd keep Rachel company, help her with homework, listen as she played the piano. "Did you always love him?"

Again, there was that small smile. "Let's just say that I didn't find it difficult to kiss him back." She reddened at her words, but then went on more seriously. "But let me tell you, Sofie, that when you're running for your life, decisions become a great deal easier. You have to revel in any feeling of warmth you can. The Nazis can take many things away from us, they can take our culture, our freedom, our lives, but there are things they can never touch: our spirit, our love, what we hold inside our hearts."

"I was glad when I heard you were married," Sofie said. "I would have worried about you more if you were on your own."

"And I was worried about you, Sofie." Rachel squeezed her hand. "Every day, I longed to know you were all right. It's part of being a big sister. I need you, just as you need me."

Sofie put her arms around her. "Whatever happens, nothing will ever separate us again."

# KATIE

THE UPWOOD KITCHEN HAD TO BE CLEANED FROM LUNCH, AND Katie needed to get started on a packed dinner to take to the underground. They were having sausage-meat pie again, but this time she was teaching her brother to make it.

"Not cooking lessons again?" Rupert said, his school uniform worse for wear now that older schoolboys had to help clear the bomb sites. It was badly needed. Every night there were more piles of bricks blocking roads, covering basements, hiding the dead or wounded buried underneath.

"You never know how useful cooking can be," Katie said, "and there's not a woman in the world who doesn't want a man who can cook. Now take out the scales." She leafed through her mother's old recipe book, which was bulging with food ration leaflets and cutouts from magazines.

It had been a week since the councilors had decided to keep the Underground Library open, and to Katie's delight, Juliet—as the new head librarian—had appointed Katie as her deputy. It couldn't be more perfect. She was doing the job she loved the most in the place she loved the most. Her schedule could work around teaching in the Underground School, which was growing by the day, and the council was considering a permanent underground primary school.

Her promotion and new salary made her bristle with pride; now her life was truly in her own hands. She hadn't given up on her studies, but any college courses would have to wait until Johnny was older. And in the meantime, she had her new job to master, grateful to be able to leave Johnny with his grandmother and Mrs. Ottley.

Sieving the flour into a bowl, Rupert joked with her, "If there's anything I miss about Dad being here, it's the way you women used to know your place, cooking and keeping quiet."

She gave him a gentle kick. "We outnumber you now, so watch out!"

The departure of their father and the return of Katie had brought the siblings together, especially since they also had to look after both their injured mother and the new baby.

"Where's Johnny?" Rupert asked as he rubbed lard into the flour.

"He's asleep with Mum. We'd better hurry up as he'll want feeding soon." She stopped to show him how to do it faster, more efficiently.

The doorbell interrupted them, and she muttered, "Who could that be?" as she wiped her hands on her apron and darted to the door.

But as soon as she opened it, her heart floundered.

There stood Christopher's mother, her eyes red from crying and her face crumpling into tears as she stumbled toward Katie, throwing her arms around her.

"What is it?" Confusion swept over Katie. "What's happened?" She pulled away from the older woman, desperate for an answer.

Mrs. Donaldson reached into her handbag and took out a crumpled telegram, handing it to her.

MR. E. F. DONALDSON
46 HATCH ROAD BETHNAL GREEN

RED CROSS CONFIRMED 46986 PVT CHRISTOPHER JOHN DONALDSON TAKEN PRISONER OF WAR IN PG 78 ITALY. DETAILS TO FOLLOW

OC RICHARDS

The world faded into the background, Mrs. Donaldson's cries of relief and joy distant as the room began to blur. Katie clutched for the wall beside her, unable to stop herself from slipping to the floor, as if her legs had simply forgotten how to stand.

Hearing the commotion, her mother limped in, her face fraught as she bent over her, Mrs. Donaldson beside her exclaiming, "He's in a prison camp in Italy. He's alive!"

It wasn't long before the three women were all huddled on the floor, their tears and cries mingling. A chilly breeze blew in through the open front door—no one had bothered to close it—and red-brown leaves flurried and settled around them.

For Katie, the world gradually came back to life, the vivid colors and sounds suddenly startling and deafening, as if she'd been living in a dream from which she'd only just awoken.

Rupert arrived on the scene, helping them into the living room, only too pleased to leave them to it while he made a pot of tea.

"When did the telegram arrive?" Katie's mother asked.

Mrs. Donaldson took a wavering breath, trying to calm her nerves. "Just now—I came here straightaway. It's just so unbelievable. I needed someone else to read it, to prove I'm not just dreaming."

Under her breath, Katie repeated, "He's alive!" as if trying to convince herself.

"Italy?" her mother said, unable to grasp it. "How do you think he got there?"

"He must have been captured by the Italians in North Africa and transferred there. My husband thinks he could have been in prison for a while. The Red Cross only receives reports sporadically, and the Italians aren't as rigorous with the paperwork as the Germans."

"But why did the army think he'd been killed?" Katie murmured.

Wearily, Christopher's mother shrugged. "I imagine he could have been split up from the others and they assumed he was dead. If he was badly injured, he would have been taken to a hospital first—the Geneva Convention demands that wounded POWs are treated—so it could have been a while before he even reached the POW camp to have a record of his whereabouts." A worried look came over her face. "I hope they're taking care of him."

Mrs. Upwood put an arm around her. "At least he's alive, and they have to return him in one piece at the end of the war, don't they? Think about it this way, if he's in a prison camp, he's not on the front line."

They sat for a moment in silence, each of them trying to take it in.

The sound of chinking cups came from the hallway as Rupert came in with the tea tray, setting it out and pouring everyone a cup.

Tentatively, Katie asked, "Do you think he'll be able to write letters?"

It was her mother who answered. "A woman in the WVS has letters from her husband every few weeks. They're not allowed to say very much about their treatment and so forth, but she says he sounds all right, if bored and annoyed that he has to work for the enemy."

"I'm just glad he's alive, that he'll get to meet his son one day." Mrs. Donaldson looked over at Johnny, still asleep in his pram.

The conversation went on, punctuated with long silences while the women let the news sink in, one minute in fraught tears, the next in frenzied delight, trying to piece together this chaotic twist of fate.

After the tea was finished, Mrs. Donaldson took her leave, bidding them an effusive farewell with promises to let them know as soon as anything more was heard.

Katie gazed down at her baby. Her mother came beside her, but Katie put her finger to her lips. "Let him sleep. I want to take him for a walk."

And softly, she pushed his pram out into the park.

The bright winter sun shone through the sparse trees. Birds were making preparations for the cold months ahead, and a squirrel hopped through the undergrowth, gathering the last of the chestnuts before hibernation. On the far side, two older men were digging over the communal vegetable garden, readying it for the next season.

She made her way to her bench, the one beneath the magnolia tree, now bare, its job for the year done.

How many times had she sat there, the seasons changing, her life shifting from one moment to another?

And now she knew that Christopher was alive. Her baby had a father.

Her eyes went to Johnny, fast asleep in the pram.

And suddenly with a new spirit inside her, she reached under the blankets and scooped him up, pulling him up and through the blue, blue sky toward her.

"Your father is alive, my darling! He's alive!"

Opening his eyes, he began to smile as she swooped him down and held him on her lap, looking into his beautiful little face.

"He's in a camp in Italy," she beamed, unable to contain her elation any longer. "He'll be coming home again, and he'll be with us—we'll be a family, the best family that ever lived."

And as Johnny looked at her, he made a small chortle, picking up on her exuberance, and she laughed as she realized that he'd never remember all that had happened. He'd never know the time when his father was lost.

All the worry, the chaos, all the pain and fear and anguish, it was now in the past. In years to come, she'd look back on this time and it would seem like a tiny black smudge in the brightness of the lives they would live together.

# JULIET

## THE UNDERGROUND LIBRARY
## NEWSLETTER

### CELEBRATION SPECIAL!

*Merry Christmas!*

*London Underground has found some extra funds to provide a special celebration, with paper hats, a Christmas tree, holly, mistletoe, and a special visitor with a surprise for every girl and boy.*

### THE FESTIVAL OF LIGHTS—HANUKKAH

*Our neighborhood is home to many Jewish families, and as Hanukkah falls the same time as Christmas this year, the theme of our celebration will be "The Festival of Lights" to salute our mixed underground community where everyone can shelter, read, and make merry together.*

### AN UNDERGROUND PERFORMANCE

*The Bethnal Green Music and Drama Society will perform Dickens's* A Christmas Carol, *and then we have been promised a special singalong with Marigold Saxby.*

I T WAS CHRISTMAS AFTERNOON, AND JULIET AND SOFIE BUSTLED
excitedly around the Underground Library preparing for the evening's
events, the smell of hot punch and fruit pies drifting in from the main
concourse.

"You must be thrilled to have Hanukkah with your family this
year!" Juliet said as they arranged some wooden crates to create a
makeshift stage.

Sofie grinned. "We're trying to make it just like the old days—
I only wish my father could be here, too. The Jewish women in
Stepney told me of a shop where we could buy a menorah, and Rachel
has been playing all the traditional songs on the piano. It couldn't be
more different from last year, sitting alone in my room at Mr. Wainwright's, praying she was still alive." Sofie came over to give Juliet a
quick squeeze. "I have you to thank for helping me get to this moment, Juliet. You came to my rescue." She let out a delighted laugh.
"The first morning I came to the library was the moment everything
changed." She grinned. "You're the one who brings everyone together."

With a brisk shake of her head, Juliet replied, "It's the library that
does that, the book club and the readings."

"But it was you that breathed life into the place. You're the beating
heart inside it."

Juliet laughed. "More like the rumbling stomach with all these food
rations."

With the stage set up, they set to work putting baubles on an unkempt pine tree standing beside the main desk, one side far bushier
than the other. Then they wove holly stems and ivy around the bookcases, singing as they went.

The crowd began to gather at around six o'clock. There was a hope
that the bombs would ease off for Christmas, but as the sirens began, it
looked as though the Nazis were trying to catch everyone off guard.

But no one seemed to mind. The routine of the Blitz was now so
entrenched that trooping down to the shelters every evening had be-

come almost a ritual—and tonight there was the prospect of high festivities.

Everyone had spent their day celebrating, children scrambling to open their presents—mostly secondhand and homemade toys this year—followed by feasts of mock goose, which was sage and onion or sausage meat stuffing shaped like a roast bird, even though it invariably looked like a brown heap of mush.

Places of worship were packed. Everyone had someone for whom to pray: the men overseas, evacuated children, young women sent to work in factories and farms, those fleeing Europe or stuck in POW camps.

And then there were those who would never come home, either missing or gone.

In the evening, the underground buzzed with new excitement, children chasing each other around the tree and singing "Jingle Bells" and "We Wish You a Merry Christmas" with increasing volume. A sprig of mistletoe beside the canteen in the main concourse received a great deal of attention and, after a while, one of the canteen ladies had to come out from behind the desk and swat couples away with a dishcloth.

By the time the band had been set up in the Underground Library, a large crowd had gathered, children sitting on the floor at the front, then a few rows of chairs, and more people swarming in at the back.

It was a sight to behold, the band playing the introduction as the star of the show arrived.

"Look, there she is!" Sofie exclaimed.

The audience erupted into applause as Marigold, dressed in a floor-length gold sequin dress, made her way to the front. The crowd parted for her as she greeted them, the music coming to a halt as she stepped up onto the stage. And as she stood before the microphone, the crowd hushed for her to speak.

"First of all, I'd like to wish everyone a merry Christmas and happy Hanukkah!" Then she turned to the drummer and nodded, and he tapped his drumsticks together—one, two, three, four—and the introduction to "Winter Wonderland" began.

The gathering erupted into cheers as Marigold began to sing, her voice full and clear, her body swaying to the music as she put her hands around the microphone.

A dance floor of sorts was quickly established, everyone dressed in their best outfits to dance into the evening.

Juliet smiled as she watched Rachel dance with Frederick. They were looking more well fed and better dressed than they had when they'd first arrived—mostly the doings of Dorothy who'd adopted them as her new family members. Rachel had started a job alongside Sofie, and Frederick was translating German coded messages.

Looking around, Juliet spotted Sofie dancing with Mac, laughing at some joke or other. They had become inseparable, sleeping on the hard underground floor next to each other every night like an old married couple.

At the side, Katie had little Johnny in her arms, her mother beside her. The previous week, she'd had a letter from Christopher asking her to marry him, and his father had arrived at the house with a ring, at Christopher's request. Even if he couldn't be there in person, at least he was there in spirit.

Mrs. Upwood had always thought that the end of her marriage would be the end of the world, but she hadn't banked on Katie. She was a girl who could make money, organize the household, and make sure the family was held together.

Beside them, Dorothy chatted away to Meg, who was wearing a lovely pink dress that Juliet had found in a jumble sale. Meg had become such a fixture in the Underground Library that her father had come to thank Juliet for giving her a second home. "It's nice to know where to find her," he laughed.

The one person missing was Mrs. Ottley. She'd been invited by her children's evacuee family to spend Christmas down on the farm in Wiltshire. A brief telephone conversation had indicated that she was enjoying it so much that she might stay a little longer.

"Oh, it's beautiful, my dear! I can see why the children love it, with the outdoor life, lots of room for them to run around, and animals, too.

I've half a mind to move down here myself, if I can find a place to live."
Then she added, "You would be all right, looking after the house for
me, wouldn't you?"

"Of course, we will," Juliet assured her, desperate to tell Sebastian.

They were to be married in a few weeks, there in Bethnal Green.
The ceremony was to be in St. John's, the big church on the corner, and
the celebration, well, that was going to be in the Underground Library,
of course.

Juliet looked around the crowd for him. He had been on ARP duty
all day, but he said that he would see her there that evening. His absence sent a wrench of fear through her. Only last week two local ARP
wardens had been killed by an unexploded bomb. But she swallowed
back her anxiety. You had to get used to it in this war, shutting out worries rather than letting them drip through your mind, ruining any life
you had left. You needed to love every day with every ounce of energy
you had—in case this one was your last.

The song came to an end, the crowd bursting into applause, a man
calling out, "Give us another one!"

Marigold gazed around the room, delighted with the spectacle. The
music had lured more people in, the place packed and the energy high.

"My next song is dedicated to all the people not here tonight, from
the factory girls and folks in the war services to our men overseas and
those who sadly are no longer with us." The crowd paused in silence.
"This one is dedicated to you."

She turned to the band, who began the introduction, and carefully,
poignantly, she began "We'll Meet Again."

Everyone turned to the stage, some linking their arms together and
swaying as the song began, joining in as the song reached the stirring,
heartfelt chorus, that hope for the future, whether in this life or the next.

Juliet felt a shiver of loneliness as she sang along with the crowd,
and she went to join Dorothy, wondering if she was missing her sister,
and she put an arm through hers.

"How are you, Dorothy? It must be hard without Irene here."

But Dorothy forced herself to smile. "At least I have friends like
you, Juliet, and there's Sofie and her family making sure I always have

good company. The library keeps me busy, and Katie's new baby has been a joy. There's nothing like seeing new life blossom, is there? Sometimes all you need is the right people in your life." She clenched her lips into a line. "Friends can make life bearable through the unbearable."

The song was followed by "Basin Street Blues," the couples taking to the dance floor once again, and Juliet was touched to see Frederick come to ask Dorothy to dance. The old lady let him lead the way.

Even though what had been taken away will never come back, sometimes new friendships spring up that can help to fill the gap left.

A tap came on Juliet's shoulder.

"May I have this dance?"

She turned to see Sebastian, and her heart exploded with joy and relief.

Together, they joined the other couples swaying to the music. As she felt his arms close in around her, she knew that this is how love should always be: her cheek on his shoulder, the smell of his neck and hair, and the slow turn of the dance.

Before she was ready, the song came to an end, Marigold announcing that the children had to line up to dance for the next song, "Santa Claus Is Coming to Town."

London Transport had donated thousands of gifts for every child sheltering in the underground, and a man dressed in a red suit came to hand them out. The atmosphere was heady with shrieks and children jumping around, unable to wait their turn, delighted to have a cardboard Snakes and Ladders game or a knitted doll handed to them— Dorothy and some of the other women had been busy making them for weeks.

Marigold's performance went on for over an hour, the crowd begging for encore after encore. Performers had been lined up for the entire evening; a mother-and-daughter comedy act, a juggling clown, a magician, and a choir with sing-along carols.

"This will definitely be a Christmas to remember!" Katie exclaimed.

At the end of the night, Marigold returned to the stage, asking for quiet before proclaiming that they wanted a word from the new head librarian herself.

A great cheer went up as Juliet was propelled onto the stage, waiting for the crowd to hush before she began.

"A hearty thank-you to all our members and volunteers for keeping this magical little library open. When I first arrived in Bethnal Green Library, I was brimming with ideas about how to improve our library with new books and departments." She paused. "But now I've realized that it isn't that simple."

She smiled around at the crowd.

"Libraries aren't only about books; they're about people. They're about human life, how books can mend hearts, comfort wounds, and inspire us. But most of all, books can bring people together. Their ideas and thoughts make us realize that we are not alone, that we are all connected."

She took a deep breath. "As a child, I imagined heaven to be a colossal, towering library, every wall coated with books. Books of the past, books of the future, books that held the true meaning of life. Here in our Underground Library, it is as if we have a small haven of peace away from the horror outside. We are here, joined by books, rising above the Nazis, above their devastation, knowing that there are parts of our culture, deep inside each of us, that they will never be able to touch."

She paused, looking around the crowd.

"Tonight we are here to enjoy and make merry. But we are not simply celebrating our festivals or our books, we are celebrating one another, our spirit, and the power of human connection—those invisible bonds joining us so tightly that no matter what our enemies do, we will always stand together."

# AUTHOR'S NOTE

THE UNDERGROUND LIBRARY IS BASED ON A TRUE STORY: THE bombing of the Bethnal Green Library only a few weeks into the London Blitz and its subsequent move underground. After the bombing, the head librarian and his deputy put together the plan to move the library into one of the shelter tunnels. There, the library became a backbone for the community as well as a much-publicized display of "Blitz spirit."

In this novel, I wanted to bring these scenes to life, showing the community spirit as well as the numerous ways that everyday life went underground, not only in Bethnal Green but in tube stations all over London. During the war, the Central Line was being built, and although Bethnal Green Station was completed and became a large underground shelter, it did not yet have trains. For the purpose of showing how working platforms functioned alongside the shelterers, I made it into the working station it would become. I kept the operations of the underground shelter and library as close as possible to the actual place.

It is estimated that over half a million people used the London underground stations as shelters during the war, many on a regular basis. The stations were up to the task, becoming underground communities with provisions and services. Bethnal Green itself boasted a makeshift theater that put on music, ballet, and opera performances, and a childcare unit to enable mothers to work. Medical facilities existed in most of the shelter stations, with larger stations housing more expansive

clinics. At least three babies were born underground, including the ce-
lebrity Jerry Springer, who was born in Highgate Station in 1944.

As you can imagine, many people who lived through the era have
stories to tell about sleeping in the underground, and it is these stories
that form the backbone of this novel. My grandmother recalls being in
London during an air raid and being surprised by the community spirit
of the underground: people knitting, playing cards, laughing, singing,
and eating sandwiches as they passed the hours. The East End undergrounds, such as Bethnal Green, were renowned for their festivities,
reflecting the mostly working class locals and their love for singing and
entertainment. Many of those living and working in the shelters were
women, and based on the gender changes in employment during the
war, I decided to add some female librarians in order to examine the
roles and difficulties they faced at this time.

The London Transport Museum is a treasure trove of information
and artifacts surrounding the use of underground stations during the
war, including letters and summaries of costs, photographs of underground schools, cooking and canteen items, designs of underground
medical units, and programs for drama and music events. The Transport for London archives also helped with a wealth of details. Likewise,
the Imperial War Museum is home to some wonderful artifacts and
records of the war underground, and I'm grateful to the staff for guiding me through their extensive document collections.

The National Archives holds a great quantity of leaflets and posters
explaining the use of underground stations and shelters, and I spent
long hours going through these, comparing them to some of my interviews, trying to patch together a good idea of how it must have felt to
have to spend every night underground.

Although Bethnal Green Station wasn't flooded, I used the flood
experienced in the Balham Underground Station to depict the water
main break. In 1940 when the main road was heavily bombed, the
water main beneath Balham cracked, sending a torrent of water into
the tunnels. It is estimated that sixty-seven shelterers were killed that
night.

Bethnal Green had a troubled war, first due to the quantity of bombs that fell in the area—more than double than in other parts of London—but also because of a tragic event in 1943, now known as the Bethnal Green Tube Disaster. One evening, just as the air-raid sirens began, some new anti-aircraft guns began pounding the sky from a local park, frightening the community. Crowds ran into the underground station, causing a stampede. In total, 174 people were killed, with more injured. Since this happened later in the war, I chose not to include it in the book, but I captured how easy it was for a stampede to occur during the scene where the water main breaks. Everyone grabbed their bags and children and ran, and when people tripped on the stairs, with no way to warn those pushing in from behind, more people fell onto them, causing a pileup. Although the tragic incident was covered up by the government for the sake of the war, a poignant monument now stands at the entrance to Bethnal Green Underground Station.

The term "cultural genocide" did not exist until decades after the Second World War, but the concept of books, libraries, museums, and even whole languages being targeted by invaders is not new. The Nazis' *Lebensraum* policy, marking out whole nations in eastern Europe to become an extension of Germany, meant that these areas were subject to "Germanification," the methodical transfer of the German language, history, and culture onto the captured populations. Polish, Czech, and Slovakian peoples had their culture systematically eradicated, from the mass burning of books to the alteration of bookshops and libraries to offer only German-language books and those that were deemed acceptable to the Reich—mainly Hitler's own books and propaganda-driven fiction by unheard-of authors. Museums saw the countries' histories changed, the German conquest glorified, while land, wealth, and national treasures were removed and dished out to Nazi "war heroes." Underground publishers and libraries sprang up as a desperate attempt to keep these cultures going—the dangerous and brave actions of subjugated people.

The Hebrew Immigrant Aid Society as well as the United States Holocaust Memorial Museum detail the flight of Jews from Germany and occupied Europe. There are incredible tales of the fortitude and bravery of the women who came alone to England to work in domestic service, as well as plenty of more positive reports, too—not all employers were as abusive as Mr. Wainwright. The experience of nuns helping to hide Sofie in the train across Europe came from the account of a young woman in similar circumstances that I read in the impeccable reference book, *Millions Like Us* by Virginia Nicholson. It was a truly touching moment that changed the poor woman's journey forever.

Information about the Isle of Man was taken from various sources, including newsreels from Pathé News, newspaper articles, and a number of books, including *The Island of Extraordinary Captives* by Simon Parkin and *Island of Barbed Wire* by Connery Chappell. My research into deserters took me into some fascinating areas, and the book *The Deserters: A Hidden History of World War II* by Charles Glass was packed with examples and the changing outlook at the time.

Among the benefits for women during the war was the opening of universities to them. With the young men at the front, rather than closing, universities offered places to bright young women who might otherwise have been limited to more "female" careers, such as teaching or nursing. Famously, Margaret Thatcher entered the prestigious Oxford University in 1943 to study chemistry, and most medical colleges saw women student bodies grow with the increased need for doctors during the war. Many city universities were evacuated, but a few remained in central London for the duration of the war, as did some secondary schools; older children were deemed useful for war work and helpful with bomb clearance.

As with all of my novels, I would never have been able to re-create the past without the voices of that era recounting real-life stories—intriguing, funny, and heartbreaking. I am continually interviewing people who lived through the war, and there is nothing quite like hearing their stories firsthand, reliving how it felt to be there. The BBC's archive "WW2 People's War" is an invaluable repository of personal stories from the war with many fascinating and heartfelt memories. And finally, thanks go once again to the women and men who wrote about their daily lives for the Mass Observation Archive during the war, all of which are now held at the University of Sussex.

# ACKNOWLEDGMENTS

"BLITZ SPIRIT" IS THE TERM USED TO DESCRIBE HOW MILLIONS OF civilians kept calm and carried on through the bombs, and through my research I've realized just how difficult and dangerous that could be. London's reduced population coped not only with war work and long shifts, but they had to take on extra duties as fire wardens and ambulance drivers during the raids and clean-up teams after them. But through it all, with the help of the community, people stayed strong. This is a tale about one such community, how they supported and helped one another, and I would like to thank the people who gave their all through the Blitz, and especially to those who lost their lives in Bethnal Green.

My warmest thanks go to Hilary Rubin Teeman, my phenomenal editor at Ballantine. Her guidance and intuition for plot and character are invaluable. Thank you so much for all your expertise. Special thanks go to Caroline Weishuhn, who has steered this book editorially and coordinated it through the publishing process. My great thanks go to Kara Welsh, Jennifer Hershey, and Kim Hovey at Ballantine Bantam Dell, and thanks also go to the wonderful team who made this book a reality: Pamela Alders, Ada Yonenaka, Kathryn Jones, and Samuel Wetzler. A special mention goes to Kathleen Quinlan, Megan Whalen, and Chelsea Woodward for working wonders with marketing and publicity.

My fabulous agent, Alexandra Machinist, combines immense charm with great wisdom and insight. A huge thank-you, Alexandra! Special gratitude also goes to my foreign rights experts in Curtis Brown and CAA, including Sophie Baker, Katie Harrison, and Sarah Harvey, and to my publishers around the world.

My talented and now much-published writing group, Barb Boehm Miller, Julia Rocchi, Emmy Nicklin, Christina Keller, and Jenny Perinovic, meets monthly to share our writing, our ideas, and our support. Their input into every one of my books is often genius and always indispensable. Thank you.

I am incredibly fortunate to meet other authors, journalists, and artists and would like to thank the community for its support and warmth. Massive thanks go to Cathy Kelly, who has become a wonderful friend as well as being an exceptional and inspiring author. Elaine Cobbe combines great writing wisdom with irrepressible character and charm. Thanks also go to vibrant and witty Vikki Valentine, whose friendship and wonderful sense of storytelling have been a godsend. My thanks also go to my teachers at Johns Hopkins, especially to Mark Farrington, Ed Perlman, and Michelle Brafman.

Immense gratitude goes to the invaluable Courtney Brown for her tremendous energy and resourcefulness, as well as her legendary hospitality and unstoppable joie de vivre. Laura Brooks and the entire Brooks family deserve massive praise and thanks for all their help. Hearty thanks go to Cheryl Harnden for her generosity of spirit and wonderful humor—your help and support have been invaluable to me.

This book is dedicated to Mrs. Irene Mussett, who we called Shakespeare Granny. Through her, we learned to dissect, analyze, and truly love literature. Born in Brazil, she went to university in London and became an aid worker around the world before settling back in Britain as a formidable schoolmistress. She was an extraordinary woman, both in her love of learning and her dedication to helping others.

Every book I write about the Second World War has to include a word about my mother, Joan Cooper, who taught me the importance of history and the secret of good stories. Thank you for everything.

Finally, my masterful sister, Alison Mussett, deserves immeasurable thanks for the flair and insight she has put into editing, reading, and advising on plot and character. Her unflagging support, humor, and spirit are invaluable, and she is a wonderful sister and great friend. And last, massive thanks go to my family, Lily and Bella and my wonderful husband, Pat, without whom this book would never have been written.

ABOUT THE AUTHOR

JENNIFER RYAN lives in the Washington, D.C., area with her husband and their two children. Originally from London, she was previously a nonfiction book editor.

This book was set in Fournier, a typeface named for Pierre-Simon Fournier (1712–68), the youngest son of a French printing family. He started out engraving woodblocks and large capitals, then moved on to fonts of type. In 1736 he began his own foundry and made several important contributions in the field of type design; he is said to have cut 147 alphabets of his own creation. Fournier is probably best remembered as the designer of St. Augustine Ordinaire, a face that served as the model for the Monotype Corporation's Fournier, which was released in 1925.